My Father's Wives

Praise for *The Book of Chameleons*, winner of the *Independent Foreign Fiction Prize* 2007:

'A work of fierce originality, vindicating the power of creativity to transform even the most sinister acts. Agualusa's writing is brought vividly home to us by Daniel Hahn' Amanda Hopkinson, *Independent*

'Elegantly written and translated' *The Times*

'It's not just Arcadia, and I, who have a good opinion of this book: it won the *Independent*'s foreign fiction award for this year, against the usual stiff competition' Nicolas Lezard's paperback choice, *Guardian*

'Agualusa's latest work, as translated by Daniel Hahn, is a triumph' *Times Literary Supplement*

'This prize-winning novel is rewarding and original with a fine sense of humour' *Daily Telegraph*

'A poetic, beguiling meditation on truth and storytelling and a political thriller and wholly satisfying murder' *New Internationalist* Books of the Year

'An unusual and charming novel; delightful and entrancing' Allan Massie, *Scotsman*

'A compelling tale … worth seeking out' *Morning Star*

'A book of lyrical intensity, deftly written' *The Good Book Guide*

Praise for *Creole*:

'Captivates with picaresque adventure and evocative impressions' Maya Jaggi, *Guardian*

'Glows with imagination' Pauline Melville

'Winged me into the lore of 19th-century Portuguese colonies and the slave trade' Lisa Appignanesi, *Independent* Books of the Year

'Unlike any other epistolary narrative of slavery you will read' *New Statesman*

'A very readable, evocative, stylish work' Margaret Drabble

'Highly enjoyable' *New Internationalist*

'Poetic and powerful' Richard Zimler

José Eduardo Agualusa

My Father's Wives

Translated from the Portuguese
by Daniel Hahn

ARCADIA BOOKS

Arcadia Books Ltd
15-16 Nassau Street
London W1W 7AB

www.arcadiabooks.co.uk

First published in the United Kingdom by Arcadia Books 2008
Reprinted July 2008
Originally published by Publiçacões Dom Quixote as *As mulheres do meu pai* 2007
Copyright © José Eduardo Agualusa 2007

The English translation from the Portuguese
Copyright © Daniel Hahn 2008

A catalogue record for this book is available from the British Library.

ISBN 978-1-905147-78-6

Typeset in Bembo by Basement Press, London
Printed in Finland by WS Bookwell

This book has been selected to receive financial assistance from
English PEN's Writers in Translation programme supported by Bloomberg.

Arcadia Books supports English PEN, the fellowship of writers who work together
to promote literature and its understanding. English PEN upholds writers' freedoms in Britain
and around the world, challenging political and cultural limits on free expression.
To find out more, visit www.englishpen.org or contact
English PEN, 6-8 Amwell Street, London EC1R 1UQ

Arcadia Books distributors are as follows:

in the UK and elsewhere in Europe:
Turnaround Publishers Services
Unit 3, Olympia Trading Estate
Coburg Road
London N22 6TZ

in the US and Canada:
Independent Publishers Group
814 N. Franklin Street
Chicago, IL 60610

in Australia:
Tower Books
PO Box 213
Brookvale, NSW 2100

in New Zealand:
Addenda
PO Box 78224
Grey Lynn
Auckland

in South Africa:
Quartet Sales and Marketing
PO Box 1218
Northcliffe
Johannesburg 2115

Arcadia Books is the *Sunday Times* Small Publisher of the Year

José Eduardo Agualusa was born in Huambo in 1960 and is one of the leading young literary voices from Angola, and from the Portuguese language today. His first book, *The Conspiracy*, a historical novel set in São Paulo de Luanda between 1880 and 1911, paints a fascinating portrait of a society marked by opposites, in which only those who can adapt have any chance of success. *Creole*, which has evoked comparisons with Bruce Chatwin's *The Viceroy of Ouidah*, was awarded the Portuguese Grand Prize for Literature, while *The Book of Chameleons* won the *Independent* Foreign Fiction Prize 2007. Agualusa divides his time between Angola, Brazil and Portugal.

Daniel Hahn is a writer of non-fiction, the editor of reference books for adults and children, and a translator. His translations include José Eduardo Agualusa's novels *Creole* and *The Book of Chameleons* (winner of the *Independent* Foreign Fiction Prize 2007) and the autobiography of Brazilian footballer Pelé.

For Karen Boswall, with whom I discovered
Faustino Manso and his wives.
For Jordi Burch, who accompanied us on our trip.
For Sérgio Guerra, who made it possible.

Part One

Oncócua, southern Angola
Sunday, 6 November 2005

I awoke suspended in a slanting shaft of light. I had been dreaming about Laurentina. She was talking to her father who – for some reason – had Nelson Mandela's face. It was Nelson Mandela, and it was her father, and in my dream this all seemed quite natural. They were sitting at a dark wood table, in a kitchen identical in every respect to my own kitchen in my apartment in Lapa, Lisbon. I dreamed a sentence, too. That often happens to me. This is the sentence:

'How many truths make up a lie?'

The light, filtered first by a very fine mesh fixed to the window, and then by the mosquito netting that surrounded the bed, slid in, utterly pure, in an incredulous torrent, contaminating reality with its own doubt. I turned my head and came face to face with Karen. She was sleeping. When she is asleep Karen becomes young again, as I imagine her to have been before her illness (before the curse).

We're in Oncócua, in a little medical centre run by a German NGO. Oncócua, like so many Angolan towns, was designed with broad avenues so that one day in the future it might grow into a large city. The future, however, seems to have been held up. Maybe it won't ever get here. I got up carefully and looked out of the window. A huge mountain, shaped like a perfect cone, floated on the horizon. Two *mucubal* women were approaching soundlessly. The taller of the women cannot have been more than sixteen years old, a narrow waist, coloured bracelets around her fine golden wrists; as I saw her I remembered a line from Ruy Duarte de Carvalho – *their breasts: fragile thorns blooming on their chests*. Ruy Duarte wrote beautifully about the breasts of *mucubal* women. I can understand that. If I were a poet I would write of nothing else. The second woman had her torso covered in a piece of green and yellow fabric. She was limping slightly.

'They're beautiful, aren't they?'

Karen was sitting up on the bed, her brown hair in disarray. I told her: 'I dreamed about Laurentina.'

'Seriously? Well, that's good. Characters really begin to exist when they appear in our dreams.'

'In my dream she was Indian. A girl with straight hair, big eyes, very dark skin.'

'She can't be. Maybe *half*-Indian? Don't forget her father is Portuguese...'

'Her father?! Which one?'

'Good question. Faustino Manso was Luandan – mulatto or black. The man who adopted her was Portuguese, and the biological one...'

'Let's not think about that.'

'You're right, let's not think about that. Who the hell was Laurentina's real father?'

(Primordial Lies)

I close my eyes and in a moment I'm back in that evening when my
mother died. My father met me at the door to her room:
    'She's very agitated,' he muttered. 'See if you can calm her down.'
    I went in. I saw her eyes blazing in the gloom.
    'Daughter!'
    She put an envelope in my hand.
    'They're calling me. I have to go. This is for you, Laurentina. Forgive
me…'
    She didn't speak again. Later Mandume arrived. I remember seeing
him kneeling beside the bed, holding my mother's hand. My father, standing, with his back to us. My father – or rather, the man who until that
evening I had believed to be my father. Now he is sitting opposite me. He
has a dry, angular face, with prominent cheekbones. Ample grey hair,
combed back. He must have rehearsed the question night after night in
the solitude of his widower's bedroom.
    'How many truths make up a lie?'
    He is silent for a moment, his gaze lost somewhere behind me, then
adds emphatically:
    'Many, Laurentina, many! For a lie to work, it must be made up of
many truths.'
    Wet eyes, shining. He smiles sadly.
    'It was a good lie, our lie, made up of many truths and all of them
happy ones. The love that Doroteia felt for you, for example, that really
was a mother's love. You do know that, don't you?'

I look at him, stunned. I get up and go over to the window. From there I can see the yard lit up by the sun. The fig tree that all those years ago I rescued from a little broken jar in a dustbin and planted in a huge clay pot is now coming along very well, there beside the long brick chimney in the middle of the yard. It has grown a lot, and very crooked, as fig trees naturally do. The bougainvillea at the back has already lost all its flowers. January is slipping away. A bad month to die – it's even a bad month to die in Lisbon where even in winter you do often find two or three magnificent summer days, astray and sleepy, like poppies scattered in a wheat field.

My father would have liked me to have been a boy. Until I was twelve, ignoring all my mother's objections, he used to buy me shorts and caps and play ball with me. We have a very strong bond, my father and I. We always have had.

'What about the Island, Dad, what's the weather like in Mozambique this time of year?'

The question didn't surprise him. I think he was relieved to be changing the subject. He sighs. 'In January,' he says, 'it's usually very hot on the Island. The sea is a luminous green, the water is hot, my girl, sometimes getting up to thirty-five degrees, an emerald soup.' He takes a coin from his pocket. 'Do you remember?' – and I do remember, of course. I hold the coin. Twenty *réis*. It's very worn, but I can still easily make out the date: 1824. My father found the coin on a beach on the Island, on the day he arrived there, the same day he met my mother. Doroteia was fifteen; Dário, forty-nine. It was 18 December 1973. I was born two years later. I think about this, about my birth, and a sudden disgust seizes hold of me. I'm aware that my voice becomes shriller and that I'm about to cry. I don't want to cry*:

'What I'm trying to understand is how you were able to hide something like this from me for so many years! Can you explain that to me?'

Dário hunches himself up like a little boy. In my study, fixed to one of the walls, I have a framed photo of Nelson Mandela and beside it another of my father. Notwithstanding the difference in their races, people are struck by the resemblance between the two.

---

* I cry a lot. I cry at the cinema, at weddings, when I read any old thing – I don't know, *Love in the Time of Cholera*, say. I'm moved by the disasters and joys of other people's loves, but I don't remember ever having cried at misfortunes of my own.

'Your mother and I spoke many times about your birth. I wanted to tell you, but Doroteia wouldn't let me. She argued that there are truths that are less truthful than any lies. Your mother, your biological mother, didn't want to keep you. She was a fifteen-year-old girl, the daughter of one of the richest men on the Island, an Indian trader. She had fallen in love with an Angolan musician who was passing through on his way from Quelimane, and she got herself pregnant. But the man left. As far as I know he went back to Luanda, and the woman went mad with suffering. She stopped eating. Her father wanted to kill her when he learned that she was pregnant, he wanted to throw her out of the house, it was all madness, but her mother stepped in. Her father hoped that she'd die in childbirth. Her and the child. He thought that that would have been best for everyone.'

'Do you remember the name of that musician?'

'I do remember, Lau, of course I do. I remember the girl's name too, she was still just a girl, your biological mother: Alima. That musician, everyone knew him. He was very popular in those days...'

'What do you mean, popular?'

'Popular, girl, you know – popular! He'd made many records, singles, and his songs were often on the radio. He was a remarkable-looking man, elegant, I remember always seeing him very well turned out. A black man – maybe a dark mulatto – dressed in a white linen suit, a handkerchief peering out of his jacket pocket, the side where his heart was. Oh, the important thing, his two-tone shoes and on his head – always well poised – a beautiful panama hat...'

'What was his name?'

'Faustino. Faustino Manso. Quite a character, Faustino Manso.'

(Letter from Doroteia to Laurentina)

My dear daughter,

I must call you daughter to the very end.

There's something you have to know, and I want you to hear it from me, because it's my fault that you never heard it till now, because I didn't have the courage.

You weren't born from out of my belly; on the day you were born I lost a little girl. In the room where I was, in a modest little clinic on the Island of Mozambique, another woman gave birth. The birth went badly and she didn't survive. The woman's parents asked me to keep the child – and I said yes. From the moment I saw you I loved you as a real daughter.

That is what I had to tell you. Forgive me for not telling you before.

Help your father. He's the one I'm worried about. Dário doesn't know how to live alone. We had our rages; I think that I was often too harsh with him. But I love him very much – do you understand that? – he was the only man in my life. It was always hard for me to accept that he had loved other women before me. Worse still, while he was with me. But men are like that.

You were the best thing that life ever gave me.

Your mother,

Doroteia

9

(The sin is not to love)

An unfortunate coincidence. I'm not sure what to call it. Faustino Manso, my father, died yesterday evening. Disembarking at the airport I bought a copy of the *Jornal de Angola*. The story – short, dry – appeared on the culture page:

'Wandering Mousebird dies – Faustino Manso died early yesterday morning, at the Sacred Hope Clinic on Luanda Island, after a long illness. He was eighty-one. Manso, known to his admirers as The Wandering Mousebird, was a popular musician through the 1960s and seventies, not only in Angola but throughout southern Africa. He had lived in a number of Angolan cities, as well as in Cape Town in South Africa, and Maputo (then still called Lourenço Marques). He returned to Luanda, his birthplace, in 1975, immediately after independence. For many years he worked for the National Institute for Books and Records. He leaves a widow – Senhora Anacleta Correia da Silva Manso – and three children and twelve grandchildren.'

I find the obituary pages more eloquent. There are four announcements bearing the name Faustino Manso. One is signed by Anacleta Correia da Silva Manso – this is the longest. The photo, too, is slightly larger, and more recent. Its words, thus:

'You left without a final farewell, my husband, and the sun in my life has gone out. The magnificent voice has fallen silent: who now will sing to me as I do my embroidery? You deceived me, you promised me that you'd stay with me till I reached the end, that you'd take my hand so I wouldn't be afraid. But I feel afraid now. As it turned out you did leave

11

me again, for such a long journey – I don't know whether I will be able to forgive you.'

The second is signed by his three children: N'Gola, Francisca (Cuca) and João (Johnny). The photograph shows Faustino Manso with a guitar in his arms.

'Dear father, we met you very late, but, fortunately, not too late. You have left us, but you have left us your songs. We sing with you today: *No roads have an end / too far from your embrace.'*

The third and fourth announcements took me by surprise. I sat down – shaken – on my suitcase. I asked Mandume to go buy me a bottle of water. It was only then that I noticed the heat, I think. It rose from the floor, thick and humid, stuck itself to your skin, entangled itself in your hair, acidic as the breath of an old man. Someone by the name of Fatita de Matos, of Benguela, had put her name to the only announcement that didn't carry a photograph; her words were brief, but explicit:

'The sin is not to love. A greater sin is not to love until the very end of love. I don't regret any of it, Tino, my Mousebird. Rest in peace.'

In the final announcement, my father appears posing for posterity, vigorous in his thirties, sitting at a table in a bar. He has a bottle of beer in front of him. It is possible to make out the label: Cuca. As I write these notes I'm drinking a Cuca too. It is good – very light, fresh. I read the words again:

'Dear father, hug our mother when you find her – Leopoldina has waited so long for that hug. Tell her that her children – your children – miss her terribly; we think of you every day, we are guided by the example of your courage and honesty, and will always be guided by it. Our world has become sadder without the joy of your double bass in it. Who will play it now? Your children: Babaera and Smirnoff.'

Mandume's parents had got married in Lisbon, in 1975; they were both twenty years old. Marcolino studied architecture. Manuela, nursing. They must have been quite naive, still are even today. Manuela said to me:

'At that time we were all nationalists, it was like a sickness. We hated Portugal. We wanted to finish our courses and return to the trenches of socialism in Africa.'

Manuela gave me old records to listen to, vinyl, of Angolan music. There are various songs that refer to the trenches of socialism in Africa. Just like that, without the slightest shadow of irony. Portuguese bureaucracy wouldn't accept that the couple's first son should be called Mutu, in tribute to a king from Angola's central plateau: Mutu-ya-Kevela. So for official purposes he was Marcelo, and Mutu to family and close friends. Mandume, the middle son, is actually called Mariano, and Mandela, the youngest, Martinho. In 1977, the year Mandume was born, Marcolino's two brothers were shot in Luanda, accused of involvement in an attempted *coup d'état*. Marcolino was very upset. He never again spoke of going back. Once his course was finished he found himself a job in the studio of an architect – himself also an Angolan – applied for Portuguese nationality and dedicated himself completely to his work. I met Mandume seven months ago. The first thing that attracted me to him was his eyes. The shine in his eyes. His hair, divided into little spiky locks, gives him the look of a rebel, in contrast with the sweetness of his gestures and his voice. I like to watch him walking. The world he moves in has no friction.

'Like a cat?'

Aline, in a whisper, her lips moist, leaning over the table. 'When we say someone moves smoothly, it makes people think of cats.' No, dear Aline, Mandume is not like a cat. There's something about the way cats move, a kind of arrogance, an imperial disdain for poor humanity, and that's nothing like Mandume. He is simultaneously humble and defiant. At least, that's how he looks to me. Maybe that's just through my eyes. Maybe it's love. Aline laughed, and I remember her laughing the first time I talked to her about Mandume. She has a lovely laugh. She is my best friend.

'And Mandume, what does it mean?'

Mandume? Ah, another king. A Cuanhama tribal chief who killed himself during a battle, in the south of Angola, against German troops. Mandume – my Mandume – isn't very interested in finding out about the historical figure who gave him his name. When I asked him what he was called he said:

'Mariano. Mariano Maciel.'

And it was Mário, a sound technician, a short, pale man with very fair hair, thinning but long, who interjected, smiling:

'So, Mandume, the whitest black man in Portugal.'

An unfortunate thing to say. I reacted violently.

'Oh yes?! Is that supposed to be a compliment?'

It was supposed to be a compliment. Today I'm tempted to agree with poor Mário, and I've even used the same phrase to Mandume myself.

There are moments when I feel truly in love with him. Others, however, when I practically hate him. I get irritated by the contempt he demonstrates towards Africa. Mandume decided to be Portuguese. He does have the right. However I don't think that in order to be a good Portuguese person you have to renounce your entire ancestry. I'm sure I'm a good Portuguese woman, but I also feel a little bit Indian; and now at last I've come to Angola to find out whether there's anything in me that's African.

Mandume came with me, reluctantly.

'Have you gone mad? What are you going to do in Africa?'

Finally he came in order to save me from Africa. He came in order to save us. He's a sweetheart, I know, I should be more patient with him. Besides which, he enjoys what he's doing. He spends the day following me around with the video camera. I tell him to film that or this, which he pretends to do, but when I realise what's going on, he's filming me.

Rio de Janeiro, Brazil
Friday, 24 June 2005

Ten a.m. – I had dinner with Karen last night. She's really keen that I help her write a screenplay for a musical film – or at least a film with a strong element of music – on the situation of women in the southern cone of Africa.

Eight p.m. – Karen came to pick me up at the hotel and we walked down to the beach. We spent part of the morning, and several hours after lunch, talking about the movie. We sketched out a plot. We want to tell the story of a Portuguese documentary-maker who travels to Luanda for the funeral of her father, Faustino Manso, the famous Angolan singer and composer. At a certain point Laurentina decides to trace her father's travels, which saw him in the sixties and seventies covering the whole southern African coast from Luanda to Mozambique Island. Faustino would spend two or three years in each city, sometimes a little more, start a little family, then get back on the road. In each city she visited Laurentina would record testimonies from Faustino's widows, and his countless children, as well as from many other people who spent time with him. The picture that begins to emerge bit by bit is of a mysteriously complex man. At the end Laurentina discovers that Faustino was infertile.

I saw Karen Boswall for the first time on stage at the French-Mozambican Cultural Centre, in Maputo. A saxophone player with light brown hair, with ethnically inspired pictures in black ink on her face and arms. The other musicians, divided between marimbas, percussion and a couple of guitars, were all very young, with identical tribal motifs painted in white

15

ink on their dark skin. The group was called Timbila Muzimba. I was reminded of the Bahian Carlinhos Brown and the Timbalada orchestra, years back, with very similar scenery and the same happy and powerful mix of traditional and contemporary rhythms. The French-Mozambican Cultural Centre occupies the building that used to be the old Hotel Clube, built in 1896, which became famous in the colonial period thanks to its broad verandas and elegant wrought-iron columns. This was in August 2003, part of the August Festival, an initiative of the Trigo Limpo Theatre of Tondelo, Portugal, in association with the Mozambican company Mutumbela Gogo. The hall was completely full. To my right was a Rastafarian elegantly dressed in a light blue suit with white stripes, nodding to the rhythm of the music. I asked him whether the saxophonist was Mozambican.

'Negative, brother,' he said, shaking his locks. 'She's Zimbabwean.'

She wasn't, but I only discovered this the following year, in September, during the thirty-first International Cinema Congress in Bahia. I had just got to the hotel, coming in from the airport, and was filling in a registration card when Karen walked in, carrying a yellow suitcase, plastic, exactly like my own, and a metal case holding her sax. I didn't recognise her. Later on someone introduced us, but even then I didn't realise that this tall beautiful woman with her thick Mozambican accent was the same I had seen playing the saxophone. Karen had come to Salvador to present one of her documentaries on popular music from Mozambique, *Marrabentando*. They told me:

'She's an English film-maker who's lived in Maputo for fifteen years.'

I saw her film on an open-air screen. Night had not yet fallen and all around the little square where the conference organisers had had the huge screen put up the traffic jostled in a noisy mechanical fury. The little I was able to see, and hear, pleased me. When the film came to an end, Karen appeared with her sax and began to play. It was only then I realised I had seen her before.

(From the roots)

My old man didn't want me to come. He told me to be very careful with everyone, in particular those who were friendliest and most well spoken, those who rather than shaking your hand open their arms to embrace you:

'First they give you a hug, son, then they strangle you.'

He didn't need to warn me. I never liked Africa. I saw how Africa had destroyed my parents. I read some of the books they kept in the study, the ones some people call Angolan literature: *Victory is assured, comrade!*, *Poetry Is a Weapon*, *Red Sabbath*. Political pamphlets, more often than not very badly written. Roots? Roots are what plants have, that's why they can't move. I don't have roots. I'm a free man. I was completely free before I met Laurentina. I say to her:

'You are my country, my past, all my future...'

She laughs derisively. She doesn't understand me. Doroteia liked me. I liked her. I gave her my hand, in the hospital, as she was dying. Laurentina suffered terribly with her mother's death. Not long after the death she was given a letter saying she had been adopted. Right away Laurentina got into her hard head the idea that she had to meet her biological parents. I was horrified when she told me she meant to go back to Africa.

'Have you gone mad? What are you going to look for in Africa?'

Roots. She wanted to look for roots.

'Roots are what trees have,' I shouted to her, 'neither one of us is African.'

She didn't listen to me. Laurentina is stubborn. Or determined, as old Dário prefers to put it. What's certain is that when she settles into something there is nothing that can budge her. I wouldn't let her go

17

alone. I suggested making a documentary about her return to Africa and the reunion with her family. She liked the idea.

And here we are.

(Dreams smell better than reality)

My father is a man of passions. For some years he devoted himself to photography and to the cinema. He bought a filming-camera, a Super 8, which he took with him everywhere. It was because of him and his enthusiasm − and also because of that old camera, which today is mine − that I became a documentary-maker. I remember, when I was a teenaged girl in Lisbon, seeing Dário setting up a little screen in the living room, and projecting slides, or a film, about Lourenço Marques or Mozambique Island. There is one in which I appear, not much more than a year old, in a swimming pool, in a float shaped like a duck, splashing at the water with both my hands. In the background, the vast indigo sea. My mother appears in another of the films, with a fishing rod in her hands. Dário would watch the images in silence, savouring a martini. At the end, he'd sigh:

'Ah, Mozambique! Those were happy years. Sometimes I dream about that time. Then I wake and can still feel the smell of Africa on the sheets. If you don't know the smell of Africa, you don't know the smell of life!'

When the plane landed in Luanda and they opened the doors, I stopped for a moment at the top of the steps and filled my lungs with air. I wanted to feel the smell of Africa. Mandume shook his head, sadly:

'This fucking heat!'

I was furious:

'We haven't so much as put our feet on the ground and you're already complaining. Can't you appreciate the good things?'

'What good things?'

'I don't know − the smell, for example? The smell of Africa!'

Mandume looked at me, confused:

'The smell of Africa?! God, it smells of piss!'

I kept quiet. It did.

(The funeral)

Faustino Manso was buried this afternoon. I wore a dark blue blouse, a black skirt, socks the same colour. My hair was held back over the nape of my neck. Mandume likes me with my hair like that. He thinks I seem taller. I am tall. I'm a metre seventy-five, ten centimetres shorter than him. I phoned down to reception asking them to call me a taxi. They explained to me that there are no taxis in Luanda, or at least not what we'd call such things in Europe, but that they could find me a driver with his own vehicle. I agreed. The driver appeared half an hour later, a good-looking man, slim body, prominent cheekbones and a square jaw. I wanted to know what he was called:

'Pouca Sorte, miss.'

I liked the 'miss'. It had been years since anyone had called me that. I found the name odd.

'Pouca Sorte? "Luckless"? That's a nickname, surely? What's your real name?'

'Albino. Albino Amador. People call me Pouca Sorte because the women don't like me.'

He said this with a roguish smile that revealed perfect, glowing teeth. Pouca Sorte has a serious voice with an accent that's happy, but discreet, more elegant than you find with most of the population. The car, a little blue van, like thousands of others here in Luanda, is called Malembemalembe. The name is engraved in black ink on the rear windscreen. I asked what it meant. Pouca Sorte showed that same happy smile again.

21

'Malembemalembe, it's like saying slowly-slowly, slowly does it. It goes slowly-slowly…'

Mandume went with me. There were a lot of people at the Alto das Cruzes cemetery. The people all seemed to know one another. They embraced. Some of the women cried on other women's shoulders. No one seemed surprised at our presence. A man with the broad beard of a patriarch, blazing and unkempt, approached the urn and raising his voice, turning to face the crowd, spoke at length about the life of my father. I managed to take a few notes:

'[…] I saw Faustino Manso for the first time, he must have been about twelve years old, and I wasn't even ten, at my father's house, on the day Joe Louis knocked out Max Schmeling. My father at that time was one of the few people in Luanda who owned a wireless set. I remember how we were all surrounding it and the delight when Joe Louis knocked out the German in the first round and became world heavyweight champion. The moment the broadcast of the fight ended we heard a piano. Then Faustino stood up and said, "When I grow up I want to be a pianist." He said it so seriously that no one laughed […]

'[…] My dear lady must forgive me, but I cannot avoid saying something about my friend's passion for the fairer sex. Faustino loved women. […] It's true that he used to say that of all the women he'd had he loved only one, Dona Anacleta, his wife, and I believe it, as it was finally to her arms that he returned, after twenty-something years of roaming across Africa […]

'[…] Friend Faustino, my old friend, life's such a quick dream. I look back and see you playing football – you played badly – with Velhinho, Mascote, Camauindo, Antoninho, the son of Moreira from the tavern, who was the captain. And I remember Little Zeca too, our goalkeeper, who later went pro, became nearly famous and forgot all about us. Who remembers him today? I look back and I see you, years later, playing piano at the dances of the African League […]

'[…] On one occasion – long after you'd left – I went to Lourenço Marques, was taken to dinner at the Polana Hotel. As I walked into the dining room the pianist started playing Muxima. It was you, with some white hairs now, but always young and elegant. You said to me, "No blacks in here," and it was true, you and I were the only two coloured people there. You let out one of those laughter-bursts of yours so full of life, full of sound and fury, and added: "I feel like a gazelle grazing among the lions. The trick is to shake your mane, and roar." The truth was, Faustino Manso always went wherever he wanted to go. He would never accept being kept out, and no one ever dared to keep him out […]'

As the old man finished speaking there was almost complete silence. Insects hummed. I noticed the frangipani, bare of leaves, but covered in flowers. Big, white flowers, with five petals, resting on the bare branches like astonished flakes of snow. A stone angel prayed, on his knees, just to my right. I moved a little forward. In front of the urn there was an elderly woman, very elegant, very fragile, supported by two others. I saw her lift up her face and begin to sing, at first in a fragile thread of a voice, then taking flight, in a language without edges that must surely have been devised especially to be sung. Bit by bit other women joined in with the widow, and then all the men, and finally the children, in a perfect chorus. The melody was of a terrible beauty. I only noticed I was crying when a very beautiful, slender girl, her hair cut short like a boy's and dyed blonde, offered me a packet of paper hankies:

'Here, cousin, keep them all. I came prepared. I always do…'

'Cousin?'

'Aren't we cousins?! I think we're all cousins here. I'm Merengue, daughter of General N'Gola…'

It was Merengue who took me to Dona Anacleta. The old lady looked at me a moment, intrigued:

'Sorry, girl, I don't remember you. You're the daughter of…?'

I filled myself with courage:

'I'm the daughter of the deceased,' I replied. 'I'm the daughter of your husband.'

I thought she was going to be angry with me. I was afraid I'd be thrown out of the cemetery with shrieks. But just the opposite happened. She embraced me with genuine tenderness, almost gladly:

'You're still very young. You must be, what, thirty? So you have to be the youngest – Laurentina. I'm glad you came, daughter. Welcome to your family.'

That's how I found myself, after the funeral, at the house of General N'Gola, Anacleta's second son. The house is at the end of a deserted, dusty, treeless street, which leads to a low hill entirely covered with little huts.

Merengue – my niece – told me that in colonial times this was a street where people from the upper middle class lived. Now you can see very beautiful residences, well looked after, though partly hidden behind high walls, side by side with others practically in ruins. Merengue also told me that houses in Luanda cost a fortune, even the ones that are the most run-down. At the time of independence many were occupied by poor country-folk who'd come in from the slums, who plundered and degraded them. Now they sell them at absurd prices, a million dollars, or more, and disappear. I was fascinated. I'd like to make a documentary about one of these people. To know what a poor person does who suddenly finds himself with a million dollars. Where does he go? Mandume, meanwhile, is horrified. He complains constantly about the noise, about the chaos of the traffic, the crowds adrift on the streets. I say to him:

'The energy!'

'Energy?'

'Energy. What I feel is energy. The city is vibrating.'

The truth is, I still don't know if I love it or hate it. Luanda, that is. The residence of General N'Gola is in the middle of a small tropical garden, with palm trees, banana trees, a round lake with a fountain and red fish. There were a number of iron tables arranged around a very beautiful swimming pool. People were chatting calmly. They ate, and drank. At the table where we were seated there was a young businessman – 'I import wines and spirits,' he said to me, introducing himself – accompanied by his wife, a slightly chubby girl with a perfect face, lately graduated in economics in Rio de Janeiro. There was also a tall lad, broad-shouldered, who greeted me with happy irreverence:

'Aunt Laurentina, am I right? Grandmother told me. Some of us were betting on how many of Granddad Faustino's children – unknown children, that is – were going to turn up at the funeral. There were two in the end, you and a soldier from the south…'

I must have blushed. He noticed my discomfort:

'What's this? Don't get angry. You're part of the family. I'm sorry you never got to know the old man alive. He was an extraordinary person. We're all pleased you turned up. Especially me, that I've got a beautiful new aunt. Haven't I introduced myself yet? I'm sorry, I'm Bartolomeu, Bartolomeu Falcato, I'm Cuca's eldest…'

Mandume interrupted him:

'How many children did your grandfather have?'

Bartolomeu laughed. The businessman and his wife laughed with him.

'According to what Granddad said, eighteen. Seven wives and eighteen children.'

'He was an African man.' The businessman winked at me, complicit. 'Here in Africa we still know how to make children, not like you lot in Europe. The people who're going to be saving Europe from a demographic implosion, it's going to be the African immigrants. The Europeans have stopped having children. They have, I can only assume, other things to do...'

'How many children do you have?'

'Me?! Only one so far, but I'm still very young...'

'Very young? You're thirty-three, man! Around here you're already past it.' Bartolomeu said this roaring with laughter. 'Don't forget that life expectancy here in Angola is forty-two. While a child born in Portugal can expect to live seventy-seven years. An Angolan of thirty-three is equivalent to a Portuguese man of sixty-eight. My aunt's right, as Africans go, you're a fraud!'

'And you, how many children do you have?'

'None, auntie. I'm a total fraud. For a start, I'm this colour, which gives me no credibility as an African. Last month I went to Durban to a writers' meeting. There were writers there from various countries of so-called "Black Africa", as well as an American, an Indian, and a young Indonesian woman, who incidentally was beautiful to die for. Some of the writers didn't hide their astonishment when I introduced myself, 'Bartolomeu Falcato, from Angola'. Two wanted to know if I was travelling on a Portuguese passport. The third person to ask me that question – who was the young Indonesian woman – struck unlucky. I exploded. I said that back in my country only border police were in the habit of asking for my passport. I asked her if she worked for the immigration service. Of course, I made myself a very beautiful enemy. D'you want to see my ID card, auntie? Read that, there where it says "race", can you see? It says "white". And the older of my brothers, over there on that table, yes, him, the dark one, he was classified as black. Son of the same father and the same mother. Well, at least we can be certain about the same mother...'

'What's all this, Bartolomeu?!' – the young businessman scolded him. 'Let's have a bit more respect for the elderly!'

Bartolomeu laughed. One would think we were at a birthday party, although I had surprised one or other of the women with a handkerchief wiping away a furtive tear. Not Dona Anacleta. Presiding over the largest of the tables, sitting very straight, very dignified, ordering around the servants with nothing but the simple authority of her gaze. Bartolomeu put his hand on my arm:

'I heard you're a documentary-maker.'

'Yes, nephew, that's what I've been doing.'

'So we already have one more thing in common, apart from our parentage. I work for a television company. Though here we can say *the* television company as there's only the one. I took a cinema course in Cuba. Apart from that, I write. I've had two novels published.'

Mandume noticed his hand. He didn't say anything. Bartolomeu continued:

'I also heard you're planning to make a documentary about this trip you're doing?'

'How did you hear that?'

'Everyone knows everything in this country. I have a proposition for you. It might be of interest…'

'I only accept honest propositions…'

'This is honest, auntie. I'd like to film with you − I don't have to address you formally anymore, do I? − I'd like to film with you, make a documentary on the life of old Faustino. A road movie. My idea would be to set off from Luanda in a good jeep, and stop in all the cities where he lived: Benguela, Moçâmedes, Cape Town, Maputo, Quelimane and Mozambique Island. We'll interview the people who knew him, the musicians who worked with him. Like Hugh Masekela, did you know that the old man played with the great Hugh Masekela…?'

I didn't know. I'm writing these notes in the room where we're lodging, in the Hotel Panorama, an elegant building built on the sands of the Island. There is sea in front of us, and sea behind us. Through the window I can see the lights of the city reflected in the black mirror of the bay. At night, seen from here, Luanda looks like a vast, developed metropolis. The darkness hides the rubbish and the chaos. I think of my father. I wanted to know what Mandume thought of Bartolomeu's proposition.

'Totally stupid!' he shouted. 'Our idea was just to film you meeting your family. We stay two more weeks, just as we agreed, then we go back to Portugal.'

I tried arguing with him. The more I think about my young nephew's project, the more enthusiastic I get. I told him I thought it was an excellent idea and that it'd be good for me. It would help me to discover my father. And in Mozambique I could look for Alima, my biological mother.

'Imagine, what if I find my mother?'

'Yes, if you find her, what will you say to her?!' said Mandume, with irony: 'Look, Mum, I'm your daughter. The daughter you thought had died in childbirth…'

I got annoyed. I shouted:

'I'm so sick of you!'

Mandume stormed out of the room, furious. He slammed the door.

It's gone one in the morning and he's still not back.

(Fragments of an interview with Karen Boswall)

'[…] I'm the daughter of a teacher and a chemical analyst. My father was born in 1924, in Portsmouth, a British navy port. Took quite a pummelling in the Second World War. The port, that is, not my dad. Dad was the son of a sailor and a domestic servant, one of those ones from Victorian times who remained below stairs with the other servants, just waiting for the master to ring a bell to summon them. His father was never at home. He had enlisted in the navy during the war, and died very young. They were poor folk. My father's sister died of tuberculosis. She must have been one of the last people in England to die of TB. My mother was born in 1927, in Beaminster, a country village in Dorset, in the south-west of England. She was a farmer's daughter. Before they got married, my grandparents had been actors. My grandmother was engaged to another man. She met my grandfather when she was playing the part of Kate in Shakespeare's *The Taming of the Shrew*. My grandfather was playing one of the tutors. They fell in love, which was scandalous, this being the twenties, as my grandmother called off her planned wedding and ran off with my grandfather. Later they moved to Portsmouth and opened a grocery store. My grandfather delivered milk door-to-door with a horse and cart. My mother is a very sociable woman, extremely pleasant company. Both my father and my mother studied, both made progress, and both are now retired, but to this day they both live with the terror of one day returning to poverty. I was born in London, fourteen years after my parents married. My mother had a son who died, then my sister was born, and then me three years later. My father didn't want children. He brought us up at some distance. I think I've become what I have today because I was always looking for some love from my father. He painted, he was a good painter, and played the violin – the gypsy violin, he was from a gypsy family. I think we're related to the famous Boswall Circus […]

'[…] I started playing the flute when I was seven, and then the clarinet. I played very well. At sixteen I was already playing professionally. I decided to continue my progress by moving on to the saxophone. I also learned to play piano. I left home around that time. I began to travel. I worked first in Austria, giving English lessons to Japanese people, interesting people, more or less on the fringes of the law. At the same time I was painting. I had my first individual show when I was eighteen. I sold the lot. I also lived in Israel for six months, where I was part of a collective of classical music composers. That was when I started composing. I came back to England and gave up classical music. I got together with an Afro-Latin jazz band, Legless – a word that in England means drunk, or that you've danced too much. Then I lived on a scholarship in New York. I painted a lot in New York. I did big multimedia installations, talking sculptures, things like that. Back in London in the early eighties I got involved with a band of lesbians, this amid the militancy of the feminist and economic movements, in support of the miners' strikes, and the protests against the policies of Margaret Thatcher. There were eight of us in the band, and the others all wanted to sleep with me. I was the great challenge. We travelled a lot. During the tours – which sometimes lasted weeks – we might never speak to a single man. We stayed in women-only hotels, went to women-only bars and restaurants. Germany, Switzerland, Holland. Walk around all those cities, you'll see a pink triangle symbol, indicating an establishment for homosexuals. There are a lot of them. Most of my bandmates ended up marrying men. Only two are still playing music. I went to bed with a woman just once. Nothing happened in the end. Just a few kisses. That wasn't for me […]

'[…] I began to be interested in African music at the start of the eighties. There was a bar where they played African music. We heard some amazing things. The first African music I started listening to was Youssou N'Dour. Then came Abdullah Ibrahim, Hugh Masekela, Fela Kuti, Manu Dibango […]

'[…] I arrived in Mozambique in 1990 to compose the music and do the sound work for a film called *A Child of the South*, by the Brazilian film-maker Sérgio Rezende. On the very first day I arrived in Mozambique I played sax with a local group. I came back to London, but when I was called back to do another job there, I stayed […]

'[…] In 2002 I was invited to make a documentary on women with AIDS. My idea was to tell the story of Antonieta, a woman who was HIV positive, modern and intelligent, who made a living – with the support of an NGO – encouraging other women to use contraceptives. During my research I discovered that many Mozambican women prefer to remain faithful to traditions even if this puts their health at risk. Antonieta, for example, at a certain point decides to take her daughter, Matilde, to undergo an initiation ritual, in a remote village in the interior of Zambézia. She knows that the teachings her daughter will receive during the course of this ritual will contradict the things she herself teaches. But just the same, the most important thing in her opinion is not to upset the spirits. So I decided to film the ceremony. I spent weeks in this community. The only way of getting there was on foot, walking for many hours. Once we managed to rent bicycles. I remember the man who rented them to us. On the way back, once he'd left us at the main road, he put one of the bicycles on his back, and off he went, back to the village, pedalling the other, fifteen kilometres, uphill and down, on a sandy track. […] I thought about going through the rite myself, though I was a little alarmed because from a young age these women stretch the labia of their vaginas; I thought that they would make me do the same. Fortunately not. […] We were a team of four, and we filmed seven days and seven nights. Drums the whole time. There's a place where the men play the drums. Only the drummers are allowed there, four drummers. We had no water, and no power. We lit big bonfires for light. I took Gita Cerveira as our sound technician. Sidónio, my husband, was producer. Cameraman was Giulio Biccari, an Italian based in Cape Town. […] Each girl has a godmother. The mothers go too. They prepare the food while the godmothers look after the girls in some secret place. The whole ritual is about female suffering. Women should serve men, bear them children and satisfy them sexually. These aren't lessons, they're symbolic rites, but I only came to understand this long afterwards. As we were filming I wasn't following what was going on. I hired seven translators, but each gave me a different version. Few people who speak Portuguese also speak the language of that region. While I was assembling the film, I could see that this was something fantastic, but that I didn't understand any of it. […] The film came to be called *Dancing on the Edge* and includes some six minutes of initiation rites. But I had much more material: I could have made a whole other documentary. However on the night the film had its premiere, on 1 December, the international day of the fight against AIDS, in a cinema in Cape Town, at the exact moment it was showing the ritual scenes, the water tank in the building where I worked – a lovely new building – burst and destroyed all the rushes. There were several rolls of film I'd sent to be developed at a Cape Town lab. The technicians called me, confused: the negatives had been burned. I began to feel ill. Less than a month after completing the film, doctors diagnosed me with a tumour in my breast.'

Luanda, Angola
Sunday, 1 October 2006

(Extract from a text I'm preparing for the catalogue of an exhibition of Kiluange Liberdade – a young Angolan visual artist based in Lisbon – to be held on the premises of the Portuguese Cultural Centre.)

Luanda. Or Lua – the moon – as it is more intimately known. Also Loanda. Literarily, Luuanda (see the writer Luandino Vieira). To give it its full name, São Paulo da Assunção de Luanda was founded in 1575 by Paulo Dias de Novais. Twenty years later the first dozen white women arrived in the new town, quickly arranged engagements for themselves, married and had children. In 1641 the city was occupied by the Dutch, who left in all haste just seven years later. On 15 August 1648 a carnivalesque troupe of whites, blacks and Indians, brought to Africa in the galleons of the vastly wealthy landowner and slave trader from Rio (originally from Cadiz in Spain), Salvador Correia de Sá e Benevides, disembarked at Luanda. Fooled by a series of bold manoeuvres on the part of Correia de Sá, more than a thousand Dutch soldiers surrendered, abandoning two forts practically intact to an exhausted army of fewer than six hundred men.

Thus began a splendid confusion of races, languages, accents, whistles, horn-honks and African drums, which as the centuries passed just got better. The chaos engendering even greater chaos.

Today the streets of Luanda see a mix of the elongated *umbundo* of the ovimbundos; Lingala – a language born to be sung – and the scratched French of the Congolese returnees. The refined Portuguese of the bourgeois. The deaf Portuguese of the Portuguese. The strange quimbundo of the last *bessangana* women. Together with this – in these new times – is a pinch of the elliptical Mandarin of the Chinese, a spice-market scent of the sunny Arabic of the Lebanese; and even some words of revived Hebrew, gathered at a leisurely pace on a Sunday morning in some of the more sophisticated bars of the Island. Plus English, in a variety of tones, from the English, the Americans and the South Africans. The happy Portuguese of the Brazilians. The enchanted Spanish of a Cuban who's been left behind.

And all these people moving through the alleyways, elbowing each other at corners, in a sort of universal game of blind man's buff. Lyrical young men. Consumptive young women. Private surety firms. Chinese people (again) aflutter. Boys selling cigarettes, keys, batteries, popcorn, padlocks, cushions, hangers, perfumes, mobile phones, scales, shoes, radios, tables, hoovers. Girls selling themselves in hotel doorways. Boys crying their fripperies, mirrors, glues, necklaces, plastic bags, hair elastics. Girls bargaining over blonde hair – 'a hundred per cent human' – in locks, for extensions. Amputees mortgaging their prostheses. Grocers marketing papayas, passion fruit, oranges, lemons, pears, apples, juicy grapes and distant kiwi fruit.

Hey, uncle! Daddy! Godfather! Hey, look, it's me, your friend! Mackerels-oh! Going for five hundred, this record, brother!

…I wash…

…I stock…

…I polish…

If it were a bird, Luanda would be a massive macaw, drunk on abyss and on blue. If it were a catastrophe, it would be an earthquake: ungovernable energy, shuddering in unison the deepest foundations of the earth. If it were a woman, it would be a mulatta prostitute, with exuberant thighs, full breasts, now a little tired, dancing away naked in the middle of Carnival.

If it were an illness, an aneurism.

Noise suffocates the city like a blanket of barbed wire. At noon the rarefied air trembles. Engines – thousands and thousands of car engines, generators, machines in motion. Cranes putting up buildings. Mourner-women mourning a dead man in long, lugubrious howls, in an apartment in a luxury building somewhere. And blows, people shouting insults at each other, clamourings, barks, laughs and groans, and rappers bellowing their indignation over the vast clamour of chaos in flames.

(The girl and the chicken)

I left the room, slamming the door. Good thing there are doors. What I most wanted to do at that moment was throw myself into the sea. Down on the beach, a few metres from the water, I stumbled on a squatting man, totally naked, defecating. That man saved my life. I'm an elegant suicide, and I'm not going to lie down and drown in a sewer. I ran along the beach until my tiredness overcame my anger. I sat down. I think I'm in the wrong film. I haven't been happy these past months, still less these past days. I think the last time I felt happy was when I travelled through Maranhão on my own, rucksack on my back, and before that in Rio de Janeiro, cycling the bank of the lagoon. I came to Luanda because I thought this trip would bring me closer to Laurentina. I wanted to understand her. I can't. She won't let me closer.

This city is a sum of horrors: poverty plus racism plus stupidity plus ignorance plus conservatism plus machismo plus intolerance plus arrogance plus noise. A lot of noise. Noise everywhere, at all hours of the day and the night. At dinner last night someone recited for me some half-dozen lines a local poet had written about blacks in America. You're in luck, says the poet, not in quite the words that occur to me now, but anyway, what matters is the meaning, you're in luck, because you were taken away from here as slaves, and now your children don't die of malaria or of hunger. I laughed. Everyone at the table laughed. That's something I do admire about people here. The capacity they have to laugh at their own wretchedness. As to the rest, I agree with the poet. Fortunately my parents stayed in Portugal. I was born in Lisbon. I'm Portuguese. There was a time in my life, between the pains and the yearnings of adolescence, when I had some doubts. I didn't really know what world I belonged to. That sort of thing. Everyone has to deal with some kind of identity crisis. Mandela, the younger of my brothers, started a hip-hop group called The Poster Heads with three high school friends. One of the guys in the group is a blonde lad, very thin and clumsy, who goes by the name MC Bué. There was one day he was at our house; after a few minutes of peaceful small talk, beer and lupine seeds, my father asked him if he'd been born in Luanda.

'No, man, I was born in Amadora.'

'You weren't born in Angola?!'

'Not me, man! I'm a hundred per cent *tuga* – a hundred per cent Portuguese, me…'

'But your parents are Angolan, of course…'

'No, they're not! They're from Amadora, both of them…'

'Get away! You talk as though you were Angolan. You have a Luanda accent and everything…'

'Man, there were only brothers in my neighbourhood. At school too. There was just me and five other white guys. Well, four whites and a gypsy. We chose between being Cape Verdean and being Angolan. I chose to be Angolan.'

As for me, if there had been any doubts still lingering, this trip would have sorted them out for me. There I was, eyes fixed on the immense night, my disorderly thoughts on my past life, on Laurentina, on what I would do next, when a girl sat down on the sand, beside me to my right. She can't have been more than twelve. Slender, plaited hair, eyes that burned in the dark like red-hot coals. An ant-thrush emerged from the darkness and nestled itself in next to her.

'*Paizinho*' – the girl's voice was happy, slightly hoarse – 'Uncle, I'm hungry.'

She was wearing a light dress in a thin, almost transparent fabric. Her legs were smooth and long. On her very small feet, plastic sandals. She gave me her hand.

'Come!'

I went. She led me to a dark house. Wedged between other even darker houses. The ant-thrush followed us. We went up two flights of stairs and came out onto a little patio with plastic tables. The patio looked out over the anxious chasm of the sea. A Chinese lad emerged in front of us, smiling a lot, bowing elaborately, and led us to one of the tables. There were only three other diners. A Chinese couple, in one of the corners, and a white man, haggard and gloomy, with his back to us. The girl ignored the menu which the waiter offered us:

'I want twenty-two.'

'What's your name?'

'Alfonsina.'

'Where do you live?'

'On the beach.'

'And your parents, where are your parents?'

'They stayed in the war…'

'Stayed where?'

'There. In the war…' Silence, a brief retrospective silence. Then an appraising look, and a slightly mocking smile. 'You're Portuguese, right?'

'I am. You could tell from my accent?'

'No, because you move like you're Portuguese.'

The waiter brought a tray with Peking duck and a little dish of rice. Alfonsina ate in silence, concentrating, as though this were her way of communicating with God.

When she had finished, she put the plate of rice under the table beside the ant-thrush.

'Is she yours, the chicken?'

'Yeah!'

'She's like a dog.'

'She thinks she's a dog. She was brought up by a bitch. The poor little thing died, and Pintada was left all on her own. She does everything a dog does, except she doesn't bark, but nearly. Want to see what I've taught her to do? Pintada, give me your paw.'

Pintada got up under the table, and extended her right leg. The girl laughed. I laughed with her. I picked up my filming camera – I'm never far away from it – and filmed the chicken.

'You make films?'

'I do.'

'I was in a film once…'

'You were in a film?'

'Yeah! One of those sex ones, you know? Me and another five girls. An Italian who came here made it.'

I looked at her with horror. I put away the camera. The man sitting in front of us turned his chair so he was facing me. From the front he looked even more haggard. He had yellow teeth and a three-day beard, wild and hard as barbed wire. He smiled. If cacti had mouths and could smile, that's what they'd be like.

'I do apologise,' he said, 'but I overheard your conversation. You should never trust a man with his back to you. I hear a great deal. In the past I used to be paid to hear. Nowadays I'm a businessman. I have investments in fisheries.'

He opened his wallet and pulled out a card. He folded down one of the corners, and put it in my shirt pocket.

'In case you ever need it. Well as I said, I heard your conversation. Don't take what the girl says too seriously. She's a prostitute, a teen whore. The city's full of them. You know, the war…'

Alfonsina got up:

'I'm going…'

She ran off. When she reached the door she whistled. The chicken gave a harsh croak, which really did sound like a bark, left its plate of rice and followed her with a commotion of wings. The man pierced me with his gloomy little eyes:

'Do you have a cigarette?'

'No. I don't smoke.'

'You're right not to. I don't either. I stopped smoking a long time ago. Smoking kills, right? It cost me one of my lungs. Now it's the boredom that's killing me. So you make films?'

'I do. I'm a cameraman.'

'I can tell. Whose son are you?'

'Sorry?!'

'Your father, what's your daddy's name? Because you might even be Portuguese, but your father's Angolan, isn't that right?'

'Why d'you want to know?'

'Easy, easy now, don't get annoyed. I was trained to ask questions. Sometimes I forget myself. I forget that that time has passed. You needn't reply, of course. But if you will allow me – about the girl – I'd forget about what she said. Fantasies. Prostitution does also exist in our country, like anywhere, and eventually child prostitution, but it's all quite random, each to his own, it's not a question of organised structures, still less anything like making films, pornography. How long have you been in Luanda?'

'Three days.'

'Ah, so you still haven't seen anything. You're young, enjoy yourself. Luanda's a beautiful city. One of the most beautiful cities in Africa. And the bay, so lovely, so lovely, don't you think? I think there isn't another city that can compare with Luanda, except perhaps Rio de Janeiro. What's more we have the liveliest nights on the continent, marvellous women, mulattas, blacks, even blondes. Artificial blondes, of course, but artificial blondes are like fake Ray-Bans, even if they aren't real you can't tell the difference.'

He got up. He took out a wad of notes and put them on the table.

'Let me get this. If you ever need me, you have my card. Look after yourself...'

He left. I asked for a beer and remained on my own for a good while. It was already gone one in the morning when the waiter came over to tell me – with much smiling and salaaming – that they would like to close the restaurant. I went back to the hotel, striding slightly alarmed, because my desire to die had passed, and in this city, at night – how can I put it? – it really is night, an ancient night, from the earliest of times, dense and murmuring and filled with dangers, even if only supposed. Supposed dangers are as frightening as real ones. Laurentina was waiting for me, very anxious. I liked to see her like that.

(Deposition of Dário Reis)

What do you want me to tell you, daughter?

My life?

Well, I've led a simple life, there's not a lot to tell.

I was a happy child. I was born right here, in Ílhavo, in a large family. I remember the house where I was born very well. Today it's a restaurant. On the main façade was engraved the date when it was built – 1900. My father bought it for a price much less than it was worth because it was haunted. The previous owner was a Brazilian, not a real Brazilian but an Ilhavan who made his fortune in Brazil, in Amazônia, and came back, by now an old man, married to a much younger woman, who was half-Indian. Well, as the story goes, this wretch found his wife with his neighbour, in bed, and shot her. The trial acquitted him. That's how it was in those days, a man had the right, even the duty, to kill his wife if he found her with another man in a situation of intimacy. The ghost of the Indian woman used to appear on nights when there was a full moon. She would appear in the kitchen, hunched over a tub, washing the bullet-wound in her chest with a drenched cloth, muttering litanies in a stammering language. My father wasn't a rich man, he never would have had the money to buy a house like that – it was a stroke of luck. The Indian woman didn't bother us boys. On moonlit nights we stayed out of the kitchen. I only saw her once and thought she was beautiful. Straight black hair, deep eyes. Now I realise that Laurentina looks a lot like her.

In that house, apart from my parents, my two brothers and the ghost of the Indian woman, of course, there also lived two of my mother's sisters and three nephews, sons of an uncle who when he became a widower emigrated to the United States leaving the children in my parents' care. For the first few years my father still received, albeit irregularly, news from his brother, and some – few – twenty-dollar bills. Then the letters began to become more scarce, and the banknotes too, until we forgot about him. Much later, now in the seventies, I went to New York, on holiday with my wife, and met him. One of those coincidences a writer would reject, for fear his fiction would seem too unrealistic – with the exception of Paul Auster who as you know enjoys coincidences. Well, what happened was that we were attacked in New York. Three young guys with knives and jeers on a street in Harlem. I started arguing with them, Doroteia clinging to me, crying, and me yelling, yelling in good Portuguese which is how I yell best, because I don't like people stealing from me, stealing my money, my dreams, my energy, when a policeman appeared and they scarpered. And the policeman – you won't believe this – was called Dário, Dário Reis, like me. See, I'm called Dário in tribute to my father's brother who emigrated to the United States. The police officer was his son. My uncle was almost a hundred years old, but he was still lucid and strong. He became anxious when his son brought me home and explained who I was. My cousins, those cousins of mine, the Portuguese ones, never got to meet their father.

I grew up happy in that house. I always wanted to have lots of children, I think because I wanted to recreate the atmosphere of my childhood. But it wasn't possible. So, on we go: do you know how I came to fall in love with books? You do, of course you do, I've told you this story many times. It was through me, or at least I think so, I'm proud to think so, that you began to be interested in books, and then in photography and – even later – in cinema, wasn't it?

Yes, I understand, this is a deposition. So I'll tell it again, just as if I didn't know you.

Let's go back to the house where I was born. In my room, which I shared with one of my cousins, Idalino, I one day discovered – we discovered, the two of us – a little door hidden behind a wardrobe. This little door, which was locked but which gave easily when we forced it, led to a rectangular cubicle, with a short run of stairs, four or five steps, no more than that, which took you to a narrow window, almost an arrow-slit, which let in a little light. Looking through the window we could see the

Malhada salt beds, or at night make out the Aveiro Bar lighthouse. If we used a little imagination we could even hear the slow unfolding of the waves on the Costa Nova beach, some five kilometres away. My parents never suspected the existence of that secret room, nor did the rest of the family, because we made a pact of silence – sealed in blood, me and Idalino, and you know, we did keep it, at least my cousin kept it, as far as I know he never spoke of it till the day he died. He died two years ago, unmarried and childless, in Canada. I kept the vow myself, more or less, at least, I didn't tell my brothers or my cousins. I did tell you. When you were small you liked me to tell you this story. In that room we found a thick bound volume, whose title I've forgotten. It was an endless novel, in which each character followed on from another in a torrent, changing name, changing sex, changing race, some of them even changing species, so that from a certain point you didn't know who was who any more, or even if they weren't actually all just one and the same character. Whatever, God knows!

Fascinating, don't you think?

I do. I still do.

Well, one day that book disappeared. I've spent the rest of my life reading old novels, tucked away in libraries and second-hand bookshops, to try and find out who wrote it, what the hell it was, that great excess, but I never succeeded. Anyway it was that book, that unlikely book, that led me to study literature. I chose Germanic literature because I assumed that the book was a translation from English. Today I'm not so sure. I graduated at Coimbra. I was twenty-three, with my whole life ahead of me. I felt shy in Portugal, as though I'd put on someone else's jacket and it was a little tight around the shoulders. I couldn't move. Suffocating. It was then that I decided to apply for the so-called General Overseas Division, the colonial service, and was sent to Mozambique. I had my debut flight in first class, ever so well installed, and to this day I'm yet to discover why. It was the first and only time I ever travelled first class. From then on the State never again granted me such courtesies. My cousin Idalino was waiting for me in Lourenço Marques, he lived in Mozambique a good twenty-five years before moving to Canada in 1973. He seems to have guessed what was going to happen. I set myself up in his house. I gave classes in Lourenço Marques for many years, then moved to Quelimane. They were happy times, there, beside the Bons Sinais

River. I went out with a lot of girls – black girls, white girls, mulatta girls, Indians, there was even an albino girl – but I never married. I always thought I was never going to marry, until I first set eyes on the woman who would come to be my wife, Doroteia, my lovely Doroteia, on 18 December 1973, on Mozambique Island. You know how old she was? You'll be shocked, that day she was turning fifteen. I remember it as if it was yesterday. I was on Mozambique Island, taking around a Portuguese couple who were based in South Africa, and one afternoon I went into a market to buy a hat and saw her. Doroteia was with a considerably older sister, but such was the poise with which she moved, such was her composure, that you'd think she was the one leading the other. I didn't say anything to her. I went back to Quelimane, my heart in distress. I couldn't admit it, not even to myself, but I'd fallen in love with a fifteen-year-old girl. But whenever I could from that day on I went back to the Island to fish, to take a boat out, to take photographs, and once in a while I would come across her. It was easy to discover who she was. I became a friend of her father's, a little Goan trader, and in that way, bit by bit, I got closer. Doroteia fell in love with me, in spite of the difference in our ages. If I told you I had to overcome great difficulties to persuade her father to accept me as his son-in-law I'd be lying. Old Justiniano was going through a complicated time in his finances and the marriage of his daughter was a relief to him. He himself had been much older than his wife. So we got married, my Doroteia and me, a few weeks after she turned twenty-six. I very much wanted to have children, as I've told you, but as you know, man makes his plans, and God breaks them. My first child died at birth, the cord wrapped around his neck, pure negligence on the doctor's part. It was one of the worst moments of my life. Doroteia got pregnant again. This time too we were unlucky. She miscarried after three months and had to be taken to hospital for a D&C. In 1975, very close to independence, in the middle of all the political turmoil, whites against blacks, blacks against whites, the Portuguese running away and whatever, and my beloved Doroteia again became pregnant. It was a difficult pregnancy. She spent the three last weeks in a hospital bed. There was a girl in the same room, also of Indian background, or half-Indian, called Alima. I remember her very well. Big, terribly sad eyes. It was said that the child's father was Faustino Manso, an Angolan musician who'd lived in Mozambique for many long years and then disappeared all of a sudden without a trace.

Alima's father – a huge man, grey-haired, with big ears, called Ganesh – turned up at the hospital sometimes but wouldn't even come into the room to see his daughter. He would pace the hall in firm strides, to and fro, his eyes fixed on the floor. Dona Renuka, the girl's mother, was a very thin woman, fragile as a dream, and yet practical, for whom I came to feel a certain affection. Doroteia and Alima went into labour at almost exactly the same time. Doroteia's labour went badly. We lost the child. Alima's labour too was complicated, she lapsed into a coma, but the little girl was saved. Dona Renuka handed the little girl over to my wife, and the nurse who had attended to the labour averted her eyes to the exchange. None of us thought Alima would survive…

But she did, she did survive…

…We never heard anything of her again. Maybe she's still living on Mozambique Island. Maybe, though, she did die…

… There is a lot of dying that goes on in Africa. Dying from malarial poisoning, yellow fever, cholera, typhoid, dying from a stray bullet, dying from sorrow or weariness. Sometimes I imagine that she came to Portugal, like us, that she married and had other children. Sometimes it happens that I pass an Indian woman on the street in Lisbon and think, 'Could that be Alima?', and then she disappears round a corner and I'm left standing there, tormented, imagining some way I could ask her forgiveness…

Quicombo, Angola
Sunday, 30 October 2005

Four thirty-three p.m. – We've stopped by the Quicombo River. I'm sure there's a picture of these huge tall earth walls in one of the four albums of the Portuguese photographer Cunha e Morais. I bought the set, a good twenty years ago, from the storeroom of one of Lisbon's main second-hand book dealers. In those days Cunha e Morais hadn't yet been retrieved from oblivion by the Coimbra Photography Meetings. Not many people knew him. The man in charge of the storeroom, an enigmatic German with a distinctive sense of humour, who in spite of never having set foot in Africa knew all about the continent, gave me the four albums at a good price. I guess he must have liked me. Cunha e Morais's photographs, gathered in Angola in the second half of the nineteenth century, helped me to put together my first novel. One after-noon, after it had been published, I went back to the dusty domains of the old German. He received me from the top of a staircase, crammed with books, that led up to the first floor.

'I hear you no longer just a student?' he said to me, smiling. 'You a writer now. Prices going to change now.'

A lot of water has flowed down this river since Cunha e Morais photographed it. The landscape, however, has remained almost identical. A group of women and children dance *kuduro* to the sound of an enormous battery radio. I recognise the powerful voice of Dog Murras:

I get up at five
back at eight at night

all day on the square
with cornmeal to sell
my back aches a lot
children back home starving
Oh, but such happiness,
peace has come to Angola

The light, very sweet, spills onto the river waters. My gaze follows a border of tall palms along the length of its slow bed. In their shade a banana tree is flourishing.

We left Luanda at the end of the morning. Contrary to what had been planned, instead of taking a jeep we're doing our journey in a little van, one of those ones that in Angola – and to some extent throughout Africa – play the part of taxis. Basically a little *candongueiro* passenger van. I pray that it'll still be light when we get to Canjala.

Benguela, Angola
Monday, 31 October 2005

Night was falling when Azarado gestured with his chin at some hills in the distance, and announced:

'Canjala.'

As though he were saying:

'Our Lady Death.'

The Canjala stretch, the setting for bloody ambushes during the war, was still being rebuilt. It still had many thousands of fierce potholes, preserved intact, perhaps the largest collection in the world. That evening they were ravenous. They flung themselves at us with the voracity of piranhas. For four hours Azarado fought bravely, with sudden lurches, but never reducing our velocity, to dodge the keen gullet of these monsters. At last, exhausted, with night already descending on us, he changed his tactics and opted to run them over instead. The damned things reacted with squeals, leaps, threatening to upturn the *candongueiro*. Then suddenly they left us, they were left behind us, allowing us to see opening out in front of us – like a miracle – a smooth stretch of asphalt. Azarado sighed, pushed the accelerator pedal to the floor, rested his chin on the steering wheel and fell asleep. The little van climbed the berm and hurled itself – jumping up and down again – on the stormy savannah ground. The suitcases jumped all around us as though alive. At last we stopped. There was a moment of disbelief – we're still alive! Jordi was the first to speak:

'That was one big hole, man!'

'It wasn't a hole,' Karen reminded him. 'We went off the road!'

I got out of the car to assess the damage. The two tyres on the right side were completely flat. Azarado shook his head.

'Bad luck. We only brought one tyre.'

I felt my blood boil. First of all, we'd agreed with Azarado that he'd bring us a jeep, and at the last minute he turned up with that kind of motorised nightmare. Secondly, he'd fallen asleep at the wheel. And finally he'd brought only one spare tyre. I exploded:

'So, old man, now what, are we spending the night out here?'

Azarado gave me a sidelong look. He murmured:

'No problem!'

He said something in quimbundo to the assistant, who pulled out a knife and started cutting grass. Then he punched a round hole in the tyre and crammed the grass inside it. I'd never seen anything like it. Jordi, excited, was taking photos.

'Cool!'

'Will the tyre take it?'

'It will, yes.'

Azarado was born in Benguela. He's an elegant man, smooth face, well-shaved. You'd never think he was a day over forty. He turned fifty a few days ago. In colonial days he tried to make a living as a singer. He set up a rock band called The Unforgettables, but it didn't work out. After independence he was a lorry driver, a fisherman, a barber, a porter at a Luanda hotel, and a lorry driver again. He has eighteen children.

'By how many women?'

The question took him by surprise.

'Uh, I don't know. I could work it out…'

Counting on his fingers:

'Anacleta, three children. Fatita, three children, Leopoldina, three children…'

Karen watched him with fascination. I could practically hear her thoughts:

'And the children? Do you know all their names?'

'Of course. All my children are named after drinks…'

'Drinks?!'

'Exactly – drinks. When my first daughter was born I was sitting in a bar with some friends drinking a Cuca beer. She became Cuca.'

Later – by now here in Benguela, at the Hotel A Sombra, after we'd said goodnight to Azarado – Karen tugged at my arm.

'Did you get the thing about his children's names? I thought it was brilliant…'

It was after midnight. The tyre lasted no more than twenty minutes. It quickly came apart into shreds, so we ended up arriving in Lobito rolling right on the rim of the hub. At the entrance to Lobito there's a good mechanic. We changed the wheel, and continued our journey. I'm exhausted. Fortunately it's a comfortable room. I've got a big bed, just for me. I'm going to sleep well.

(The departure)

Mandume woke me up at five-thirty. Washed, dressed, cologned and (strangely) in a very good mood.

'Shall we?'

At six on the dot we came down to the lobby. Pouca Sorte was sitting in an armchair waiting for us, legs crossed, reading a newspaper. He got up, greeted us, and helped us to arrange our bags and rucksacks in the van. I bought ten bottles of water yesterday, a litre and a half apiece, as well as beer, soft drinks, chocolates and packets of biscuits. I also bought medication. It all fit. No shortage of space. Bartolomeu was late. At six-twenty I called him. He told me he was on his way. Half an hour later, with Mandume already beginning to get impatient, a little gold-coloured jeep pulled up in front of the hotel. Bartolomeu got out of the jeep, his rich black hair flustered, deep bags under his eyes, as if he hadn't slept at all that night. I only noticed who was driving the jeep when Merengue got out to greet us. She too looked as though she'd only just woken up. She was wearing a red-and-black tracksuit, yellow trainers. I noticed she had a bruise on her neck. She hugged me:

'Have a good trip…'

I smelled a lively scent on her skin, chocolate and pepper, an explosive mixture. Bartolomeu began to walk around the van, with an expression of disgust:

'This is the rusty tin we're crossing southern Africa in?'

I was the one who suggested we take the Malembemalembe. It's really expensive to rent a car in Angola. So a good jeep goes for an impossible price. Pouca Sorte asked for only fifty dollars a day. He told me he often went to Benguela, to see his family again or to do little bits of business, and always in this van. He also assured me — and other people said the same — that dozens of *candongueiro* drivers face challenges like this every day and on the whole they manage to make it. Bartolomeu's comments annoyed him:

'It's a solid vehicle,' he roared. 'It's already been to Benguela so many times it doesn't even need a driver. It knows the way all on its own. Sometimes I fall asleep in Porto Amboim and when I wake up we're arriving in Lobito.'

'I'd rather you didn't fall asleep...'

Pouca Sorte looked at him angrily, then shrugged his shoulders and got into the car. He spoke little all the way to Porto Amboim. Apart from the odd stumble on the road, which was in a poor state, it was a pleasant journey. The landscape is incredibly beautiful. At last I feel I'm in Africa, in the vast edgeless spaces my father felt such nostalgia for, the open horizon, the red earth, and the giant postcard baobabs. I'm writing at the table of a restaurant, on a little esplanade, facing out to sea. Magnificent sunshine. Saturday. The beach is bustling with people. Children, muscly lads, fat women with their children in their arms. Mandume and Bartolomeu have gone off to swim. Mandume a little suspicious — 'You think the water's clean?' — Bartolomeu really excited. I can see them from here. Mandume is far away. He's swimming along the coastline, a perfect crawl. Bartolomeu is in animated conversation with a tall girl. I can make out the limpid brilliance of his teeth. I feel (stupidly) a prick of jealousy.

Lobito, Angola
Monday, 31 October 2005

A girl is sleeping, squatting down, on a pedestal, completely covered by a piece of yellow fabric. She is showing herself – and covering herself – there as a work of art. Jordi gets out of the car, fascinated, and shoots his camera. Flamingos pass dully, in the distance, drawing out the evening's languor. The girl wakes up and her startled eyes appear brightly under the cloth. Jordi takes a step back. He returns to the car.

'Did you frighten her, or did she frighten you?'

He doesn't reply. Taking photos is trespassing. I suspect that occasionally Jordi feels this like a blow.

I met Jordi Burch in October 2004. We worked together on a feature on Barcelona for a Portuguese travel magazine. We chose to construct a little story – a sort of photo-story – with the help of an Italian girl, a young student who agreed to take the part of the main character. 'Autumn in Barcelona' tells the story of Montserrat Montaner, a Portuguese girl, who after losing her mother comes to Barcelona bringing with her – in the place of a guidebook – a collection of letters from her father, who had died years earlier in an Indonesian prison and whom she had never been able to meet. I created the character of Montse from Jordi, himself also an orphan of a Catalan father and Portuguese mother. I remembered this story again later, when I met Karen in Rio de Janeiro to think of a screenplay that would bring together effortlessly the two main subjects she's been working on these past years as a documentary-maker: popular African music and the difficult lives of women in southern Africa. So in a way *My*

Father's Wives begins in 'Autumn in Barcelona'. Jordi Burch lost his father at sixteen, and his mother at twenty. He also lost the older of his two brothers. This sum of tragedies might have made for a cynical character, one inclined to shadows, with a tendency towards solitude. But to the contrary, it strengthened him:

'The worst that could happen to me has already happened. Now I have the right to be happy.'

I've never seen him annoyed. His happiness is contagious. When I decided to invite him to travel with us, that counted for as much as the quality of his work. It was a good decision. Jordi has been taking photos that might come in useful to us later, whether during the writing of the screenplay or as part of the promotional work for the project.

Why are Jordi's photos so extraordinary?

To photograph is to illuminate. Jordi had taken against Sebastião Salgado, because he once heard the great Brazilian photographer protesting, in a brief aside, criticising his younger colleagues who in order to get an original perspective are prepared to climb up into chandeliers, to practice contortionism and other arts of the circus. My friend took the comment to be directed towards him. I don't think it was. Jordi illuminates his objects in unexpected ways. In his images it's not the perspective that surprises you, it's people's internal light.

I saw the Hotel Terminus in Lobito again. I remember as a child having lunch there a few times. What I remember:

- The waiting-staff, standing very rigid, in resplendant white uniforms. Today whenever I see an admiral I remember the men waiting tables at the Hotel Terminus. Not that I've ever seen admirals looking that dignified.
- A conversation between my parents and some friend about a dish served at lunch which mixed meat with fruit. To them this seemed like an eccentricity. My parents' friend commented that he'd eaten exactly the same in South Africa. For many years I entertained great illusions about the originality of South African food.

However much I try, I can't remember any more.

The Hotel Terminus was completely restored by a private Angolan bank. Round the back, on the perfectly pure sands of the beach, a bungalow-bar has now been put up. I also remember a square, opposite the port, where I was reunited with a massive cement turtle, looking a little dislocated. We had lunch, eating very well and for a good price, at Tamaris, a decadent but decent restaurant, the property of a woman with the same name as my paternal grandmother: Rosa Maria Carvalho. A small casino operates on the upper floor. We also had a walk through the Restinga. Really beautiful beaches. We ended the afternoon with a swim in the warm waters of Blue Bay.

(The accident)

The holes leapt out at us without warning. Malembemalembe went lurching forward, maddened, belying its name. Suddenly the car roof seemed to me to be too low. We tried to protect our heads with pillows. I thought my body was going to come apart. Mandume was holding me. I felt his body tense, sweaty. In the middle of all the noise he was shouting something, but I couldn't tell what. Night hurtled across the windows. Bartolomeu, sitting at the far end, facing us, was roaring with laughter. I raised my voice and asked Pouca Sorte to take it easy.

'He can't hear you,' Mandume shouted in my ear. 'Actually, he's asleep!'

'What do you mean "asleep"?'

'He's asleep! Look in the rear-view mirror! He's got his eyes closed. He's been asleep for a while now.'

'I can't see anything…'

'Just believe what I'm telling you, he's sleeping!'

'Then fucking wake him up! How is it possible for someone to fall asleep and stay asleep at the wheel on a road like this?'

Bartolomeu hurtled forward. Mandume grabbed on to him, to prevent him from bashing his head against the door. The two of them shouted something to one another. Bartolomeu took a few moments to understand what it was that Mandume was saying to him; then, turning towards the front, he shook Pouca Sorte. The five seconds that followed were the most alarming of my life. Malembemalembe climbed the berm and went on a good fifty metres, in huge leaps, knocking over the grasses and termite hills, before finally coming to a halt, leaning over to the right, in a thick cloud of dust. The light from the headlamps, struggling to make it through the red dust, allowed us to see – some two metres ahead of us – the hard wall of a baobab.

'That was close,' sighed Mandume. 'I thought we were going to die…'

Bartolomeu turned to Pouca Sorte, shouting:

'Fucking hell, old man, didn't I tell you not to go to sleep?!'

'It was your fault!' Pouca Sorte's voice sounded strangely calm, a voice of velvet in the total silence of the great night around us. 'You startled me…'

'Startled you?! I woke you up, is what happened…'

'Yes, you woke me up. If you'd just let me sleep none of this would have happened…'

Mandume opened the door and got out, stumbling. I got out too. My chest hurt, and I felt as though all my internal organs had changed places. I leaned, trembling, against the wrinkled trunk of the baobab. It was huge. As far as I could tell, there wasn't another tree around. The moon was barely visible, but the light from the stars lit everything up, millions and millions of them, like I'd never seen before, occupying all of space, right up to the edge of the horizon, up to the level ground, shining and multiplying, and crackling in silence in the endless immensity of the universe.

'God!' I almost prayed. 'It's so beautiful!'

Pouca Sorte was hugging the car. He was speaking softly:

'Please forgive me, my Malembe.' He turned to Bartolomeu, in the same tone: 'You shouldn't have shaken me! I told you I do this route practically in my sleep. I really do. Do you think I'd be able to put up with all that jumping about if I were awake?'

Bartolomeu came over to me. His rage had passed; he was smiling:

'And now, Pouca? We've lost three tyres and we only have one spare, how do we make more?'

'We'll wait…'

'Wait for what, man?'

'Wait. Someone will come.'

Fortunately I had remembered to bring a torch (a gift from my father), which doubled as an alarm clock/radio. It doesn't have batteries. To operate it you turn a crank. Turning it for five minutes gives you light for another five, and in addition I can listen to the radio. I found an Angolan channel. I listen to it sitting in the car while I write these notes and eat chocolate. Cadbury's with mint, made in South Africa. I don't think it's available in Europe. In Luanda you can buy it on the street. Tastes good. Relax.

On the radio I hear:

'[…] It's two weeks today since the death in Luanda of singer and composer Faustino Manso. Together with the nostalgic N'Gola Rhythms from Liceu Vieira Dias, and the Ouro Negro Duo, both groups now practically forgotten, Faustino Manso went to the folklore of the Luanda area in search of inspiration for his compositions. The Wandering Mousebird, as he was known, learned to play double bass from an American musician who had escaped from a warship at the start of the 1940s and settled in Luanda. His passion for jazz took him to Cape Town, in 1958, where he played alongside musicians like Hugh Masekela and Abdullah Ibrahim, then called Dollar Brand. Today, in The Cicada Hour, we're going to listen to some of the tunes that made him famous […]'

Someone came – a decrepit Volkswagen with two soldiers – while Faustino Manso was singing *Luanda at Twilight*. The soldier at the wheel was tall and ungainly; the other, short and plump, a full broom-shaped moustache. Don Quixote got out of the car and stretched. Sancho Panza got out too, lazily, made as if to arrange his huge belly in his trousers, gave up, went over to the baobab and urinated uproariously. Don Quixote reprimanded him:

'Captain, the girl!'

He held his hand out to me:

'An accident?'

I explained to him what had happened. Don Quixote shook his long gaunt face, pensive.

'You can't stay here, in the middle of all this night. Especially not the girl, a delicate girl like her. We're in hostile territory. Yes, the war's over, but in these forests round here there are still half a dozen stray bandits. You know I nearly died here in '99? It was this baobab that saved me.'

'You would have died in an ambush?'

'No ma'am, it was my wife who almost killed me.'

'Your wife?'

'Affirmative. I was inside the car fooling around with a Benguela girl called Mil Flores – a thousand flowers – a fair mulatta girl… like this girl here… I was already completely – how should I put it – fully operational, when my wife appeared. As I learned later the person who'd given us away had been another girlfriend of mine, severely afflicted by jealousy, by the name of Anunciação. Maria Rita, my wife, appeared armed with a katana. I didn't see her coming. I only realised she was there when the driver's-side window smashed. Mil Flores opened the door on the other side and ran off, stark naked – a lovely sight to see – towards Lobito. God made me as you see me now – thin and agile – like a little goat, but I'm old, my wife is much younger, not so quickly out of breath, and it was only a matter of time before she caught me. And if she caught me – yikes! – there I was, unarmed, so I climbed the baobab.'

'It's not possible! How did you do it?'

'How do cats fly?'

'Cats don't fly!'

'They don't fly over there in Europe, miss. Here they do fly! Put a greyhound behind a cat and see if it doesn't fly. A dogged cat can climb any tree, even a eucalyptus. And depending on the dog, scale even a smooth wall. What's for sure is that I flew, up I went. I stayed up there – stark naked – or maybe I should say, given my vantage point, "*stork* naked" – till night fell and Maria Rita tired and went away.'

(Fatita de Matos, the unhappy lover)

In the spacious living room of the house of Fatita de Matos, Sis' Fatita, in the tropical forest of Lobito, there are five oil portraits, each measuring a metre by a metre and a half. In every one Fatita de Matos is seated in the same wicker chair, in an almost identical position, with a book in her lap. The first canvas was painted in 1946. Fatita is twenty years old, still a virgin, she's reading *Love of Perdition* by Camilo Castelo Branco. In the second she is thirty, she has four illegitimate children, and she is reading *Love of Perdition*. In the third she is forty, she's dressed in black for the death of her youngest son, and she is reading *Love of Perdition*. In the fourth she's fifty, she has seven grandchildren, and she is reading *Love of Perdition*. Finally, in the fifth picture, she is sixty, she has twelve grandchildren, three great-grandchildren, and she's reading *A Hundred Years of Solitude* by Gabriel García Márquez. She painted all the pictures herself.

'There are two missing,' I say to her. 'Did you stop painting?'

Fatita smiles. She has a young smile. The smile is the same in all five pictures. It hasn't aged:

'No, I didn't stop painting, I just don't like painting old ladies.'

She falls silent. Her elder daughter, Dr Pitanga de Matos, interrupts the silence. She says that her mother suffered a lot because of Faustino Manso. She talks about her mother's love as though she had suffered it herself. Fatita de Matos just limits herself to smiling, every once in a while, somewhat mockingly, or otherwise nodding her head in confirmation, her eyes lowered. Pitanga de Matos is a robust woman. Her burnt skin reflects the light like a mirror. She has very lively grey eyes. She studied socialist economics in the former Yugoslavia. For two or three years she was deputy finance minister. Today she's the successful director of a fishing company, based in Lobito, and a fish-flour factory in Tombua. She speaks in a firm, slightly nasal voice:

'Mother met Daddy at a Carnival dance. Love at first sight. His band was playing a bolero, *Bésame Mucho*, of course you know it, everyone knows it.'

She sings. The way she sings, the timbre, something about it reminds me of Faustino Manso:

Bésame, bésame mucho
como si fuera esta noche la última vez
bésame, bésame mucho
que tengo miedo a perderte,
perderte después.

And then Dad started singing, he started singing turned towards Mum, his eyes fixed on hers…

Quiero tenerte muy cerca
mirarme en tus ojos, verte junto a mí.
Piensa que tal vez mañana
yo estaré lejos, muy lejos de tí

Think that perhaps tomorrow, I'll be very far, very far away from you… He meant it, he really did, but she, poor thing, didn't realise it. They started going out, in secret, first the odd kiss, then some feeling around, and five months later Mum turned out to be pregnant. Scandal! Mum, an only child, had always been treated as a princess. My grandfather worked for the Benguela Railroad, Goan, a huge man – you see that photo? That's him. We look alike. My grandmother, a Benguela lady, with a very conservative attitude, stayed home, devastated. Granddad closed Mum in her room and ordered the maids to give her nothing to eat or to drink until she denounced her seducer…

…That's the word he used – seducer – I think it even sounds rather lovely…

…Finally on the third day she gave them a name. Faustino Manso. Granddad went in search of him, armed with a pistol, but didn't find him.

He had left for Luanda. So Granddad took a steamer to the capital, deter-mined to bring Faustino back to Benguela by force – kicking him all the way if needs be, he said – and to oblige him to marry Mum. He arrived too late. Faustino had got married two days earlier...'

Fatita de Matos smiled.

'I liked Faustino. He was a sweet man...'

'Really sweet, yes, he must have been that. Pure chocolate! So sweet, so sweet that in spite of the fact that he'd got married you continued to see him, always in hiding. There were three more children after me. My little brother died of malarial poisoning aged fifteen. Balantine, the second, lives in Rio de Janeiro. Malibu is in Luanda...'

Fatita de Matos lifts her face, defiant:

'When Malibu was born I was already married to Faustino!'

Pitanga shrugs her shoulders:

'Married? In a manner of speaking. Married in the manner of these parts...'

This is how it was. Fatita de Matos awoke early one stormy morning and found herself looking at Fausino Manso, sitting on her bed, completely drenched. A lightning-flash illuminated him and she saw him as he would look forty years later: a filthy, shaky old man who leaned on walls to keep himself upright. She wanted to know what had happened. The old man replied, 'Nothing.' Then he ran his fingers through his hair and said he was never going back to Luanda. He added:

'I must be yours until the hour I die.'

Fatita had dreamed of that moment for seven years. She got up and went to the window to look at the storm. In her dreams Faustino had appeared on just such a night. He would embrace her, rest her head in his lap, plait her hair, and she would cry. In the morning, very early, she would wake up to find her pillow damp with tears. Faced with reality, however, Fatita de Matos did not cry. On the contrary, she suddenly found herself wanting to laugh. She laughed with rage, in harsh, explosive bursts, remembering the nights she had spent alone, and the shame of facing people in the street, the sound of laughter behind her, and the fierce silences of her father and her mother's fainting spells, and as she laughed she gripped a chair and with a strength she didn't know she possessed brought it down onto the head of (and to the shock of) her lover. In films, especially in westerns, it's common practice to throw chairs at other people's heads without the victim appearing to suffer all that much. But in the reality we live in, we know that chairs are harder – or heads softer, or perhaps both – than in the fantasy universe inhabited by film stars. Faustino was hospitalised and remained unconscious for three days and two nights. When he finally opened his eyes, dazed, he saw Fatita de Matos sitting before him. She was sitting in a chair, in a corner, reading *Love of Perdition*, completely dressed in black, like an old widow, and so concentrated that she was startled when she heard his fragile voice:

'You're right,' the man murmured. 'I promise to be yours after death too.'

He didn't manage to keep even the first part of his promise.

Faustino Manso only became a professional musician after he'd left Luanda. In the capital he'd worked (vaguely) as an employee of the postal service. He played double bass, as part of a jazz band, at private parties or in one club or other, almost always at weekends. In Lobito he managed to find work as a pianist at the Hotel Terminus. Up till that point he had never played piano in public before. It was relatively well-paid work that allowed him a lot of time off. One night a young South African came over to congratulate him. His name was Basil du Toit. His father, who owned a chain of hotels in South Africa, had sent him over to Angola to study the market there. Basil, who was originally from Cape Town, talked to him with enormous enthusiasm about Sophiatown, and about how jazz back home was changing its colours. He assured him that if one day he wanted to visit South Africa he'd give him every support.

Two years passed. In 1965, one hot, humid December morning, Faustino set off on his bicycle. He usually stopped by the post office where he would spend some time chatting with his old colleagues. He returned just minutes later, very excited, waving a letter from Basil in his hand. The South African had offered him a good contract to play in Cape Town for three months. Seeing him so enthused, Fatita did not even try to dissuade him. A month later, right after Christmas, Faustino Manso boarded a ship headed for South Africa.

The house is in the middle of a huge, badly kept plot of land, and is surrounded by five skinny palms and a young mango tree more or less dying of thirst. It is a fine example of colonial architecture – it has a cement base, with elegant arches on which a light wooden structure rests, in faded emerald green. The broad, fresh veranda circles the whole way around it. I've seen similar buildings on the Caribbean islands.

'I wasn't born in this house. We moved here when I was fifteen. But I got pregnant and went to live with a spinster aunt in Benguela. I came back after my father died…'

'And your mother? Did she get on well with Faustino?'

'No, no! She ignored him. She acted as though he didn't exist. Never addressed a single word to him. I ended up convincing myself that she actually couldn't see him…'

'It was as though Daddy was a ghost,' Pitanga agrees. 'Once she went into the bathroom while he was in the tub. Daddy started shouting…'

Fatita laughs:

'It's true. I'd forgotten about that. Faustino started shouting and I went to see what was happening. And there was Mother calmly having a pee. I said to her, "Mother, for shame! Look, Faustino's here!" And she, shrugging her shoulders, "Faustino? What Faustino? There's no Faustino." It was like that the whole time.'

We arrived in Lubango yesterday morning. We're set up in an apartment, in the centre of the city, with three rooms, a bathroom, a kitchen and living room. It's on the third floor, without a lift. This morning we had breakfast at the Café Huíla, on the ground floor of the same building and which also belongs to the owners of the apartment. It seems to be a meeting place for the local bourgeoisie. It's almost always full. A lot of whites from the area come here; they're known here as 'chicoronhos', an ironic corruption of 'senhor colono', that is, 'colonial gentleman'. They look at us with some mistrust. They don't get close.

We spent yesterday visiting the 'tourist sites' and some possible locations for the film: the Huíla Grand Hotel, Christ the King, Leba's serpentine forest road, the Tundavala Gorge. Jordi took a lot of photographs. We're travelling with a taxi driver, she's called Dona Augusta, whom we met right as we were coming out of the airport. The Huíla Grand Hotel is now painted in the Sonangol colours, red and yellow, an anxious yellow, sudden as a shot, which makes the whole building stand out from the cityscape. The interior retains a certain colonial elegance. The roads here are in very good condition. Christ the King, a slightly crude dwarf replica of the magnificent Christ the Redeemer that keeps watch over Rio de Janeiro, has been completely restored. From there you have a view over the whole city. Then we went to Tundavala. The sky was stormy. Huge flakes of dark cloud ran agitated towards the east. The light from the sun, illuminating them sidelong, accentuated their texture and their vigour. All of a sudden the road opened out into an enormously broad plain completely covered in huge grey rocks. The size and arrangement of these rocks suggested deliberate disorder, an act of intelligence, if convulsed, like a letter written by a madman. It is only after this that the gorge appears. No photograph can do it justice. Faced with this sudden abyss we felt as though our reason was escaping us. That just is not possible. And yet, there it is.

Afterwards we went on to Chibia. I wanted to show Karen Inês's Bar. It's on the main road. There aren't many roads in Chibia. The owner, a man now of a certain age, a very fair *mestiço* – mixed race, that is – 'struck with whiteness', according to Dona Augusta, was born in Malanje and came to live in Chibia straight after independence. He has eyes of diaphanous blue, almost transparent. A staunch Sporting fan, he'd painted the little space in green and white, and put a plastic lion in one of the corners. He told me he clearly remembers the first time I came into his bar, four years earlier, accompanied by the writer Jorge Arrimar, a native of the town, back home after thirty years away. I sat down with Karen at one of the tables:

'Do you understand why I've brought you here?'

She didn't understand.

'This, my dear, is going to be Leopoldina's Bar, the bar of Faustino's third widow.'

She shook her head.

'This could be the bar. But it's not going to be in Chibia, it's going to be in Namibe. Namibe is a coastal town. It has a port. Our man, don't forget, is a kind of sailor, a woman in every port.'

(Conversation with a humble-looking man, very drunk, on the way out of Inês's Bar.)

'Old man, I need your help, I'm suffering from the image…'

'How so, suffering from the image?'

'I'm suffering from the image. I want to ask the scientist: might there be other people who're also suffering from the same thing I am?'

'I don't understand, what exactly is it you're suffering from?'

'You talk to the person on the wall. The image talks to you.'

'I don't talk to images…'

'That's right, scientist; I do.'

'And what does the image say?'

'He says he is going to die. But now, now, the voice is starting to disappear. The shirt's like a snake walking across his body. You people are scientists, you'll pass it on, my name is Elídio Cabinda.'

(The first mermaid was dead)

A short dog, sand-coloured, ran past. Behind him trailed a strong smell of wet hair and dry fish. The smell seemed to be the only concrete thing about him. Other dogs, further ahead, burst from the dunes and joined the first. Mandume headed off in long bounds, down the beach, in an attempt to film the pack. I shouted after him to be careful. He waved back to me with his free hand. He was shirtless, a red kerchief tied round his head.

'There's no danger,' Bartolomeu assured me. 'It's just those dogs here, and they won't attack a man...'

The Bay of Tigers. I read Pedro Rosa Mendes' book. I should have brought it with me. I already can't remember what he wrote about this old population of fishermen, today dead and buried (or almost buried) by the living dunes of the desert. All I retained was the metaphor. We're doing the journey to Namibe, or Moçâmedes – which is what the city used to be called in colonial times, after already having been called Angra do Negro – in one of my niece's trawlers. Mateus, the captain, has dropped anchor outside the Bay of Tigers and we've disembarked to visit some ghosts. Mandume reappeared half an hour later, tired of running after the dogs. He looked mysterious.

'I want to show you something...'

He sat down on the sand, his back against the sun, throwing some shadow on the screen of the video camera:

'You see?'

I laughed.

'Good one. It really does look like one of those Fontcuberta mermaids...'

'I didn't do this, I swear! I found it like this.'

The Spanish photographer Joan Fontcuberta attained notoriety by setting up – with a great deal of humour – images of mythical beasts. Among his collection highlights include a strange series of mermaid fossils. The images recorded by Mandume remind me of them: the upper part of the skeleton of a man, or of a monkey, including the skull, linked to what seem to be the clean bones of a dolphin. The discovery managed to excite our hosts. From time to time I can hear Bartolomeu's shouts:

'Over there, over there, look, jumping in the water, a mermaid!'

At first Mandume pretended to be amused by these jokes. He doesn't laugh at them any longer. He gets irritated by Bartolomeu's irreverence (which is sometimes a little brutal, I grant you), and everything that through his gestures and laughs show him ungovernable and immoderate. He hugged me. He whispered in my ear:

'This guy's an actor, he's playing the part of a black man, or what he thinks a black man's meant to be. I'm a black man and I'm not like that.'

'Maybe you're not a black man.'

'You don't think?'

'Don't know. After all, what's a black man, anyway?'

Pouca Sorte continued over land with Malembemalembe. It will take him two or three days to reach Namibe. We'll do the rest of the journey with him. It was Pitanga who suggested we come by trawler. Curious, I accepted, because I wanted to experience what Faustino would have felt. The sea may even be the same, but it's a different boat, certainly a more comfortable one, and a different time too. We weren't very lucky. At four o'clock the sky darkened and it started to rain. The wind lifted the waves. Howls and hisses and the heavy agitation of the water striking the wood. The trawler danced dangerously. If I leaned over the main rail I could see the sea getting closer, till I could almost reach it with my fingertips, and then moving away, further away, exposing almost the whole back of the vessel.

'Oh no!' Mandume sighed. 'Not back to Canjala again!'

He said this, and threw up over the side. Bartolomeu copied him. I managed to refrain. I think it's genetic…

And of course, no, I'm deceiving myself – I forget so often that my father isn't my father; that is, that Dário isn't my biological father. Dário's father was a captain in the merchant navy. My paternal grandfather died fishing for salt cod. Everyone in Ílhavo has some connection to the sea. It's only now, as I write these lines, that it occurs to me, I don't actually have any sailor's blood in me. Pity, it's something I'd been so proud of...

And then suddenly everything was serene, the sea confused with the blue of the sky. I don't know if we were sailing or flying.

Perhaps we were flying.

Land sighted. A golden sheet floating on the horizon. The sea has calmed. We slip, as in a dream, across the splendid evening. Mandume films the group of white houses in the distance. Bartolomeu shouts:

'Namibeeeeeeeee!'

Old Mateus smiles. A gentle smile. Warm as an embrace.

'Good place, Moçâmedes. Here I was born.'

(The silence of chess players)

Silence.

No, silences.

I could write a short essay on silence. Or rather, a catalogue of silences illustrating them for deaf people*:

The silence that precedes ambushes;
The silence at the moment of taking a penalty;
The silence of a funeral march;
The silence of sunflowers;
The silence of God after massacres;
The silence of a whale suffering on a beach;
The silence of Sunday mornings in a little village in the interior of the Alentejo;
The silence of the ice-pick that killed Trotsky;
The silence of the bride before the I do;
Etc.

There are placid silences and others that are convulsed. Happy silences, and others that are dramatic. There are those that smell of incense, and those that stink of manure. There are those that savour intensely of ripe guavas; those that are kept in the inside coat pocket together with the

---

* Assuming that someone who lives in complete silence doesn't know what silence consists of. Does a blind man know what darkness is?

photograph of a dead son; those which go naked through the streets; arrogant silences, and the ones that beg.

The silence of chess players is different from any other. These two in front of me now, unlikely adversaries, are between them producing a silence I recognise from halls very different to the one we share now. The first player has a huge pumpkin head, baked by the sun, and wears what little hair he has left arranged into rebellious ruddy locks, loose over his shoulders. The second could earn his living as a model for tourists in search of typical African characters, if it weren't for the fact that this largely abandoned city does not have many visitors: he's a *mucubal*. He's one not in the way I'm Portuguese, you understand, but in the way that a *pauliteiro* folk dancer from Miranda dressed up for a folk festival is Portuguese. There's actually a difference: a *pauliteiro* from Miranda isn't really a *pauliteiro*, he's a *pauliteiro* for the time he spends on stage; then he takes off his typical outfit and replaces it with jeans and a T-shirt with the face of Bob Marley or Che Guevara. Once, in Santiago de Chile, I filmed a homeless man who dressed like a Mapuche Indian. He even wore a sign at his chest: 'Authentic Indian. Made in Chile.' All that the man sitting in front of me now lacks is the sign. He's tall, elegant, broad-shouldered, with well-drawn features, long sideburns like a seventies' rock singer. His hair is covered by a coloured cloth, and around his waist he's wearing a sort of loincloth, also made of fabric. Two glass-bead necklaces, one of which carries a safety pin, attract attention (they attracted mine) to the solid neck and strong chest. He greeted us, when we arrived, in faultless Portuguese. He asked Bartolomeu if Sporting had won. He was pleased with the reply:

'Good old Sporting!'

In this place, as far as I can see, everyone is a fan of Sporting. Leopoldina's Bar is painted green and white. In one of the corners, fixed to the wall, in a kind of shrine, between lit candles, I came across a green-painted stuffed cat. 'What do you want?' retorted the *mucubal* when he noticed my surprise. 'It was the only lion we could get hold of.'

The *mucubal* talks to his companion in a language that is dry and sibilant, which seems to me like Russian. Victória, the daughter of my father's third wife, serves the players another two beers. I ask her for three for us. I ask her:

'Are they speaking Russian?'

She nods, expressionless. It wasn't hard to find Leopoldina's Bar. Even before we arrived someone had warned us that Leopoldina had died.

Victória, her youngest daughter, runs the establishment. She receives us in a friendly manner, but as soon as I give my name and tell her what I've come for, the smile disappears:

'I never met your father. I don't remember him. He abandoned us even before I was born. I never wanted to meet him.'

I'm going to have to work hard to get her to talk to me.

The redhead is called Nicolau Alicerces Peshkov. His grandfather served under Nicholas II as a cavalry officer. He fled to Paris after the October Revolution, and from Paris ended up in Luanda, as a boat dragged by a storm finds itself washed up on some nameless island, and there set down to rest and lick his wounds. He married a German woman, from Namibia, set up a photography studio, and had one son, whom he named after the last tsar. The lad continued in his father's line of work. He was also interested in the cinema and in the middle of the last century moved to Benguela where he hired a hall to show films. Unfortunately he was a heavy drinker, he gambled, and had something of a propensity for unhappy love affairs. He died in the arms of his elder son, Nicolau II, the redhead, who received as his only inheritance a projector and half a dozen films in very poor condition. For some years, both before and after independence, Nicolau earned his living showing movie classics – black and white – in the poor neighbourhoods of Lobito, Benguela, Namibe and Lubango, and in country villages along the route of the railroad. He was defeated by television and later by video. To find an interested audience he had to travel to ever more remote places. He went around by bicycle, always accompanied by a thin, shy adolescent lad, called James Dean. I can see him right now, little James, sitting out there, in the shadow of a wall, reading a book. I wanted to know what his real name was. He looked at me strangely:

'My real name is James, auntie. James Dean.'

He showed me his identity card. He is indeed called James Dean, black, born in Lobito on 4 July 1990. Nicolau II and James Dean know the desert well. They cross it by bicycle. They stop at any shepherds' camp, attach a sheet to a wall or to two big trees when there is no wall; they set up the projector, and run the film. James Dean pedals throughout the showing to produce electricity.

'On a moonless night there's no better cinema,' Nicolau assured me with conviction. 'And the film's very good too.'

The film is a rather random collage of photograms. Nicolau assembled it with the patience of a saint from what was left of his father's films: *The African Queen, Casablanca, Vertigo, On the Waterfront* and, naturally, *Rebel without a Cause*.

His companion at chess, 'You can call me João', was kidnapped by Angolan armed forces when he was twelve or thirteen years old. He learned to fire a gun at the same time as he learned to speak Portuguese. Later he spent fifteen months in Moscow, studying 'Persuasion Techniques', whatever they are (I'd rather not know), and left fluent in Russian. Demobbed in 1998 he returned home, to the desert, and went back to being a simple shepherd. 'A simple shepherd' is his own phrase. 'Persuasion Techniques' too, obviously. Whenever he comes to Namibia he passes through Leopoldina's Bar to play chess with Nicolau II. He gives him Russian lessons. The other teaches him about the history of cinema.

(Fragments of the interview with Victória Manso)

Me: Did your mother used to speak to you about Faustino Manso?

VM: No, I never think of him as my father. He abandoned us before I was born. Then my mother had other husbands. This man didn't look for us even after he came back to Angola. Do you think he helped my mother even once? Nothing. Nothing of anything. When I think about him, I get the feeling of a lot of anger in my heart.

Me: Do you know how your mother came to meet Faustino Manso?

VM: I know what they say, that he kidnapped my mother. Stole her away from her people. Took her to Sá de Bandeira. She worked for him.

Me: Do you know your family on your mother's side?

VM: They're *mucubals*.

Me: Yes. Do you know them?

VM: No, they have their own lives there. And we have ours.

…

Me: Have you ever been to Luanda?

VM: No. I've been to Oshakati.

…

Me: When Faustino left Lobito he was heading for Cape Town. Do you know why he stayed here?

VM: He didn't stay here. The bastard left us, he went away…

Me: He stayed three years…

VM: Yes, he stayed three years… No, I don't know why. I don't want to know. Ask my brother, Babaera. You'll find him in Lubango. Go there and ask him.

(A hero by the side of the road)

Malembemalembe was making a determined effort to climb the Leba mountain range. Mandume had installed himself with the video camera by one of the windows. For the first time he was visibly excited by the landscape.

'Amazing curves!'

'Amazing curves!' Pouca Sorte agreed. 'This road of ours has more curves than a beautiful woman.'

The boys laughed. Bartolomeu slapped him on the back.

'You believe in fidelity, bro?'

'Me? Not me! I don't believe a man can like just one woman for his whole life.'

'Hear that, auntie? That's the perspective of a real African. As for me, I think that a man who only ever likes one woman, it's because he doesn't like any. There's no such thing as faithful men, only men who are unable to be unfaithful. I've heard that the only mammals that are monogamous are whales…'

'Not even whales!' Pouca Sorte said. 'It's just that they're very discreet creatures…'

All three laughed. After this, there was silence. Mandume distracted, filming the landscape. Bartolomeu suddenly serious; at a certain point he asked Pouca Sorte to pull the van over. He got out into the bright afternoon light. I went with him. He beat a path through the tall, golden grass till he reached a spot with a small stone cross. At the base of the cross there was a marble plaque. I read: 'Here fell Bernardo Falcato defending his country. Rest in peace, commander.'

Bartolomeu turned to me:

'He was my father.'

There were tears in his eyes. In 1975, at the start of the civil war, Bernardo Falcato, then a young medical student, hurriedly made commander of the FAPLA, tried to hold an armed South African division. He had five *mucubal* warriors with him. When he ran out of bullets he threw away his gun and ran down the road, arms open, baring his chest, to meet his horrible death.

'No one remembers him anymore.'

Bartolomeu wiped away the tears with the back of his right hand. I hugged him, hard, not knowing how to comfort him. At this moment Mandume appeared, holding the video camera.

'Can someone tell me what's going on?' His voice trembled. 'Is this guy bothering you?!'

I had a desire to hit him. I shouted:

'Shut up, idiot!'

I'd never called him that before. But worse than that was the tone of my voice when I'd said it, a blade of ice that cut my lips. Mandume looked at me, shocked, turned his back to me and moved away. A short while ago, here in the hotel, I asked him to forgive me. I explained to him what had happened. It didn't do much good. I feel we're moving apart.

There was a time Lubango prided itself on having the largest swimming pool in the world. And if it never was actually the largest in the world, it must at least have come close. Today, even empty, it retains its immensity and continues to astonish visitors. A silence of separated trees surrounds it. Sharp cypresses are staked on the ground, here and there, beside round, leafy mango trees. Just behind these you can see eucalyptus, then pines. It reminds me of a big international airport with all races together, inadvertently, but determined not to mix.

Going up a stone staircase you come to an elegant building painted in a gentle pink and white – the Lubango Casino. Colonel Babaera, Victória's older brother, was waiting for us at the entrance. A bearded bear. I liked him at once. It was as though I had always known him:

'Sis?! If you'd warned me you were coming – not to mention that you existed – I would have had an ox slaughtered...'

Babaera took us in his car, a black Hummer, to a spacious residence, beautiful and half hidden behind a well-kept garden. The wall is low, like those of almost all the remaining residences in the city, which came as a nice surprise to me. In Luanda I sometimes felt I needed more air, trying to find a bit of green, a bit more blue, as I raced through a confused labyrinth of high walls. You breathe here. The fresh, clean air does you good, like a hosepipe shower that washes your soul.

'Luanda?!' Babaera laughed when I told him of my discomfort. 'The capital is a horror, sis. First God created Angola, then the Devil came along and created Luanda.'

Babaera was only three when Faustino left. But for all that he speaks of him with admiration. He says he saved him from being a simple ox-herder. With affection he keeps a handful of memories – going for walks, in the late afternoon, hand in hand, his father naming the songs of the birds, teaching him to spin a top, playing piano with him on his lap, talking to people on the street. He knew everyone.

'I'm going to show you a treasure, sis…'

He showed me a collection of records of Faustino that he'd acquired in various countries over a number of years: twelve singles and three LPs. Only one single is missing – a rarity, recorded in South Africa. One of the LPs has on its sleeve the picture of a young *mucubal* woman, tall and thin, in front of the Tundavala Gorge.

'Let me introduce you to my mother, Dona Leopoldina…'

Babaera has three daughters, Muxima, Rosa Maria and Belita, and they have all inherited the lofty posture of their grandmother. The latter two are twins. Muxima, an agronomist-engineer, already married, played in the national basketball team. She's a metre eighty. Rosa Maria and Belita are almost identical miniatures of their sister, though with lighter skin and straighter hair. They're studying hotel management in Cape Town. They had come back to spend a few days' holiday. They dragged Bartolomeu into the kitchen, demonstrating a rather excessive enthusiasm for their cousin (which irritated me a little), and after half an hour served us a fish broth which was one of the best dishes I have ever eaten in my life.

After lunch Babaera took us to a little room which had chairs arranged around a huge flat-screen TV. He turned the TV on and put a DVD in the machine. He dimmed the lights:

'What you're going to see is a bit of amateur footage. I bought it from a Portuguese trader in Lisbon, half a dozen years ago. Then I had it transferred to DVD. It was filmed near Tundavala, in 1957, probably in December…'

Yellow grain. A sky with rips in it, sudden flashes of brilliance. Dark rocks, tall and wrinkled, thrown onto a flat ground. A path drawn like a labyrinth between the rocks. And then, coming up on the left, a bicycle. A man, on a bicycle, carrying a double bass. The image jumps. You see three couples sitting on the ground, in relaxed poses, around a cloth with plates and food. They eat. They laugh. The image jumps again. What you see now is a slender man embracing a double bass. The man is sitting on one of the strange black rocks that emerged at the start of the film. In the background, like a screen, a dark storm sky. The man plays. You cannot hear what he is playing. The film has no sound.

It is like an image stolen from a dream.

(Fragments of an interview with Col. Babaera Manso)

Me: Victória told me you might know why Faustino stayed for three years between Moçâmades and Sá da Bandeira, rather than going straight on to Cape Town, as he'd originally intended...

BM: Because of a woman, why else? A Portuguese lady he met on the boat. The lady in question was married to a prosperous planta-tion-owner, based here, in Lubango, but who spent whole seasons in Lisbon and in Luanda. Daddy fell in love with this woman, and instead of continuing his trip he decided to wait for the next boat. He planned to stay three weeks at most. He ended up staying three years.

Me: How did you find this out?

BM: Daddy told me...

Me: Told you?! When?

BM: In Luanda. I spent some time with him in Luanda, after independence, obviously, for the whole time I was stationed in the capital. We used to have lunch at the old Biker – d'you know it? – a beautiful old beer place opposite the *Jornal de Angola*, I think they've closed it down now. I saw him for the last time five or six years ago. We used to talk a lot, about music, about travelling, about women. We were good friends.

Me: And the Portuguese lady Faustino fell in love with?

BM: She was called Perpétua. Her husband discovered the two of them were having an affair, he intercepted one of Dad's letters and did the most stupid thing a man can do in circumstances like that – he killed himself! He put a bullet in his head. This was three or four months after Dad disembarked in Moçâmedes, though I don't suppose anyone noticed the coincidence, no one understood the gesture of the poor man. And Dona Perpétua, she sold the farm and was never heard of again. But my mother appeared and my father fell in love with her. He fell in love very easily.

Me: And why did he leave?

BM: Basil du Toit, the friend who'd invited him to go to Cape Town, started insisting again. So Dad packed his bags and left...

Me: I presume in Cape Town he found another woman...

BM: Naturally. Seretha du Toit, Basil's younger sister...

Me: A Boer?!

BM: A white woman, and blonde, and this in the middle of apartheid. Dad was a brave man. Seretha was just twenty years old. I've seen photos of her, very pretty. A choreographer. She's well known today. Very well respected.

Me: Do you have contact details for her?

BM: No. But it shouldn't be hard to find her. As I've said, Seretha is a public figure. She was imprisoned during apartheid. Today she directs a contemporary dance group. Our dad corresponded with her for many years.

(Albino Amador's secret)

Just days ago, in Luanda, a Chinese *candongueiro* driver passed me – yes, Chinese!

A skinny, nervous little man, with sharp eyes. He threw himself forward, a blind leap, like a drunk turkey after its head has been cut off. I braked, unbalancing a fat grocer-woman who was sitting next to me, a little goat on her lap. The animal hit its horns on the dashboard, poor thing. I thought that wasn't on, and shouted to the Chinese man:

'Careful!'

Just that: 'Careful.' I never swear. I had (I thank God!) a very fine education. Then the man stuck his head through the window and shrieked:

'Go back to the Congo, *Langa!*'

I swear to God! To me, Albino Amador, a pure Luandan, practically an island native. I was born in the Workers' Neighbourhood, but my father was a native of the Ilha. To go back to the Chinaman, I'm mentioning this episode to show you that this business of being a *candongueiro* driver is a lucrative activity, one that everybody wants, so much so that even a recently arrived immigrant to the country risks driving through Luanda's hellish traffic. It already paid well even in the difficult times of socialism. I don't wonder that there were ministers – and no small number of them – who put vehicles into service. And today there must be too, as well as actors, artists, engineers, traders *et cetera*, that is, and many others. But even I haven't always been a *candongueiro* driver. There was a time when I had a future, a good future, just like the best of the best of them. My old mother used to talk of me with pride, she'd show her friends the photos of when I entered the seminary; she'd say:

'This son of mine will go far.'

It could have been like that. Sometimes I fall asleep and dream of it. I see myself as a bishop, a cardinal. But man makes plans and God... God just breaks wind.

God, God, God! We should stop talking of God. I'm tired of God: Out, God! Out, God!

He who tends to all the monsters of the sea, and all living beings that drag themselves along, which the waters produce in abundance according to their species, and who tends to the birds that fly, and to the plentiful shoal of living things, and who for all that abandons my thoughts, just as he abandoned my life so wretchedly. Out, God! Out, God!

I made my own plans, with my right hand, and with my left unmade them all.

I do mean to tell you the truth. But not just yet. I crave your patience.

Before the scandal (the thing I don't want to talk about yet) I was a happy man. I still am, from time to time, at the moments when I forget myself. This is what happens to me: I'm alone on the street, me and Malembemalembe, and the great silence of nature is around me, and I get it into my head to sing. At the wheel of a *candongueiro* you do, sometimes, meet interesting people, and I do like to travel. This job with the film people, for example, that was a gift from heaven. The young Portuguese couple is nice. Though the little Angolan annoys me a bit, I must confess, with that propensity he has for exaggeration and his constant praise and exultation of mulatta womanhood. I have no sympathy for mulattos at all. But he does know how to tell stories and to make everyone laugh. The girl, Laurentina, has fallen for him, poor thing, and she's going to suffer a bit.

Canyon, southern Angola
Thursday, 3 November 2005

Six p.m. – There's not much light left for me to write. I came back to the jeep a few moments ago. I can hear Karen playing *Muxima*. The sombre cry of the saxophone echoes long on the high earth walls. *Muxima*, a traditional song, first popularised by the group N'Gola Ritmos, from Liceu Vieira Dias, and then in a slightly different version, a bilingual version, by the Ouro Negro Duo, means 'heart', in quimbundo. The song makes reference to the Church of Our Lady of Muxima, on the left bank of the Quanza River, some hundred and forty kilometres from Luanda. As the legend goes, the church sprung up miraculously, from one moment to the next, somewhere in the first half of the seventeenth century.

I don't know what this place is called.

The Canyon.

His name is Johan.

Johan is twenty-three years old. He looks at least thirty-five. Cold, green eyes. He reminds me of Joaquin Phoenix as Commodus, in *Gladiator*, without the armour, naturally, and without the harelip. He admits to being 'the crazy one in the family'. He speaks Portuguese with the accent and the same happy awkwardnesses of an Angolan rustic. His father, a South African, came to Angola some fifteen years ago in search of diamonds – he told me this himself. He didn't find diamonds, and set up a fish-flour factory in the old town of Porto Alexandre, what's called Tombua today. After losing the factory, following a complicated court case, he built half a dozen huts a few kilometres from Moçâmedes:

Paradise Lodge. Johan grew up around here. He studied in Canada, and returned. He has turned out to be an exceptional driver.

The Canyon: a pass that runs parallel to the coast. There at the end, where at just this moment Karen is executing her intimate concert, entirely dressed in white, like a New Age fairy, the big earth walls outline the image of Africa in the sky.

On a rock I saw a dead scorpion. It was at least fifteen centimetres long. It was splayed out and dry, but even so instilled fear. Johan told me that his father was bitten in this same spot by a snake. He and his father go barefoot. Once, many years ago, I interviewed a Boer businessman. He told me that he'd been born into the heart of a very poor family. His father had been the first person in his family to wear shoes. According to him, apartheid allowed Boers to provide shoes for their whole tribe. I suppose that in some of them there must be a perverse sort of nostalgia for the time when they didn't wear shoes.

Eight p.m. – I'm now in the dining room of the Paradise Lodge. A fat, bald man is playing guitar and singing in Afrikaans. My whole life I thought there could be nothing worse in the world than country music. It turns out there is: country music sung in Afrikaans. There's another Boer couple, who work here, and two adolescents. They all seem very excited at the fat man's performance. I'm assailed by an uncomfortable feeling: I feel exceedingly foreign. I'm in Angola and I feel foreign. On the walls are posters with pictures of fish, and photos of fishermen each proudly bearing his trophy.

(Place and identity)

I'm not from here. I'm not from here. I'm not from here.

I repeat this silently through the day.

I think that people hear me, hear what I'm thinking, because they look at me strangely, rather sidelong, like a bird sizing up its prey. Some of them ask:

'You're not Angolan, right?'

Others don't ask anything. I tell them anyway:

'I'm Portuguese!'

The reaction varies. One or other might smile:

'I'm a Sporting fan.'

Or Porto, or Benfica; either way. One old man wanted to know what had become of Eusébio, the Black Panther. Another retorted, seriously:

'I used to be too, mate. But then I grew out of it.'

I was hired once to film a documentary about far-right groups in Portugal. At one point we had to film an anti-immigrant protest in Lisbon. Maria, the director, a dry, harsh woman, but one whose coldness hid a huge heart, instructed me to position myself in front of the protesters, then to wait as they surrounded me and then moved past me. I counted some fifty young men, most of them muscly, many of them skinheads, with skulls and swastikas tattooed on their arms. Most were wearing black T-shirts. On them I could read: 'Things here are looking *black*.' I didn't feel any fear, didn't even realise that I was in any danger, not until it was too late. Suddenly one of the men stuck himself in front of me, shouting:

'Hey, *black man*! Black man! Go back to where you came from, black man!'

'Shoot it!' the director ordered me through my earpiece. 'Shoot it! Don't stop shooting.'

I gritted my teeth and did what she was telling me. Today, looking back at what happened from this distance, I think it was the right attitude. A calm sort of guy, with a moustache and goatee, put his arms round the other lad and whispered something in his ear, and moved him away. The others ignored me. As I saw them from behind I began to shake. I was shaking so hard I couldn't stay on my feet. I had to put the camera down and sit down in the alleyway. Maria, anxious, came to be with me.

'You OK?'

I felt the furies overcoming me:

'Get out of here!' I shouted at her. 'Get out of here now or I'm going to thump you!'

The furies, yes. Alecto, Megaera and Tisiphone, the ancient furies of the inferno, I could feel them descend on me and control me, with their appalling heat, their acidic smell, the harsh lash of voices in anger. I got up and kicked the camera hard. It was a good kick. I limped for a week, but it calmed me down. The furies left me, left behind an immense sadness. I sat down again, and cried. Maria sat down beside me. She wiped away my tears with a paper tissue. She said to me:

'I've lost a lot of struggles in my life, and some important ones, but there's one I know I'm going to win. It's as if I'd already won it, and you know which it is? It's the struggle to make this country what it was for many centuries, a place of meetings and mixtures. Those guys, we can't even consider them our enemies, they're a mistake, an aberration, like a bird without wings…'

I laughed:

'A rainbow in shades of grey.'

'Or worse! A voiceless nightingale…'

'A carnivorous sheep…'

'A happy *fado*-singer!'

'A blind photographer!'

'Oh, blind photographers really do exist!' she laughed. 'I know a Frenchman – of Slovenian background – called Evgen Bavcar. Blind in both eyes. And he's pretty good…'

This became a sort of game between us. We continued to play it whenever we met again. I remembered those shaved heads recently when, not long ago, in the middle of a violent discussion about the qualities and defects of the Portuguese, Bartolomeu wanted to know if I'd never been the object of any sort of racist violence in Portugal. I said no, without thinking, and then immediately remembered that guy. I corrected myself:

'Yes, I was. You're right.'

'Yeah!' shouted Bartolomeu in triumph. 'You see, all racists, the *tugas*!'

'Yes, of course, all of them!'

'OK, not all of them, obviously. But they'll never treat you like you're really Portuguese.'

'I am really Portuguese.'

'Don't give me that crap. You're an Angolan born in Portugal...'

'No! I'm not from here.'

(I'm not from here. I'm not from here. I'm not from here.)

'And when you sing the national anthem – 'our distinguished grandfathers, etc.' – what do you feel? Hell, your grandfathers were Angolan! They certainly weren't the distinguished ones, whoever the hell the distinguished ones were.'

'And what do you feel when you sing your national anthem? "Angola, advance! Revolution, through the Power of the People! Fatherland United, and Liberty, one people, one nation!" What do you feel? Do you feel more Angolan or do you feel more Marxist, whoever the hell the Marxists were?'

'Look, man, know what? I give up. You can keep your mistake...'

Mistakes! Ah yes, I know about mistakes. A rainbow in shades of grey. A voiceless nightingale. A carnivorous sheep. A happy *fado*-singer.

(The Chameleons' Secret)

I'm alone in the dining hall, a simple wooden terrace with a view of the sea. On the path that takes you to the huts that make up the Chameleons' Secret you pass under an archway made of two enormous whale ribs. Other whalebones are arranged along the route, together with gigantic turtle shells.

I find it frightening.

From here I can also see the other huts. I can count five of them, sad, orphaned things like those whalebones. A sort of discouragement, slow, insidious, comes up to me from them. I can't work out what led Andries to build a set-up like this here.

'We get a lot of visitors,' Brand assured me, feigning (badly) an enthusiasm that is belied by everything around him. 'Fishermen. A lot of fishermen come from South Africa and Namibia. Here in these waters, my friend, there are a fuck of a lot of fish.'

I don't like him. I said this to Lau, and she got offended. She gets offended with whatever I say to her. Truth is, I don't like Brand. He has icy green eyes, and his harelip gives him an expression of permanent disdain. Bartolomeu's arguments won out: we need a good guide to get us to the border, at Ruacaná, and besides that it's not good to make the journey in just one car. So we arranged to spend the night at the South Africans' little hotel, this 'Chameleons' Secret'. Tomorrow morning Brand will take two guests back home, to Cape Town. We'll follow his jeep.

Laurentina thought it better for all of us to stay together, me, her, Bartolomeu and Pouca Sorte, as each hut has four beds. That way, she says, we save some money. She's evading me. Evading. I write the word again. I write it slowly. I look at it as one might look at a rock. It's a dark, gnarled word that weighs in your hands. Laurentina doesn't evade, she eludes, slipping like a fish, slipping far away from me. I say this to her and she isn't listening to me:

'Did you hear what I said?'

'Of course I did. Don't be a pain…'

'What did I say?'

'You're being an idiot. I'm not going to play that game.'

When I touch her she recoils. I insist. I touch her hair, gently, as she sleeps. My love's hair is strong and smooth. I bury my fingers in her slowly up to the roots, and there it's soft and dense. I smell her hair, the back of her neck, and she sighs. She talks, as she sleeps, in a language I don't understand. I stay awake watching her sleep. It's been like this these past few nights. I fall asleep – exhausted – as the first light alights on the sheets. She wakes me:

'What have you been doing all night? You have bags under your eyes…'

How can I answer her?

I've been watching you, my love. I watch the dreams slip in light flight across your eyelids. I let my fingertips wander down your back, from the light down of your neck, to below where the flesh rises firm and proud. Laurentina tells the story of how one day at university one of her professors asked whether as it happened she was part African?

'As it happens I am,' she retorted, 'it's the part I sit on.'

Tonight we slept in separate beds.

Espinheira, southern Angola
Friday, 4 November 2005

We camped in the bush, in the middle of the Iona Park, in a place called Espinheira. It appears on the maps (at least, on the good ones), like this:

Espinheira

Nothing around it, no other name, not even a fictitious one like this. Ten minuscule black letters on the distressed ochre surface of the paper. The reality is even more stripped down: there are some very clean ruins, all that's left of two houses and a water tank. Tin walls, no doors and no glass in the windows, which are painted orange. The paintwork looks new. There's no sign of a roof. All around, as confirmation of the name of the place, which means 'bramble', it's all spiny bushes. A lone acacia or two. Mountains in the distance.

I think: this place fits within its name.

I sit down, leaning on one of the walls while the sun batters against the horizon. A picture-postcard moment. The sky turns amazing colours. I shout to Jordi, just to annoy him, that he should go get the camera. Today we've driven through many other picture-postcards which he refused, horrified, to photograph. I was particularly pleased by the stretch along the coast, running along the beachfront, great dunes to our left. We saw dozens of seals, bands of flamingos, enormous turtle carcasses.

Johan pitched a little tent for me and Karen. Jordi prefers to sleep out in the open, with the Boers. He wants to see the stars. Not long ago, around the fire, Harry – a fat bloke, middle-aged, who's been accompanying us in his car since Namibe – explained that Boer children are educated very strictly, taught respect for their elders, because it's the only way of ensuring that they'll survive in a hostile territory: Africa. I didn't reply, but kept thinking about his words.

I was born in 1960, and for most of my life, until recently, I've lived through – and as a journalist seen from close up – the war in Angola. I struggled against political intolerance and suffered for it (thousands of others, of course, suffered far more). I still don't think of my country as hostile territory. When I look back, back to my childhood, the first thing I remember is the freedom. Everything was (and is!) immense. I remember my father waking me up in the early hours on Sundays to go hunting with him. I never liked hunting. What I liked was the feeling of travelling long deserted roads, through the illuminated haze of the morning, with the smell of wet earth and dog hair. Once someone asked the Polish writer and journalist Ryszard Kapuściński what struck him most about Africa. Kapuściński, without hesitating: 'The light!' That's it: where some see light, others see only shadows. Those who see shadows build walls to protect themselves. They have a tendency to be fanatical wall-builders.

Oncócua, southern Angola
Saturday, 5 November 2005

I got up early. All night that vast silence had seemed strange to me. I imagined that in the middle of the bush the arrival of the shadows was accompanied by an infinity of minuscule noises: the twittering of some owl, the dragging of a snake through the grass, the creak of the branches, the rustling of the wind in the crown of the trees, crickets.

But no, nothing. Nothing of anything.

Just a bottomless silence. The stars, mute in the dark abyss.

I remember hearing old hunters talk about Espinheira as a place vibrant with life. They claim that there are kudu running about here, and *olongo* antelope, mountain zebras, springboks. There's even one who claims to have seen black rhinos. What troubles me the most is the apparent absence of birds, even of insects. I can understand how war, and abnormal, unbounded levels of hunting, can have kept the larger animals away.

But the birds?

We gave a lift to a woman, Avelina, one of whose feet is injured. No sooner had we said that she could get into the car than her husband and a number of other relatives appeared with a thousand and one bundles that they immediately began to arrange, demonstrating extraordinary zeal and skill, on the roof of the jeep. Johan, desperate, sought to stop them. Trying to contain his anger he assured us that the excess weight would delay the journey. Then he took against the stench of dried meat that was escaping from one of the bags and threatened to throw it out of the window. Soon afterwards the car broke down. We all got out into the hot sun. We were in the middle of an immense patch of open country. The stony ground. Dry. A little plaque affixed to a bush caught my eye. It said 'Shelter of Chief Tchimalaca-Lutuima'. The most stripped-down real tribal shelter I'd seen till now. After almost two hours Johan was able to improvise a solution to the breakdown, and we continued on our journey. Avelina, a tall, very beautiful woman, was born in Huambo. She has eight children and none of them can speak the language of their parents – they speak only Portuguese. After some insistence she agreed to sing to us a few traditional and religious tunes in *umbundo*. I was struck by how beautiful her voice was. The melodies simple, contagious.

We arrived at Oncócua at nightfall; it's a small town, broad red-earth roads, which has its own school and hospital and even – as Jordi has discovered – a little disco. We managed to find lodging at a health centre run by a team of three Germans: an older man and a young man and woman, all of them nurses. Tonight we're going to have a bathroom – albeit not a very clean one – and a bed with a mosquito net. We've had a good dinner, around the fire, and then Karen went to get her saxophone, and Harry accompanied her on the guitar. The German nurse, the girl, sang a few old Jacques Brel songs.

(Another beginning)

I awoke suspended in a slanting shaft of light. I turned my head, and saw Mandume's face beside me. He was sleeping. When he sleeps, Mandume is a little boy again. When I see him like this I want to put my arms around him. I wanted to love him just like at the very beginning.

And how was the very beginning?

Ah! The Bairro Alto, the moon high in the sky. A twisting alleyway. Young people sitting in the alley, cup in hand. Laughter, a diaphanous happiness (it was summer). I was out with a friend, she trying to recover from an amorous disaster, when, all of a sudden, a figure leapt into my path, a young man with his hair stuck into little locks:

'Got a light?'

'No. I don't smoke…'

'Me neither. Not before. I was going to start because of you…'

He was good-looking, a stylish shirt with coloured stripes, jeans torn at the knees. He knew how to talk to people; and, rarer still, he knew how to kiss.

I got up carefully and looked out of the window. Two *mucubal* women (can they have been *mucubal?*) were approaching soundlessly on a very long dirt road. The taller of the women cannot have been more than fifteen years old, a narrow waist, a waist I wish I could have again, coloured bracelets around her fine golden wrists. A huge mountain, shaped like a perfect cone, rose up at the horizon. Seeing it reminded me of some lines from Eugénio de Andrade:

They sing too, the mountains,
only not one of us
can hear them, distracted
by the dull syllables of the wind.

I dreamed about the morning they arrested my father. It's my worst memory, a recurring nightmare. Doroteia thought it impossible that I should remember that episode.

'There's no way,' she said to me again. 'You were just three years old.'

And yet I do remember. My father had finished his breakfast, buttered toast, chocolate milk, had got up from the table and was getting ready to go out when there was a knock on the door. They didn't ring the bell. They knocked on the door hard, three times. My mother, alarmed, went to open it. A strong man, uniformed, moved her aside in an expansive gesture and came in:

'Comrade Dário Reis, you're under arrest!'

There were two other men waiting at the door. My father wanted to know what they were accusing him of. Doroteia hugged him, screaming. The policeman said nothing. He wrenched my mother from my father's arms and threw him out the door. The other two men held Dário by the armpits and forced him into a green jeep with bars on the windows.

Some neighbours watched the scene. One of them spat with loathing as my father passed. In my nightmares I see him with different faces. I recognise him by his cruel, twisted smile, revealing a row of little yellow teeth:

'And not a moment too soon, settler! Now we're going to re-educate you…'

At that time we were living in Quelimane. We left the city and took refuge in the house of a brother of my mother's, in Maputo. Doroteia didn't rest. She moved heaven and hell till she was able to get my father transferred from a 're-education camp' in the north of the country to a penitentiary in the capital. Before he was arrested he'd been teaching me how to whistle; I made a huge effort, but to his utter disgust, nothing came out. Then I spent a few days practising on my own, and when, for the first time, we went to visit him in prison, me in my flowery little dress and blue hat, I whistled *Casa da Mariquinhas* for him. Dário cried. I hugged him. Those tears still burn my skin today. I also remember the evening we went to say goodbye to him at the airport. I remember very clearly my father, handcuffed, on his way up the steps to the plane. At the top of the steps a policeman took off his handcuffs. He turned and gestured to us, raising both hands up to his face as though still wearing the cuffs. Then he boarded the plane, and I didn't see him again till three months later.

I was four years old when I discovered Portugal. My first image: an apple. An apple that my father offered me when I arrived, still in the airport. I bit into it, and it tasted sharp.

Brand. Brand Malan. A pretty mad bloke, is what I think of him, but deep down a good guy, heart in the right place. On some days he wakes up Angolan. On others, white South African. On others still he wakes up Angolan and white South African and Boer, all at the same time, and then, right, then it's best to keep your distance. Tonight he came up to me, cigarette in the corner of his mouth, laughing uproariously:

'Bartolomeu, old man! I've got a good bit of weed here – you smoke?'

He rolled a cigarette and offered it to me. We went off to smoke round the back of the medical centre. Laurentina, Mandume and the two Boers Brand had brought from Namibe (father and son) were improvising a little party round the other side. They'd lit a huge bonfire and were dancing and singing with the German doctors. People had gathered to watch. Brand finished his cigarette in silence, sitting on his feet, a position which to me looked very uncomfortable.

'Shall we go dance?'

'With them?!'

'Fuck no, not with the whites! With some birds from the crowd here…'

'Where?'

'At a club. You've never heard of the crazy nights of Oncócua? Here they seriously dance like fuck.'

I thought he was kidding. He wasn't. He took me to a bar called O Máximo, a decrepit place, with posters of naked women stuck to the walls and crates of beer leaning up against the corners. In what little light there was you could see faces floating, dazed by the alcohol. Bare-chested guys, with a sort of leather loincloth around their waists; very young girls, their hair laboriously plaited, necklaces of shells and glass beads, and the hard points of their breasts piercing my eyes. Our entrance was greeted with shouting and laughter. Brand ordered half a dozen beers and handed them around to the guys and girls. He passed one to me.

'*Tarrachinha*,' he said, pointing to two couples in front of us. 'Up in the capital do you dance the *tarrachinha*?'

Yes, they do dance the *tarrachinha* in the capital, but they do it more heavily clothed. It's a violently erotic dance. It greatly surpasses everything I've seen (and I've seen plenty) in the *funk* dances in the Rio slums. The girl coils herself around the guy's chest, holding him round his neck, and screws herself around him with super-slow movements of her hips. Can you imagine that? Now try and imagine that they're dancing the *tarrachinha* bare-chested, with a girl who's just fifteen.

'It's better than making love,' Brand sighed, anguish in his voice. 'You're not going to dance?'

I? I, Bartolomeu Falcato, was terrified. To hide my fear I moved over to the other end of the bar and sat down on a crate of beer, next to a skinny, worn-out old man, his face cut by tiny wrinkles. The old man threw me a curious look.

'Angolan?'

'Yeah, man! My name's Bartolomeu Falcato…'

'Pleased to meet you. I'm Máximo, owner of this here establishment. You like the vibe?'

'I like it… It's different…'

The old man laughed. A beautiful, clear laugh. He was missing teeth, and the few he had were dirty and neglected. But when he laughed, he was a child again; it was as though, under the dark, rough skin there was a little boy.

'Are you from here, sir?'

'Me, from Oncócua?! Course not, son! I'm from Timor…'

'From Timor?'

'You find that strange? My father was Portuguese. Anarchist-unionist. Salazar sent him to Timor, exiled, like so many others, and he married a Timorese woman and had five children. I'm the oldest.'

'And how did you end up here?'

'End up? I didn't end up. I just stopped. Like a car that runs out of petrol in the middle of the road. This is the middle of the road between nowhere and no place at all.'

He fixed his curious eyes on me, and it was only then I noticed there really was something about him, in his little features, something oriental. Nonetheless people like that do appear here in the south, people with stretched eyes and prominent cheekbones. *Mucancala* tribesmen. *Mucuissos* from the bush. Very ancient peoples. Máximo smiled, a boy again:

'You're the son of Bernardo Falcato, I'm sure of it. I knew your father well. I was looking at you and remembering him, and then you sat down and introduced yourself. A brave man, your father, but a terrible player. You play?'

'Play?! Play what?'

'Dice, cards. Anything you can bet on…'

'No. I've never played. I don't like it.'

'Pity. I was going to bet this establishment of mine against your car. If I won I'd get your car and go back, back to the life I left behind.'

'And if you'd lost?'

'Hell, I'd still have gone back. I'd have gone back on foot.'

Part Two

A short while ago we arrived in Swakopmund. There's a rough, dry cold that moves up the deserted, pristine streets. This is the moment someone is meant to say:

'You wouldn't think we were in Africa!'

It's what the Brazilian president, Lula da Silva, said when he visited Namibia, scandalising some very good people (there are some who believe that what he really thought was, 'This doesn't even look like Brazil!'). I imagine it's the phrase most repeated by travellers, in particular those who come in from the north, in their jeeps. We came in across the border at Ruacaná.

It took a lifetime to get there from Oncócua, over roads that had been dead for thirty years, and vague ox trails which only the eye of a very experienced driver like Johan can make out between the loose rocks and dense, sharpened bramble bushes. The frontier-post, a doorless and windowless hut, seemed to be abandoned. Eventually a boy appeared with the information that the guards were at lunch. We waited for the guards. One came, in his shirtsleeves. He smelled of alcohol. The next one to emerge didn't even have a shirt. He was tremendously nice. He'd been born in Luanda, into a family from the north, and studied in Cuba, on the Isla de la Juventud. He told me an anecdote about Fidel Castro in rocky Spanish. He challenged me to a game of draughts, on a cement board on which the pieces were beer-bottle tops, Cuca versus Ngola. We played two games while his colleague filled in the paperwork. Halfway through the third game a little *mucubal* girl appeared. She started to argue with the guard. She grabbed a broom and knocked all the bottle tops to the floor. The man smiled at me, as if in apology, and followed her without even picking up the bottle tops first. On the other side of the border, the Namibian guards, rigorously suited, received us coldly and professionally. The road: a smooth black strip, drawn perfectly onto an even landscape, with barbed wire fences on either side. The sensation this produces in the spirit is contradictory – simultaneously of freedom and claustrophobia. There's that immense horizon, all around us, and it is forbidden to us. All that remains to us is that narrow corridor of tarmac.

Johan prefers the chaos:

'The Angolans – tsch! – total confusion. But they've got soul. Here people are cold, like this landscape, all very organised, but with no surprise.'

That's not true. There are surprises. Wlotzkas Baken was a surprise.

We passed it on the way. I asked Johan to stop a moment and took a few photos. Jordi too, though reluctantly. I think we could go there to film a stray scene. The setting is ready: dozens of little houses, each with a water tower beside it, all painted in different colours. No one on the streets. No sign of human activity. 'Hopper,' Karen suggested, and she's right, it does remind you of an Edward Hopper painting. Solitude and melancholy. These are holiday homes, Johan explained to us, the property of Namibian Germans who occupy them during the Christmas holidays. At that time of year, he assured us, the town gets really very lively. The Germans, after a few drinks, circulate from house to house.

Nonetheless we don't have to explain this to the people watching the film. We don't have to explain anything. We can restrict ourselves to showing our audience the town as it appeared to us.

Inexplicable.

(Wlotzkas Baken)

Laurentina with her arms around me.

'Calm down, my love, calm down! I think you've flipped.'

I don't know where the idiom comes from, but I can imagine. This is what I imagine: 'flipping' over to the other side, the other side being the dark abyss where we go around with a newspaper hat on our head, dragging an empty Coke can on a piece of string.

The psychiatrist: 'So, Mandume, taking the dog for a walk?'

'Dog?! You raving lunatic, can't you see this is an empty Coke can?'

The psychiatrist moves away, thinking to himself:

'This one is cured. He can go back home now.'

And us, to the can:

'Good one, Bobi, we've fooled another one!'

Yes, I've flipped, I really have. Let me explain myself:

First, the exhaustion. For several nights now I've hardly slept. Sometimes I dream without even closing my eyes, or think I'm dreaming. I hear voices, some of them I recognise, others I don't; I can distinguish the real ones from the false ones, because the latter break up in my fingers like echoes when I try to decipher them. I also see shapes, swift shadows, that appear on the scene, top left to bottom right. Then they beat their weary wings and leave the stage.

Second: the landscape. Hours and hours sliding across this emptiness, with the sun shrieking above us, in a splendour that makes it impossible to see anything. Light blinds more than darkness.

In the far distance I heard the amazed voice of Laurentina:

113

'What's that?'

I looked, and what I saw looked like what I see at those moments when – without closing my eyes – I become distracted and fall asleep, or think that I'm falling asleep. Lively-coloured houses were floating (are floating) in the desert air, absorbed, like little tropical fish escaped from an aquarium. There a dry garden of bones, over there a swing-chair swinging on its own. Footprints in the sand that don't lead to anyone. The wind softly moaning in the deserted streets. And in the background, always, always, these flaming mirages. We stopped. They all got out, and I got out too. The sun beating down on my head. I took two steps forward, three to the side, as though I was dancing. That's what Laurentina asked me:

'You dancing?'

'This black man doesn't know how to dance,' teased Bartolomeu. 'He's just pseudo-coloured. I bet he eats *muamba* with rice.'

Yes indeed I do (I've never liked manioc flour). I could have said this to him, I could even have said nothing to him at all, I could simply have gone back inside the car and drunk a warm beer. But I didn't. That was the moment I flipped:

'I want you to leave me in Windhoek,' I shouted. My voice shook, so changed that even I took a few moments to recognise it. 'I'm leaving. I'm fed up of all this shit! Fed up!'

'Now what's happened?'

'I'm sick of this guy, with his non-stop racist insinuations!'

'Hey, no way, man! Racist, me?! No way!'

Pouca Sorte got out of the car, both of his hands raised. He was shouting something, but whatever it was was lost in the tumult of voices in my head. The sun was shouting louder. The wind had begun to howl. I had too:

'I want to go to Windhoek and I want to go now! I'm not spending one more day with this fucking racist...'

'We'll take you to Windhoek, it's all settled, pal, but first we're going to talk about this racism thing. Nobody calls me a racist.'

'I do. Racist, yes, a racist! And on top of that some sort of provincial Don Juan. And if you fancy a beating you can come right over here because I'm not scared of you...'

Bartolomeu took two steps forward, fists clenched, as though he were about to hit me. He didn't. Quite the opposite. He stopped in front of me, and began to laugh. Genuine laughter, broad bursts of laughter that were happy out in the air like rockets and then rolled out along the empty streets. He sat down in the sand and wiped his eyes. He was crying from laughing so hard, the fucker.

'I'm sorry, bro, I'm really sorry. I think you've had too much sun.'

It was worse than if he'd hit me.

I ran – round the streets, at random, dazed by the sun and my shame. Eventually I tired. I stretched out in the salmon-coloured shade of one of the houses. Laurentina soon appeared, breathless. She sat down next to me. Then she hugged me.

'Calm down, my love, calm down. I think you've flipped.'

I noticed there were tears running down my face. I didn't want to cry in front of her.

'Did you call me your love?'

'I did, you are my love.'

'No. I'm not. It's over, isn't it?'

Laurentina sat up again. She hid her head between her knees.

'I don't know. I swear I don't know. I know what I ought to do. I ought to stay with you. You're a good person. You're one of the best people I've met in my whole life…'

'I've heard this speech before,' I said to her. 'It's all used-up. Even I've used it. Try another one.'

Laurentina got up:

'I'm very sorry.'

She turned and vanished. When I got back to the car the three were eating lunch. They were talking, their voices lowered. They stopped talking when they saw me. Pouca Sorte held out a piece of bread and chorizo to me. Laurentina waited till I'd finished eating:

'You still want us to take you to Windhoek?'

I tried to smile:

'No. Not worth it.'

I feel tormented. Empty. A short while ago Brand appeared with the two Boers. 'This place,' he said, 'is called Wlotzkas Baken.'

If I were a town I'd be just like this.

(Moose's Bar)

The trip from the ghost town where Mandume flipped out was just ever so slightly – how should I put it? – gloomy. Everyone silent. Mandume and Laurentina in front of me. Him pretending to be asleep; her pretending to be reading; and me actually reading. The roads in this country are smooth, and have almost no curves, with one car here, another a hundred kilometres further down, so that even in a mechanical ruin like the one we were travelling in it's possible to read almost as if you're at home. I'm finishing a book (which I pinched from Laurentina), *Another Day of Life* by Kapuściński. I know some of the characters personally. They're friends of my mother's, people who visit our house. I find it a bit strange seeing them now in the pages of a book that you read as though it were a novel.

Night was falling when Pouca Sorte drew our attention to a bar on the side of the road. It looked like the setting for an American road movie, something like *Thelma and Louise*. A petrol pump with a bar behind it, with neon lettering:

Moose's Bar.

The desert all around. The shallow light throws the grain into relief. A sky of a vibrant blue, though broken with dull creases, like a creased photograph of a vibrant blue sky. We went in. There was just one person inside, on the other side of the counter, a man in his fifties, large and fat, with blonde hair, now a little greying, pulled back into a ponytail. We asked for orange juice and ham sandwiches with tomato for the four of us, and sat down in one corner. The man brought our juice over on a tray. He stopped, stood a moment to look at us, as we talked. He smiled.

'You're speaking Portuguese? Sounds like Russian to me but I think that's not likely…'

'Yes,' Laurentina confirmed. 'We're speaking Portuguese.'

'Are you Angolan?'

I said yes, but before I could add anything else Mandume came out with his shining English, which I presume he polished in London in the years he studied cinema at the National Film and Television School:

'No, I am Portuguese. Me and the girl. Them, yes, they're Angolan.'

The man looked at him, amused. He pulled up a chair, and turned to me and Pouca Sorte:

'I know your country,' he said. As he talked, his voice became darker. 'I was in Angola at the beginning of the war, in '75. A bad time. We had no choice. I was part of an armed column from the South African army, as a driver. I happened to be up front. Suddenly a white guy appeared in front of me, on his own, in the middle of the road, and started shooting at us. When his bullets ran out he threw his gun away and held his arms open, baring his chest. I asked our captain what I should do. "Keep going," he said, "iron him." And I kept going. Today when I fall asleep I see that man's face. I never slept peacefully again.'

I got up and went out into the fresh night air. I sat down on a bench. What had just happened? I wasn't sure I'd understood it right.

A few minutes later Laurentina came out to me.

'You OK?'

I told her yes, I was. I asked her for a bit of time to put my thoughts in order, I closed my eyes and leaned back. Then I heard the voice of the man who'd killed my father. He was standing there, in front of me, very upright, like a man preparing to face a firing squad.

'I'm so sorry. I'd give anything to be able to go back…'

'What would you do if you could go back?'

'I could have refused to follow orders.'

'What would've happened to you?'

'I'd've been arrested, accused of treason and failure to follow an order. I'd've spent a couple of years in jail, probably.'

'And my father?'

'They would have killed him anyway, obviously!'

'In that case, what's the difference?'

'No difference to you. But it would have made an enormous difference to me.'

I told him to sit down. I felt no hatred for him at all. I feel no hatred as I write these lines. He sat down, and offered me his hand.

'I want to ask you for forgiveness. You and your family.'

I took his hand, a broad, bony hand, a little calloused. I noticed his face properly now. He had light eyes, hazelnut-coloured, clean and sincere, with little wrinkles at the corners. Deep bags under his eyes. I remembered an old turtle from my childhood. He went by the name of Leonardo because he really liked listening to Leonard Cohen. Sometimes he'd disappear for weeks. But to bring him back all you had to do was put on the record of the Canadian singer – at the first lines of *Famous Blue Raincoat* – 'It's four in the morning, the end of December, / I'm writing you now just to see if you're better...' – Leonardo would emerge from some unknown abyss somewhere, still dragging behind him the torpor of a long sleep, he would get up onto his tiptoes next to one of the columns, he'd stretch out his neck, and for brief moments would seem to be completely happy. Then he would go back to being sad again. A sadness like the sadness of the deserts. This man in front of me now, he looked like Leonardo looked, the turtle, when the music came to an end.

'Tell me about your father.'

I never got to meet my father, nor he me. We still speak a lot. I'm naturally a sceptic. Even as a child I made fun of Father Christmas, of ghosts and monsters. I don't believe in God. It's a solid disbelief. I do believe, however, that my father watches over me, protects me. I collect photographs of him, the books he read and annotated. I think I'm an animist, in my way. A while ago, Laurentina provoked me:

'Your father's an invention!'

'Yours too,' I retorted. 'That's something we have in common.'

'Tell me about your father,' the man insisted. 'I think about him so much. I've been thinking about him for thirty years...'

My father was a good man. Maybe a bit wayward. He loved the desert. He used to say that in the desert he felt complete. My mother used to retort (she told me) that he only liked the desert because there weren't any people in it. Cuca has a fierce sense of humour. My father gave himself heart and soul to all lost causes, to the defeated in life, to places without salvation. He would have liked to live here. I hugged the old soldier; I said to him:

'I think you and he could have been friends.'

We remained like that a while. The wind blew, inflating the stars.

Gita Cerveira remembers the drums. Yes, there were drums. Bonfires too. Ah! And an excellent kid-goat barbeque. He'd chosen the kid himself. Any other memories? 'There was this guy, a strange guy, the tribal chief of the Quimbo, who would always walk around – even under the noon sun – dressed in a long, thick black overcoat. We noticed afterwards that he had an enormous *bumbi*. A monstrous thing, that came down to his knees. Sorry, man, the thing I remember best is the guy in the cloak.' Gita laughs. His laughter is contagious. In the film world, in Portugal and Portuguese-speaking Africa, everyone knows him. He's lived in the United States, in France and in South Africa, before returning to Angola after the end of the civil war. He worked as a sound technician on many of the documentaries and feature films made in Mozambique in the last twenty years. He met Karen on one of those trips and they remained friends. The days when they were filming *On the Edge* didn't seem any harder to him than so many other similar situations.

I tell him Karen's story. He looks at me in surprise. He'd heard about her illness, but didn't know the episode of the flooding, and the sum of dramatic coincidences that began to unravel after they'd filmed the female rites of passage in that remote village of Zambézia.

Gita is on his way through Lisbon. I am too. He phoned me and we arranged to meet at the Brasileira café in Chiado. I arrived before the appointed time, sat down at a free table on the esplanade, beside the statue of Fernando Pessoa, ordered an orange juice and at that exact moment found myself face to face with Jordi, lately arrived back from a six-month trip around South America. We embraced noisily. I was glad to see him again. Gita appeared, elegant as ever. He's forty-seven, but looks much younger. Jordi met him in Luanda. I invited him to join us for lunch. One of us suggested the First of May Restaurant, and here we are.

'One thing I didn't understand.' Good old Jordi. 'What's a *bumbi*?'

Jordi is getting to grips confidently with Angolan Portuguese. It's something he's proud of. But *bumbi* is a word he's never heard before, has no idea what it means. Gita laughs loud. His laughter shakes the air:

'You explain it to him…'

'An inguinal hernia. Basically a part of the intestine travels to the inside of the testicles. If you don't get it treated the testicle increases in size…'

'Yeah! In the case of the man in the coat it seriously grew like fuck.'

'God, I'm eating! Spare me the details…'

Bumbi is a sickness that only afflicts the very poor, like elephantiasis. I remember as a boy accompanying my grandmother to the market. One of the traders had elephantiasis. I looked down to his feet, that immense encumbrance, and I envied him. I firmly believed that the man was part-way through being transformed into an elephant. That seemed like a pretty good destiny to me. Humanity horrified me. They used to ask me:

'What do you want to be when you're big?'

And I, without hesitating:

'An elephant!'

Then I grew up, and conformed.

Sérgio Guerra's apartment in Salvador, Brazil
Monday, 31 July 2006

(Still on the subject of strange coincidences, which is where life triumphs over literature.)

Sérgio told me this afternoon, as we were taking some sun in the pool after lunch, about an odd thing that happened. A few years ago one of his best friends fell sick and died, confirming the gloomy prediction of a fortune-teller. He was (as I am) a chap who liked lizards. He kept some, at home, and talked to them. Always happy, in a good mood, he'd send letters and postcards to his friends and sign them simply 'Me'. A few days after the funeral, Sérgio went to a little beach they used to frequent together, and which it was only possible to reach on foot after crossing a piece of private land. There was a gate, invariably closed, which they would open to get onto that land. On that day, however, Sérgio found the door wide open. He approached it sadly, his head lowered, thinking of his friend and how much he missed him, when suddenly a lizard ran out along the wall, causing him to raise his eyes. Only then did he notice a recently graffiti'd phrase: 'Still here!'

Signed: 'Me'.

(Of civilisation)

Not long ago we passed the border between Namibia and South Africa. We're now in a little restaurant on the roadside. We're planning to go directly to Cape Town. Brand, on the other hand, means to stop first at a little town in the interior to drop off the two tourists. As soon as we had sat down, our young guide stretched himself out and announced that he wasn't speaking any more Portuguese. It was our turn to speak English now. Then he added with a broad smile:

'Welcome to the most civilised country in Africa.'

Bartolomeu's response was sarcastic, in Portuguese:

'Oh, super-civilised. Just don't forget this is the country that invented apartheid…'

Brand coloured. He retorted furiously:

'Apartheid is over!'

'You're right,' I said. 'It's over. But that doesn't mean it never existed. Let me remind you that in the most civilised country in Africa, as you call it, no woman is ever safe. Do you know how many women are raped here every day?'*

'It didn't used to be like that!'

'Used to?' Bartolomeu is shouting. 'You mean in the time of apartheid?'

'South Africa used to be a safe country.'

* According to data from the South African Institute for Race Relations, 147 women are raped in South Africa every day.

125

'People *used to* die every day,' Mandume reminded him, 'in clashes with the police. There was practically no foreign investment. South African products were boycotted the world over. The economy had stagnated. And most of all – you remember? – racism was the official ideology.'

'I'm not defending apartheid!'

'Of course not,' Mandume – ironic – 'You're just defending the *time* of apartheid.'

'I studied in Australia,' – Brand was speaking Portuguese again. He shook, nervous, tears coming to his eyes. 'My mother lives in Melbourne. If I'd wanted to I could have stayed there. I came back because I love Africa. I was brought up in the middle of the bush, in Angola. You – Mandume – you live in Europe, you're Portuguese. You don't understand anything of what's going on here. Nothing of anything at all. And you, Bartolomeu – you live in Luanda, which is a kind of Lisbon in the dark. You don't speak any African language. I do, I know the depths of Angola. I'm much blacker than any of you.'

The discussion was losing its thread. The two tourists Brand was travelling with, father and son, looked at him, and then at Mandume and Bartolomeu, anxious, trying to understand the reason for the quarrel. The word 'apartheid' turned in the air like a funereal bird. I asked permission to intervene. I said to Brand that maybe the word he'd used – 'civilisation' – hadn't been quite the right word. South Africa is undoubtedly one of the most developed countries on the continent. Development, however, has never been a synonym for civilisation. Not even, unfortunately, for civility. For its day, Nazi Germany was a very developed country, but I'm not sure it was all that civilised. I added that among the victims of the old regime there weren't only the blacks and *mestiços* and Indians, but also the whites, all the whites and particularly the Boers, who would have to live the following decades chained to the ignominy of that dead time. Brand looked at me with surprise. He agreed vehemently:

'Yes, yes! I'm fed up of people talking to me about apartheid. I'm nothing to do with apartheid. I don't have to apologise for being white, do I?'

The discussion died away then. Bartolomeu said goodbye to Brand without even shaking his hand. The gesture, or rather, the absence of any sign of warmth, struck me. Over the past days a sort of friendship had been struck up between them, I thought. A short time ago, after we'd got back in the car, I criticised him, quite harshly. He shrugged his shoulders, annoyed, and said nothing. Mandume muttered softly:

'Yes, is what I think, actually, I don't think it'd be a bad idea at all if the whites were to apologise to the rest of the population of South Africa.'

(Long Street: where the rainbow begins)

It was Brand who told us about the hotel where we are now.

'Very good!' he insisted. 'Different. You'll see, it's not like anywhere else, it's kind of like a film.'

The expression 'kind of like a film', and the fact that he wasn't able to explain himself any better, decided me; or rather, my curiosity prevailed. The hotel is called Daddy Long Legs, after the crane fly, and it's on Long Street. One of my guidebooks, the *Time Out*, talks of Long Street with positively childish enthusiasm: '*Long Street is the main artery of Cape Town's cosmopolitan culture*'. On the next page they call it 'the spiritual heart of the city'. No sooner had night fallen – or maybe it would be better to say, no sooner had night *risen* – than we understood the enthusiasm of the *Time Out* writer. Down Long Street are a succession of restaurants, bars and clubs, almost all of them full. We had dinner at Mama Africa, a restaurant serving regional cuisine, while a marimba and drum orchestra with growing euphoria accompanied a young singer able to intersperse – with equal enthusiasm – snatches from famous operas and old Bob Marley songs. We then – somewhat adrift – went on from bar to bar. At the first, which was calmer, there were only middle-aged couples, all of them white. In the second a noisy press of young people of all colours pushed and shoved their way around: blondes, redheads, mulattos, blacks, Chinese, Indians, whatever! You'd think it was a Benetton models' convention.

'My God,' Mandume sighed. 'You get the twentieth century right next to the twenty-second on this street, in a space of less than fifty metres.'

We returned to the hotel. What makes it remarkable are the themed rooms. One of them, for example, pays tribute to a band that is very popular in South Africa, Freshlyground. The group, which was formed in 2002, brings together musicians from various regions of South Africa, white and black, as well as from Mozambique and Zimbabwe. I'd have liked to have had that room, but Mandume preferred another, inspired by hospitals – will never understand men! In the bathroom there's a very conspicuous glass case filled with surgical instruments. Hanging beside the bed on two clothes hangers are nurse and doctor outfits (overall, stethoscope, etc.). While Bartolomeu's room is a kind of cellar. It's scary.

Needless to say, I refused to put the nurse's outfit on. But Mandume wasn't upset.

'You're right,' he said. 'You'd be better in this…'

He handed me a gift. Something soft, elegantly wrapped in dark blue silk paper. I removed the sticky-tape that was holding the paper. Silk pyjamas, so beautiful, in black, with golden stripes, from La Perla. I put them on and looked at myself in the mirror (the room is full of mirrors); they looked good on me.

'Now take them off!'

I took the pyjamas off. Then I took off his. Mandume kissed me. A long kiss, like the old days.

It was good.

I first visited Cape Town in 1994. I came to film the party for Nelson Mandela's accession to power. Now just imagine a twenty-year-old cub reporter, at the start of his career, experiencing a moment like that. At that moment I discovered the aphrodisiac effect of revolutions. I remember an amazing mulatta woman, very tall and elegant, with a Black Power hairstyle – an anachronism in those days. Her name was Martha – a TV journalist. When she walked into the room the men stopped talking. I didn't, of course, I'm Angolan. Martha told me a joke I often remember. There are jokes capable of revealing more about a particular period in history than any dense essay packed with numbers. This (I think) is one of them. Question: what was the contribution of the different races to the struggle against apartheid? Answer: the whites thought up the fight. The Indians paid for it, the blacks embodied the manifesto, weapons in hand, and at the end the mulattos had the party.

It's important to remember that the official party was actually in Cape Town, dominated by a *mestiço* majority – just like the rest of the region, actually and – what a surprise! – this is where the National Party won the first elections of the new South Africa. Mandume didn't laugh. He asked me, very seriously:

'Do you really think that whites preserve the exclusive privilege of thought?'

I was irritated:

'What I really think is that you have no sense of humour. If I told you a joke about a flying pig you're quite capable of arguing that pigs can't fly…'

Pouca Sorte didn't seem much troubled by the joke. He was troubled by something else:

'And the journalist? Do you still have a number for her?'

What I do think is that Creole societies have a natural vocation for happiness. *Mestiçagem* – the mixing of races – produces happiness like a glow-worm produces light. Carnival, for instance – where in the world do people play at Carnival with the greatest happiness?

Have you guessed?

That's right – in Brazil, in the West Indies, and in New Orleans. In Goa it used to be in the capital, in Panjim, in the Fontainhas neighbourhood, inhabited predominantly by Portuguese Indians. Then the *mestiços* – referred to by the rest of the Indian population as 'the descendants' – went away, and Carnival died.

And in Africa?

Answer: in Luanda, Benguela, Cape Verde, Cape Town and Quelimane!

The Cape Town Carnival, known as the *Coon Carnival*, is celebrated in the first days of January. We saw a documentary on the *Coon Carnival* at the house of Serafim Kussel, in Observatory. The different troupes carry coloured parasols as they progress, singing, dancing and getting in the way of the traffic, through the streets of the city. It reminded me of the Carnival in Olinda, with its *frevo* orchestras, parasols and acrobatic moves. If it weren't for the Calvinists and the Muslims, Cape Town would be Brazilian.

Observatory – Obs, to close acquaintances – was in the time of apartheid a neighbourhood exclusive to the *mestiço* population. Nowadays all the guides refer to it as a bohemian suburb, which at night the young university students transform into an enormous party hall. On the afternoon we went to Obs to visit Serafim Kussel there was a splendid summer sun. The person who'd put me in touch with Serafim was Martha, the journalist with the Black Power hair. She didn't seem surprised when I called her in Johannesburg:

'Well, look who's just emerged from the past! My Angolan!'

She told me that Serafim had been the owner of a jazz bar in the fifties and sixties and that he knew everybody linked to the Cape Town music scene. Perhaps he'd remember Faustino Manso; and he might also be able to put us in touch with Seretha du Toit.

Serafim Kussel was awaiting us seated (very much seated) in a swing-chair. In the garden, between papaya plants, a brood of chicks was scratching around. I liked the old man. Tall, greyed hair, an untended beard. He moved a book from off his lap, got up and greeted us all with a firm handshake, a sonorous 'Good day!' in Portuguese. Then he took us inside, to the living room, a spacious area, airy, a little chaotic, like a teenager's bedroom. Three old sofas backed onto the walls. There was a low table that limped in one leg; in one corner a piano, very dignified-looking, reminding me of a butler in tails. Serafim brought us juices and beer. Finally he sat down, opposite Laurentina, and told us the curious story of his life: in the sixties, just as apartheid was becoming organised, his wife – a *mestiça* like him – chose to get herself classified as white and abandoned him with four children in his arms. I was struck by a phrase he used several times: 'after my wife became white'. He'd say it without irony, with the same tone you might use to say 'after my wife put on weight'. It was just the statement of a fact. The woman, then, became white, a choice common to many lighter-skinned *mestiços*, breaking all the ties that had bound her to the world of the not-chosen ones. She disappeared.

'It was as if she'd died.' Serafim Kussel said this, and was silent for a moment. He shook his head. 'No. It was rather as if she'd never existed. Someone who dies rarely disappears so completely. They leave a name on a tombstone. Photos. She left us nothing. She just went…'

His hands drew a quick circle in the air, like an illusionist disappearing a white rabbit (or perhaps a black one – I don't want Mandume accusing me of being racist), and repeated:

'She went…'

Up till that day Serafim had survived – without any great effort – managing a jazz bar (no, he wasn't the owner), playing piano and playing cards. He borrowed some money from his mother and some more from two or three friends, and set up a little nappy factory. Today, aged sixty-five, he is still – as he says – 'making money from shit'. A few months ago he met his first wife again. She'd gone back to being *mestiça*, actually, boasts about how much she suffered during the apartheid regime. She nurtures political ambitions. Serafim laughed:

'Other countries have turncoats. Here in South Africa we're more radical: we turn skin…'

Laurentina asked him if he'd known an Angolan musician called Faustino Manso. Serafim got angry, or rather, pretended to get angry:

'Patience, girl! We're coming to Faustino…'

Serafim Kussel goes at his own pace and won't allow for any interruptions. We still had to hear – over the course of a good half-hour – his discursions on the origins of Cape Town and defence of the proximity of the different Creole cultures of the world:

'I don't know Luanda, but I'm sure I'd feel at home there. Last month I played with Cuban musicians. They'd never heard our rhythms, the *goema* – do you know the *goema*? You don't know it either? Ah, we'll fix that right away.'

He got up and put a CD in the machine. I saw the case: *The Goema Captains of Cape Town: Healing Destination*. I liked the sound, sweet, swinging, something about it reminding you of the best Afro-Latin jazz.

'What was I talking about? Ah, yes, the Cuban musicians. In just a few minutes the Cubans were playing with us as though this was what they'd been doing their whole lives. It was very good!'

He fell silent and the five of us listened to the recording. Finally he got up and left without saying where he was going. After a few minutes had passed he returned with an old photo album. He put the album down on the little lame table and began to leaf carefully through it. At a particular page he stopped. He called Laurentina:

'Recognise this man?'

In the right-hand corner, hidden behind the piano, you could see Faustino Manso playing double bass. As well as the pianist the image included a guy with a trumpet resting on his lap. I seemed to recognise the pianist's face:

'And him?'

'Ah, him! Yes, he's exactly who you think he is: Dollar Brand… In those days he still called himself Dollar Brand… When he was here he played colonial stuff, but then he went to New York and became African … I took this photo exactly at his leaving party, let me think, in January 1962… The next day he was on a plane to Paris. The rest is history…'

I would have liked to have heard more at leisure about Dollar Brand, alias Abdullah Ibrahim. I've been listening to his piano-playing for years. In January 1976, the month I was born, Abdullah Ibrahim launched an album called *The Children of Africa*, which includes what is today my favourite number of his: *Ishmael*. I fooled around with an awful lot of girls while Abdullah Ibrahim played *Ishmael*. Unfortunately Laurentina interrupted him:

'Sorry, and Faustino Manso?'

'Your father, right? Beautiful Martha told me Faustino was your father. It doesn't surprise me that he left children scattered across the continent. That man liked women. I like them too, of course, but his passion was something else. He liked women so much that no woman could fail to like him. Also he was an elegant man, with a voice of silk, a perfect gentleman…'

'Did you ever hear him play?'

'Did I ever hear him play?! Of course! Many times. Who do you think took this photograph?'

'Was he a good musician?'

'Yes, a very good musician, really very good, an excellent musician, but he was more at ease on the double bass than on the piano. When Faustino put his arms around the double bass something quite strange happened, a transformation. It was as though the instrument were using him, and not the other way around.'

'How so?'

'How should I know, my dear?! Voodoo! A kind of possession… What do they call voodoo in Brazil – you'll know – ?'

'…Candomblé…'

'That's it – candomblé.'

'You're kidding…'

'No. You don't believe that some kind of spirit can manifest itself through the body of a living man?'

'I don't, no!'

'No one's told you the story of Faustino's double bass?'

'No…'

'You don't know who taught Faustino to play double bass?'

(Devastated) 'No, no, I don't know…'

'Ah. Well! Then, my dear, you don't know very much about your father.'

(An uncommon calling card)

A short while ago, while I was arranging my clothes, I found in the pocket of one of my shirts a calling card: 'Magno Moreira Monte – Businessman, Poet, Private Detective – No. 13 Frederick Engels Street, Luanda – Tel. +244 222 394 957'. For a few moments I was confused, and amused, studying the card. Where could it have come from? Finally I remembered the sallow little man in the Chinese restaurant in Luanda, the night I lost my temper with Laurentina. I saw him open his wallet, take out a card, and put it in my shirt pocket.

'In case you ever need it. Well as I said, I heard your conversation. Don't take what the girl says too seriously. She's a prostitute, a teen whore. The city's full of them. You know, the war...'

I showed the card to Laurentina. I told her about that episode. She wasn't very impressed. She said I should keep the card:

'Poet and private detective? I find that an unusual combination. Maybe he'll be useful to us.'

I put the card away in my wallet.

It still (and I'm not sure why this is) disgusts me slightly having it there.

The Daddy-Long-Legs Hotel, Cape Town
Tuesday, 15 November 2005

This afternoon we visited the District Six Museum.

District Six, today a windy, desolate area, made up of a series of fallow plots of land, was in the fifties a neighbourhood famous for its cultural vitality. There were countless jazz bars there, in which white musicians, black musicians, mulatto musicians and Chinese musicians (there were a few) played side by side. In 1966 the neighbourhood was declared a residential area for whites only. Nine years later all the houses were demolished and most of its inhabitants forced to seek accommodation in distant suburbs.

'They destroyed District Six because of the hatred they felt for mixing,' we were told by Vincent Kolbe, one of the founders of the Museum. The District Six Museum preserves the memory of those days, including the street signs, which an employee responsible for the earthworks was able to save. There is also a huge map, hand-painted, with the names of all the streets and all the families who lived in the neighbourhood.

Established in 1867, District Six originally sheltered a population made up of former slaves, European and Asian immigrants, traders and artisans. In its golden times, people mixed in its streets and squares – as Noor Ebrahim recalls in his short volume of memoirs, *Noor's Story: My Life in District Six* – painters, musicians, businessmen, Catholic priests and Muslim imams, juvenile delinquents and sportsmen.

Noor described how in 1975, just before the start of the demolitions, he managed to buy a residence in Athlone. He took with him – as well, of course, as his wife and children – his racing-pigeons, which had won various prizes, building his second pigeon-house out of the wood recovered from the first. After three months he decided to release the birds. None returned. Anxious, after a sleepless night, Noor drove over to what had been District Six. There, in the middle of the immense ruined space, he could clearly make out the sound of wings. Some fifty birds were awaiting him, quite perplexed, on the exact site of the old pigeon-house. To this day a similar wonder hovers over the scar – on the empty ground – where the houses should be.

(Faustino Manso, according to Serafim Kussel)

Walker!

That was the name of Faustino's double bass: Walker.

Martha told me that Faustino died. She told me that you were at the funeral. I'm very sorry…

Do you know what they did with the double bass?

No, no, of course you don't. When you get back to Luanda, ask after the double bass. Walker – the double bass – had belonged to a sailor, a guy – if memory serves – from New Orleans, who'd jumped ship from the American navy, in Luanda, at the start of the Second World War. I heard Faustino tell that story a hundred times – usually rather euphoric, when after a show we'd hang around in some bar and celebrate life. I still can't remember the sailor's name…

…Archimedes… It was Achilles or Archimedes… something like that, I have a notion it was a Greek name…

Anyway, let's say it was Archimedes. New Orleans. Yes, definitely, the guy was from New Orleans. He'd been a jazz musician, before he was called up, and later in the navy he continued to play bass with a sax player and a drummer to entertain the troops. Archimedes lived in Luanda illegally. He played weddings. He did little odd jobs. Something here, something there. He earned just enough not to starve to death. His greatest treasure was Walker.

You know the difference between a violin and a double bass? You don't? You get a much bigger bonfire out of a double bass. Ha! It's an old musicians' joke. I remember another – there's this man who's shipwrecked

141

and he manages to make it to a Pacific island inhabited by a little tribe. One night he awakes to the sound of drumming. He can't sleep for the noise. In desperation he seeks out someone to tell him when it's going to stop. 'You don't want that,' an old man replies, 'something bad will happen when the drums stop.' Again and again he asks the same question and the natives give the same reply. Finally, his nerves completely shot, the poor shipwrecked man puts a knife to the throat of one of the drummers and orders him to tell him what will happen when the drums stop. 'Something very bad!' the lad sighs: 'When the drums stop, the double bass solo starts …' Ha! You know what the difference is between a double bass and a coffin? The dead man! With a coffin, the dead man's on the inside… I could spend the whole day telling you double bass jokes… Well, on we go, what I was going to say was that Archimedes often thought about burning the instrument. He didn't… This is what Faustino said… He didn't do it because Walker wasn't just any old double bass. Walker had belonged to Walter Sylvester Page, a jazz pioneer, the leader of the Oklahoma City Blue Devils, and Faustino believed that his spirit sometimes possesses those who touch the instrument.

Maybe. I don't know.

(The militant)

My fourth-grade teacher was a thin, pale, authoritarian woman. She had a great impact on me. She defined a sort of pattern in my spirit, or rather, I'll admit, a prejudice: thin pale woman – authoritarian woman. I can't imagine a fat woman being brusque, especially if she's dark. Seretha du Toit is slender, her skin almost transparent, with fair, very straight hair, running like honey down over her slim but muscular shoulders. When I saw her I remembered my fourth-grade teacher. Serafim phoned her, explained to her who we were, and she agreed to receive us in her house, a discreet residence at the foot of Table Mountain. In the hall, decorated with pieces of African craftwork, there is – above a sofa – a very noticeable photograph of Seretha next to Nelson Mandela. What I found most unusual were the two greyhounds, sitting down, absolutely immobile, like pieces of porcelain, beside a glassed door – glass eyes lost in the sky.

'You're Faustino's daughter?' Seretha studied me, curious, before holding out her hand. 'You don't look like him.'

We had only just settled in when a woman with yellowed skin and prominent cheekbones came to bring us tea. She served us in silence, looking at no one, and disappeared. Seretha, sitting very upright on a little stool, wanted to know what we made of South Africa. I was interested to hear Bartolomeu talk about his experiences during the first multi-racial elections. Then she turned to me and said – changing the subject abruptly – that she was sorry not to have had a child with Faustino:

143

'I'm looking at you and wondering what my child – Faustino's child – might have looked like if I'd become pregnant. They'd be much older than you today, naturally…'

I didn't speak for a moment. Only one question occurred to me:

'What would have happened if you had become pregnant?'

She looked at me, serious:

'I did try, you know? I very much wanted to have a child with Faustino. In those days, I'm sure you understand, giving birth to a mixed-race child was an act of subversion. It implied a direct confrontation with authority. You risked getting yourself arrested. I think they'd have exiled me, probably I would have gone with Faustino when he left. But anyway, that didn't happen. I don't have children. It's an old wound. I ended up dedicating myself to dance, and to politics…'

Bartolomeu took advantage of the moment:

'I think *mestiçagem* – mixing races – is by its very nature revolutionary. Cultural *mestiçagem*, biological *mestiçagem*, they inevitably presuppose a breaking with the system, the emergence of something new from two or more separate realities…'

Seretha smiled, impressed:

'You're very bold! In Angola do they take you seriously?'

Bartolomeu – contrary to what I feared for a brief moment – didn't get annoyed. He laughed with an enchanting simplicity:

'No, Seretha. Not me, fortunately no one takes me seriously.'

'That's what I thought. You are, however, correct. Sex is revolutionary, and mixing races, naturally, is all about sex. Apartheid failed, it was a project that had failed from the outset, because there's no law in the world that can impose itself on the force of desire.'

While the two of them discussed the role of sex in the revolution, and of *mestiçagem* in the redemption of the world, I got up and looked out of the glassed door in front of which those two greyhounds were positioned. The view of the street from the front of the house is unprepossessing. Simple, elegant lines, with a narrow garden. Beds of roses and araceae. A white orchid, resplendent, in a shady alcove. The back garden, however, seemed to me a real paradise. A carpet of soft grass leading to a small swimming pool in tones of emerald. Behind that, a border of palm trees. Bird of paradise flowers, like arrogant crested cranes, loom giant over the world, their crests the colour of old gold. In the distance, between the green and the sky, shines the deep abyss of sea. I returned and sat down.

'And my father...' I asked, making the most of an angel's passing – 'Was my father interested in politics?'

Seretha looked discouraged:

'Faustino? Faustino was never a militant, he wasn't that type. Everyone thought him a fine person, good and caring. He worried about other people's happiness. He expended all his militancy in favour of humanity. And for the rest, what can I tell you? He was... a rarity, especially in those days... He was a man who liked women...'

Serafim had said the same thing, I think he'd used just those words, but in Seretha's mouth the phrase seemed to have a very different meaning. I saw her get up, with the pretext of going to look for some old photographs, and suddenly saw her much older, even a little stooped. Mandume leaned over to my ear:

'My God, she's moved, the iron lady?!'

When she returned, some ten minutes later, Seretha du Toit was once again my primary-school teacher. She handed me half a dozen photographs. She had also brought with her a large envelope, which time had yellowed. She opened it and showed me a pack of letters tied together by a light blue ribbon.

'They're some of the letters that Faustino wrote me after he left. We didn't see each other many times after that, but we went on exchanging letters, at first every week, then once a month, and, in the later years, at least at Christmas. I'm not going to show you the letters, of course. Maybe one day, when I know you better, if I think you deserve it...'

Bartolomeu interjected, with his number three smile, the one he uses – and this is his description – to charm dragons:

'She deserves it all, you can be sure of that. Laurentina is an angel.'

'We'll see. Be that as it may, these are intimate letters...'

Unsure how to respond (thin, pale women have a gift for making me nervous) I set to studying the photographs. There was one in particular that I liked, in black and white, in which you see Seretha with her arms around my father. Behind them, a little out of focus, two couples are dancing rock'n'roll. The image conveys simultaneously a kind of solemn innocence and a kind of energetic affirmation of love. Seretha noticed my interest. She took the photograph from my hand:

'A simple photograph like this – would you believe it? – could get someone sent up to a tribunal.'

In the sixties there was a certain number of mixed-race couples all over South Africa. To escape the snares of apartheid the black or *mestiça* wife of a white husband would often be registered as a domestic servant, in order that they might be able to continue living under the same roof. A white man or a white woman could also request a change of race, so that they pass to being considered *mestiços*. There were also cases of *mestiços* who managed to get themselves reclassified as whites, and blacks who managed to get themselves reclassified as *mestiços*. But these cases were rare.

The conversation left me tormented. When we left, promising to return another day, with more leisure, I asked Pouca Sorte to take us to a nice restaurant. Pouca Sorte knows the city well. He's been here before, I don't know how many times nor in what circumstances. He doesn't talk, doesn't like to talk about his past. This arouses my curiosity even further. He took us for tea to the Mount Nelson Hotel, a building (to use the expression of a number of guidebooks) of 'striking colonial splendour'*, on a large veranda hanging over a (another) dream garden. Cucumber and smoked salmon sandwiches, raisin scones covered with cream, dozens of lavish and fatal cakes. I succumbed, and now I feel sorry for it. Before that, though, before we'd sat down, the pianist started playing *Luanda at Twilight*. Tears came to my eyes – moved and incredulous – until I understood that Pouca Sorte, who seems to have lots of friends around here, had sent him a text message alerting him to our arrival and requesting that tune.

Ah, that mysterious driver of ours… The more I feel I don't know him, the more I like him!

---

* It's an expression that pleases and intrigues me. You wouldn't say of a modern building that it possesses 'a certain post-colonial splendour'. It sounds ludicrous. It's assumed that splendour is something that can only have happened in the colonial period.

(A rape, or almost)

I felt my feet burying into the drenched darkness. Something was pulling me down. A dark smell of rotting leaves, damp moss, rose in hot gusts, numbing my senses. That is how I was, sinking, my heart galloping, when three dry blows dragged me away from there – wherever that was. I leapt out of bed, wrapped a towel round my waist, still dizzy with sleep, and went to open the door. Laurentina came in, her eyes shining, took me by the neck with her long nervous fingers and kissed me on the lips. She tasted of alcohol. Before I could say anything at all, she had torn off her T-shirt and was pressing her small breasts, moist and trembling, to my chest, heart abandoned. I should have said something then. Perhaps:

'It's very late...'

Something that I could have grabbed onto as a formidable force dragged me down, a river floating in the dull morning, with all its fish, the dead yield of the foliage, somnambular crocodiles stumbling in the mud. Palm trees shook herons from their tall tousled hair. A kingfisher, with a metallic-blue breast, crossed like a lightning flash the heavy shadow of the waters. On the opposite bank, the vegetal dream of the trees asphyxiated the light. Death, all of a sudden, seemed easy to me, so easy. I gave myself in to the current, and let myself be carried away.

(Of love and death)

O amor, a morte. Have you noticed how in Portuguese the words for love and death are so similar? With the end of *amor*, love, being the beginning of *morte*, of death? I've been thinking about this for years. A curious phonetic coincidence, or rather, for would-be cabbalists and other such – myself not included – the protruding tail of a fat metaphysical cat. There is no love, no great love, that doesn't always have the cold shadow of death lurking beside it. Pedro and Inês. Romeo and Juliet. Orpheus and Eurydice.

It was like that with me. I had a great love, and lost it. It wouldn't have been a great love if I hadn't lost it. I think of him all the time. I lie down, to sleep, and I see him. I fall asleep, and see him. Wake up, and see him, sleeping, beside me. My mistake. My sin. The scandal that destroyed the future my mother dreamed for me. Today I can't love anyone, can't give myself over with truth and passion to anyone at all, however hard I try, closing my eyes, practising forgetfulness, I can't stop myself from comparing the bodies I take to bed with the body of my lost love, and in all of them I am nauseated to discover unbearable flaws. The firmness of the skin, the exact colour of the eyes, the teasing laugh with which he pushed me away, the way he tilted his head to look at me, the tall, long legs, the voice of dusk between the sheets.

'Where did you sleep?'

Laurentina, curious. The only person in this group who really worries about me. I replied enigmatically:

'I don't sleep. I dream and walk. My nights are more sleepless than your days.'

What I didn't tell her: that I go from bar to bar, with the anxiety of a predator, looking for bodies in which I can forget, even while knowing that there isn't one in which I can forget my love. I have dinner – a vegetarian dish – at Lola's. I park opposite Angels, or the Bronx Bar, and I wait. Club 55 has also merited some of my attention. Then there are a certain number of shady places – which out of delicacy I will not name or describe – where a man can go in alone and invariably come out accompanied. I don't drink. I never have. I guess my horror of alcohol saved me from a fall; or rather, if you'll allow me to use a word much appreciated by my teachers at the seminary, from abjection. Because to tell the truth I am falling. The problem, however, is not the fall, as he kept saying as he fell from the twelfth floor – more or less – that character in a very good film I once saw in Luanda in a cycle of French cinema: 'The problem isn't the fall, the problem's the impact.' The impact is what we might call abjection.

Shocked?! Ah, yes, I too like the cinema.

(No one ever falls in love with someone they know)

I open my right hand slowly, and then my left. I smell them. The only proof that she was here is the distracted ardour of a slightly sweet perfume, on my skin, on the sheets and pillows. The echo of a phrase, '*Your hands were made for the cup of my breasts*', the vague memory of lips on fire and a light body resting on mine.

When I woke up, the bed was too big.

Women say I have beautiful hands. I like them, my hands, I like what they give me. I think about Laurentina. Maybe it was a dream, after all. A perfume – something impossible to capture – is no kind of material proof. Still less the memory of a voice whispering in my ear, '*Your hands were made for the cup of my breasts*', a fragile silhouette against the slight clarity of the window. Another phrase occurs to me now – 'My name is abandonment' – but that's accompanied by a different scent. 'Come on! Come on!' I don't know if that's part of the same dream. I remember there was a force dragging me down, a river, or something like a river, a deaf current. There was a woman with liquid hair who called me in the voice of a bird. I can see the mermaid that Mandume saw. I see her with his eyes, but she isn't dead; she rises up triumphantly, her teeth sparkling with sunlight. I try to connect the dots on the page to form a picture. Fish floating between the leaves of the trees. A crocodile laughs at me, and only then do I notice just how broad a crocodile's smile is. Before going to sleep I was smoking the weed that Brand gave me. A solid bloke, the South African, even with those recessive racism genes. Maybe it was the weed. God, that was good! They say it's the desert sun that does it. Then

I see the kingfisher again, a metallic brilliance, calling me, from the opposite bank. I open my eyes and it's as though I were closing them. Laurentina gives a prolonged shudder, her arms around me.

I'm a guy who falls in love easily. I also, if truth be told, lose interest with equal facility. I'm fickle, is my mother's accusation. Perhaps. What attracts me in a woman is what I don't know about her. Some women use silence as they would wear a burqa. A man imagines what's behind that heavy, dark, sealed silence, which barely allows you to guess the shape of their thoughts. To imagine is already to love. Then there are the women who speak, but with a voice that is somehow so seductive, slightly hoarse and at the same time luminous, which is as if they didn't speak at all, so that we men can only hear the voice itself and not notice what it's saying. 'How can you fall in love with someone you don't even know?!' asks my mother, annoyed. That's precisely why, I answer, because no one ever falls in love with someone they know. In fact what I think is that passion ends the moment you come to know the other person. I think it was Nelson Rodrigues who used to say that if we all knew each other's intimacies no one would ever so much as greet anyone else. Then, of course, there are those women who seduce us through the brilliance of their thought. But even in these cases there comes a moment when we've turned the final page. Rereading a classic can be a pleasant exercise, without a doubt, but discovering a new young author arouses quite different feelings. Women who think are the most dangerous kind of all (and now I'd just better hope this diary never falls into the hands of a woman).

We usually have our breakfast in a happy, brightly lit café on Long Street, right next to our hotel. This morning, as I came down after a quick shower, there was only one customer there – Lili, a Portuguese historian, doing some work related to the restoration of old books in South Africa's public libraries. She greeted me with a splendid smile. I told her that her smile made the sun jealous. She smiled a confirmation. I sat down at the table next to hers. Lili has an oval-shaped face, full of freckles, and untamed red hair. She wears a piercing in her lower lip. When she leans over I see the tips of her breasts under her loose T-shirt. She has beauty spots on her chest, but no freckles. It's as though the freckles were little golden flowers that only opened up in direct sunlight. I wonder whether her hair is red down below too.

You understand now? With imagination, we're lost.

Mandume came in as I was finishing my food. He remained standing in the doorway a moment, with a strange look at me and Lili. What do I mean by a strange look? Well, a sort of sidelong look, dark and appraising, like a little bulldog looking at a big bulldog. He understood that he had no choice but to sit next to me. He sat down, with a sigh.

'Have either of you seen Laurentina?'

I shook my head. I explained that I'd just woken up, and that I'd slept like a stone all night. Lili said she'd been with her the night before:

'We were talking about you two! A women's conversation. We had a long talk…'

Mandume sighed again. I felt for him. I said:

'I dreamed about your mermaid.'

'Don't piss me off…'

'Seriously. I dreamed I was drowning. Then she appeared and dragged me to the bank. But it was the wrong bank…'

'Wrong? What d'you mean wrong?'

'No idea – but I know it was the wrong bank. That is, in the dream I knew it was the wrong bank.'

'And then what happened?'

'I don't remember. I've been trying to remember, but I can't.'

'Know what your problem is? You smoke too much. Your head is full of smoke. It destroys your neurons…'

'*Dagga*! Here in South Africa it's called *dagga*. But if you ask for grass people also understand you. Or *boom*, *zol*, dope, weed, ganja. There are still people who call it *swazi gold*, or just "poison". You see, when people come up with lots of names for something, it's because they really love it. In Africa people love weed.'

Lili interjected:

'Not just in Africa. I like it too. Have you got some?'

'I do. Really good. Very pure. Want some?'

Lili laughed willingly:

'I'm going off to work now. Why don't you come by my room at the end of the afternoon? We'll have a party, the two of us…'

Mandume was livid. This guy has about as much sense of humour as a mongrel with scabies. He can't appreciate life. If you ask me he's spent too long in Portugal. Look, I like travelling to Lisbon too, I go to the bookshops, to the cinema, I see photography exhibitions, and I think that's all great for washing out the soul. But I never stay more than a couple of weeks. Three, maximum. Portuguese melancholy corrupts your spirit, darkens it, just like autumn cold yellows and kills the leaves on the trees.

(Where we first speak of Elisa Mucavele)

Nine women covered by black burqas moved onto the stage in a sort of blind dance. A tenth woman, naked, or nearly naked, an intense, perfectly drawn body, burning under a bronze light, was fleeing backward from them. I recognised the music: *Nkosi Sikelela Africa*, the South African national anthem, in an enchanting interpretation by the Alexandra Youth Chorus. But I feared I hadn't correctly understood the intent of the choreography. Seretha du Toit refused to enlighten me. I shrugged my shoulders, a little annoyed, when at a café table, less than an hour after the show, I asked her about that particular piece of choreography. She muttered something vague about the ancient suffering of African woman. I insisted:

'And the burqas?'

She ignored my questions. Seretha prefers to ask the questions herself:

'Are you sure Faustino's your father?'

I found the question strange. Her tone of voice I found even stranger:

'You seem to be sure that he wasn't. Is there something I should know?'

She smiled. A gentle, pacifying smile. She put her right hand on my left shoulder. A mother's gesture:

'My dear, this world is full of traps.'

She was wearing a wine-coloured dress, silk, maybe a little too tight and low-cut for her age. It looked good on her, however. 'Elegance doesn't age,' my father used to say. Which one of them?! Good question. I have – or had – several fathers and the feeling that I no longer have any. But in this case, of course, I'm referring to the man who raised me.

'From South Africa you're going on to Mozambique, right?'

'Yes. We're going to Maputo.'

'Lourenço Marques! You want to go to Lourenço Marques. Maputo came later. Faustino went to Lourenço Marques, by train, in 1962. But do you know who you should be looking for?'

'No. Well, we have some ideas. One of my brothers told me that our father – that Faustino… that he played piano at the Hotel Polana…'

'That's true. He was the first black man – or rather, the first non-white – to play piano at the Polana. I can't imagine you'll find anyone from that time, anyone who remembers him, at the hotel. I'll give you a much better lead: Elisa Mucavele. Do you know who she is?'

I didn't know. Bartolomeu, however, assented at once, interested:

'Elisa Mucavele, the Health Minister?'

'Exactly. Back in 1962 she was a nurse. Faustino lived with her for seven or eight years. They had a number of children.'

'The nurse?! Babaera, my brother, also told me our father had lived with a nurse in Lourenço Marques, but he didn't know her name. So she's well known now…'

'Well known?' Bartolomeu laughed at my ignorance. 'Elisa Mucavele is an extraordinary person; and like any extraordinary person she has many enemies. A person who has no enemies doesn't deserve to have any friends.'

'A nice phrase, but pretty stupid.' Seretha doesn't weigh her words. 'That woman doesn't even deserve enemies…'

Bartolomeu looked at her, scandalised:

'Don't say that. Elisa writes, she published two or three very interesting novels, about the state of the Mozambican woman. I met her in Barcelona, at a meeting for writers from the southern countries, and I found her fascinating. And besides, no one's ever been able to prove anything against her…'

'Proof? What better proof is there than the life Elisa leads?!'

'What are you talking about?'

'Today Elisa Mucavele is one of the richest people in Mozambique. How do you think she managed that?'

'How?'

'It's all speculation. She could have inherited it…'

'You don't really believe that.'

'Her ex-husband was a pretty rich man.'

'So he was. And him, how did he become so rich?'

'Right!' Bartolomeu raised his voice, excited. 'And how were all the big fortunes made in the United States of America? In Brazil? The whites killed the Indians, robbed and skinned them, and now their grandchildren are respectable people. All the whites in Australia descend from thieves and prostitutes. If that happened in those countries, why wouldn't it happen in ours?'

'Any moment now you're going to tell me that denouncing corruption in African countries is just a manifestation of racism.'

'To a lot of Europeans the only good black man is a poor black man. They don't accept that a black man can be rich. First they attack us for having allied ourselves with the socialist bloc. Now they attack us for being good capitalists…'

'You don't shock me.'

'Sorry, I got carried away. I don't mean to say that you think like that ma'am; I know your story.'

'No. You know nothing. You don't know what you're talking about. You're a boy, drunk on your own impertinence. Accepting that you can't criticise someone because that someone is black, that's called paternalism. Paternalism is the elegant racism of cowards.'

Knock-out. The bell rings.

Bartolomeu slunk out of the café.

I've been feeling a little anxious. I've started thinking that maybe we won't be able to complete the journey. Last night I lost my temper with Mandume again. I left him in the room – watching *Magnolia* on television again – and went down to the hotel bar. There was a girl sitting alone on one of the sofas. I thought she looked improbable there, dislocated, a bit like those greyhounds at Seretha du Toit's house. In fact she did have just the same distant and aristocratic bearing. She looked at me deeply. A precipice, those eyes of hers. The most striking thing, though, was her hair. Red, down her back. She introduced herself: Lili, Portuguese. She invited me to have something. I asked for a caipirinha. Lili lives in London. She's a specialist in restoring old books. She's in South Africa as part of a project financed by some European institution. She fell in love with a Namibian of German origin, one of those types who takes tourists out to see the elephants, boats buried in the sand, genuine *himba* tribesmen and authentic postcard bushmen. She showed me a photo of him. Good-looking. With that kind of insolent, very blonde charm of a Robert Redford. She went with him to Etosha. On their return she discovered – by accident – that the man was married, and the father to three children.

'A son of a bitch!'

I ordered another caipirinha. Lili was on her second whisky. I rarely drink alcohol. I don't know at what point it was that we started exchanging intimate confidences. I don't remember very well what happened after the third caipirinha. I woke up this morning with a terrible headache, and the confused feeling of having done something appalling.

Trans-Karoo Express, somewhere between Cape Town and Johannesburg,
South Africa
Thursday, 17 November 2005

I like the sort of places where nothing happens, not a thing passing, a place at an impasse. Of course, I like them as I pass through them, pace by pace, on my slow passage, or on wheels, slipping quickly through. I like the static silence, the still light, in the various shades of rust – an old photograph stained with tears.

Early this morning I awoke rather bewildered, stretched out on my back on the narrow berth of a train compartment, and looking out of the window saw just that sort of light. Yellow grasses, and slow, curly-haired bushes. Mountains came down from the sky, delicately as giraffes. Jordi was sleeping face down, in the lower berth. I climbed down carefully so as not to wake him, I opened the door and stepped into the corridor. In the restaurant car two men were having coffee. A loose phrase reached me:

'It's not the right life, but it's my life.'

I kept wondering what incorrect life that man was living, and envied him. Incorrect lives have always interested me. I ordered a coffee, fried eggs with bacon. The train had stopped in the middle of a naked landscape. Pure silence.

'In Cradock,' the man continued, 'the remote village where I lived as a kid, we used to hear secret sounds, melodies from another world, carried to us by the harsh wind of the Karoo. There was a time I thought I was the only one who could hear them. A sort of ghost song. But one day my grandmother said to me: "That thing the wind's blowing, that's the bell of the tomb of Tribal Chief Ntsikana. It's a bell carved into the rock itself, there, right in the Xhosa country." Many years later I went in search of this bell. I found nothing. Nothing that resembled a bell. What I did discover was a large smooth boulder, covered in aloes. Then a very old woman came with a stone and struck the boulder and I heard it again, pure and strong, the great bell of Ntsikana. There's a legend. You probably don't know it. One afternoon as Ntsikana was tending his flock, the Lord God came down from the clouds and spoke to him. Strange prodigies were seen those days, clouds dancing in a fiery sky, snakes were seen flying, but Ntsikana remained silent in his *kraal*. Then one afternoon he got up and began to sing. They say his songs calmed all around him.'

The man stopped. Silence settled again over the landscape. The wind tousled the harsh hair of the bramble bushes, making the dry grass wave. A plastic bag rose up into the blue like an apathetic bird, inflated with light. A narrow dirt path ran alongside the train tracks. Then it curved to the right and led to a wooden house. I hadn't noticed the house immediately, as it was the same colour as the earth. A convulsive red. Big open windows. The light, in a burst, illuminated a black lad, tall and angular, inside the house, sitting on a sofa. I waved to him, and the lad waved back. I thought – as I often think when I find a place like this – 'That's a house it'd be good to live in.' Then I imagine myself living in that house, a day, a whole month, watching the trains pass, counting the trains, waving to the distracted passengers in the restaurant car, and I flee in horror. Yes, I like places where nothing happens, not a thing passes, but I like them only as I'm passing through. I'm brought my fried eggs with bacon. A cup of coffee. Behind me I hear the man's hoarse voice again:

'Today, around the tomb of old Ntsikana, the landscape is sad and hopeless. A graveyard of car engines, mechanical parts. There are pigs foraging in the ground and goats gnawing at telephone directories. Yet whenever someone strikes the boulder and the bell awakes, Ntsikana's songs are heard again, and this unsettles the clouds, and it sometimes rains. At least, that's what they say. I don't know. I've heard the songs. They still echo in my heart.'

It was cold. I returned trembling to my bed. Not long ago I found among Jordi's books an anthology of South African poetry: *The New Century of South African Poetry*. Leafing through it, distracted, I came across some lines by Frederick Guy Butler that refer to Ntsikana's bell. Not long afterwards when I was listening to Abdullah Ibrahim I noticed for the first time that the first track on one of his collections, *Celebration*, is entitled

Ntsikana's Bell. It explains in the sleeve notes that it's a traditional song. Jordi wasn't surprised by any of the coincidences:

'I have a friend who has never left the little town where he was born and knows the whole world through poetry. He can talk for hours about Alexandria, about the Greeks of Alexandria, and with such feeling that people are moved. They ask him how long he lived in Egypt, or whether he'd only been on holiday. No, he'd read Cavafy.'

Perhaps he's right. After all, what's left in us when our journey is done? In me, less than the simplest line of poetry, undoubtedly. Disparate images, the diffuse memory of a smell or of a colour. Apart from that, as Jordi reminds me, poetry is cheap and relatively safe. No one ever contracted malaria from reading the poems of Rui Duarte de Carvalho. They should produce guidebooks that are simply collections of poetry.

(The red house)

We spent the night on the road. It was five in the morning – a bit earlier or later – when Malembemalembe fainted, drained completely dry, somewhere in the middle of Karoo. Laurentina was sleeping, her head in my lap, wrapped in a blanket. Bartolomeu was up front, next to Pouca Sorte, with the task of ensuring he didn't fall asleep. Suddenly Malembemalembe shuddered, coughed, and a thick smoke began to come out of the engine. We got out. Our feet in the red dust. The smooth sky, immense, a prodigious blue singing above our heads.

'And now?'

The inevitable question. Laurentina smiled, still half-asleep:

'I've never seen so much nothing.'

Bartolomeu pointed ahead. Some hundred metres away, at a bend in the road, was a little wooden house in faded red, its windows open. It looked as though it had sprung out of the ground, like some ancient flower. It was the only building in the middle of the enormity of landscape. Pouca Sorte leaned dejectedly over the engine.

'The head gasket's blown…'

I don't understand anything to do with cars. I don't drive. I do have a driving licence, though. One of my ex-girlfriends, a doctor eight years older than me, signed me up to a driving school. I passed the theory exam easily, but I was sure I'd fail the practical part. Naturally my greatest ambition was to fail. I made two or three minor faults, but so calmly that the examiner gave in:

'I could fail you. But it's obvious that you've already been driving for a long time. You have all sorts of drivers' vices. If I fail you you'll just keep driving without a licence. It would be better for me to give you your licence.'

I drove for a week. One afternoon the car started rolling down a slope. The horns started their assault immediately. There I was, nervous, trying to resolve the situation, and those morons behind me shouting obscenities and blowing their horns. I pulled up the handbrake, got out of the car, locked it, and walked slowly away, to general stupor. Then I phoned my girlfriend, told her what had happened, and she went to rescue the car. Our relationship ended that day.

The four of us walked to the house. The door was half-open. We called, but no one answered. Bartolomeu pushed the door and went in. I went with him. A very clean room, almost unfurnished: two leather sofas covered in transparent plastic, and a low, rustic table in elaborately worked wood, with an erotic frieze made up of little African figures. One door opened to a narrow bathroom; another led to the kitchen. In a shed, round the back, there was a series of tools arranged on metal stands. Pouca Sorte whistled:

'Everything I've ever wanted. At last God has heard my prayers…'

He chose the tools he needed and put them in a bag.

'We can't do that,' I protested. 'It's not right. And if the owner turns up?'

Bartolomeu laughed.

'If that happens we'll have to kill him.'

I don't appreciate his humour. I sat down in the living room. The sky was coming in, in a blue torrent, through the open window. There was an exercise book on the table. I opened it and read:

'I went up to the biggest ravine and closed my eyes and listened to the silence, and felt myself in an instant liberated from the fury and the noise, from the torrent of days. A few metres ahead of me I saw a couple of eagles: they cried their urgent love to the world. A lizard looked at me with eyes of an intense blue – I was certain that he was happy.'

A thick clamour of metal tore me from my reading. I hadn't noticed that the road ran parallel to the train tracks. The train passed, very slowly, piece-o-turf, piece-o-turf, piece-o-turf, in a long lament of silk and smoke. A dark man, tanned, in one of the windows of the restaurant car, waved to me. I lifted my hand and waved back. Pouca Sorte returned with the tools.

'All done. We can continue on our way.'

'Who do you reckon lives here?'

'I have no idea.'

'It's a strange house. It doesn't have a bedroom. It doesn't even have a bed…'

'Maybe he doesn't sleep. Maybe he doesn't need to sleep…'

'Everyone needs to sleep.'

'Not everyone. I practically don't sleep.'

'I can believe that. That's why you fall asleep at the wheel.'

Pouca Sorte looked at me, offended:

'That accident, back at Canjala, it only happened because you people startled me. Yes, I sleep little. I go weeks without coming anywhere near my dreams. I had a serious problem, some years ago, and since then I've scarcely closed my eyes. And when I close my eyes I can still see. I see even better with my eyes closed.'

I gave up. Sometimes I think this guy's crazy. At first he surprised us with his careful way of speaking which seems to be so apart from the job he does. But actually, if George Bush who talks like a stevedore can be President of the United States of America, why not the other way around, why shouldn't someone with the eloquence of a bishop, the same gentle gestures, the same tamarind voice, why can't he be a *candongueiro* driver in Angola? What troubles me, though, is not the incoherence with his job. What troubles me is the feeling that we're not moving in quite the same world.

As for me, I would like to know who lives in this house. Before leaving I tore a sheet from my notepad and wrote, in English: 'We found the door open and came in. We used your tools to fix a problem with the engine of our car. I used the window to look at the sky. Thank you very much – Mariano Maciel.' I put the sheet of paper down on the table, and left.

Part Three

(Fragments of an interview with Ricardo Rangel)

'I began to have contact with jazz in the forties. I was only little, and I liked music. There was a moment, here, in this city of ours of Lourenço Marques, when a convoy of ships was detained in port. The sea, that whole sea there, it was packed with American ships prevented from getting out by German submarines. There were huge sailors. And I, being a smart kid, went out to sell the guys weed. In those days the cleaning of the city was done by people who came from Gaza, but I don't know where exactly, somewhere in the interior, and the city was always incredibly clean. There were blokes living in a camp, where Third of February School is today, who cultivated weed, and I'd go there and buy a few little rolls for five *escudos* and then sell them to the Americans. And the guys, 'Bring more!' and they'd say to one another, 'We're going to make a fortune in the United States,' because they didn't intend the weed for consumption but to sell it on later. But I didn't want money, I preferred it when they gave me records. Seventy-eights. Thanks to that some guys came over twenty years ago, who knew I had certain records, records I still have today, guys came who wanted to buy those records from me. I didn't sell. They'd heard I had a few V–Disc recordings – you know what they are? When the United States came into the war they recruited a number of musicians. They wanted them to play music to entertain the troops. The navy department invited the most incredible musicians and they'd play together. They managed to bring together some extraordinary musicians. When the war ended the big publishers went to the navy to ask them for the masters. The navy refused, and simply had the masters destroyed. So today those records are a rarity. I have a few.

' [...] South Africa already had some jazz. Every once in a while some guys would come here. Whites. And during the war, that is, in the forties, in '45, Jewish musicians began to spring up – they'd fled from Hitler, they were Czechs, Austrians, Germans, the guys came to shore here, and they'd stay, two of them became part of the Mozambique Radio Philharmonic orchestra. They were classical musicians. There were also the guys who played jazz, in the cabarets, in the casinos, on Araújo Street. Dance music. Big Bands, with orchestra. There were two casinos that from time to time hired bands. They used to dance in the casinos. Araújo Street had huge cabarets. When they knocked off work in the casinos, they'd take their jackets off, take their ties off, and they'd go to the bars. It was in these places that the masses began to get used to jazz.

' [...] In the fifties, at the end of the fifties, it was American policy to send jazz groups to Africa. Herbie Mann came once, with a Big Band of nineteen people. I covered the three days of their visit. When he saw the photos in the paper Herbie Mann wanted to meet me. He took three of my photos to publish in the most important jazz magazine of the time, *Jazz Beat*. There are still musicians who come to seek me out today.'

(The pianist without hands)

Georgina assures us that he is eighty-two years old. It's hard to believe. He looks like a young man who's just lived to excess. Of course, I already knew him, through his work and his reputation: Ricardo Rangel. Mutter that name and before long someone will offer the tag 'The Father of Mozambican Photography'. It implies a certain responsibility, that tag, as Mozambique has a handful of excellent photographers. I like Sérgio Santimano a lot, a half-black, half-Goan guy, with a stunning lyrical eye. I like Kok Nam too, in this case a Mozambican of Chinese origin, who accompanied Rui Knopfli to the airport on the day the poet abandoned the country; this is important only because Knopfli left us a poetic record of the event:

It's the fateful month of March and I
am upstairs looking at the void.
Kok Nam, the photographer, lowers his Nikon
and looks obliquely at me, into my eyes:
Not coming back? I just say, no.

I won't come back, but will always remain,
somewhere in little illegible signs
Safe from all indiscrete futurologies,
only preserved in the exclusivity of private
memory. I don't want to remember a thing,
all that matters to me is to forget, and forget

171

the impossibility of forgetting. You never
forget, everything is remembered secretly [...]

I don't know the poem by heart, obviously, I went to get it off the Internet.

But let's leave aside the oblique gaze of Kok Nam and return to Ricardo Rangel (ironic, almost always, and in love). He's also been given another label: 'The Jazz Man of Mozambique.' The bar where we went last night bears his name: Chez Rangel. After nightfall it operates in one of the most beautiful colonial buildings in Maputo – the Mozambique Central Railroad Station. Places like this discredit even the best dreams. You go in through the illuminated night-time (oil lamps on the walls) and come to a little stage with tables and chairs, arranged on the cement of the platform. The iron of the tracks glimmers, just alongside, unreal, like the rather extravagant setting for a film. Rangel was seated at a nearby table. He was drinking something. He was laughing with an overly blonde woman. Long legs. During the moments that the double bass lowered its big hollow voice a few loose phrases fell to our table, arousing my curiosity: '... There's this one group here, the best Mozambican group, the only foreigner is a Belgian...', '...Our best musicians are in South Africa...', '... A Danish woman brought us another...' I thought about getting up to say hello to him. I didn't have the nerve.

I met Georgina at the house of the writer Mia Couto. That was four or five years ago. I'd found myself in Maputo, for the second time, filming a documentary on AIDS orphans in southern Africa. On the third night I ended up – I don't know how – in the middle of a really lively birthday party, in an immense yard, surrounded by palm trees, dancing *kuduro*. I'd had a lot to drink. I remember I'd started drinking back at the hotel, with the Angolan journalists I was with, and I must have kept on drinking later as we went from bar to bar, revealing the city – but of that I have only fleeting images. So there I was in that party, when someone pushed me (I'm sure that someone pushed me) and I lost my balance and fell into the swimming pool. I was immediately lucid. It wouldn't have been so bad if I hadn't become lucid. I got out of the water flustered, but laughing, no one would think that that would affect my good mood. Mia and his wife, the lovely Patricia, who didn't know me at all, were exceedingly kind to me. They had me take a hot bath, gave me tea and lent me a pair of jeans and a white T-shirt that was a little big for me. Even lucid, however, I still couldn't remember practically anything that had happened before my fall. There were dozens of people at the party, and not one of them could even remember seeing me arrive. No one knew me, and I couldn't recognise anyone. Let's just say I turned into the Mystery Man of the night. The feature attraction. It was Georgina who offered to take me to the hotel.

'I'm a bit mad!' she shouted as she drove. A huge smile opened on her face. 'To tell the truth, I'm really very mad. Really, really wild. Sexually speaking. I think that in bed anything goes, anything at all, so long as it's done with love.'

I didn't know how to reply. There I was, recently saved from the waters, crossing a sleeping city, driven at high speed by a very young, very beautiful woman, who had just confessed to me – shouting – in an ecstasy – to be completely wild in bed. I felt insecure. Maybe I, Mystery Man, wouldn't be able to fulfil her expectations? What the hell could Georgina mean by 'anything goes'? All the same, when we arrived I invited her up. The girl looked at me, surprised:

'Up?'

'Up to the stars…'

She laughed:

'I won't go to bed with anyone but my boyfriend.'

Georgina is nineteen years old and is studying law. In between times she sings. She made a record, in Cape Town, with some of the continent's most famous songs, such as *Pata Pata*, *Malaika*, *Stimela* and *Diarabi*, in an elegant style that falls somewhere between jazz and Afro-pop. At that point, however, I had no idea about this talent of hers. This is the little I knew about her, apart from the name that comes from the famous *marrabenta* song: that she frequented the house of the most famous writer in Mozambique; that she was, or claimed to be, a lover totally without any preconceptions; that she had a boyfriend, and that she was faithful to him.

This last piece of information restored my spirit. This might be pathological, I accept that, but the women who ignore me, or who reject me, they're invariably the ones that attract me the most. I said to her that if she didn't come up with me to my room, and eventually beyond, up to the stars, she would spend the rest of her life wracked by the doubt. Women are excited by curiosity. It didn't work. Actually, none of my manoeuvres worked. I went up alone (and no further than the second floor); fell into bed and slept uninterruptedly for eleven hours. A Lisbon-São Paulo flight.

I went out with her the next night, to get to know some live-music bars, and another time for lunch, to the O Coqueiro restaurant in the Popular Market, but the best I could get out of her was a pious promise that she would think of me and that she'd write to me after I went back to Luanda. She really did write to me. Today she's one of the few people I chat to on Messenger. That was how I came to know that her mother, Fátima Saide, in the sixties and seventies found a certain fame as a singer and composer of *marrabenta* music. After independence she left for South Africa, settling in Johannesburg, where for many years she worked as a manicurist in a beauty salon. Georgina was born in Johannesburg. Her father, a piano tuner, a South African, who never stayed long in the same city, is irregularly in contact with her. Her mother died two years ago, a victim of the so-called virus of the century. When she learned she was infected she returned to Mozambique with her daughter, then a little girl a few months old. Even while she was sick, Fátima went in search of some musicians she'd worked with before independence, and started singing again. Without much success this time.

I told Laurentina the whole story. I thought she'd be excited. After all, Georgina knows huge numbers of people connected to the Mozambique music world, including the odd historical name who must have shared with Faustino Manso those years of colonial euphoria. But Laurentina refused to meet my friend. She exploded, a complete breakdown:

'If you want to sleep with this woman, you don't need a pretext. Apart from that I don't have to have anything to do with it. Go, get out of here!'

I looked at her, stunned:

'I never slept with her!'

The moment I said this I realised how absurd the situation was. Either I'd take it seriously and get angry or make a joke of it. I tried to joke about it:

'So we're arguing like a couple now? It seems to me that's much more serious, and certainly much more dangerous, than going to bed together. Now before I know it you'll want to marry me.'

Laurentina got up (we were having breakfast in the hotel) and left without finishing her coffee. This happened yesterday. Last night I went with Georgina to Chez Rangel, and met a pianist who didn't have any hands, who assured me that one of his closest friends had been Faustino

Manso. By this point Ricardo Rangel had already left. The overly blonde woman with the long legs was dancing alone with a glass in her left hand. A small, skinny young man, his thin legs in very faded and extremely tight jeans, came up to our table and asked Georgina to sing something. He was the double bass player. Georgina agreed. She sang – turned to face me – a song by Lura: *Nha Vida*. She sang it with the same impetuous despair of the Cape Verdean, with a similar sensuality in the way she moved her hips and her arms. As I lost my eyes in her eyes, it felt as though she really were doing it with her heart in flames, 'hold my hand / take me with you / let me rest my head in your lap', as though the impossibility of anything at all happening between us linked us more strongly than the strongest love. As the final note was extinguished, however, the magic was broken. Applause for her, and many curious glances in my direction.

The pianist without hands was sitting at a nearby table. He didn't restrict himself to glancing. He raised both stumps up to the level of his head, accompanying his gesture with a complicit smile, and although he didn't have hands I could almost see him giving me the thumbs-up. I smiled back. A waiter brought him a glass of whisky with a little straw. When he came back right away to bring me my beer (a dark Laurentina) I asked him quietly who the man was.

'Him? The pianist, of course!'

I try not to be shocked at what the continent offers me. I've had some practice at that over the past couple of years, filming the strangest episodes in remote places in the interior of Angola and neighbouring countries. Nonetheless that perplexed me. Georgina came back after singing another two or three songs. She didn't know the pianist. Then he got up and came over to join us. He pulled up a chair, dragging it over with his feet, and sat down:

'Marechal Carmona! That's my name. Like the old president. My father wanted to make the Portuguese happy…'

He turned to Georgina:

'Congratulations. Miss sings very well. I hope you don't mind if I say that your mother at the same age sang even better. Ah, the wonderful Fátima! Fátima Saide, the *Marrabenta* Queen. After she came back from South Africa it was never the same. I lost my hands, but never stopped being a pianist. She didn't lose her voice, but stopped being a singer.'

I couldn't resist and asked him out of the blue whether he'd known the Angolan musician Faustino Manso. Now it was his turn to be astonished. He leaned back in his chair, closed his eyes and breathed deeply.

'Faustino Manso? How many years has it been that I haven't heard anyone mention Faustino? Do you know him?'

I explained to him that Faustino was my grandfather. I told him that Faustino had died a few weeks ago, in Luanda, after a number of years struggling against a cancerous tumour in his lungs. He smoked his whole life. I told him about the funeral. The pianist put out his stumps. He held them in front of my face:

'See my hands?'

I didn't.

'They are the hands of Faustino Manso!' He said this, and then stopped talking. Leaving me completely intrigued. He leaned back again and changed the subject: 'Do you know which tune is most requested from pianists in hotel bars? *Casablanca! Play it again, Sam.* I've seen the film seven times. Ilsa doesn't say that. She says: *Play it, Sam. Play "As Time Goes By".* Rick – Bogart's character – is rough when he makes the same request: *You played it for her, you can play it for me.* You can only imagine how many times some idiot has come up to me and said that quote that's not actually in the film. Many times! Only once, at the Polana, after Faustino left and I took over from him, just that one time! – a woman came up to me and said it right: *Play it, Sam. Play "As Time Goes By".* The next morning they found her in the bathroom, her wrists slit. *It's still the same old story, a fight for love and glory, a case of "do or die".'*

Before I had the chance to put more questions to him, a thin, shy teenager appeared, dressed in a blue overcoat. I noticed the overcoat because it was enormous on him.

'Come on, Dad, we've got to go. Mum's waiting.'

Marechal got up; he bobbed a little apology with his head:

'If I don't go now I'll turn into a pumpkin.'

I got up too, unsure whether or not I should hold out my hand to him and take his stump. I opted for giving him a couple of pats on the shoulder, somewhere between a hug – which would have been too much – and the impossibility of a trivial handshake:

'Can we meet again some other time? I'd like to talk to you about my grandfather.'

He smiled. A smile of triumph.

'Certainly, young man. Be here, tomorrow, same time. You're buying the drinks, obviously.'

(A ghost with a stole)

A short while ago, at lunch: a little shock.

The four of us were in a restaurant serving Zambezian food, in the Popular Market. Laurentina dreamy. Mandume downcast. Bartolomeu, very excited, telling us about a meeting he had last night with a handless pianist who used to play at the Polana Hotel.

Barbequed chicken for the four of us.

Barbequed chicken, Zambezi-style, is one of the best dishes – notwithstanding its simplicity – that you can get in Mozambique. The chicken is seasoned with salt, lemon, pepper and *gindungo* chilli. The milk is extracted from a coconut, the pulp is grated and mixed in with two spoonfuls of oil. The chicken is then grilled over a low flame, constantly basting it with the mixture of coconut and oil. It's good to make use of the sauce that runs off down the grill, and with which you can baste the meat again when it's time to serve. Chicken *à zambeziana*, then, and beers all round.

Then without warning a dark figure appeared before us. I didn't notice until it was too late:

'Father Albino?!'

I sat bolt upright. Right in front of me, with black suit and an ecclesiastical stole: the past. It could have been worse. In my nightmares it's always much worse. The past – in this case given inferior representation in the form of Father Lírio from the congregation of Espírito Santo – lives in meditation and exile, over in the outskirts of Lichinga, in Niassa, praying to the giraffes and the rhinos – more to the latter than to former,

179

as they're boring animals little given to the sacred – and he doesn't hear the world's gossiping, still less what's happening in Angola. So I restricted myself to replying succinctly to the half-dozen questions he had for me on the health of one or other illustrious prelate with whom we'd both spent time during a short stay in Luanda by Father Lírio, following which we bade farewell with the grace of God. Of course, I wasn't able to escape the curiosity of my clients.

'So, it's *Father* Albino?'

'I always suspected…'

'Ha! No way, I think you owe us an explanation…'

I didn't owe them any sort of explanation, of course. I could have left them burning in the hell of their curiosity. But I thought that revealing a small part of the truth might save me from having to reveal the whole truth later – if the past were to return. I told them that I had in fact been a priest, but that having tired of God I abandoned the church.

Laurentina was interested:

'You lost your faith?'

Bartolomeu tried to make light of it, but not too convincingly:

'What you lost was your chastity, wasn't that how it was, father? Behind any big decision taken by a man, there's always a woman.'

I let them speak to me like this, familiarly. A mixture in their tone now, respect and incredulity. A priest never completely stops being a priest. In the evening Laurentina came over to me. She seemed restless, disturbed.

Perhaps she was expecting me to hear her confession.

(The triumph of authenticity)

I remember her in Barcelona, during a writers' gathering, an enormous woman, magnificent silver hair, opening the inaugural debate with a song which – she explained – would call in the good spirits and drive away the bad. Her voice, now moaning, now humming, now in a vague cry, unfolding mysterious vowels into the air, left the Spaniards numb with astonishment. They listened utterly still, and utterly still they remained after she had fallen silent, not knowing whether they ought to applaud or maintain a respectful silence. They chose the silence. As soon as the session had ended I asked her if she'd received any kind of initiation as a medicine woman. Elisa Mucavele laughed. A little laugh:

'Oh, for the love of God, my dear Angolan! It's just a song my mother taught me. A song to get children to sleep. It's nothing to do with spirits. But the whites loved the number. It's just the number they would expect from an African writer. Why shouldn't I give them this little pleasure?'

At another debate she wept full tears as she recalled the death of a giraffe. Many in the audience cried with her:

'You've got to practise tears,' she confided in me later, as we were drinking beers in the hotel bar. 'If you manage to get them to share a moment of mourning with you, you can get anything from them, in particular you can get them to buy your books. Make them laugh with you, move them with you, and they will follow you to your very last book.'

Barcelona was hosting a gathering of writers from southern countries – illustrious unknowns – that was being promoted by an NGO for development support. Over the three days that followed they talked about nothing but that extraordinary Mozambican writer, the woman who sang to appease the spirits, so sensitive that the death of a giraffe could bring her to tears.

I saw an old woman, with diaphanous sky-blue hair, holding Elisa in a protracted hug, on the way out of the first debate:

'Thank you for being genuine,' she said to her, tears in her eyes. 'Here in Europe we've killed God, and now we're all orphans. We've lost our connection to the sacred.'

A solemn, sad girl, very thin, whom we'd called The Cypress, asked for her help in appeasing the spirit of her mother, who'd died weeks earlier in a car crash. Another offered her a giraffe, in cloth, made in Botswana by an organisation supporting children who were victims of AIDS.

It wasn't hard to get hold of Elisa's mobile number. As soon as she heard my voice, she shouted, pleased:

'The Angolan! I already knew you were in my country…'

But when I told her what I'd come for, her voice darkened. She seemed amazed, yes, but also a little fearful:

'You're Faustino's grandson?! Amazing! So you're the nephew to my children. I can hardly believe it. Life creates the sort of plots that you could never pull off in fiction.'

She agreed to meet us, tomorrow, early afternoon. I took down her address: Sommerschield – the glorious neighbourhood of the *haute bourgeoisie*, where Graça Machel and Nelson Mandela live. Laurentina was pleased with the news. She also agreed to go with me tonight to Chez Rangel, to meet the handless pianist.

Lovers' Garden, Maputo
14 September 2006

(A mulatto Clark Gable)

Elegant, with almost straight white hair, cropped close, a small grey moustache, like a circumflex accent over his fine, well-drawn lips. During the sixties and seventies João Domingos, leader and vocalist of the João Domingos Band, was a very popular figure in Mozambique. The João Domingos Band played in dance halls: the Ateneu Grego, now the Wedding Palace; the Chinese Club, where the Visual Arts School is today; the Casa do Minho; the Casa das Beiras; the Comorianos Club. In any case there was no shortage of work in those days for someone who wanted to – and knew how to – earn his living from other people's leisure.

'In the old days there used to be much more live music,' says João Domingos with a resigned sadness. After independence they only wanted us to play revolutionary music, so that's what we played, but to dance rhythms. Even President Samora liked it…'

The conversation is taking place in a nice café in the Jardim dos Namorados – the Lovers' Garden – with a stunning view over the Indian Ocean. João Domingos was present at the birth of *marrabenta*, the one Mozambican rhythm to achieve some sort of international renown:

'The name "marrabenta" came from Mafalala. There was a man there called Fernando. He had the best electric guitar and he played it louder, though every once in a while he'd snap a string playing *majika* music. He played tangos and rumbas too. So people would say to him, "Play that one that breaks 'em – that is, *aquela q'arrebenta*." The name came from there, but the rhythm is what we called "majika". At the Comorianos Club, where we also used to play, there was another guy who danced tap very well, just like Fred Astaire. He was called Jaime Paixão. He developed the tap dance, sliding as he danced, and that's where we got the way you dance the *marrabenta*.'

Karen praises his elegance. The good shape he's in. João Domingos tells us he was in a serious accident as a child, playing with a rocket, and spent two weeks unable to see. Then he recovered and never had any more trouble. But a few years ago, feeling his eyesight tiring, he went to see a Cuban ophthalmologist. The doctor studied his eyes; he said he'd never seen the like before:

'Technically, sir, you're blind. There's nothing I can do to help you. I find it hard to believe that you can see anything at all. If you really can see, it's with the eyes of the soul – and them, well, them I don't know how to treat.'

João Domingos laughed and went to consult another doctor. This one seemed to him to be better equipped. He sat in front of a complex arrangement of movable lenses linked to a computer. He looked at it, and looked at it again. Then he held his hand up a few inches from his face:

'How many fingers?'

He got him to read letters on a poster. Eventually he sat down (perhaps he felt more secure sitting down), shook his head, and – quite incredulous – confirmed:

'You're the first blind man I've ever come across to complain of tired eyesight...'

I look into his eyes, distrustful, dark. I'm thinking what it must be like, the world he sees. And it's true that no two ways of viewing the world are alike.

Ahead of us, the light seems to be rising up from the sea.

(The lost hands of Faustino Manso)

Marechal Carmona has the voice of an airline pilot[*]:

'Can I see your hand?'

I held out my right hand. He ran his eyes over it, carefully. He smiled:

'You have no country, miss; the country quadrant, a tiny image you usually find between the life line and the luck line, you haven't got it. Faustino didn't either. Your destiny is to travel.'

I denied this vehemently. I'm tired of travelling. I look in the mirror and don't recognise myself. My hair is dull, spoiled. Bags under my eyes, bigger than my eyes. I like to travel, but anything in excess is tiring. I feel terrible homesickness for my flat in Lapa. I dream about it. The calm light on the patio. The orchids organising the silence. But I can't complain. I was the one who insisted we stay at the Polana Hotel, even if we risked going over our budget, as I wanted to film the piano my father played. Some of the people he touched too. They told me of a porter who would have known him, but he's at home sick, with malaria. So I agreed to speak to the handless pianist Bartolomeu discovered at Chez Rangel.

Marechal Carmona lost his hands in the war. He'd taken a bus to go and visit his mother, who was very ill, in a village near Beira. Halfway

---

* One of the main requirements of a good airline pilot is the voice. When the plane takes off, at that moment when everything shudders and creaks, there's nothing more soothing than hearing that phrase, 'Good afternoon, ladies and gentlemen, this is your captain speaking…', spoken in a voice that's firm, and utterly safe, but at the same time warm too. Imagine an airline pilot with a voice like Woody Allen? Would you feel safe? I'm asking my female readers, especially. I'm a woman, and I want my pilots to have a voice like a pilot.

there the road vanished; or rather, to believe what he says, it changed from solid state to liquid:

'There was a river that began where the tarmac had been. We all got out and just stood watching that slow water. The river seemed to be carrying more shadows than water. Someone pointed into the distance: "Look, there, a crocodile!" Then we saw another a little further ahead, then another. They approached, heads down, greenish and slow. But as they rose out from the damp shadows of the river they weren't crocodiles at all. They were almost men. They were carrying weapons. Katanas. Spears. The leader, a thirteen-year-old boy, maybe younger, was carrying a rifle that was bigger than he was. Some of us they pushed to the river. They made us kneel. The first five, they cut their heads off. I was the sixth, and I was luckier.'

He looked at his stumps. He looked at me:

'In 1973 I was no one: the skivvy. I cleaned the floor. The first time I saw the piano, in the hotel lobby, I was speechless. I'd never seen anything so beautiful in all my life. To me, it was as though I'd seen a flying saucer, just landed there. And then, the first time I heard your father play – ah! – I remember it as though it were yesterday, you know, girl, I've even got goosebumps, it was as though I'd heard the voice of God. From that day I was always trying to find a reason to go to the lobby when Faustino was playing. I have a very good ear. One morning Faustino met me on the patio. I was leaning over a piano. I'd drawn a piano on the concrete with a piece of chalk, I'd drawn all the keys, and I was trying to play it. Without much success, as you can imagine. He was there behind me, for a long time, standing listening to me play. "God has given you an enormous gift," he said to me. "What you need is someone who can teach you how to use it." And from that day I began to have piano lessons. Five years later we began to play together. And when he left, when he went to Quelimane, I never really knew why, I stayed behind and took his place – there at the Polana. Those were the happiest years of my whole life.'

(Malaria)

I look at myself in the mirror. I run my fingers through my hair. It's rough and dry, all split. I've made an appointment at the hairdresser's. I lie down on the bed and try to read. I'm not well. I'm really cold. I cover myself with a blanket. A short time ago Mandume came in – he'd been swimming in the pool – and was alarmed at how I looked:

'What's up with you?'

I put my arms around him, crying:

'I don't know what's up with me. Cold, very cold. My whole body hurts.'

I try to make some notes. That helps me to think. To keep me lucid. I can't get sick now. I can't read what I've just written. Loose images appear in my memory. A boy with a weapon in his hands. Hands lifted up to protect, or to protest, and blood. A lot of blood. I worry suddenly that these memories aren't mine, that they were injected into me like a sickness. They're the memories of old Marechal. Hell of a name – hell of a man. He's contaminated me with his nightmares. I close my eyes and see everything more clearly. The sharpened line of the katanas. In my head I hear the women wailing. And then, a voice:

'You OK?'

I open my eyes to find Mandume. Beside him there's a smile. It was the smile who spoke. A man with a nice smile. Grey hair. Glasses. The Smile puts his hand on my forehead. His hand is icy. Icy hands. Hands that fall – detached – onto the grass.

'You're burning up, my dear. Let's do a blood test…'

'A blood test?'

'Probably malarial poisoning. The baptism of the tropics…'

'My father. I want my father!'

My father's name is Dário. Dário Reis. My father's name is Dário Reis. You should be here with me, Dad, why aren't you here with me? I tell him:

'My father's name is Dário Reis!'

The Smile starts slightly:

'Dário Reis?! I knew a Dário Reis. Is he a teacher, your father?'

He opens a little case and prepares a syringe. He pierces the needle into my arm and takes some blood, without ever losing that smile. I see Bartolomeu standing at the door, looking unhappy. Mandume pushes him out. Shuts the door. The Smile says to me:

'Your father, in those days, was a very handsome man. He broke a lot of women's hearts around these parts.' He smiled more widely still. 'Ah yes, broke a lot of hearts!'

Malaria. The word fascinates me. The evil – the *mal* – in it.

My whole life I assumed I was immune to malarial poisoning. I used to brag about it. And then, three or four years ago, I woke up with aches all over my body, trembling with fever and cold. I took some pills and a couple of days later I was back on the beach, surfing, at the clubs, dancing, and with girls in various beds – all the best that life has to offer. Those pills, it's true, nearly killed me: a nausea of the soul. That's all I remember. I tried to calm Mandume, reassuring him that really soon, really soon, Laurentina would be fully recovered. He shouted at me, terrified:

'You know how many people die of malarial poisoning every year in Africa?'

Yeah, bro, many thousands, maybe millions. But look, they mainly snuff it because they're not treated in time, they kick the bucket because they're weakened. Basically they drop their rump in the ungrateful earth – as my grandfather, Faustino Manso, used to say – because they're poor. Mandume looked at me, his eyes wide, made as if to say something but then was silent. Suffocated by his rage. I like seeing him like that. Like a drowned man. For us – us, Angolans – annoying *tugas* has become something like a national sport.

I looked back over some of the material I've filmed over the last few days.

Laurentina. Laurentina. Laurentina. Laurentina. Laurentina.

Why must I film the world if I can film her?

You can see the progress of the illness. A sort of wonder, a slow faint-ing, the skin tired. I love her even more like this, enfeebled, delirious. I spent the night watching over her. Taking her temperature. Cleaning the sweat from her face. Filming her: the dry lips that mutter loose phrases, dizzy birds in the desert air. For example:

'…I can't. I'm very sorry, I can't…'

'…*They walk on stones…*'

'…*Your hands were made for the cup of my breasts…*'

(Elisa's eyes)

Do you remember Gloria, the friendly hippopotamus from *Madagascar*, the DreamWorks cartoon?

Elisa Mucavele reminds me of Gloria.

Everything about her is excessive – her breasts, like lush papayas, her big full hands, her happy eyes – everything, except for her voice: the sweet chirping of a little bird. There are women with power, and women of power, as well as the so-called Iron Ladies – like Margaret Thatcher, for example, whose nature is really much closer to that of metal, of iron, steel or copper – take your pick – than to that of women.

Can anyone imagine being in bed with an iron lady?

Elisa is a woman of power. She exercises her power like a great mother, one of those olden-days big mamas, a bourgeois *bessangana* woman, at once maternal and rigorous. She uses her laugh more than her whip. You only have to look at how she runs her own household. Her servants wear smooth white overalls, immaculate – almost aglow – light cotton caps, such that they look like nurses. But they fulfil their domestic chores in a state of somewhat foolhardy joy, which I suspect would be impossible in the house of a rich person in any European country.

The house? Oh, it takes some imagining – complicated, dissonant furniture, heavy salmon-coloured curtains smothering the sun in every window, candlesticks with crystal tears, reddish sofas, and on the walls – the very white walls – cheap reproductions of famous paintings expensively framed. That tiny attentive voice:

'Have a seat. Something to drink?'

Before we could say anything, though, Elisa had decided that I'd have a whisky and Mandume a Coke. She said she was sorry Laurentina wasn't there. She said that as Minister for Health she felt personally responsible for Laurentina's sickness. She told me that, if we felt it necessary, we could place her in a good clinic at the expense of the Mozambican government. But it seemed to her that she'd be better off at the Polana, with a good doctor.

'As of now you're all my guests. You stay as long as you have to for the girl to get better. She's really Faustino's daughter, is she? I find that so unbelievable. I knew, of course, that Faustino had had other children in Mozambique. I know one of his girls, the daughter of the medicine-woman...'

'Of the medicine-woman?'

'Oh, yes. He lived with a medicine-woman, over in Quelimane.' She gave a little laugh. 'Faustino Manso had no judgement whatsoever. But I'll admit, he did know how to make a woman happy...'

She remained, pensive, in a lit-up silence. It was as if my grandfather's lack of judgement – her memory of it – made her happy. In the evening calm you could hear – coming from that distant past – long moans of pleasure. At least, I could hear them. Shouts and laughter, two hearts galloping in unison, the urgency of flesh and then hallelujahs. I believe Mandume could hear them too, for he interrupted her, unsettled:

'This other woman, the medicine-woman, do you know if she's still living in Quelimane?'

Elisa Mucavele looked a little annoyed, like someone who's been tugged out of a beautiful dream. She said she didn't know, we'd do best to ask Juliana, the medicine-woman's daughter, a relatively popular theatre actress. She'd give us the girl's phone number. She turned to me:

'You've taken after your grandfather, right?'

'What?'

'I should have guessed when I met you, in Barcelona. All those girls buzzing and buzzing around you. I remember one day when someone asked you what you did to manage to stay so young. And you – "It's easy. I love women a lot!"'

I don't remember that episode. I don't think myself capable of saying such a thing, even if I was drunk, not because I think it's nonsense but because of the arrogance of it. I'm not so arrogant. But I didn't have the nerve to contradict her. It takes a lot of nerve to contradict Elisa Mucavele. Mandume laughed. A mocking laugh, aggressive, which irritated me. I changed the subject:

'How did you meet, you and my grandfather?'

'In hospital. I was a nurse. One day that beautiful mulatto man appeared, burning up with fever. Malarial poisoning. Like the girl, your friend. Malarial fever has always been a problem in our countries. I already knew him, Faustino, his songs played on the radio. I took his temperature and was horrified. But the devil was still strong enough to tempt me: "It's not fever," he said to me. "It's fire! I've been like this since I first saw you." In those days I weighed forty-eight kilos. I was a beautiful woman. I believed him. We started going out two or three days later…'

'And how long did you live together?'

'Eight years! We had four children. But Faustino was always a real scoundrel. One afternoon I got home early from work and found him in our bed with the maid, a fifteen-year-old girl. It was the final drop of water that made the cup overflow. I struck him, then threw him out of the house. Then he went to Quelimane.'

She fell silent again. Elisa Mucavele is more expressive when silent than many people who never shut up. Her eyes, huge, very black, continue to speak even after she has stopped. In this case, Elisa's eyes were saying:

…Men are such bastards…

(Alien thoughts)

I revived. It's me…

Or isn't it?!

Five kilos thinner. My head is full of thoughts I don't recognise as mine. I feel as though I've accidentally brought someone else's purse home with me. The purse is just like mine, or almost, but when I open it I find myself looking at a series of objects that don't belong to me: that's not my lipstick, no, red lipstick, so bright.* The photographs of children – what children are these? – or, more serious, another of a man I've never seen before, his arms round me, round someone who looks like me, his right hand over my left breast.

Some of the alien thoughts in my head:

(1)

I see myself (me, the other one, the one with the strident lipstick) making love with Bartolomeu. I kiss him furiously, his beard scratches my face. I push him to the bed as I tug the towel off his body. He sighs:

'It's very late…'

He's afraid. It's his fear that makes me bold:

'Very late, my love? Not too late, I hope…'

Bartolomeu has a swimmer's shoulders, a strong chest, large, well-defined nipples. Nipples are the most feminine things about

---

* It's not that I don't like lipstick, I like it a lot. As Aline says, 'We – we, women – we like lipstick because with a minimum of effort you can have a maximum of impact.' A good lipstick always looks good on a washed face, and there's never any doubt about where to put it.

195

a man, and the most useless too (they serve only to remind them that they're failed attempts at women).* I kiss his nipples. I bite them. Bartolomeu tries to push me away, his voice grey:

'I don't think it'll work.'

Now, yes, now he's very afraid. It's not the alcohol intoxicating me, but power and desire. I place his hands on my breasts. I say to him:

'You see? *Your hands were made for the cup of my breasts.*'**

(2)

A violent argument between my parents. Doroteia shouting, as she ironed clothes. Suddenly lifting up the iron and holding it close to Dário's terrified face:

'I'll burn those eyes of yours, you hear me, you son of a bitch?! Look at another woman again I'll burn your eyes!'

Maybe this memory really is mine. I don't know. It might have been forgotten for a time in some dark attic of my poor brain. They argued a lot. Doroteia was sick. She suffered from jealousy and migraines and confused the two pains with each other. All it took was for my father, in the street, to make some charming comment about some woman for her to lose her head. She'd return home in agony, dazed by the light, wishing she could actually lose her head, not to have it on her shoulders, barking and throbbing like a fierce animal, she'd close all the windows and lie down on her bed till nightfall.

---

* Not long ago I read in *Pública* magazine, issue 547 of 12 November 2006, an interesting interview with sexologist John Bancroft. I quote: 'In the development of the embryo, the basic pattern is female. The male has to be added. In this process a number of feminine character-istics are suppressed. Others are not, though, as there is no need to suppress them. The clitoris, for example, has the same origin as the penis, the same nerve endings. It did not develop in the same way because there was no need. It remained, however, and can still be used. The equivalent in men are the nipples. They are not needed, but there was no reason to eliminate them either. They are there, and some men can be brought to orgasm by stimulating them.'

** It's a line from the Angolan poetess Ana Paula Tavares. I'll let you have the whole poem: 'I should have looked at the king / But it was the slave who came / To sow my body with creeping plants / I should sit in a chair by the king's side / But it was on the ground that I left the mark of my body // I combed myself for the king / But it was to the slave that I gave the locks of my hair // The slave was young / He had a perfect body / His hands made for the cup of my breasts // I should have looked at the king / But I lowered my head / Sweet, tender / Before the slave.'

(3)

Two girls in a garden. A hosepipe. The girls are watering the flowers, the lawn. One of them (the one who looks like me as a child) turns the spray of water on the other. The second girl runs away. She opens the gate and runs out into the alley. The first girl chases after her with the hosepipe. The second girl tries to cross the street. She's halfway across when a car lurches into view. In this fragment of memory – which can't be mine, which I don't want to be mine – the last part has no images, only sounds: tyres that squeal on the tarmac and then the noise of metal striking the little body. A shattering of glass. Silence.

Elisa Mucavele came to visit me this morning. After that discussion between Bartolomeu and Seretha du Toit, in Cape Town, I'd prepared myself to dislike her, but I couldn't.

Imagine a gentle hurricane. You can't?

I understand. There are some paradoxes that are hard to understand. Elisa Mucavele is one of them. A very big woman with a very small voice, and this amazing hair made up of an infinite number of rebellious silvery locks. The whole ensemble produces a contradictory feeling of defiance and gentleness. She sat down opposite me with the authority of an empress, or of an emperor, either way, let's say Gungunhana before the fall, and took in her broad hands my little right hand. She rested her eyes on mine:

'How is it going, my child?'

By the time I realised what was happening I had my arms around her, in tears again, exposing my poor torn heart to her, my most intimate anxieties, telling her what I'd felt when I read my mother's letter. Elisa stroked my face, set about plaiting my hair:

'Men, my child, have as much usefulness out of bed as a seaplane on a motorway. They just get in the way.'

As far as I could tell Faustino Manso got in the way an awful lot. Elisa had collected (after it was all over) a list of all the women my father had seduced while he'd been living with her. She summarised for me all the ones she thought the most interesting:

(1)

Tiny Matilde, a nurse, Elisa's best friend. Married, no children. Matilde's husband found a letter from Faustino Manso in her purse, 'My jewel, you make me so happy!', and started beating her meticulously on Saturday nights. Elisa thinks that Bernardino beat his wife on Saturday nights out of sheer boredom. He'd drink two or three beers as he read the paper, then he'd get up, drag her to the bedroom, tear off her clothes, take off his belt and beat her. He was a lonely, silent man, a little dull, who worked as an accountant in a big civil construction company. The only child to a Chinese father and a Goan mother. An orphan. No friends. He took independence badly. No one ever saw him with his fist raised. He died in 1978. Heart attack. Disgust. Both those things. Matilde sought refuge in religion. She became a nun.

(2)

Valentina Valentina – really just so, even her name redundant – a potter. In the sixties, in the restrained colonial environment, she was a kind of circus attraction. Half a dozen intellectuals – that is to say, almost all those who lived in the territory – recognised her talent and praised her originality and the energy of her little creatures. The bourgeoisie were startled by the wild sexuality of those clay women, who would copulate with two or three men at the same time, with serpents and donkeys, or joyfully loved one another. The women – horrified – would remark on the scars and tattoos on the face and body of the artist. Valentina Valentina was somewhere in her early twenties, and needed no food to maintain her fragile silhouette, the lit light of her imagination, nothing more than a little bit of air and sun, pure water, a plate of manioc leaves with white rice. She had come from a little village, in the north, a few kilometres from Quelimane. She had been brought over by a Portuguese architect, a very well known, well respected man, who happened to come across some of her clay figures at some market somewhere. The architect took the works of Valentina Valentina to the galleries of Paris and New York, and managed to interest art critics and journalists. Unfortunately he died in 1973, run over by a taxi on the streets of Lourenço Marques, without seeing the artist's first major exhibition. Valentina Valentina is today one of the rare Mozambicans recognised abroad.

(3)

Camilla Sandland, the wife of an elderly English railway administrator, looked at people – and especially at men – with one green eye, and one blue. Faustino liked both. The husband approved of the general admiration. He collected the anonymous letters – and there were plenty – denouncing his wife's supposed attentions for one admirer or other. He enjoyed reading them at dinner, when his closest friends were together. Only he laughed, however. Camilla Sandland's green eye sparkled, and the blue sparkled even more.

(4)

Ana Sebastiana, professional widow. She buried three husbands in ten years, inheriting some money that allowed her in Lourenço Marques – in those vertiginous sixties – to live a very comfortable life. She married again, after Faustino Manso had left for Quelimane, this time to an officer in the Portuguese navy. The husband shot her. Arrested and brought to trial, he offered a plea of self-defence. The judge acquitted him.

(5)

Sylviane Dzilnava, French journalist. Little, and very well put together. Whenever anyone teased her over her height, she'd retort at once: 'Small? Yes, but I'm really deep.'* She spent a few weeks in Mozambique, in 1968, gathering information for a set of reports on the Portuguese colonies in Africa. She was one of the first foreign journalists to interview Valentina Valentina. She returned to Lourenço Marques seven years later, with the aim of witnessing independence. She stayed another week, then another, and yet another. An affair with the Minister of the Interior allowed her to gain a truly deep understanding (if you'll pardon the pun) of the functioning of the apparatus of the state. Then she fell in love with a famous local poet, and wrote an award-winning report on young Mozambican literature. For a few years she was with a film-maker. She made a documentary – also award-winning – on child soldiers. One day she awoke and realised she'd been dreaming in

* God! I find that disgusting. But Elisa laughed a lot as she told me this.

Portuguese. She applied for a Mozambican passport and burned her French one. By this point she had already become known everywhere as 'the Girlfriend of the Revolution'. Today she's the director of a news agency specialising in subjects relating to southern Africa. I saw her one night, in an effusive yellow dress, having dinner here at the Polana. With her was a man in his early thirties, in suit and tie, very elegant. Bartolomeu greeted him warmly. 'He was a good journalist,' he said to me later, 'now he's a bad politician'. And her? 'She's Sylviane Dzilnava. They say that the best interviews she ever published were given in bed.'

(6)
Alma Nogueira, pilotess. Native of Moçâmedes, she became famous in the sixties for having crossed the continent, from Cairo to the Cape, in a little twin-engine plane. She was in Mozambique various times. In 1974 she had an accident while flying from Benguela to Moçâmedes. She managed to land the plane, but fractured a leg. They found her dead, two weeks later, in the cockpit of the craft. She must have suffered horribly. Elisa showed me a cutting from the *Diário de Luanda* with the news of the accident. According to the article, Alma had with her an autographed record by Faustino Manso. The autograph said: 'For my Alma – my soul – somewhere in the skies of Africa.'

(7)
Bela Paixão, 'a businesswoman in the field of night-time entertainment'. Elisa punctuated this euphemism with a tiny giggle. She added: 'Amazing as it may seem, her name, Beautiful Passion, was real.' I didn't reply. I've come across stranger names. 'Here's the best part – Bela left for Brazil after independence. She returned five years ago, transformed. She's made herself a pastor in the Evangelical Church Hide-Away of the Most High. She's rich. Exceedingly rich, they say. And be that as it may, she certainly earns more money in the Jesus business than she ever did in the Mary Magdalene business.'

(The medicine woman's daughter)

We arranged to meet at the Café Surf. I didn't know how I was going to recognise her. In fact it turned out to be easy: I recognised her, recognising myself. Juliana is me after a sleepless night. A woman of thirty-four, distracted almond eyes, the bags under them a little wider and deeper than mine. Full mouth, straight black hair, burnt skin. Voice as gentle as a Sunday morning:

'Sis?! Can I call you that?'

Bartolomeu didn't hide his amazement.

'Granddad really knew how to make daughters!'

Juliana studied in Lisbon, at the Conservatory, but returned to Mozambique before completing her course. She works with an independent theatre group and has already had a supporting role in three feature films. She's heading off to Johannesburg now. She's been invited to join the cast of a new television series. I heard her speak with contagious enthusiasm about the part they've offered her, of a Mozambican journalist committed to solving the mystery of a plane crash, an aircraft in which President Samora Machel was travelling. Finally I presented our project to her. She smiled at me:

'I don't remember Daddy... Well, I remember vaguely, a handsome man, picking me up and dancing with me. Mamã thinks it's better like that... Forgetting...'

'Your mother, she... Elisa Mucavele told me that your mother...'

'...that she's a medicine-woman?'

'Exactly.'

201

'We're descendents of the country's original matrilineal landowners – did she tell you that too? Mamã is one of the last Donas of Zambézia, one of Zambézia's "Ladies of the Land". We've been rich. My grandfather used to refer to the good old days saying: "Back in the days when we were white." Ha ha ha!* When I was born the only wealth remaining to us was our name and our house. Mamã always had a great facility for communicating with the spirits. A girl of six, seven, she'd sit on the stairs talking to herself and people thought she was funny. She wasn't talking to herself, of course. Then she began to guess at certain events – well, I say 'guess', but you could equally say 'predict' – but they're no more than simple memories of events yet to come…'

'Memories?!'

'Time isn't like a river. Time's a sphere. There's no source, and no mouth. It has no beginning, or end. Everything repeats incessantly. Just as you remember things that happened yesterday, so you can also remember things that are to happen tomorrow…'

'Never in my case. I'm blind to the future.'

'Naturally. Few people are prepared to look into the future. We've been educated to think of time as linear. It begins there, at that point, it dies over there, and, somewhere in-between, this thing and that thing happen. People like Mamã train the spirit to remember events that are to happen in that place in time which we call the future. Future, past or present, it's all just a question of perspective. But be that as it may, Mamã revealed when still a child certain gifts that alarmed my grandparents. Old Paulino punished her cruelly whenever she insisted on revealing what would happen the following day, and made a huge effort to contradict her. Later, after their deaths, Mamã met an old medicine-woman who helped her to guide this natural talent. She's very sought after. People come from Maputo, even South Africa, to consult her.'

She's called Ana, the medicine woman. Dona Ana de Lacerda. I very much want to meet her. Perhaps she can tell me something about my divided heart. And also about my father, things that no one yet has told me. I'd like to know why he left Mozambique Island, suddenly, and returned to Luanda.

And why he left me?

---

* Very poor onomatopoeia. Juliana doesn't laugh like this. No one does, actually. Juliana's laugh is a little bit of silent splendour. Like watching fireworks with your hands over your ears.

(Lady of the Land)

Palm grove after palm grove.

Kilometres and kilometres and kilometres. Hours on end. I close my eyes. I open my eyes. Lying down on the back seat, my head in Laurentina's lap, what I can see are the big leaves cut out against the brilliant blue of the sky. I hear the piano of Faustino Manso, opening a luminous path – note by note – the voice singing, radiant, now in a surge, now in a whisper:

So much sky in your mouth.
I drink the day in it.
So much sea in your hair
Slender palm tree.

So much sun in your desire
I kindle myself in it.
So much glow in your eyes,
Lady of the Land.

I start to understand old Dário. Through the windows comes a thick, damp perfume. I breathe deeply and feel my heart beat faster.

The famous scent of Africa?

I don't know. It brings a wild happiness into the car. I feel an urge to hug Laurentina. I look for her hand. I hold it in mine. She looks at me, smiles. She hums along with Faustino:

'So much sun in your desire…'

I sit up and put my arms around her. I kiss her mouth. She has soft lips, hot, her tongue touches mine. Bartolomeu, in the front seat, nods. With a glance, in the rear-view mirror I spot Pouca Sorte's closed eyes.

He's asleep?!

Well, let him sleep, so much the better

Laurentina is wearing a denim skirt, a white embroidered blouse I bought her in Salvador. I caress her legs. The higher I go towards her thighs, the more heat there is in her skin. It's smoother inside, very soft, like hot wax. I whisper in her ear:

'*You touch me; I hear the sound of mandolins. You kiss me; with your kiss my life begins…*'

The night we made love for the first time, in her apartment in Lapa, Nina Simone was singing *Wild Is the Wind*. Laurentina sighs. Puts her arms round me.

Malembemalembe slips – as in a dream – through the perfumed shadows of the palm groves.

(A mermaid in the Bons Sinais river)

I returned to Mozambique, two days ago, with the intention of getting to know Quelimane, the only city on our tour (the Faustino Manso Tour) we weren't able to visit last year. Karen, who'd just got in from London, came with me. I'm enjoying it. It reminds me of Corumbá in the Pantanal, Mato Grosso do Sul, Brazil; or Dondo, in Angola; old towns asleep beside a big river. An identical melancholy dejection, a torpor of the end of the world – or rather, of the end of time.

Quelimane lies face down on the riverbank. Waters that flow unhurried between cane fields and rusty carcasses of old ships. It boasts the loveliest name in the world, this river: the Rio dos Bons Sinais. The river of good signs.

At the end of the morning we interviewed Sr Palha, an elderly public functionary, eighty-four years old, born and raised here. We wanted to know more about life in the city in colonial times. 'Old things?' he asked me, and began talking with passion about life in Quelimane in the forties. When I tried to drag him up to the seventies, to the period just preceding independence, he got fed up:

'That was yesterday. Weren't we meant to be talking about the old days?'

At a certain point he launched into a kind of exotic foods challenge:

'…boa constrictor…' the old man wanted to know. 'You ever try boa constrictor?'

'Yes, I tried boa in a hotel in Kinshasa…'

'And elephant trunk?'

'No, not that.'

'Ah! Elephant trunk, it's like salami.'

'…I ate armadillo, in Pernambuco…'

'Well I've eaten red grasshoppers. Have you?'

'No, never eaten grasshoppers.'

'And mermaids? Once we caught a mermaid on an island not far from here, a little animal, this size' – he held his hands some fifty centimetres apart. 'Tail of a fish and face of a person, an ugly beard. You ever eaten mermaid?'

'No, no!'

'Well you should. Good meat. I quite liked it. I found zebra bitter, though' – he gave a grimace of repugnance – 'zebra is no good at all.'

Karen interjected, confused:

'It was probably a baby dugong. The mermaid, I mean. Dugongs are mammals with a fish-tail and a snout that's almost human. They're often mistaken for mermaids…'

'No, no!' the old man replied, upset at the interruption. 'I know perfectly well what a mermaid is. And that was a mermaid!'

And he went back to his zebra meat.

(Let's talk!)

There's a low wall, painted white. On one side, our side, runs the road. On the other, a silent explosion of nature: a tousled vegetation, submerged in the mud.* Then comes a solid mass of water, of a gloomy blue, and still further into the distance the harsh green of little islands; finally, like a backdrop cloth, the great calm of the sky.

The city ends at the wall

A frontier.

Nature accepted the contract, it doesn't cross the wall, but nor does it allow civilisation – we'll call it that – to set foot on the other side. Rusting ships lean onto the solid concrete quay like dead dreams.

We're seated at one of the little plastic tables of a café-restaurant which has undoubtedly seen better days. The river opposite. Bartolomeu points to an advertisement phrase painted on the facing wall: 'Let's talk! Lower rates, only with Mcel.'

* I think about what there is hiding under the bushes, under the twisting roots, under the successive layers of bushes and roots and heavy centuries of mud and slime: very ancient monsters, with copper scales, blind, with long retractile whiskers, adapted to life in the depths. Ugly bearded mermaids, the skeletons of slaves who tried to escape. The armours of Goan noblemen, resting in there with the noblemen themselves. Their greyhounds, with gold necklaces around their necks. Treasures in chests. Barges and boats. Dário, my father, believes – or pretends to believe – that under a river's waters a world like our own has developed, but one where everything happens in reverse, as in a mirror.

'Let's talk! That's a good suggestion. Now that we're alone at last, let's talk. A serious talk, you and me...'

I look at him, mistrustful. Mandume has gone with Pouca Sorte in search of some part for Malembemalembe's engine. We've rented two rooms in a little family hotel called Vila Nagardás. Dona Ana de Lacerda is not in Quelimane. We phoned her – the medicine-woman has a cellphone! – and she explained to us that she's gone to the north to buy herbs and roots. She's back tomorrow. I try to smile:

'What is it you want to talk about?'

'About us, and not s...'

'About knots?! I'm not a sailor, I've never even been a girl guide. I don't know anything about knots...'

'Oh really? How about ties, the ties that knot us together?'

'If you want to talk about ties and knots you'd do better to ask the writer Alçada Baptista. They say that once at a book fair some guy came up to him, really excited. "I've been looking for this book for years!" he said, holding out a copy of *The Ties That Bind Not*. He was an old sailor.'

'It's very funny, your story, but I'm not going to let you get out of it. Tell me, in Cape Town did you come into my room and make love to me, or did I dream it?'

'Of course you dreamed it. Was it a nice dream?'

'It was. So good that I kept your scent on my skin for the whole day. Even today I can smell you, do you believe that? I could recognise you from dozens of other women just by scent...'

'God! I've never been so humiliated! But I thank you for your sincerity. I'll take to bathing more often, and I also should change my deodorant.'*

'You're really blushing!'

'Blushing, me?! I'm a mulatta, I don't blush.'

'Yes, you're a mulatta. I noticed that when we made love too. Very mulatta, and in a new way, even for me. And yet you're blushing. Does this subject bother you?'

'It does. If you know everything, tell me why they gave this river the name Bons Sinais? Why 'good signs'?'

---

* This business of a scent remaining on your skin has always bothered me. Still, the praise of smell is very popular. Ridicule is too, especially – as Fernando Pessoa observed – in declarations of love.

'When a man and a woman sit beside it and talk about love, and the woman changes the subject, this is a good sign. It means the man can have some hope.'

'Ha! I thought you were a better liar. Aren't you supposed to be a writer?'

'There's another legend. One evening, as the sun was setting, a man came across a woman here – more or less where we're sitting now – looking fixedly at the river. She was so beautiful that he fell in love with her. On that day he didn't have the courage to speak to her. The next evening, though, he met the woman in the same place. Then he approached her and declared himself to her. The woman looked at him in silence. Her silence had the effect of driving the man even deeper into love with her. He would keep coming back, always at the same time, bringing gifts for the woman – flowers, mirrors, cloths, necklaces of glass beads. She accepted them, but never spoke. Until one fine evening, the sky clear and the river waters totally smooth and very, very bright, the woman turned to him and said: "The signs are good – are you coming?" And she jumped over the wall, beat a path through the vegetation, stripped off her clothes and entered the water. The man – hugely excited – tore off his clothes and followed her. The woman turned into a mermaid and devoured him.'

I laughed. He makes me laugh. I think that's his main weapon for seduction:

'And was it good, the man's flesh?'

'According to the mermaid she found it a little bitter…'

'You've improved. I liked your story. Deep down it's taken from the myth of the praying-mantis woman. You're afraid I might devour you. Is that it?'

'I guess so. I've fallen in love with you, you know that? I don't know how it happened, not with me, I'm always so careful not to mix up love and sex. I've fallen madly in love with you…'

'Nonsense! You're a hunter. Hunters hunt, they don't fall in love with their prey.'

'Obviously, you're right. I assure you this has never happened to me before. I'm quite alarmed. Part of me wants to be with you forever, to get old in your arms, you see? This gets me talking utter nonsense – it's patho-logical – and another part of me wants to run away like before, to disap-pear, to go back to my old life. Never talk utter nonsense again. Apart from that I'm jealous of your boyfriend, and I'm not someone who's ever suffered from such *petit-bourgeois* feelings, or such petty *bourgeois* feelings if you'd rather. I can't bear to lay eyes on him.'

'Behave yourself. The trip is almost over.'

'And then? What will happen then?'

'Then you'll go back to Luanda, to your little life…'

'I don't know if I still have a life, even a little one…'

'More nonsense?'

'I mean it. You think this is easy for me?'

'How do you expect me to respond? If Mandume comes to suspect anything I'll kill you. Nothing happened between us, understand? This conversation isn't happening.'

'Please, Laurentina…'

I got up and left him there, talking to another Laurentina – this one a blonde, in a bottle, and the reason I have my name. 'The girl is called Laurentina,' Alima's mother said when she put me into Doroteia's arms. 'It was the name my daughter gave her. The name that the child's father wanted her to have, they were sure that it'd be a girl.' This is what Dário told me. Probably – this is how I imagine it – Faustino Manso was drinking a Laurentina beer in some bar on the Island when Alima told him she was pregnant. My father baptised his children with the names of the drinks he was having at the moment he learned of their existence.

(The house)

Seen from the road, the house resembles a big weary animal. A solid stone staircase leads to the main door. All the pride of the old building rests in that staircase; everything about it that is still intact, that resists, and persists, and insists on fighting against time and bad days, like a woman, poorly dressed, holding – under a hard sun – a little silk parasol. In the main hall, Dona Ana de Lacerda's grandparents look down at us, solemn, from inside heavy gilt frames. A half-dozen intricate wooden chairs have also survived from the old luxury, in the Indo-Portuguese style, as well as a table – extremely long – which takes up the whole centre of the vast hall.

'This house' – I observed – 'has a soul. It seems alive.'

Dona Ana de Lacerda looked at me, directly, as though only then seeing me for the first time:

'A soul? Say souls, rather! You noticed, then? Ah, I think you did. You're a sensitive girl. Give me your hand. Put it here, on the wall. Do you feel it?'

The heat! I drew my hand back – astonished – dumbstruck – not knowing what to think. The woman watched me, her eyes shining.

'You understand? This old house of mine has raging fevers. Sometimes, on some rainy nights, I feel her tremble. Sometimes that can be a bit alarming, as well as the voices, of course...'

'Voices?!' Mandume looked at her, in terror. 'What voices?'

'Juliana didn't tell you? All these people...' – and she pointed to the paintings on the walls – 'All these people talk to each other during the night. Well, talk to each other in a manner of speaking. Have you ever slept in a room full of sleepwalkers? One of them says one thing, another replies, but more often than not there seems to be no connection between what seems like the question from one and the answers given by the others…'

Mandume shook his head:

'Rubbish! I don't believe it!'

Bartolomeu silenced him with a look:

'I'm sure there are lots of things you don't believe in, pal, but your disbelief doesn't stop them from thriving, all over the place and especially here under African skies. Reality has more imagination than you do.'

Dona Ana de Lacerda smiled. A teasing smile. Her little round-rimmed glasses, in silver with dark lenses, give her the air of a rebel intellectual. Her haircut and dress confirm this: a Black Power hairstyle, an orange blouse, a patchwork Indian waistcoat, a large, wide skirt down to her feet, with lovely pictures of orchids, and hanging down over her chest a coloured torrent of glass beads. You'd think she was a hippy exiled from her time.

'Son, this house is full of voices…'

She told us that her mother, Dona Consolação, as a child used to hear moans and laments coming from the wall which ran alongside the bed where she slept. To her father, Pascoal de Menezes e Lacerda, an embittered widower, that little girl was his whole family. He denied her nothing. Having decided to appease the girl, showing her that there were no such things as ghosts, he had the wall knocked down. They discovered a tiny compartment, a kind of cupboard, with an iron ring solidly soldered to the wall, to which was attached the skeleton of a woman. Beside her they found the fragile bones of a baby. Pascoal de Menezes e Lacerda remembered a story that had terrorised him during his childhood: his grandfather had told him that a young, very beautiful slave-girl had been walled-in alive, on the orders of her mistress, after the latter had discovered her in daring amorous entanglements with her (that is, the mistress's) husband.

'Legends!' Mandume muttered. 'This grandfather of yours must have read Poe.'

'No doubt,' Dona Ana de Lacerda agreed, sweetly. 'Do you want to see the skeletons?'

There weren't actual skeletons any longer, just a half-dozen melancholy bones, kept in a metal box from Delespaul-Havez with a picture on it of eight children stuffing themselves with chocolates. The box was kept in the 'slave's cupboard', underneath the iron ring. I found it scary. Mandume didn't speak the rest of the afternoon.

(The garrulous shells)

Thin, long fingers. Nails carefully painted in cherry-red. An unlit cigarette between the ring finger and the middle finger. Dona Ana de Lacerda looks nothing like I'd imagined. She served us tea and slices of cashew cake. While we talked she put on a CD of the João Domingos Band, *Live in Macao*:

'It's what we used to listen to. I've danced a lot to the music of the João Domingos Band...'

'Do you miss those days?'

'Miss them, girl? I'm sorry I no longer have breasts like yours, that's for sure. I miss the days when men would look at me and sigh. In those days if a man came up to me, in the street, it was to throw me a compliment. Nowadays they just want to know the time.'

'That's not true! Ma'am, you're very well preserved...'

Dona Ana de Lacerda brushed away my compassion with a small gesture of annoyance:

'Not counting the breasts, no, there's nothing I miss. The present is just that – a present! We just have to open it up, and enjoy it. I never look back to the past. I look to the future. I earn my present by looking to the future. But you haven't come to this place at the end of the earth to hear me philosophising about the past, present and future. You want me to tell you about Faustino, right? Ah, Faustino Manso! He died, didn't he? He wasn't what he seemed...'

'How so?'

'That's something you'll discover for yourself. He must have made a few enemies, of course, like any of us. In his case, particularly a few unhappy husbands. But there's one thing I can assure you, you'll never find a single woman who slept with him who'll feel bitter or regretful in the slightest. Faustino was like a flattering mirror. A woman looked at him, and saw herself always beautiful.'

She laughed. When she laughs she's just like Juliana (well, the opposite, of course, I know). She poured herself some more tea. She passed me another slice of cake. At that moment for the first time I felt Mozambican, in perfect harmony with that old house, and this city where over the centuries – for good or ill – Arabs, Portuguese, Indians, have come together, along with the various African peoples who in 1498 received Vasco da Gama when he made port here. Dona Ana de Lacerda guessed what I was feeling:

'This house is welcoming you.' She took off her glasses and I saw her clear sphinx eyes. 'It's your house.'

Then she got up, and taking my right hand pulled me after her.

'I'm very sorry, boys,' she said to Bartolomeu and Mandume; 'Laurentina and I have to have a talk. A long talk. There's a chessboard over there. It belonged to my grandfather. Why don't you play a little? It's a kind of gentlemen's duel, but no one gets hurt…'

The bedroom where she took me burned in a thick silky dusk. The only window was covered by a long red curtain. A second curtain, even ruddier than the first, almost completely covered the opposite wall. At the head of the bed an old mirror in a copper frame – very elaborately wrought – repeated the brilliance of the curtains. In one of the corners, on a sort of little altar, an exquisitely beautiful picture of the Virgin praying, very pale, her eyes upraised, while a dragon slept like an invalid dog between her delicate bare feet. Red candles, black candles, the falling wax sculpting fantastic shapes. Sticks of burned incense, a cedar perfume, fine smoke in the still air. I sat on the edge of the bed. Dona Ana de Lacerda took a little bag out of a drawer in the bedside table, pulled a stool and a chair up to the bed, and sat opposite me. She covered the stool with an embroidered cloth and tipped the bag onto it. Shells. A set of shells, black, polished from use.

'Relax,' she said to me. 'Don't be afraid. There's no need to be afraid of what's going to happen. I'm not the one who reads the shells, it's my grandfather, Old Pascoal.'

She took off her glasses and put them down on the stool. Then she was silent, a good few minutes, caressing the shells. Then she suddenly rolled her eyes, her body shook, and I could clearly hear the clicking of her bones in her thin body. She stretched herself out, her face changing its expression, her chin pulled forward, eyebrows arched. She cleared her throat. She began to speak with the voice of a man, deep, hoarse, a thick local accent:

'Good evening! Well, well! Good evening!'

214

She grasped the shells with both hands and threw them onto the cloth. She leaned over them:

'Well, well! Well, now!'

She shook her head, unsatisfied. She looked at me, very serious. Muttered a few words in some round, glowing language. Then she threw the shells again. This was repeated several times. I began to feel nervous.

'What's going on?'

'Take it easy, girl,' she murmured. Her right hand twirled an imaginary moustache. 'Take it easy, take it easy – I can see you're at a crossroads. Ha ha! At a crossroads. A beautiful woman, a mysterious woman – ha! – how men like mysterious women …'

She threw the shells again. She followed the shape they made with the tip of her index finger. Now she was extremely focused. Her face shone with sweat:

'Your mother, your adopted mother, she passed away recently, didn't she?'

I nodded, shocked.

'She died in January.'

'She died angry with your father. They argued a lot, didn't they? This affected you more than you know. Men frighten you. You never give yourself up completely. The keener they are, the more in love they turn out to be, the more you try to keep your distance. And of course, the colder you are, the more distant, the more in love the men are… No, you needn't answer… Either way we have to do something to appease your mother's spirit… Ah, your journey won't be ending all that soon, but by the time that end comes you'll be a quite different woman… On an island, Mozambique Island, I imagine, you will find your real mother, she's waiting for you… You've lost one mother, but you'll gain another, few people have that good fortune… I see a danger… Death, yes, definitely death… A stranger –' She sighed. She twirled her imaginary moustache again. 'Don't worry, it doesn't relate to you directly… As to your heart, you will have to choose, but this you know already and this I can't help you with… Life is made up of choices, one door opens, another closes… Yes, I know, it's a cliché and you don't like clichés… Let's just call it free will, then – ha ha! – we can choose the path we want to take, and that's what makes this game – the game of life – so interesting. You do, though, have a third path: you can try and keep both. You laugh? Dona Ana de Lacerda, my granddaughter, had two men on the go at once, she first met

Faustino – yes, yes, the Angolan! – but immediately afterwards fell in love with a Portuguese man. They were very different from each other, different virtues, defects too, and she was unable to decide. She ended up telling both. Faustino told her he understood, that in the past he'd loved two women at the same time – more than two, even. "I'm the world champion on this matter…" he insisted. It was a lie, of course. His whole life he loved just one woman, the first: Dona Anacleta. As for my granddaughter, well, I think he took her as an abbreviated version of her – Faustino in his passion would sigh, "Ah, Ana! Ana!" and she'd hear the rest of the name… Women still liked him. The old rogue, ha ha! Yes, yes, they still liked him. They said, "Even if he doesn't love us, he still loves us more and better than most men." But to go back to the matter in hand, Faustino accepted the situation, but it was the Portuguese man who was none too pleased, but he really did like my granddaughter. The agreement held for a while, Dona Ana with her two husbands, without the rest of the town being any the wiser. She'd rent rooms – she still does – that's what she lived off, and would often have a number of guests. But alas, the Portuguese lover couldn't bear it. One day he went. He left behind a letter of farewell. Dona Ana still cries when she re-reads it, to this day. There's nothing sadder, nor more beautiful, than a letter of farewell.'

The sun had set. It had got dark without our noticing. Dona Ana de Lacerda put down the shells. She shook herself, a prolonged shake. Her face took on its usual expression. She got up, and turned on the light. Her hands trembled with the effort. With a white handkerchief she wiped the sweat from her face. When we returned to the living room Mandume announced 'Checkmate'. He turned to me, triumphant:

'*Bam* – killed an Angolan!'

No, with these two there's no chance the Third Way is going to work.

(The Aphrodisiac, or Afrodisiac)

The owner of the restaurant where we usually eat is a lively-eyed old man, thin and very upright, with an elegant felt hat always on his head. He said he remembers Faustino Manso well:

'He was a very relaxed man, discreet, but you couldn't let him catch sight of a beautiful girl. If your mind wandered even for a moment he'd be screwing your wife, your daughters, your mother – depending on the age. There's quite a crowd here who can't listen to his music. I know one man who's allergic. I just have to put on, say, *Twilight in Luanda* and he starts coughing, choking, unable to breathe. Does the girl know what Faustino's nickname was here in Quelimane?' He winked at me as he poured me another beer. 'The Aphrodisiac. Or rather, the Afrodisiac…'

(Beer, lupine seeds and stories)

Faustino, the Afrodisiac!

Or to be more accurate: Faustino the Luso-Afrodisiac.

Laurentina didn't find the nickname funny. Granddad would definitely have laughed. He liked to make fun of himself. Whenever I turned up at his place he'd take me out to the veranda, gesture to a chair and offer me a beer and lupine seeds; more exceptionally a little plate of shrimp; eventually he'd sit down opposite me and tell me stories from his life. I liked to listen to him. He talked a few times about Quelimane. Hunting, fishing. He told me that once he received a gunshot wound to the leg; he showed me the scars. A hunting accident.

'A hunting accident, Granddad, or a deceived husband?'

'No, no, son!' – a big laugh, with a complicit smack – 'A husband who wasn't deceived at all!'

A fat man, an employee of the Mozambique Railways, married to a bitter woman who was known for her bad breath – such an evil stench, Faustino assured me, that the very trees lost their leaves as she passed. The fat man shot him in the leg so that his colleagues would think that he too had been cuckolded by Faustino. He was offended by the possibility that his wife should be the only virtuous woman in the neighbourhood.

I was sometimes left with the impression that Faustino was teasing me, that he was making up his stories just to impress me, and that later he'd be at the Biker laughing with his friends at my naivety. I do believe that he received a gunshot from a hunter – the scars were there, in his left leg, next to the knee, to prove it; but as to the rest, I'm not sure.

Mozambique Island
Saturday, 19 November 2005

This evening we arrived on Mozambique Island. The plan had been to do
the whole journey over land, but unfortunately we were running late, and
besides that we'd gone over our budget. So we opted for skipping
Quelimane – the sixth city of the Faustino Manso Tour – and going on
by plane from Maputo to Nampala. In Nampala – another city abandoned
in the middle of some colonial fantasy – broad, though empty, streets, an
invincible tiredness sagging the houses – we hired a taxi. The driver was
called Bem – that is, 'Well' – which he explained to us was a diminutive
of Benigno, Benigno Meigos. Benign Sweetnesses – this seemed to me to
presage extremely well. The Island was Mozambique's capital till 1898.
Peopled by Arabs, Portuguese, Indians, as well as the African peoples come
over from the coast, over the centuries it accumulated a rich embroider-
ing of memories. Few places of such limited dimensions can have thrilled
so great a number of poets. Nelson Saúte and António Sopa collected
dozens of poems inspired by Muhipiti – the indigenous name of the
Island – in a book published in 1992 in Lisbon by '70 Publishing':
Mozambique Island in the Voice of the Poets. The extracts that follow, with the
exception of the lines by Jall Sinth Hussein, I found in that volume:

Tomás António Gonzaga – 'I have come exiled here to
Mozambique. / Head uncovered in the burning sun; I brought
through derision hard punishment / Before the African woman,
pious, good folk. / Thanks, friend Alcino, / Thanks to our star! / I
did not beg, no beggars here; / the Africans their breasts kindly /

219

Before the unhappy hand is held out to them, / Run eagerly to help you. / Thanks, friend Alcino, / Thanks to our star!'

Rui Knopfli: ' […] very slowly I resume your slow streets, / paths always open to the sea, / white and yellow, filigreed / with time and salt, a slowness / Brahmin (or Muslim?) lasting in the air, / in the blood, or in the oblique way the sun / falls on things wounding them gently / with the light of eternity.'

Jall Sinth Hussein: 'The deserted streets full of wind / like a god the enormous fort walls watching it all / the long smooth sand and the shyness of the sea / the tongue lost like ruins / in the hand the sea horse and the dreams / time without arrival and without departure // my life later will have to be thus.'

Glória de Sant'Anna – ' […] It is a whole island / with a silver clasp / – its fortress / very well worked // in pale stones / that were transported. // And palm groves and houses / at the foot of other neighbourhoods / down in the earth / which carves and shapes itself // for black people / so svelte and grave.'

Alberto de Lacerda – 'Island where the dogs don't bark and where the children play / In the middle of the street like pilgrims / From a more open, crystalline world.'

Luís Carlos Patraquim – ' […] It is where we are useless / pure natural objects. A palm tree / of glass beads with the sun. Singing […] '

Mozambique Island is linked to the mainland by an extremely long bridge, so narrow that two cars cannot pass one another on it. It's necessary to wait for a light before moving onto the roadway. From afar you would think it was a cable. If it were to snap – something I fear could happen at any moment – it would surely leave the coast, adrift, towards a dead time. The degraded houses, the trees, the statue of Vasco da Gama in front of the old Governor's Palace – all this is democratically covered in a veil of dust and forgetting. We went to wander the twisting streets. Jordi photographed an old man, in the Christian cemetery, beside an urn. A good portrait: the man, in big dark glasses, kufi on his head, a blue shirt with the first few buttons undone, revealing a hairless chest and the unexpected gifts of an actor. He photographed a boy, in a market, standing on the counter with the coloured shelves as a background: soaps, tins of conserves, bottles of water, packets of biscuits, bags of crisps. The television was broadcasting a programme sponsored by the United Nations. He also photographed a tailor in his shop. Walls of lath and plaster, a calendar with the picture of a little orange wooden house in the middle of a stripped-bare landscape. I recognised – or thought I recognised – the little house. I felt as though I'd lived through that exact moment sometime before. The man smiled (he smiles forever in the photograph) behind an old Singer machine.

We returned later to the Omuhipiti Hotel, where we're staying, we changed our clothes and made our way down to a little beach wedged between the São Sebastião Fort and an old ruined warehouse, round the back of the hotel. They call it the Nacarama beach – that's lion in *Macua*, because in the ruins of the warehouses you can still see – at the very top – the little statue of a lion. This is the only beach, Bem assured us, where we can bathe at all safely, because all the others have long been used as vast public latrines. I was reminded of lines that Jorge de Sena wrote (which not long ago I could have quoted) remembering Camõens' passage through this small piece of ground where Mozambique began:

[…] They all passed by here – Almeidas and Gonzagas,
Bocages and Albuquerques, even Gama.
In those days people wondered
at this little civic village
of whites, blacks, Indians and Christians,
and Muslims, Brahmins and atheists.
Europe and Africa, Brazil and the Indies,
it all crossed paths here, in this heat as white
as that of the lime fort on the patio, and so crossed
as the elegance of simple ribs
of the little bulwark chapel.
Here lie on lost stones
the names of all those people who,

like the blacks today, approached the rocks,
lowered their pants and left in the sea
the foul-smelling dross of their being alive.
It is not in bronze, blonde-haired,
nor in writing verses, that I see you here.
But in a nook in marine grunt-fish
releasing the nymphs who lick the rocks
Such is the hunger and the glory of the epic
are digested in you. […]

Jordi wasn't alarmed by these lines of Sena's. He entered the water, attempted half a dozen energetic strokes of his arms then remained floating on his back. I went in too. He said to me:

'What I'd like would be to be able to photograph the colour of this sea.'

'You can't photograph everything, sea-boy. And taking photographs isn't the truth, it's just an approximation.'

'No. It's another truth. They're different truths.'

He's probably right.

(The frangipani veranda)

Laurentina has been really anxious lately, drained. She felt ill and fainted last night just after we'd arrived at the little hotel. I made her some tea, massaged her with almond and chamomile oil (my own recipe), gave her a hot bath and finally got her off to sleep. She woke up in a good mood. This morning we circled the Island in an old fishing boat. Seen from the sea it looks even smaller and more isolated. We had lunch at the O Paladar restaurant, belonging to Miss Kiu-Kiu, daughter of a Chinese man and black woman, who married an Arab and had five children. One of the daughters married an Indian, the others mulattos, etc., in an example of multiculturalism that predictably enough delighted Bartolomeu. I wanted to ask Miss Kiu-Kiu if she knew a woman on the Island by the name of Alima, but Laurentina stopped me:

'Don't do that,' she asked me. 'I'm not ready yet.'

Bartolomeu shrugged his shoulders, sceptical – or distracted, or both:

'There are probably lots of women with that name, it's a common enough name here, and it may be that none of them is this woman you're looking for.'

'I'm looking for my mother!'

'No, Lau,' I said to her. 'Your mother died. The woman you're looking for doesn't even know that you exist.'

'You're right! What should I do?'

'It's your decision. We'll do whatever you think best.'

'No! We're in this to the end.' Bartolomeu raised his voice, already regretting his former scepticism. 'This isn't just a little whim. We've

223

travelled to the ends of the earth to film a documentary about the life of Faustino Manso. Now we have to look for this woman, and if we find her, interview her.'

'No, no we don't have to find her.' I felt the mustard rising to my nostrils. 'We're going to film the Island. Record two or three more depositions. Alima's testimony isn't vital.'

Laurentina looked at me, looked at Bartolomeu, and for the first time I could see she was unable to take a decision. I paid the bill, and we left.

As night was beginning to fall I came across Bartolomeu on the patio, beside the pool, under a summerhouse incandescent with bougainvillea. He was talking to the owner of the hotel, a very red-headed Italian called Mauro. In the rosy light, filtered by the flowers of the bougainvillea, it looked as though Mauro's rebellious hair had caught fire.

'This is our Portuguese,' Bartolomeu said, pointing to me. 'A tropical Portuguese.'

Mauro held out his hand:

'Hello! I'm Mau,' he smiled, showing surprisingly glowing teeth. 'Not *mau* as in bad, Mau for Mauro. I'm really not that bad at all. It's just that in this country people like to economise on their words.'

Mauro, or Mau, is quite the opposite, and has no appreciation for any kind of economy, still less verbal economy. Everything about him has a tendency towards the literary. The hotel itself, in fact, is called The Frangipani Veranda, like the novel by Mia Couto. I wanted to know if he'd done it on purpose. He smiled even more widely:

'We have a veranda, and a frangipani, haven't you noticed?'

I had. But – I don't know – he might have called it The Bougainvillea Summerhouse. I'll admit he's done a good job. The hotel retains the charm of an old house: high ceilings, a wooden floor of worn planks, big wicker chairs dozing in favourable shades, and on the walls, baskets, mats and pieces of local craftsmanship; and at the same time it offers every comfort of modernity, including the beautiful pool on the patio and wireless Internet in every room.

Mau has an unusual hobby: he creates mechanical insects. Or rather, what he does is he penetrates the shells of hornets – and all kinds of coleoptera – with minuscule mechanisms taken from old watches. He has an impressive collection, spread all around the hotel, in 'demonsteration cases', as he calls them, with glass covers. There are beetles that beat their wings, move their pincers, others that blink delicate blue, red or yellow lights. Two or three squeak when you touch their heads. They're like creatures from sci-fi films, like *Blade Runner* or something, or from Enki Bilal's graphic novels. They give me the shivers; watching Mau in his office dissecting beetles alarmed me even more. There's a mixture of sophistication and cruelty about it, the patience of a loving and experienced torturer.

'What did you do before you came to the Island?'

He looked at me, distrustful:

'Nothing. I was very good at it.'

I insisted:

'Back in Italy, what did you do there?'

'I left Italy many years ago. In a different incarnation. I'm Mozambican now.'

'You never went back to Italy?'

'I've told you already, that was a different incarnation. No one ever returns to their old body.' He pointed to one of the beetles. 'I'm like these bugs, you get it? All that's left to me now of the life I lived – when I was Italian – is this shell. What moves me now isn't a heart, or any living muscle, I only get up in the morning out of sheer inertia. Or otherwise – who knows? – maybe I'm also half-animal, half-machine. When they autopsy me they're going to discover that someone's replaced all my organs with mechanical parts.'

The idea seemed to amuse him. He spent a good fifteen minutes explaining what sorts of mechanisms he'd implant in his own carcass if only he could. On a cork board on the wall were pinned some ten beetles, cicadas and praying-mantises. There were also pencil drawings of coleoptera, alongside sketches of how they would end up once their mechanical parts had been inserted. A few photographs: Mau on a camel; Mau in a bathing suit, his arms around a beautiful woman; Mau fishing, on a boat, with another man. This last picture caught my eye:

'I know that guy!'

'You know him?! That seems very unlikely...'

'I do know him. I met him in Luanda...'

'In Luanda? Then perhaps – he is Angolan.'

'I'm sure of it. Monte, he's called Monte. Magno Moreira Monte. Businessman, poet, private detective...'

'A private detective, Monte?!' Mau laughed with delight. 'Life is full of surprises. I lived in Angola a few years, at the end of the seventies, after leaving Italy, before settling in Mozambique. I met Monte at that time. He collected butterflies and coleoptera. He had an incredible collection. It was with him that I started getting interested in beetles. We still exchange samples today.'

'And what did Monte do in those days?'

'As I say, he collected insects...'

'I get it. But you were surprised when I told you the guy's a private detective now. Magno Moreira Monte. Businessman, poet, private detective. That's what's written on the card he gave me. I haven't forgotten.'

'You know, the world's changed a lot. And people – in order to survive – have been forced to change with the world. In the seventies Monte was already a detective, although I don't think that's what it would have been called then. But he didn't defend private interests, no. We were communists.'

Bartolomeu, who'd been distracted looking at the mechanical beetles, came over to look at the photo too:

'Ha! I know this guy well. A tremendous cop...'

Mau shook his red hair, disordering the evening:

'Fuck, you people all know each other?! Angola's one small country...'

'No, no!' Bartolomeu retorted, indignant. 'Angola's big. It's the world that's small.'

(Aline's dreams)

Aline, my best friend, is an excellent dreamer. Dreaming well is a rare talent, little recognised, at least in European countries. Here in Mozambique, on the contrary, people who know how to dream tend to be quite well respected. Aline's dreams are intricate, with sudden about-turns, and in them there are often realistic details which trouble me more than the plot itself. Aline doesn't limit herself to dreaming about an angel – something quite trivial – but is capable of discussing with him Fermat's Last Theorem, and describing precisely the form of his wings; the mathematical angel, for example, had transparent ones, like those of a dragonfly.

In my email today I found a message from Aline, informing me about her latest dream. I transcribe:

'There's a lad, standing up, playing a kind of flute, curved and sharp as a sabre, while a fish sits at the other end singing. A second lad, spread out on his front on the ground, is playing the harmonica; a third, squatting in front of the other two, is holding a bird. There's also a cage, in which a shadow – or perhaps a heart – is palpitating. Houses unfold in the distance. You're sitting in a chair, watching everything. A man approaches you, from behind, dishevelled hair burning. He looks like a firebrand. I say to you, pointing to the cage, "It's mine, the heart!" and then something snaps and the man falls. He had a secret, I can tell by the darkness of his spirit as he falls. When you look again, you notice that the cage is empty. A beetle takes flight with the sun caught between its jaws.'

227

The strange thing is that when I finished reading the message I looked up and saw – fixed to the wall – a silkscreen print of Chichorro*: a lad standing up, playing a kind of flute, etc. I turned around, anxious, expecting to see the torch-man approaching – but nothing happened.

(A shot at dawn)

Early this morning I witnessed a crime.

I spend my nights in the car. Not so much to save money, but simply because I don't like the idea of paying – however little it might be – for the doubtful pleasure of stretching myself out in a public bed to pretend to be sleeping. I'm troubled even more by the possibility that I actually will succumb to sleep, and dream all the dreams someone has left behind. Hotel mattresses – especially those in the cheaper hotels – tend to accumulate the residue of quick, poorly dreamt dreams, and there's no way of ruling out the possibility of contracting some stray nightmare or other. Do you know any promiscuity worse than dreaming a second-hand dream?

I – who have been so promiscuous – hate promiscuity.

There's nothing remarkable about that, when you really think about it. Smokers who love cigarettes are few and far between, smokers who're prepared to defend them, who show themselves willing to die for them with the same enthusiasm as, say, a suicide-bomber sacrificing his life for the holy name of Allah and His prophet.

So I prefer to spend the nights in my Malembe. I lie the seat back, and look at the stars. I park now round the back of the hotel, now on the beach, then finally in some calmer hideaway. In every place I've witnessed strange scenes, or at the very least scenes that are not morally very edifying. The devil – as my teachers at the seminary liked to remind me – enjoys shadows. Two nights ago a car stopped in front of me. A woman, still young, in a black jersey-dress, was at the wheel. Beside her was a tall,

---

* Roberto Chichorro, one of the best known Mozambican painters, who has lived in Lisbon for many years. Some people have called him the African Chagall. Like Marc Chagall, Chichorro very much likes music and brides, blue and people levitating. Once, at one of his exhibitions, I heard one lady remarking to another: 'This man must be happy. He only paints happy people.' I look at those women he paints, all wide-eyed, dreamers, in their tropical languor, and think that I'd like to be one of them.

distinguished-looking man, grey hair, a white linen suit. They didn't see me. The woman pulled the dress over her head and was completely naked. She opened the car door, got out, and lay down in the sand. The man got out too. He didn't take his clothes off. He simply lay down, in silence, beside the woman. They remained like that, quite still, watching the moon, which was very round and bright that night. Then the woman got back into the car, dressed, and left. The man remained lying there for some time. At last he too got up. He walked with slow steps towards the sea until I could no longer see him, swallowed up by the darkness and by the gentle murmur of the waves.

I also saw, on another night, an old lady taking a fish for a walk. She had the fish in a little round tank. She put the tank down beside the breakwater and with the help of a glass changed the water over. It was a blue fish, that glimmered in the darkness, as though by its own light. The old lady talked to it.

'It's just you and me, Senhor Bonifácio,' I heard her say as she passed just centimetres by me, not seeing me – 'There's no one in the world who can hear us.'

A lot of people turn up having to satisfy their physiological needs. They squat down by the water with total assurance. Sometimes there are as many as six or seven, even more, at once – and they chatter. A veritable defecators' congress.

But this is what I witnessed just recently – not so much as five hours ago. A man in an orange tracksuit, dishevelled hair the same sandy colour as our Luanda slums, came out of the hotel and went off in the direction of the beach. He stopped, standing, for some time, under the fragile lace of an acacia tree. The sun was opening onto the horizon, petal by petal, like a rose. You could hear the purring of an engine and straight after that a red scooter pierced the twilight. It stopped right beside the redhead. The motorcyclist was wearing a helmet, also red, which partly hid his face. The two talked for a few moments, very calmly, like old friends. The one from the scooter pulled out a cigarette. He lit it and offered it to the redhead. With two firm gestures the redhead threw down the cigarette, stepped on it. Then he did something strange. He straightened himself up, raised his right fist and began to sing. The motorcyclist took a pistol from his belt, pointed it at the redhead's chest and fired. Then he put the gun away again, switched on his engine and left. The redhead didn't fall right away.

He spun around in slow motion, right arm to his chest, the left sticking out as though dancing a waltz with an invisible girl. He clung to a tree and, finally, slid down to the ground and remained there, face down, fingers in the sand. The report of the shot in the liquid calm of the early morning had attracted people. First a woman came out of the hotel – young, pretty, in a simple see-through slip. She fell to her knees beside the body of the white man, threw her head back as though she was about to shout out, but there was no sound to be heard. Bartolomeu burst out next. He pushed the woman away, with a gesture that was gentle but firm, and took the wounded man's pulse, like in a film. It was as though he did this sort of thing every day.

'Help!' he shouted. 'Call an ambulance!'

People began arriving: Laurentina, Mandume, other guests. Only then did I approach. Bartolomeu told me to help him put the man into the car. We laid him out along the back, on a beach towel the colours of the Angolan flag.

'What now?'

'Man, we've got to get him to the hospital. Anyone know where the hospital is?'

The woman wearing the see-through slip nodded her head up and down without a word. Perhaps the shock had left her voiceless. She sat down next to me, sitting up very straight, struggling to cover the firm outline of her breasts with her left hand while she pointed the way with the other.

(The return of The Smile, and two or three extraordinary revelations)

Mauro is between life and death. This afternoon he was taken by military helicopter to Johannesburg. It seems he has good friends in the armed forces. Pouca Sorte told me he saw the shooter – a man on a red scooter. But he refuses to give evidence to the police. As soon as I mentioned this he looked serious and back-tracked, no, he'd been mistaken, he hadn't seen anything. I thought it would be pointless to insist. Each to his own secrets. Mauro must have many. His girlfriend (I presume she's his girlfriend), a girl of twenty-something, seems unable to contribute anything to the solving of the mystery. Indeed, she's mute! Bartolomeu is ironic:

'A man who chooses a mute woman for company – that's a wise man.'

Mandume's observation seems smarter to me:

'No, that's a man with a lot to hide.'

I remembered Mauro's shock when we suggested recording a deposition from him about the Island and his experiences since buying the hotel and setting up here:

'Me?! No, no! No filming, no photos. I'm too ugly…'

He isn't ugly, quite the contrary. He runs, cycles, swims, fishes underwater and works out – his body, then, is in impeccable condition for his age. His face reminds you a lot of Sean Connery's – that is, if you imagine (which I know isn't easy to do) the old actor with a head of rebellious red hair. According to Bartolomeu, Mauro dyes his hair. Mandume disagrees. As for me, I think it's his natural colour, precisely because it looks so fake. If I wanted to disguise myself, and especially if I wanted to go unnoticed, I would never dye my hair that absurd colour.

At the hospital I met an old friend. I didn't recognise him immediately. But he recognised me:

'And how are you? It's good to see you looking well…'

He smiled, and then, yes, then I did recognise him: The Smile, the doctor who'd treated me in Maputo. I hugged him and thanked him. I'd left Maputo without thanking him. To tell the truth, I didn't even know his name. He introduced himself, very politely, with a slight bow:

'Amândio Pinto de Sousa, my princess, at your service…'

His age already weighs on him. He walks slightly hesitantly. His straight, very white hair is in strong contrast with the burnt colour of his skin. Amândio Pinto de Sousa comes from a Goan Catholic family, like my mother. He wanted to know if I was on the Island for tourism or on business. I explained to him that I was making a documentary on the life of the Angolan musician Faustino Manso. Did the name mean anything to him?

Amândio Pinto de Sousa gave a start:

'Faustino?! Of course! Faustino was one of my best friends!'

I told him my whole story then. The old doctor listened to me in silence. Right there in his office he keeps a photo of him with Faustino. The two of them at a table in a bar. Amândio had a luxuriant mane of beautiful black hair which fell straight down his back; it rather surprised me. Yes, in the seventies young people used to wear their hair long, but Amândio must already have been in his late forties.

'We were useless,' he said to me, suddenly melancholy. '"Pure natural objects…"'

He took my hand.

'I know your mother, Dona Alima, I can take you to her house. But first I think I should entrust you with a secret.' He sighed. 'I don't even know where to start… When you were sick, with the fever, delirious, you said your father's name was Dário. Dário Reis. I knew Dário Reis too. Now you tell me that after all your father wasn't Dário, it was Faustino… Well, what I'm going to tell you will perhaps disturb you even more. It happened that after Alima had got pregnant, apparently by Faustino, Faustino had a problem, a very unpleasant one, and came to see me to treat him. I made the most of his visit to run a few tests, and it turned out that he was infertile…'

'He'd become infertile because of this problem?'

'No, no, my princess! He'd always been infertile.'

'That's ridiculous! He left eighteen children! I've spoken to some of them…'

'I know. Eighteen children, but none of them biological. Faustino was devastated when I told him. A wreck. You can imagine. His whole life thrown into doubt.'

'And my father? So who's my father?'

'That I don't know, my princess, I don't know! You'll have to ask Dona Alima.'

The two of us were alone in his office. Amândio Pinto de Sousa made some tea. I drank it slowly. I felt dizzy, unable to think things through with any clarity. At one point Mandume knocked at the door. He'd come to look for me. The doctor got up, said something to him in a rough whisper, and came back to sit in front of me.

'That's why Faustino went back to Luanda. Because of this, and for another reason I can't be the one to tell you. He went back to his first wife, Dona Anacleta, in a state of extreme anxiety. Try to see the positive side of things. Your father, as you told me, is, always will be, Dário Reis. It was he who brought you up, and brought you up – according to what you've said – with all the love in the world. I missed both of them. They were quite alike.'

'Alike, how?'

'Don't be offended. What I mean is that they both really liked women. On the whole the women reciprocated. Be that as it may, I must tell you, you got a good exchange. Imagine if Faustino had stayed with Alima. It wouldn't have worked out. It couldn't have worked out. You would have suffered a lot.'

'And my parents' marriage, you think that was a success?'

'I don't know. You tell me. In any case I'm sure the first option would have been more painful for all concerned. But tell me, then, is that why you've made this trip? Did you want to see how things would have turned out for you, what Plan A would have been like?'

'No! Of course not! I wanted to meet my biological father. I thought if I got to know him, it might help me to know myself better.'

'I understand… No, my dear, no, I don't understand any of it. What you are has everything to do with who brought you up, and very little to do with your genes. But that's your issue. Let's move on to Alima now –

if you'd turned up a year ago I wouldn't even have taken you to meet her. I'd have said, "Alima? Don't know her." Back then Alima was a married woman. If she'd suddenly had a daughter by another man turning up, it would have put her in a very difficult position. But her husband has died. Today Alima is a widow, childless, living alone. That is, I mean she's childless apart from you. We have to explain the situation to her very calmly…'

'I've been worrying about that. I've hardly been sleeping. To tell the truth, I'm not even sure it's worth it. I mean… Troubling this woman… maybe it would be better just to leave things as they are. Actually, after what you've told me about Faustino I don't know what to think any more.'

Amândio Pinto de Sousa shook his head:

'I do understand. You need to rest. You've been through so many emotions…'

'And Mauro?'

'There isn't a lot we can do for him here. We'll lose him. But if we can get him off to Johannesburg, and if he makes it there alive, perhaps he'll survive. I've had people brought to me in worse condition who've survived. Mau's strong. Incredibly strong.'

'And what was that, was it a mugging?'

'There, at that time? And what was Mau doing out at that time anyway?'

'He ran…'

'At four-something in the morning?!'

'I don't know. It seemed strange to me too.'

'You know what I think? I think the shot came from far away, from another time, that's what I think.'

'How so?'

Amândio Pinto de Sousa lowered his voice:

'Immediately after independence, Mozambique became a sort of promised land for socialist revolution. For the first few years we received revolutionaries from every part of the world. People who were persecuted in their countries of origin: South Africans from the ANC and the Communist Party, Basques with ties to ETA, guerrillas from Peru and Argentina, Red Brigades Italians…'

'You think Mauro belonged to the Red Brigades, is that it?'

'I don't know. I'm not even certain he's really Italian…'

'Why do you say that?'

'No concrete reason, just the odd thing I saw, some things he told me, and mainly an old man's sense. Or perhaps just because I like spy novels. Don't take me too seriously, princess. I'm a free spirit. I have no obligations to reality.'

Back at the hotel, Mandume found my silence strange:

'What's up with you? You're like a whole funeral cortege on your own!'

Maybe I really was a dark silence on the outside; but on the inside I felt like a big-city main street at rush hour. Ideas hurrying, jostling past. Memories spinning vertiginously. Horns blaring. Traffic lights flashing. I couldn't make out a face. Make a connection. Recognise a place. I didn't sleep. Or perhaps I did fall asleep a few times, but always within the same narrow turbulent space. Waking up, very early in the morning, Mandume looked at me, and was shocked:

'You're not like this because of the Italian, I'm sure of it. Tell me what's wrong?'

So I told him:

'Faustino Manso isn't my father!'

'I know he isn't, my love. I've been telling you from the beginning…'

'You don't understand. He really isn't my father. Faustino was infertile!'

I told him about my conversation with the doctor. Mandume shrugged his shoulders scornfully:

'The great African macho man! And now we find he was the biggest cuckold on the continent!'

'I won't let you talk like that!'

'Come on! This man is nothing to you, Laurentina! You don't have to defend him.'

He's right, I know it. Faustino Manso is not my father, he isn't anything to me, and no one in the family has given me their proxy to defend him. He never came to find me. He didn't even wait for me before dying. But over the past days I've been getting fond of him. I know his voice and the places he went. I've spoken to his wives with whom he shared his joys and sadnesses, and begun to see him through their eyes. I learned to love him too. It's as though he'd been stolen out of my heart.

'I feel like I've been plundered!'

Mandume took a step back. He was in his pyjamas (he never gets into bed without changing into his pyjamas) and his shock, pure as the early morning light, filled the room:

'What?!'

I dressed, and went out. Mandume came behind me.

There was blood on the tarmac. In the background the sea, apart from everything. Malembemalembe was parked under the broad foliage of a fig tree. I noticed the anxious movements of shadows inside. Voices. Then a teenager – some sixteen years old – got out of the driver's door, bare-chested, looked at us with a challenge in his eyes, did up his shorts and left, whistling. I realised (with surprise) what the tune was: *Xigombela*, by Faustino Manso.* Mandume shook his head, shocked:

'You see that?! That guy, Pouca Sorte, he's a well of surprises.'

A well, yes. Infinitely deep.

---

* I know the words by heart: 'I live the other side of the mirror / Where it's left, I turn right, / they want my blue, and I am red. / The mouth says yes, the heart refuses. // My heart refuses / Both lash and leash, / Insult or affront. / Dance, dance, the xingombela.' This name, xingombela, is what they call a traditional dance from the south of Mozambique usually danced at dusk. It's a circle which individual couples move into and out of. Some dance love, and others represent valour. *Xigombela* must have been one of the last songs composed by Faustino Manso in Mozambique.

(My mother, Dona Alima)

I think: so this is my mother. I don't know what to say. Alima seems even
more bewildered than me. We avoid looking at each other. She rolls up into
herself like a hedgehog. She's a very thin woman, faded, perhaps half my
height. People like that stop existing, after a certain age, thanks to an effort
of silence and annulment, till they reach almost complete public invisibility.
Amândio Pinto de Sousa spoke to her before bringing me. He told me that
Alima received his news with no apparent surprise. She wanted to know if
I was happy – if I'd been happy with my adopted family. At one point she
had weakened a bit, wiped away a tear on a white handkerchief; at last she
agreed to meet me. The house is small, stuck into a row of others, a door
and a window, a door and a window, all the same. Two leather sofas, very
worn; a television set, in one corner, on a little wooden table, and on the
television an embroidered cloth and a little bronze statue of Ganesh*, sitting
on a kind of throne, a little mouse at his feet. Hanging on the wall a calendar with the image of the Virgin Mary. Amândio came with me. He installed
himself on the other sofa. He drank his coffee in silence. He tried the
chocolate biscuits Alima must have bought in the market (I bought the
same ones a few days ago). Finally he got up:

'I'll leave the two of you alone. You must have a lot to talk about...'

Alima made as if to get up, but the doctor stopped her with a gesture:

* I've always felt for Ganesh, the boy, son of Parvati and Shiva, who lost his head following
a domestic misunderstanding, it being replaced with that of an elephant. Ganesh is the
protector of homes, and it is also to Him that believers go when they need obstacles remov-
ing from their way.

237

'There's no need, dear lady, I know the way.'

He opened the door, winked at me, and went out. The two of us sat there facing one another. It was my turn:

'Listen: I imagine this must be very difficult for you. After all, you thought I'd died in childbirth...'

Alima shook her head:

'No, child! I knew you were alive. Don't ask me how. My heart knew. There wasn't a single day I didn't think of you. When you were younger I used to make up stories about you, trying to guess from other children's faces what your face would be like. I even bought you toys which I would later hide.'

A sob shook her fragile body. I got up, took two steps and knelt down beside her. I buried my face in her lap. I felt Alima's hands slipping like light butterflies over my hair. My mother's lap smelled of incense and sea air. We both cried. A tiredness came over me, a desire to forget, to have no time and no universe, and not even the shadow of a God over all this.

....

Alima was Doroteia, all the mothers, and I all the daughters of the world.

Part Four

Luanda, Angola
Saturday, 11 March 2006

Yesterday I went to a party at Orlando Sérgio's flat. He phoned me two hours beforehand to invite me. I hadn't heard from him in months. He gave me the name of the street and the number of the building. He told me the flat was on the seventh-and-a-half floor. I was surprised at the half:

'Yeah! You walk up to the seventh floor – the lift doesn't work – and my flat's wedged between the seventh floor and the eighth.'

It was an old building, a sombre façade, deep black bags under its eyes, which remained standing only out of sheer stubbornness. 'Dignity, my friend, say rather out of dignity!' Orlando retorted. 'It still remembers happier days.' The entrance was frightening. Dirty, broken steps. Various flights in darkness. Candles panting in the gloom. The wax melting over the flagstones. Naked boys playing cowboys on the landings. A rapper sitting on a step, hurling rhymes at the wall as though they were stones:

A dog is man's best friend, it's said –
But I know that it's booze instead.
I'll drink until I drop down dead.

A little girl in a blue dress, with trimmings, with little pointed plaits, ran by me. She shouted to someone (someone I couldn't see) inside the house:

'Dadddyyyyyy! This music huuuuurts!'

It really did. Orlando was waiting for me at the top of the stairs, wearing old yellow shorts, a bottle of beer in his left hand. He'd come back days earlier from a long stay in Rio de Janeiro. I found him rejuvenated. His glasses seemed odd to me, with their thick black frames, squareish, like an anachronistic prop from a dressing-up chest. There are some actors who act all the time, compulsively, changing their face, and their personality, from each moment to the next. Perhaps it's a kind of professional weakness, or – the contrary – a sign of great efficiency. Orlando Sérgio was the first black actor to play Othello in Portugal. We've been friends for over twenty years. We clasped each other in a tight hug:

'Tired?'

He showed me his flat. A clear living room, kitchen, bathroom and three bedrooms. The only piece of furniture in his bedroom was a narrow iron bed. In the others there were mattresses laid directly onto the cement, and wires to hang out clothes attached to the walls. The rooms were rented to two artist couples. One of the girls, with a swollen belly, moved about the flat as though she were floating, lit by the calm, enraptured light of a mother-to-be. There was also an extensive veranda leaning out into the cool night. A thin guy – long, stretched out on the cement – blocked our way.

'Dead?'

Orlando shrugged:

'Could be. I found him like that this morning. Don't you know him?'

I recognised the name: an Angolan stylist who's lived for years in New York. The pregnant girl offered me a beer. I asked her for juice. She brought me a caipirinha and a dish of spicy fish soup. She introduced me to a man with lively green eyes, light brown hair. He'd disembarked very early that morning, coming in from Lisbon. I asked him what had brought him to Luanda.

'I want to be Angolan,' he told me. 'Always have. I think I've got the knack for it.'

I congratulated him on his courage. I added that it struck me as a terribly ambitious thing to be aiming for. I stressed the word *terribly*. Coming to Angola in order to be Angolan isn't the same thing as coming to Los Angeles aiming to be a famous actor. For a guy to become a famous actor, that's easier. But this lad didn't lose heart. He didn't even lose his smile. He was born in Porto, he explained, but his parents – both of them from Benguela – always talked to him about Angola. He said he knows more about the country than most Angolans. He got up and went to dance *kuduro* – I'll admit, he does dance well. A tall, thin girl, glowing skin, very black, an enigmatic expression like a Quioca mask, sat down beside me. She was wearing a tight white T-shirt, and very scratched jeans. She didn't introduce herself. She didn't say anything. I got up. There were two young guys rolling a joint in the kitchen. In another group a famous artist and art dealer was speech-making at the top of his voice. His grey hair almost gave credibility to the torrential speech with which he was crushing his audience. He was discoursing on the contribution of traditional African art to the revival of European painting, cubism, globalisation, on the narrow cultural nationalism of many of our intellectuals, who're pleased when they're told that Pablo Picasso was inspired by traditional African art, or that Bahia begins in Luanda, but get annoyed that some of our Carnival groups are based on Brazilian models. I have no patience left for these sorts of discussions. Traditions, they say, you have to respect traditions. What traditions? The people who brought Carnival to Angola, it was the Portuguese, along with the language, Jesus Christ, salt cod, cassava, palm oil, corn, guitars, accordions, football and roller hockey. The Portuguese also brought syphilis, tuberculosis, chigoe fleas and even The Devil. They burned witches in *autos-da-fé*, giving rise to a tradition that exists to this day. They set up the slave trade, and from this another set of massively respected traditions was born. Tradition. Just the word gives me the shivers. I went to sit back down. I served myself another plate of bean stew. The tall girl, beside me, was in the same position I'd left her an hour earlier.

'Are you a friend of Orlando?'

She looked at me, surprised.

'No, no! I'm the Dancer.'

Oh, right. There had to be some story. Hours later I met Orlando on the veranda, sitting in a plastic chair, eyes lost in the vast darkness. I wanted to know who this Dancer was. My friend smiled. An engrossed smile.

'No one,' he said. 'She lived here…'

'She lived here?!'

'That's it. She lived here. She lived with a sapper. The Dancer and the sapper. Can you imagine a stranger love story than that?'

'What happened?'

'What do you think happened? One day the sapper went to work and never came back. One of the mines exploded while he was defusing it. The next day they found her dancing, naked, on the minefield.'

'Naked?!'

'Yeah, naked. Starkers, pal. As God made her…'

'And what's she doing here?'

'Just sits and breathes. She doesn't do anything any more. A while ago she knocks on the door and I let her in. She's a sort of ghost, but without that impertinence that ghosts have.'

I found her again this morning, on the beach, her feet in the lace trim of the sea. Gesturing flower shapes with her hands. I got the impression that only I could see her.

(The Dancer)

I never learned her name.

'The name doesn't matter,' Monte, the copper, used to tell me over and over again. 'What matters is the nickname.'

Strange guy, Monte: a sharp, scrutinising gaze, like those guys at the airports who check your passport. He moved silently, making no impact on the ground, and yet securely, tremendously securely, the angel of death walking in the twilight. A voice that is too agreeable – frightening – you can talk, my child, talk all you want, we already know everything. I remember his nickname too: the Dead Man.

What matters is the nickname.

But let's get back to the Dancer. I used to see her on the Island, opposite the Café del Mar, dancing alone. She danced alone, not like someone dancing on their own in a party crowded with people; but rather with the intimacy of someone dancing alone in a desolate, empty room, hours after the party has ended. Her feet in the glimmering sand, long arms raised, eyes tightly shut. Her embroidered white dress, very fine, describing the slight curves of her body. People kept their distance from her – as from an abyss. I, on the other hand, was attracted to her. A few times I tried to strike up a conversation:

'D'you come here a lot?'

She never replied. Her gaze went right through me, as though I didn't exist, as though no one around her existed, no sign of human activity. The feeling of being a mere spirit in transit isn't very pleasant, believe me. One afternoon I tried touching her arm. Perhaps after all she was the one who was a spectre. Then she did give a shudder:

'What do you want?'

I didn't know how to reply. I lied to her:

'I think we know one another...'

She drew back, in a moment of alarm:

'I don't know anyone anymore...'

I invited her to sit with me. I ordered a passionfruit juice for her. Another for me. Passionfruit has a calming effect, they say. I wanted to know who she was. I was burning with curiosity. The Dancer drank her juice delicately. Then, as though choreographed, she unhooked the strap from off her right shoulder, unhooked the other, got up and the dress slipped in a gentle caress to her feet. She had a perfect body. Round breasts, with little brown tips, a flat belly, her navel like an exclamation mark above the dark forest of her sex. There was a silence, a stunned silence, like that of a boxer at the moment his opponent's fist strikes him between the eyes, and the blood flows, a light that links everything together, and I was aware of the whole city looking at us. I knew I ought to get up and cover her up with a towel. I didn't. I remained silent in my place, as she crossed the narrow strip of sand and into the sea. She dived in head-first, disappeared, and the whole city sighed – ôôôôôôô – just like that, their mouths open, little hats on their heads, after which they all started speaking at once. Only then did I grab the towel and go to meet her at the water's edge.

I took her home. She lived in Largo do Quinaxixe, on the sixth floor of the so-called Cuca building, one of the emblems of the city in the last years of the colonial period. Today it's a melancholy ruin, waiting to be knocked in – it will then be replaced by a much larger building – but by night it still proudly shows the big illuminated neon Cuca which made it famous. The best thing (a complete luxury) in the Dancer's apartment was the light. The Swedes would pay good money to have light like this coming into their apartments in Stockholm. It came in for free through open windows, lazily, and then stretched itself out into the generous empty compartments. All the rooms were meticulously clean, which in contrast with the stains in various tones of sepia on the ceilings and walls – the products of slow work of successive infestations – induced in the spirit (or at least induced in mine) a lively anxiety. The Dancer went to the kitchen to prepare coffee. She brought two cups and put them on the floor, in front of the bed, a noisy iron contraption which was actually the only piece of furniture in the whole apartment. I sat down on the floor and drank the coffee, attentively, in little sips. She drank hers. When I'd finished she took my cup, put the saucer onto it, turned it over, withdrew the saucer and hunched over the coffee-dreg pictures that had been left on the sides and bottom of the vessel:

'See this little square? You're about to get involved with a married woman. This one here, that looks like a horse's head, this means you're soon going to take an important journey, and that this journey's going to change your life. I also see that you're going to lose someone you love.'

The following week my grandfather died and I met Laurentina. A few days later, we set off on our journey.

(The return to chaos)

We returned to Luanda, by plane, via Johannesburg. Pouca Sorte will have to come back on his own, retracing the whole journey with Malembemalembe. It's a shame, as we're missing the car, and the patience, kindness and skill of its driver in this horrid city. After everything that happened on Mozambique Island, the return to Maputo and the journey following were somewhat like the end of a party: a great tiredness, dirty crockery strewn across the whole house, the sense of there being something that's been broken or lost forever. Lau is hardly speaking. Bartolomeu doesn't understand what's going on, but he can tell that there's something. He's been nervous. We decided, me and Lau, after a long discussion, that we'd keep Faustino Manso's secret from him. Lau argues (and I understand her) that this revelation would affect a lot of people – including Bartolomeu himself – and she's afraid of the family's reaction. She refused to interview Alima for the film. I don't know what they talked about; I don't even know if Alima revealed the name of the man who got her pregnant. The refusal to interview Alima, as might have been predicted, annoyed Bartolomeu even more. He thinks without her deposition the film will be mutilated. Laurentina is ignoring him. Yesterday she spent the day at the home of Dona Anacleta. Today she went for lunch with her and still isn't back. I see her – the old lady – as a sort of guardian of all the secrets. She has the keys to the closet. We just need to know whether she's prepared to show us the skeletons. I am of course referring to metaphorical skeletons, but, well, actually nothing would surprise me. Didn't Dona Ana de Lacerda show us real bones?

(An epiphany – or rather, its opposite)

A stroll round the Island for some distraction. I came across Alfonsina
again. Or, well, I really came across Pintada, the chicken, and she took me
to the girl. Pintada was on the beach, half buried in the sand, drunk on
sun. She jumped as I approached, and hopped away, with little piercing
cries, but in spite of all this maintaining a certain dignity (as much dignity
as a chicken is capable of). I followed her. I came across Alfonsina asleep
in a ruined bandstand. I made to wake her up but Pintada attacked me
with two vigorous pecks. The first tore my trousers. The second injured
my hand. The ruckus woke Alfonsina. She sat on the ground, adjusted her
dress and smiled:

'You came back? Ha, uncle, Luanda is cool!'

'No, I don't like Luanda.'

'So you came back because of me?'

'No!' I laughed. 'That's not why either. I came back because I have to
finish my work here.'

'A film?'

'Yes, a film. About a man who had seven wives.'

'At the same time?'

'No, not at the same time.'

'Ha! My father has three wives.'

'Has? You told me your parents died in the war…'

'They didn't die. They stayed there, in the war, in Cuíto. I don't hear
from them.'

'And your father lives with three wives in the same house?'

'He does. He's an old man. Older than you.'

'Do you miss them?'

'No. My father beat me. I ran away… That on your hand, is it blood
or what?'

'It was the chicken, she pecked me. She's a fierce creature. You should
muzzle her.'

Alfonsina laughed. She whistled to call Pintada over:

'I warned you. Like a dog, this one. She protects me.'

I sat down beside her.

'That other time, at dinner, you told me you'd made a film…'

She looked at me in terror:

'No, no! I've never made any film…'

'You told me you'd made a film with an Italian…'

'It was a lie!'

'Did you see the other guy again, the white guy, did he threaten you?'

'No, no, I haven't seen anyone. I never see anyone. I'm on my own here.' She got up. She shook the dirt from her dress; I thought she seemed to be wearing more dirt than dress. 'Bye then! I'm going to hospital…'

'Are you sick?'

'Is hunger a sickness?'

'You want to eat?'

Alfonsina smiled, a woman's smile, lightly ironic. Only then did I notice she'd lost weight. Her eyes seemed larger, they shone, reflecting the radiant light of the morning like two mirrors.

'No. It's not just hunger, uncle. I really am sick. Fever.'

I touched her forehead. It burned.

'Sick like this no man wants to go to bed with me.'

I didn't know what to say to her. At that moment, there, I had the opposite of an epiphany: a revelation that came to my spirit, like a darkness exploding under the broad midday sun, of the implacable absence of God. I sighed:

'If you want I'll go to hospital with you…'

'You have a car?'

'No.'

'Then give me a hundred *quanzas* for a *candongueiro.*'

I pulled out my wallet and took out everything I had. Two hundred dollars. The girl looked at me astonished:

'What's this?'

'Take it. Buy food, medicine, whatever you need.'

'What is it you want?'

'Just want you to get well.'

Alfonsina took the money from my hand, took the shoe off her right foot and put the notes inside. She put it back on. Then she hugged me, leaning her head against my chest. I felt her heat, her bones light and fragile as though they were full of warm air. I felt ashamed, alarmed that someone might see us like that and think I was taking advantage of her, and I pushed her away. Perhaps I did it too sharply. Alfonsina was scared:

'What was it?! You afraid of getting fleas?'

She put the chicken in a bag:

'I can't leave her here alone. They'll kill her and eat her. They ever kill and eat a friend of yours?'

I walked with her as far as the *candongueiro*.

'You know in the city there are also *costangueiros* now?'

'*Costangueiros?*'

'Yeah! They're like *candongueiros*, but don't have a vehicle. They cross flooded streets with passengers *às costas* – on their backs.'

(An unpublished uncle)

I returned to the hotel dazed. My head was heavy. I closed the blinds and lay out on the bed. I was already half-asleep when the phone rang. I answered:

'Hello?! I'd like to speak to Mariano Maciel...'

A voice just like my father's:

'Yes, that's me...'

'Mariano? Man, it's your uncle, how're you doing? I had a hell of a job tracking you down.'

'Uncle?!'

'Nelito, your father's older brother.'

'My father never told me he had an older brother.'

'No?! Well, I'm not surprised. When Mariano and Martinho died in '77, they were on one side, along with your father, and I was on the other. There wasn't anything I could do to save them. I couldn't. Your father never forgave me. He broke off relations with me. I tried to see you all once, in Lisbon, but he wouldn't let me.'

'...'

'Hello?! Listen... Don't hang up... I want to meet you, to introduce you to your cousins. What's past is past. You lot, the kids, you shouldn't be punished for it. It's not fair.'

'I have to speak to my father.'

'Yes, speak to him. Tell him I send my regards. I'll leave you the number of my cellphone, you got somewhere to make a note? Call whenever you want.'

I put down the phone. I tried to focus on the purring of the air conditioner. Laurentina had thought that she had one mother and one father and they said to her, no, it was another mother, another father. Then they said to her, we're really sorry, that second man isn't your father either. She's looking for him. As for me, I learn now that my father has been hiding his elder brother from me. I have an uncle, cousins (how many?), and I never knew. I sat on the bed and called Lisbon.

'Dad?'

'Mandume? Everything OK?'

'Nelito, does the name mean anything to you?'

'No!'

'No?!'

'I had a brother with that name. He died.'

'No, sir – no, he didn't die! Why did you never tell me about him?'

'Nelito tracked you down? I don't believe it…'

'The fact that my uncle tracked me down really doesn't seem all that strange to me – it only reflects well on him. The strange thing is that you hid his existence from me.'

'Don't you go anywhere near that man!'

'Why not?'

'Because I don't want you to!'

I hung up the phone. I counted the seconds. Twenty-eight, before it started ringing. I unplugged the cable and lay out on the bed again. I tried to separate the sounds that were coming to my ears – the air conditioner, the cars speeding dangerously along the street outside the hotel, the remote beating of the waves, a long burst of laughter. Whenever I pay attention to sounds, here in Luanda, it's not long before I hear a burst of laughter. I'm not saying that that means anything. I'm just stating a fact.

(A cenotaph)

The house: a cenotaph.* Guests are received, in the living room, by a portrait, in oils, of Faustino Manso with his arms around his double bass. I knew who'd painted it even before seeing the timid signature in the bottom right-hand corner: Fatita de Matos. Walker, the double bass, fills the room with its solid presence. On the piano sit dozens of framed photos: Faustino Manso, at the end of the fifties, with Raul Indipwo. Faustino Manso, probably at the end of the sixties, early seventies**, on an esplanade in Lisbon with Rui Mingas, of whom he was a great admirer. Faustino Manso next to Nelson Mandela. This last photo caught my attention. Between Mandela and Faustino, her back to the photographer, and apparently in animated conversation with the legendary South African leader, is a blonde woman. Her face is hidden. Her elegance, however, gives her away at once:

'Yes,' Dona Anacleta offered, guessing my thoughts. 'It's Seretha du Toit. The photograph was taken in Pretoria, when President Mandela took power.'

---

* Tomb or funerary monument in memory of someone whose body does not lie there; an honorary tomb. Etym. Fr. cénotaphe (1501); from Lat. cenothaphium, honorary tomb, from Gk. kenotaphion, or 'empty tomb'; see cen(o)-e-tafo, var. syn. of sepulcro. Definition taken from the Dicionário Houaiss. I think that for users of the Portuguese language Houaiss is rather like a woman's handbag: indispensable, life-saving, and filled with an infinity of tiny articles that are utterly useless but wonderful. Cenotaph, for example – for me that was love at first sight. A few days ago, in the airport at Johannesburg, we came across a very dense border guard, a man quite without a soul. 'He looks like a cenotaph,' I remarked. Bartolomeu agreed with a laugh: 'I haven't the foggiest idea what a cenotaph is, but he definitely looks like one.'

** The waiter serving them has long hair, long sideburns, bell-bottom trousers. I don't think men have ever been quite as ridiculous as in the late seventies.

She next showed me three albums with family pictures. Her and Faustino, the afternoon they were married, outside the Nazaré Church. The groom very thin, very dark, like a shadow at evening lengthening across a wall. The bride was the daytime beside him, radiant, in a lovely satin dress. Faustino appears in another photo with his arms around a slightly younger man with a long face, sincere eyes, with delicious, very well-drawn lips:

'His name was Ernesto; he was Faustino's brother, two years younger. He died in 1975 poor thing, killed by a stray bullet. He was at home, a fire-fight started up and he went into the yard to fetch Irene, his youngest daughter, who must have been six or seven at the time. He took the bullet in his heart. At the funeral someone remarked – I think it was the priest – that it was no wonder the bullet had hit his heart, as he had such a huge heart. He really did have a huge heart. I think of him as a kind of angel.'

'Was he Faustino's only sibling?'

'Yes; well, the only sibling by the same father and the same mother. Old Guido, their father, had many other children outside his marriage… Don't make that face, my dear. In this country even the lame jump the fence.'

A thin, timid lady came in to announce that lunch was served. We ate in the yard, in the generous shade of a huge mango tree. The woman sat with us.

'This is Irene, my niece,' Dona Anacleta introduced her. 'Remember what I told you? Her father died in her arms. She never married. She lives alone. She moved here these past days to keep me company.'

The rest of the afternoon Irene can't have said more than a dozen words. She limited herself to nodding and quickly agreeing on the rare occasions Dona Anacleta addressed her. There were times I forgot she was there. Her aunt too, I imagine. It was as though she was speaking only to me:

'I thought you'd always lived in Mozambique,' she said. We ate a soup and a dried-meat *calulu*, very well seasoned, then moved on to the sweets: banana cake, mango mousse, cassava pudding. I chose the banana cake. Dona Anacleta opted for the mango mousse. Her voice softened. 'The truth is, I thought you were Mozambican. But you tell me you're not, that you were raised in Lisbon, by a Portuguese couple. I also heard you were on Mozambique Island, with my grandson, Bartolomeu, and that you met your mother. Your biological mother…'

'Yes, that's true.'

'Was she pleased to see you?'

'She was, I think so. It was a bit strange. Hard for me as well as for her, but I think I did the right thing in tracking her down. We talked a lot.'

'I understand. Is there anything you wanted to say to me?'

'There really is. I met a doctor, on the Island there, who told me about my father... – about your husband... – he said he'd been a good friend of his.'

Dona Anacleta sighed:

'Irene, please go and buy my medicines.'

Irene got up, kissed me goodbye and left. A fat maid, with very smooth, stretched-out skin*, came to clear the table. Dona Anacleta asked her to bring us some tea. She brought her face close to mine:

'And this doctor, does he have a name?'

'Amândio Pinto de Sousa...'

'Yes, Faustino spoke of him a lot. And what did Doctor Amândio tell you?'

'Listen, I don't even know if I can believe what he told me. He told me...'

'I know what he told you...'

'Well, he also told me he felt no obligation to the truth.'

'He did well. The truth is a stupid, awkward, troublesome old woman. And also deaf – not stone-deaf, as you can get some pretty attentive stones, plenty of them, but deaf as God, to whom everyone begs and who hears no one. And you, you're looking for the truth?'

'I think so.'

'And what use will it be to you knowing the truth?'

'It's not a question of being useful. What use is the beauty of stars to me? They make my soul glad. I think truth has something to do with beauty.'

'I don't agree with you, my child. There are many ugly truths. Some bring only pain.'

'Yes, there are truths that bring pain. But perhaps the pain is necessary...'**

'You don't believe that!'

---

* She looked like she was out of a picture by the Colombian painter Fernando Botero: glad to be fat!

** I'd just said this when I remembered some lines from the South African poet Breyten Breytenbach: 'There is no need for Pain Lord / We could live well enough without It / A flower has no teeth [...] Let us regularly taste the sweet evening air / Swim in tepid seas, be allowed to sleep with the sun / Ride peacefully on bicycles through bright Sundays // And gradually we will rot like old ships or trees / But keep Pain far from Me o Lord / That others may bear it [...]' (from *In Africa Even the Flies Are Happy: Selected Poems 1964-77*, translated by Denis Hirson, publ. John Calder, 1978).

'You're right. Pain is useless. We can get along without it.'

'Indeed we can!' She laughed. 'A flower has no teeth.'

'Ma'am, you've read Breyten Breytenbach?'

'You can't imagine the things I've read. You suppose that because there isn't a single good bookshop here in Luanda, since independence, you suppose that's made us all stupid?'

'No, of course not...'

'No? Well, you should suppose it, girl, we really have become stupid. I have the good fortune of having good friends in Lisbon, in Rio de Janeiro, in Paris, who send me books. But returning to truth, and its traps. The truth is a recourse for people with no imagination. And besides, lies can be to the general good. Your bait of falsehood takes this carp of truth...'

'Shakespeare?'

'Indeed, old William himself. Tell me, do you like love stories?'

'I do. Very much. I like good stories.'

'I'm inclined to tell you a love story, I want to tell you this story, but not today. Today I feel tired and my story might be rather long. It will wait for another day.'

'And what does this story have to do with truth?'

'Everything, my dear. It's the true life story of Faustino Manso. A demonstration of how you can have perfidious truths and benevolent lies. Life is neither grey nor rose-tinted. It depends on the lenses through which you look at it.'

(Delay)

My period should have come three days ago. I'm absolutely sure of it. I'm starting to worry. I'm planning to go by a chemist's, soon, to do a pregnancy test. At my gynaecologist's suggestion I've stopped taking the pill. That was six months ago. I'm normally very careful. But even if I weren't I could trust Mandume. I feel completely sure of him. Unfortunately it happened that night in Cape Town. I look back and still don't understand how I was capable of knocking at the door to Bartolomeu's room. My memory of those hours remains imprecise. Fragments. Once, many years ago, I was in a car, with my father, on a street in Lisbon, when a taxi hit us. It was a Sunday morning, in January, and there was hardly any traffic. The taxi shot suddenly out of the fog, as though coming from another world, parallel to ours, and struck the driver's-side door hard. I associate that accident with another, a smaller one, when my father accidentally let go of me as he was spinning me around holding me by the hands, in the living room of our house. I was thrown backward against the wall. I wasn't hurt. In each case, what I remember is the world spinning quickly around. A taste of blood in my mouth. They took me to the Santa Maria Hospital in an ambulance, with a blow to my head, and the only image I can call up between the taxi striking our car and the moment I came to in the emergency room is of a nurse in the ambulance* looking at me and saying, "It's nothing, child, it's nothing." However hard I try I'm also unable to remember leaving Bartolomeu's room. But I do now remember, I think I remember, meeting

* This scene has a soundtrack: the howl of the ambulance. However, the image I retain of the disaster, the world spinning around me, is silent and black and white, like an old documentary.

Lili in the hallway. I think it was her who took me to my room. Mandume must have been asleep already and didn't wake up. Strange, I think of Lili and Mauro's face comes to me. In a short space of time a red-headed man and a red-headed woman came into my life and left it again – one of them with a gunshot. Red, as we know, is the colour of danger.

(What distinguishes life from dreams)

I want to tell you what I saw, just this past night, in Quelimane. I arrived yesterday. I'm having to stay a couple of days preparing for the trip back. I don't mind returning alone, me and my faithful Malembe. I empty my thought as the road passes. To travel is to forget. I have a lot to forget. What happened on the Island, for example, after that early morning when I witnessed the murder attempt (or the murder – it depends; the hotel owner remains in a coma in a Johannesburg hospital). A young man came up to me, asking if I wanted to buy some old coins, then he offered to sell me glass beads, and finally images of the saints. We chatted for a bit, before he realised that my only interest in him was in him. I have no curiosity about old coins, still less about glass beads. As for saints, I said to him, the only ones that interest me are the ones that don't have wings.

'And this?!' he asked, dropping his shorts. 'Does this interest you?'

Ah, the arrogance of adolescents! Abdul spent the night with me in the car. As he left he stumbled upon Laurentina and Mandume. It was ill luck. That afternoon the Portuguese man came up to me:

'I don't know who you are, if you're a priest or a *candongueiro*, if you're both of those things or neither. And it's also not up to me to judge you on your sexual choices. All I ask is for you to be more discreet.'

I kept quiet. I am discreet.

I close my eyes as I think about this. My heart hurtles, blood burns my face. I was saying: that night, in Quelimane, I saw something very strange. I was thinking about a phrase. I can spend hours at night thinking about a phrase. 'So weird are my dreams when you're away from me.' The person

261

who said this to me, his mouth to my ear, was a man I met, a long time ago, in Cape Town. I think if I were to meet him on the street today I wouldn't recognise him. But the phrase, I've never forgotten that, nor his scent, the rough beard scratching my neck.

'So weird are my dreams when you're away from me.'

Then I opened my eyes and saw the hyenas. There in the square, as dawn broke, between the wonder of the river and the very white silence of the little church. Five hyenas. Panting. Some thin crying, like women already tired mourning a dead man. At this distance, in the twilight, I could hardly make out their shapes, vague smudges, the solid horse neck, the too-small back legs, and running around, around, moaning. As they approached the car I could see they had their jaws trapped in a sort of muzzle, made of sisal hemp, and at their necks strong iron chains. Three dwarves, tiny, but muscular, dressed darkly, were holding the chains. Night raised its dark wings, dissolving bit by bit into the dense, damp air. I waited till the group was about thirty or forty metres away, opened the car door, without making a sound, and got out. I followed them. I was terrified, but wanted to know where this madness would go. The city slept. A late-night drunk, sitting on a corner, lifted his head when he heard the moaning of the hyenas. He rubbed his eyes, also incredulous. Perhaps he'd promised himself that he would give up the drink. The cortege proceeded, moving away from the centre, ever faster. They were afraid of – who knows? – the morning light, which lighting them up would reveal their madness. We passed through old groups of houses with broad iron verandas, roofed in zinc; by elegant residences in a 1950s style; and then past a succession of humbler white houses, doors painted green or indigo, big yards with palm trees. A dog fled in panic faced with the hyenas. Then, suddenly, a clearing opened up, and I saw the enormous striped tent: white, yellow, orange. The sight took me back to my childhood. I saw again – with my very round eyes of a nine-year-old boy – the terrace, in wood, filled with people. I saw again the women with their extremely short skirts, lace stockings, selling popcorn and smiling at me. I found them amazingly beautiful – that was how I imagined angels to be. I saw again the jugglers, the illusionists, the contortionists, the fakirs, the knife-throwers, the animal-tamers, the clowns who spoke Spanish. At that time I thought Spanish was a language invented by clowns. To this day I can't take anyone seriously who speaks to me in Spanish. I can't conceive of a tragedy in Spanish.

'Boswall Circus' was written on a board placed at the main entrance. Around the tent there were four or five caravans, two lorries and three cages on wheels. The dwarves opened the doors of one of the cages and made the hyenas get in. In the middle cage a very old, thin lion was sleeping. A gorilla occupied the last. The dwarves went into one of the trailers, laughing, exchanging quick phrases in a language that I didn't recognise at all. I sat in front of the gorilla's cage. The animal was awake. He picked his teeth with a piece of kindling as he watched me. Cloudy yellow eyes. He looked at me with his head high, like a prisoner of war struggling to maintain his pride; I really think he was watching me with a certain amount of scorn:

'*Rust never sleeps…*'

I turned, startled. It was one of the dwarves. I hadn't noticed him approach. His voice shone in the morning. His teeth too. Rust, the little man explained to me – quite unnecessarily – was the name of the gorilla. The fur of the poor animal really did have a rusty tinge to it, which emphasised his air of abandonment, of being something left behind, like the carcass of a car on the shoulder of a minor road.

'Where are you from?'

The dwarf shrugged his broad shoulders:

'From everywhere. Circus people don't have a homeland. I'm Nigerian' – he pointed to the hyenas – 'them too. I'm here with my brothers. Why don't you come see our number this afternoon?'

I agreed. Life is no less incoherent than dreams; it's just more persistent.

(Enemy brothers)

Sunday in Luanda.

In the early morning Nelito came by the hotel to take me to meet the family. My father looks like him, without a doubt, though not as you'd imagine a younger brother would resemble his elder, but like a shadow resembles the body that casts it. He hugged me, delighted:

'Been so long, nephew!'

Been so long? It was the first time we'd met! His wife, Ondina, had come with him. She also greeted me as though she'd always known me, though with less warmth, a mist darkening her gaze (beautiful eyes, actually: deep, and very black). They took me to a naval club, a few kilometres from the city, where I saw a lot of pleasure boats, some on a quite considerable scale. The oldest of my cousins, Manolo, was already waiting for us, on an elegant launch, white as a swan, to take us to Mussulo. Nelito has four children: two girls, Mimi, aged fifteen, and Mulata, seventeen, and two boys, Miguel, twenty-nine, and Manolo, thirty-one. Manolo is the commercial director of a new bank. He's rich, I'd imagine, as he's had a huge beach house built on Mussulo, a house in wood and bamboo which – in his words – 'is in harmonious dialogue with the environment'. It is in dialogue with it, and not just a little. It gorges itself on conversation with the coconut palms, dozens of them, which extend from the door to the shore of the sea. My rich cousin also owns a spacious apartment in Luanda, and another in Rio de Janeiro.

Miguel, Mimi and Mulata were already waiting for us. Mulata isn't a mulatta, they call her that because she was born with skin slightly lighter than that of her brothers. She's pretty, with a calm, sweet prettiness, without the impertinence that sometimes annoys me in young Luandans. We had roast chicken for lunch, prepared by Miguel and Manolo, perhaps a little too peppery for my taste but nonetheless very good. I was the one who moved the conversation onto the subject of the disharmony:

'There are some things my father's never told me. So many years have passed now. I think I have the right to know. What exactly happened to my uncles?'

Nelito sighed. He opened a bottle of Cuca and filled his glass. He drank down a long draught of it:

'Mariano died in the very first few days. Martinho was only young, he can't have been more than eighteen. He was studying in Cuba. They ordered him back and he was held for a few weeks in the São Paulo prison. I only managed to see him twice, after that they sent him to a concentration camp, somewhere in the south. I tried to get him out of there, I did what I could, but you don't imagine, you can't imagine, what our life was like in those days. We lived drowning in fear. We fell asleep exhausted, terrified, and in the morning, when we woke up, we'd be even more tired than before, because we'd been trembling and grinding our teeth all night long. Even today I still sometimes wake up with nightmares. Fear is tiring. It can break a man. I was on the right side, but I had three brothers on the wrong side, and that counted against me. My comrades looked at me askance, like this, sidelong, you see? And I know a lot of them doubted my convictions. You could hear it, behind me, the damned word, 'Fractionist! Fractionist!' or I only imagined it, perhaps. I slept in my clothes in case they came for me suddenly in the middle of the night. I didn't want to be arrested in my underpants…'

Mulata interrupted him:

'I think a man with dignity is still a man with dignity, even in his underpants. Real dignity can withstand nakedness.'

Everyone laughed. To me it seemed a very sensible statement. I returned to the hotel feeling differently about the Angolans. I phoned my father and told him what had happened. I heard the silence taking shape on the other end, like clouds getting denser in a stormy sky, and prepared myself for the worst. His voice, however, revealed not even a trace of rage, only hurt:

'What do you want me to say to you? You probably did the right thing. In any case, you're a grown-up. I don't have the right to impose my bitterness on you. I've lost three brothers, I don't want to lose a son.'

'You've lost two brothers, Dad. Nelito is alive!'

A new silence. In the background my mother's voice in a harsh murmur. A car horn (they must be stuck in traffic). Finally a long sigh:

'When do you come back?'

Night was falling and still no sign of Laurentina. She told me she was going to spend the day at the house of Dona Anacleta. It would appear that the old lady promised to tell her the true story of Faustino Manso. I was curious myself. I spent a good while sitting in front of the TV, skipping from channel to channel, until I realised I wasn't really watching anything. Then I decided to go out. I went to look for Alfonsina. I found her in the abandoned bandstand, with the chicken sleeping between her legs. She'd bought a new dress, a little white dress, with a huge rainbow drawn from the right shoulder to the pleat, blue trainers with little yellow flowers. A broad smile opened to me:

'You think I'm pretty?'

I told her yes, I did. I wanted to know what had been the results of the tests. She shrugged her shoulders:

'I got AIDS.'

'What?'

'Yeah! They gave me a fuck of a lot of pills to take. Now I feel fine.'

'It can't be AIDS, Alfonsina!'

'I'm fine, man, don't worry. The fever's gone, I feel fine.'

I asked her why she was always on her own, why I didn't see her with other children. Street children usually go around in gangs. She told me that the boys hit her. They accuse her of being a sorceress and they hit her. A sorceress?! She didn't notice my astonishment. Yes, a sorceress, she insisted. Once they tried to set her on fire while she was sleeping. They threw gasoline on her, then a lit match. She woke up and rolled in the sand. She showed me the scars on her belly. I was agonised, disgusted; it was the final straw. My voice came out hoarse:

'Get your things together and come with me.'

I acted without thinking. Now that I consider what I did I'm slightly alarmed. The girl followed me in silence. At the hotel I took another room in my name. The receptionist looked at me with distrust, shaking his head, as he watched us go upstairs. We were halfway up when he shouted after us:

'No, there's just no way!'

I was startled:

'No way that what?'

'The chicken. The chicken can't go up. We don't allow animals in the rooms.'

I went back down, put my hand in my pocket and took out a ten-dollar note. I put the note on the desk:

'And now, can it?'

The man started shaking his head again, in reproof:

'I saw nothing.'

We went up. I opened the door to the room and let Alfonsina go in.

'Am I going to stay here?'

'You are.'

'You want to have sex with me?'

'Fucking hell, no!'

'Because I'm sick or because you don't like me?'

'Neither one nor the other. I don't want to sleep with you because you're still a child. I just want you to be well. You can't stay sleeping on the street.'

'I've always slept on the street.'

'We'll go to find your parents. Your family...'

'My parents disappeared. They disappeared when the war came back, after the elections. I never saw them again...'

'In 1992?'

'Yes...'

'Don't lie, Alfonsina. In 1992 you weren't even born.'

She fell silent. She sat down on the bed, her head in her hands.

'You don't know anything about me.'

I pulled up a chair and sat opposite her:

'You want to tell me?'

(Pregnant)

It's confirmed: I'm pregnant. I did the test. Then I did it again. I should talk to Mandume, tell him everything, but I don't have the nerve. The best thing would be to talk to Bartolomeu first, but just thinking about that overwhelms me with rage. I hate him. I hate myself. Of course, I don't really hate him, don't really hate myself, and no sooner do I re-read what I've just written above than I realise how ridiculous it is. I lapse into the ridiculous easily, what do you expect? I lived my whole childhood and adolescence inside a kind of Mexican soap opera with Portuguese subtitles. Exaggeration thrived in my house. My father liked *fado* music and lively parties, guitars, bullfights, blood'n'tears dramas. My mother, Doroteia, liked Indian movies. She listened to Roberto Carlos and Júlio Iglésias as she did the housework. And I'm the result of these immoderate loves.

I called Aline. She heard me in disbelief (I can picture her in her little apartment, in Chiado, twisting her hair with her left hand, as she always does when she's nervous). She shouted:

'This kind of disaster doesn't happen to you! Not to you!'

'I'm sorry to disillusion you, but it's happened to me...'

'Well, now what are you going to do?'

'I called you in the hope that you'd tell me what I should do.'

'Me?! OK, look, let's think this through calmly. When do you come back?'

'I don't know. There's so much happening. Dona Anacleta, Faustino Manso's widow, told me a marvellous story. I want her to agree to tell it for our film. If she won't tell it, the film will be a fake; to me, at least, it'd be a fake. Fake, like a fake jewel. What I mean is, even though it still glitters, and it fools everyone with its shine, I still won't be happy with it because I know the true story. On the other hand I'd understand if Dona Anacleta didn't want to speak. It would be a big shock to a lot of people...'

'I don't understand, are you worrying about your pregnancy, or about your film?'

'About everything, Aline, about all this at the same time. What do you want me to say? I look at my life and what I see is a huge mess. You know how I hate things to be messy. My God, what should I do?'

'You're not speaking to God, you're speaking to me, your best friend. But even so I can't give you an answer either. You still have a few days to think. You don't want to be a mother now, do you?'

'I don't know. Incredible as it may seem to you, there's a bit of me wants it very much. Let me explain: if I start thinking about what's happening at this precise moment, if I start thinking that there's someone developing inside me, and if I then think about a child, a baby, I feel such tenderness, an ecstasy, I don't know, yes, I really want to be a mother...'

'It doesn't sound like you...'

'You're right, maybe I'm just going mad.'

'Are you going to tell Mandume?'

'Can I not tell him?'

'The boy doesn't deserve it. I'm the one who should have had him.'

'So why don't you take him?'

'Because the poor thing's in love with you! He only has eyes for you. See if you can recover your good sense, Laurentina, guys like Mandume only come along once in our lives. You'll never find another like him again. This Bartolomeu, from what you've told me, seems he's the Big Bad Wolf. You should run away.'

'I think it's a bit late now.'

'Late, pal? Then look: Go to hell!'

She said this and hung up. I suddenly understood what I could say to Mandume: 'Guess what, you've got me pregnant!' or even – without having to lie, 'Guess what, I'm pregnant!' and no doubt he'd receive the news with great pleasure. He very much wants a child with me. I realised that if I did this I'd be acting just like all the wives of my father – that is to say, of Faustino Manso. Me, in the role of these women; Mandume in the role of Faustino. Bartolomeu in the role of the many faceless fathers to whom all those women surrendered themselves.

Dizziness.

Alima, my mother, didn't tell me my father's name. I didn't ask her. I imagine she doesn't even know Faustino was infertile. She probably doesn't know to this day why it was that he left her.

(The words of Alfonsina, who loves the sea)

I was born in Bailundo. You won't know it, Bailundo is a secret place on the map of the country. The sky: the bright hugeness! The blue of a blue that doesn't exist anywhere else. The blue of the sky in Bailundo – Father Cotovia used to say to us – is the same as at the beginning of the world. Sometimes I dream of the sky in Bailundo, brilliant and wet, and then I turn into a bird and I fly. I wake up and I sing like a bird. I become just like Pintada. At those times I can speak to her in rural birdish. There's a lot of green there, timber of every species, don't even know what they're called but always really sweet sounds because *umbundo* is the language the angels use for romance – that was also Father Cotovia who said that, it must be true. Luanda, if you just compare it to Bailundo, it's like a dried fish next to a live fish. In Bailundo life is very full of shinies, you wear your Carnival clothes, little mirrors, glass beads round your neck, bells on your ankles, and always – night and day – dancing. But I was unlucky. Mamã stepped on a mine – not one of those exploding ones that mutilates you, takes your foot off, takes your leg off, no, uncle, not one of those, a witch-craft mine, ever heard of them? Never? They're something we make round here, traditional weapons, Mamã stepped on a mine when she was pregnant, and I was the one the mine hit, in the soft silence of her belly. I'm not a sorceress, I hope you understand, I've just been enchanted, but we only found that out later when I didn't grow. You don't believe it? Don't you have sorcery in Portugal? It's everywhere. Jesus Christ, for example, he walked on the waters. He cured the blind. He got a glass of water and commanded it – Water, you're going to be wine! – and the water accepted it and changed colour and smell and turned into a good wine. Jesus Christ got a little mackerel, and said you're going to be a fuck of a load of mackerels, and that little mackerel was transformed into a fuck of a load of mackerels, each scale a new mackerel, and with them he fed a whole village. And me, ha! If I walked on water what would people say? That girl – tsch – she's a witch! They'd throw stones at me. They'd want to burn me. It happened that I turned eleven years old and I stopped growing. I became a girl. Like I am now. The rains came, and then the dry season, and the rains again, and I was just the same, and then a few of them, some of the people, they started saying, that's witchcraft, this girl will bring us bad luck and sickness, and war, here in Bailundo, but my mother defended me, my father defended me, held up his katana and as he was a strong man – he was like Rambo – and very respected, a teacher at a priests' school, the others were afraid of him and left me alone. In 1992 when the war started up again they came for my father. They took him into the jungle to be a guerrilla fighter and I never saw him again. On another night, a while later, the war came to our village. Gunshots, confusion. Howitzer fire came through the wall of our house. We ran out screaming, my mother, me and my cousins, someone hit me on the head or something, and when I woke up I was alone. I wandered aimlessly. Then a nun saw me and put me with other children in a bus and brought us to Huambo. No one knew me, people treated me not as if I was a dwarf, an evil, ill-made thing, but rather as a little stray girl. They felt sorry for me. I spent four years there, then some people began to get suspicious because I didn't grow, and started hassling me again. I fled to Lubango, and then to Namibe, and there for the first time I saw the sea. So much water, and its foam, like a cloth of lace, a bride's dress – me, the bride? All I want is to live at the shore of the sea. When they asked my age I always said eleven, I hid the other years of my life away. I tried to forget myself. I forced my thoughts to forget me. After a while I succeeded. I remembered Bailundo now only as a dream. The Lubiri Mountain in the middle of the fog. And if they asked me, I'd say, Bailundo? No, don't know it, never been. A family took me in. An old woman and her daughter, sort of mulatta. The old woman treated me well, she was my friend, we laughed together. She gave me curdled milk. She combed my hair with *mupeque* oil. The daughter didn't like me, jealous, her little soul, I can see now, was very inclined to shadows. I helped clean the bar, cooked, served the customers, and at night I stretched out a mat behind the counter and slept right there. One day morning broke and the old lady was dead, just suddenly like that, her heart had stopped. The mulatta started to provoke me. She made me work twice as hard. She hit me. I ran away. I met a lorry driver, Captain Basílio, that's what he's called, and he took me to Lobito. I spent two years there, worked in a restaurant, swept, washed the floor, I even had a room just for myself. But this time my luck didn't hold out long either. One night the owner grabbed me, tore my clothes off with his teeth, hit me and raped me. This happened once, then it happened again. And again. I waited for Captain Basílio to pass through again and asked him to help me. Captain Basílio went to find my boss and gave him a thrashing with a stick. Then he took me, put me in the seat beside him, and brought me to Luanda. I'd never seen so many cars. The streets, a raging, roaring river, full of teeth, after the rains. A country creature like me, I covered my ears with my hands, closed my eyes and tried to think about the blue sky of Lubango and the great silence of the early mornings. Captain Basílio, I'm sure you don't know him, he's a cripple. He lost his right leg to a mine when he was in the army. But even so, completely peg-legged, he drives his lorry, travels the whole country, meets people in every city, has friends in every bar in this Angola of ours. A cousin of his, or the friend of a cousin, whatever, works in Roque Santeiro, the biggest open-air market in all of Africa, our great pride, and he gave me a job, I sold fruit there. Two years, three years, then it all started again – people looking sidelong at me, so this girl doesn't grow? She must be a young woman by now. So where are her breasts then? I left Roque and came to live on the Island. I began to sell my body. It makes me sick, sometimes, the dirty men, smelling bad, but at least there's no one telling me what to do. I'm almost free. I live listening to the sea. The sea washes me. I bathe in the sun. I learned it from Pintada. You dig into the sand, make a nest, and then huddle into it. The sun warms you, and then you begin to forget, it's better than sniffing glue. Even better than smoking dope. I brought Pintada from Roque. There was a little dog there, a bitch with really long white hair, called Maria Rita. She was really good-natured, nice and gentle. One day someone brought me an ant-thrush egg and as a joke I gave it to her to hatch. The bitch would spend the whole day lying on the egg. When Pintada was born, Maria Rita was really pleased. She looked after the chick as though it were her real child. That's why Pintada thinks she's a dog.

My age? Well then, uncle, I must be almost thirty.
You believe me?

(The man on the red scooter)

I arrived, after an uneventful journey, at the border with South Africa. A confusion of people. Some trying to get across. Others, coming from the other side, laden with all kinds of junk. A white man, with a parabolic antenna on his back, wanted to know if I'd help him carry his heavy burden to Maputo. Two black guys tried to sell me a stove. An old woman in traditional Ndebele dress – striped robe, blue, yellow and brown; neck completely hidden by metal necklaces and over these another set of thick necklaces of glass beads; ankles similarly covered in metal bracelets – showed me a monkey who according to her was able to whistle *Nkosi Sikelele Africa* very well, but he only did it on rainy days. I asked her what the hell I'd want with a monkey who could whistle *Nkosi Sikelele Africa* on rainy days. The old woman laughed:

'He has more use than my husband, who can't even whistle.'

I waited in line a good half-hour. I was seen by a woman in her early thirties, pretty, very well put together. She looked at my passport and smiled.

'Good morning, Senhor Albino! You're Angolan?! Can I ask what's brought you to Mozambique?'

'Tourism. I've been as far as Quelimane.'

'Alone?'

'No. I was taking some Portuguese tourists. They stayed; I'm returning to Luanda. Do you want to come with me?'

She gave a little glowing laugh:

'Don't ask me that again, I'll say yes.'

The difference between the border police in South Africa, Mozambique and Angola is that while in South Africa they're efficient but disagreeable, in Mozambique they're incompetent but pleasant; in Angola, meanwhile, they're both disagreeable and incompetent. On the other side I stopped at a supermarket and bought drinks, biscuits and sandwiches for the journey. I drank a Red Bull. Two hours later I drank a second. It didn't take long to feel the effects: a kind of anxiety, an urgent need to be on the move, to lose myself, to dissolve into the air. After drinking two Red Bulls I'm quite capable of driving for twenty-four hours non-stop. I rolled on for a long time. Night was falling when I saw the red house, appearing from nowhere, where on the way we'd managed to find the materials to repair Malembemalembe. I thought it would be nice to thank the owner for involuntarily having helped us. I parked and got out. The door was open, as it had been before, but this time there was light inside. I saw a very pale man, straight, grey hair combed back and held with gel, sitting on one of the leather sofas. He had a book resting on his lap and his gaze was fixed on me. He didn't say anything; nor gave any sign of getting up. I greeted him:

'Good evening!'

'Good evening!'

'I'm sorry, I hope I'm not bothering you...'

'Do you need something?'

He had a strange accent. I recognised the accent from some film, but I couldn't place it. In South Africa, English has a lot of different accents, sometimes it seems like a different language.

'No, no! I don't need anything! I was just passing, I saw the light, and as there wasn't another house around...'

I wished I hadn't stopped. In this country it's still dangerous for a black man to stop in some remote spot just to say hello to a white man. You never know what sort of white man you're dealing with. The man got up, put his book down on the table and held out his hand:

'Come in. Want a beer?'

I accepted. A beer would go down very nicely. The man invited me to sit down, on the other sofa, and went to the kitchen to fetch the drinks. I looked out of the window that opened onto the porch, and saw a red scooter leaning on a post. I saw the helmet too, the same colour, hanging off the scooter handlebars. Holy God! This was the man I'd seen shooting the hotel owner! My heart raced. I wiped the sweat from my brow with a handkerchief. The man returned with a tray – three or four bottles of beer, a plate of prawns, a lemon and a few *gindungo* chilli-berries. He put the tray down on the little wooden table in front of us.

'Castle Lager or Black Label?'

'Castle, thanks very much.'

'You're not South African, I'm sure of that – Mozambican?'

'No, no. I'm Angolan.'

I wanted to get out of there quickly but didn't know how. It occurred to me that the man might have noticed Malembemalembe, and maybe even me lying inside it, on the morning I saw him shoot the Italian. It would be easy to kill me. No one would hear the shot. Then he could bury me somewhere, between the bramble-bushes, and burn the car.

'Angolan?' The man opened one of the bottles of Castle Lager and held it out to me; then he opened a Black Label and drank a draught, slowly, through the neck of the bottle. A deep wrinkle ran across his forehead. 'My Lord! You're very far from home…'

'Do you know Angola?'

'Do I know Angola?!' He looked at me wonderingly. 'Oh yes! You think I was a soldier? Yes, there are a lot of men in this country, white men, who were in Angola during the war. But no. I'm not even South African. I'm very far from home too.'

He sighed. In the pure silence the sigh sounded deep and a little hoarse, like something emptying out. A falling star crossed the night. If we'd paid attention we might have been able to hear it fall, gently – *puf!* – onto the soft mattress of grass faraway.

'This is a perfect night for dying.'

'What?'

'Nothing. I like the night. I'd like to die on a night like this. And you, how'd you like to die?'

'I'd rather not die, at least not yet. There's no night more beautiful than life.'

'Oh no? You must be a very happy man, or very given to lying, or perhaps both.'

'I was, yes, I've been happy a few times. Now it happens rarely. Only when I forget. From a certain age we're only happy through an effort of forgetting. This doesn't stop me loving life and thinking it's beautiful.'

'You can't separate life from death. If you really love life, then you have to love death too. Loving life without loving death is like loving only half a woman. Loving her only from the waist up, or from the waist down, whatever.' He set about sadly peeling prawns. He cut a lemon in half, did the same with the *gindungo* berries and seasoned the prawns. He held out to me a plate of prepared prawns. 'Can you imagine a perversion like that, someone who falls in love with only half a woman?'

I thought of mermaids. There are those who fall in love with mermaids. But I kept quiet. The prawns were excellent, the beer too and the night was, indeed, worth dying for. I remembered a song by Faustino Manso, which Laurentina forced us to listen to for a good part of the journey. I know it by heart:

> *Life is not sad*
> *Sad is dying without having lived*
> *a great love.*
> *Death only exists*
> *far from the heat of you.*

....

Then I said to him:
'Death is just as sad as life, but it lasts longer.'

(Saturday lunch)

I guess for most people the feeling of returning home, after a long absence, is something they experience as soon as the airplane doors open. For others it takes longer. You have to sit in your favourite armchair and savour a good cigar. Make love to your wife. Have a peaceful sleep. Take the dog for a walk in the park. Have an espresso in the café on the corner. Etc. For me, it's *funge* for Saturday lunch. The long wooden table, on the patio – with my brother, my two sisters, and their respective girlfriend and boyfriends, uncles, aunts, cousins, and Cuca, my mother, presiding over the assembly, in a white dress, silver necklaces, mother of pearl earrings, like a queen in her summer palace. Anecdotes are told, old stories unravel. Sometimes someone will bring a guitar and songs are remembered from the days of the struggle, or even older ones, the songs of Granddad Faustino, the ones he wrote for Grandma, and which she sings, hands clasped together, eyes closed, with a voice of well-ripened persimmon. If I arrive in Luanda on a Monday I go through five days in a state of anxious incompleteness: I wander the city, conscious of it manifesting itself bluntly around me, the hard concrete corners growing up about me, the fierce baby-blue metal of the *candongueiros*, the squares where the cripples fight with their canes, or their heads, depending on whether or not they have arms. Heads they do usually have. Something is still missing for me, though, and this absence makes me nervous, my heart tight with anxiety, like a parachutist after falling who approaches the ground vertiginously and realises he is missing his chute. I only feel I have really returned after I've sat down, on Saturday, at the big table, on the patio of my mother's house.

Last Saturday was like that. I sat down, I drank, I ate and chatted, and drank again, ate and chatted. I laughed till I cried, between one glass and the next, at what one cousin – a military pilot – told me about the national air force, which having acquired six or seven planes nonetheless forgot to assemble new crews. Finally I sat back, and felt myself ready to proclaim, satisfied:

'People, I've arrived!'

It was at that moment that Merengue appeared. She gestured to me, an imperious 'Come!' from the other side of the table. I got up and went to her. She dragged me into the house by my arm. Then she pushed me urgently along the corridor to my old room. She threw me against the wall and silenced my protests with a long, wet kiss.

'My loooove! Bad news…'

I guessed what she meant.

'Are you pregnant?!'

'Very pregnant, at least two months…'

'And why didn't you tell me before?'

'Because you were travelling. To begin with I wasn't sure, sometimes I go for days waiting for my period, and then, when I'd confirmed it, I didn't want to tell you because you'd gone to work out there deep in the bush in South Africa, in Mozambique, wherever, with our new aunt, and you might have been annoyed.'

I sat down on the bed:

'Annoyed?! So you thought I might be annoyed?'

'You see what you're like?! Love, you're going to be a father! You should be happy!'

'I'm not going to be a father! And anyway, you're on the pill, what happened?'

'I'm sorry, I thought I was never going to get pregnant, I thought I was infertile, and I stopped the pill for a few days, just as a test. And, well, now it's too late. There's nothing we can do now…'

'Yes there is!'

'No! No, there isn't! We're going to have this child. I want to be a mother. What we can do, the best thing we can do, is accept the baby, get married. I'll make you very happy…'

'We get married and have a child, or have a child and get married afterwards?! And what will your parents say?'

'Don't worry. I'll talk to them.'

I looked at her, incredulous. My uncle N'Gola is a general. For many years he was one of the most powerful and most feared men in the country. I can never look him in the eye. I get nervous whenever he says hello to me with an energetic handshake, a big slap on the back:

'So, nephew, always battle-ready?'

And I, yes of course, searching for a phrase that might please him, a joke, a *fait divers*, as I look at his feet, enormous feet, so solid you'd think they were firmly screwed down to the ground. Everything about General N'Gola, my uncle, is immense and compact – a triumphant war tank, which imposes total domination wherever it appears. The world shrinks around him, the air runs short, and maybe that's why he bothers me so much, anxious for a gulp of oxygen, and I scramble my words, and stutter, and almost inevitably end up by coming out with some idiotic comment on the state of the weather:

'God, it's hellishly hot!'

In any case, he doesn't hear me. He doesn't hear anyone. He gives me another slap on the back, and orders:

'Make me a Martini, kid, and don't skimp on the gin. You know how I like my Martini.'

And I run off to make his Martini. The gin, a little vermouth, three cubes of ice and a green olive, served in a long-stem conical glass, because if it were in a normal glass he might pull a pistol from his pocket or his underpants or his socks or wherever he keeps it and shoot me. I lie back on the bed. Che looks at me, from the other end of the room, in a poster that time has already rather faded: '*You have to get tougher, but never losing your tenderness.*' At sixteen I swore that that would be the motto for my life, and till now it's always worked out. Merengue lies down beside me. She rests her head on my breast. 'Daddy's doll', as General N'Gola insists on calling her.

'Your father is going to kill me!' I say to her. 'I already feel half-dead. I already smell of a dead man.'

'You smell of meanness, that's what. The old man likes to talk loud, makes a big fuss about being tough, but open his chest up you'd find a heart as soft as butter. He does everything I ask…'

'Fucking hell, Merengue! We're first cousins, almost brother and sister! We were brought up together. Your father will kill me, he will, and then my mother will kill him, and somewhere in the middle of all the shooting your mother will also die, of sadness. You'll see, there are going to be a lot of casualties. It's not worth it…'

There's no point arguing with a stone. Merengue left hissing threats:

'I'm talking to Dad. I'm really sorry, but I'll have to tell him that you got me pregnant and now you won't admit paternity.'

I was at home, desperate, thinking about what I could do, when a friend phoned me – Jordi, a photographer, Portuguese of Catalan origins, who's in Luanda working on a report on Angola's new bourgeoisie. I explained to him that I didn't have many hours of life left to me, and Jordi suggested we go and celebrate my wake at Elinga's bar. We went. The Dancer danced alone, eyes closed, face raised, her body undulating to the rhythm of the music. People kept their distance from her, in a frightened murmuring, as though afraid of being contaminated by her… by her what?

It was Jordi who resuced me:

'Voluptuousness?'

That's it – *voluptuousness*. In Greek mythology, Volupta was the daughter of soul (Psyche) and love (Eros), a sprite who was transformed into an evil siren when a drop of water touched her skin. On her back she had large coloured butterfly wings. We decided that from now on the Dancer would be called Volupta. Jordi went to fetch her. He had some trouble as she didn't want to open her eyes, nor did she seem to hear what my friend was saying to her. Eventually she came out of her trance and – seeing me – a smile opened up and she agreed to have a drink with us. It's hard to talk to Volupta, at least when you're trying to do it conventionally. You can't expect her to respond directly to any given question. Asking her, for example, 'So you like this place?' she might reply, 'It's easy being stone – what's hard is being glass'. After a while, after some practice, conversation flows. Jordi was fascinated. Unfortunately neither she nor three whiskies and a caipirinha were able to make me forget Merengue and her threats. I returned home, at four in the morning, alone, and even more distressed than when I'd left. I woke up a short time ago, close to midday, to the shrill sound of the telephone. Half-asleep, I recognised the trembling voice of Cuca:

'Son, what have you done?!'

I listened to her in silence. Then I hung up the phone, and took a cold shower. I'm writing these notes now in the hope of calming myself down. It's raining out there, a thick rain, and at moments there forms a kind of…

– not silence, which is something only the deaf can enjoy in Luanda, but a benevolent clamour. I open the windows and allow the freshness in. At the end of the afternoon I'll have to appear before a family tribunal. I'm expecting the worst.

(Fragment of an interview with Karen Boswall)

'[…] When it became clear to me that I'd have to do an exorcism, because of what had happened in Quelimane, my husband, Sidónio, told me that he knew a very powerful medicine-man in Catembe and I went – I went with him. We first had a consultation, the medicine-man threw some bones, and then he said, 'Look, she's got some evil spirits.' And then we did a series of ceremonies on various early mornings, which was amazing, very beautiful, crossing the bridge together for the rituals. I already knew the exorcism rituals, I'd already filmed them several times. The medicine-man looks for the spirits while he sings. He took some eight spirits out of me with the aid of a little tool, like an oxtail. Can you feel it?! Yeah, you feeeel it, I swear!! A very strange sensation. I remember one well, it was almost orgasmic. Beforehand you have to bathe in the blood of two white chickens mixed with medicine. The medicine-man makes little cuts in various parts of your body and injects you with ash to protect you from the evil spirits. And the spirits, they leaped out of me shrieking, shouting in different voices, speaking different languages, some of which Sidónio knew. Today I feel better. It might have been just suggestion, of course, but I do feel better. My relationship with Sidónio improved a lot too.'

(The dispenser of justice, or the praise of euthanasia)

I arrived in Cape Town yesterday with my spirit empty. Empty in the sense that the sky in the desert is empty of clouds – that is, filled instead with light and a vibrant blue. Ah, the sweetness of forgetting. I felt happy as a migrating bird after conquering the sands of the Sahara. Kilometres and kilometres of slipping over the slow rusting of the evening. The hills in the background. The bramble tufts, like lazy hedgehogs. The electricity lines running alongside the road. An eagle followed me, very high in the sky, for more than half an hour. I parked the car at a sort of belvedere, on the slopes of Table Mountain, put my seat back and closed my eyes. I must have slept a few minutes, as I dreamed about the man in the red house. Now, looking back, I'm not even sure whether I dreamed about the vestiges of reality, or whether on the contrary in Karoo I stumbled on the remnants (or revenants?) of some alien dream. Let's go back, then, to the point where I paused my story. There we were, the two of us, drinking and talking. One beer after another. Big meaningless phrases about life and death, about man's destiny; anyway, basically the conversation of drunks – or of seminarists (there's not much difference). At a certain point I got up. The alcohol, the tiredness, or the two things together, gave me courage:

'This house doesn't have a bedroom, a bed?'

'No,' the man replied in a very sweet voice. 'What for? They stole twenty-five years of my life. I decided then that I'd abolish sleep. I no longer sleep. Sleeping eight hours a day loses us about three months of the year, lying unconscious in bed. I want to recover the years they took from me, to take advantage of every remaining moment.'

'I sleep very rarely, and never more than a few minutes. Sometimes it happens when I'm driving and the car decides to keep going on its own. She – that is, my car, Malembemalembe – knows almost all Angola's highways by heart. But you won't believe that, of course…'

'Why not?!' The man shrugged his shoulders. 'This gentleman under-estimates me. I'm a great believer. I've believed in extraordinary things. Look, I've been a communist, for example. Sometimes I still am, especially when I've had too much to drink.'

I don't like communists. They ruined my country. But I didn't say this to him. It seemed impolite. I went to the door and stood there watching the spectacle of the stars a-spin in the firmament. The man got up and came over to me. I felt his hot breath, a strong smell of tobacco.

'You were there, on the Island. In the car. I saw you. I never forget a face.'

All my nervousness vanished at that moment. I turned towards him and confronted him:

'Are you going to kill me?'

'Come on! I thought it was the opposite, that you'd come here to kill me!' He took a step forward. His eyes just a few centimetres from mine. 'Brian McGuinness was the last man I killed. I spent thirty years looking for him. A private matter between us. When I found him I realised I would have to kill him somehow, so many crimes, and so horrible, Brian McGuinness had committed before he fled. He betrayed his people and then, over all those long years, betrayed all the principles and beliefs he'd grown up with, the values of our religion. It had been corroding him. I think he was seeking out death. In his eyes, when I pointed the gun at him, there wasn't any fear. You know what there was? Relief. What you saw was no execution. It was an assisted suicide: euthanasia. But tell me, after all – who is it you work for?'

'For myself. I drive tourists around.'

'And my house attracted you? You found me by pure chance?!'

'Chance… Yes, let's call it that. If I'd known you lived here I wouldn't have come anywhere close. I don't like getting involved in other people's problems. I have plenty of my own.'

'I understand. In any case, the bastard survived, you know?'

'He was alive when he reached the hospital. I took him myself in my car. Then they sent him to Johannesburg, more dead than alive…'

290

'He'll live, the papers are saying. No matter, to me it's as though he'd died. It's over. It's all over, actually, our time has come to an end. You can tell that to your bosses.'

'I've already told you, I don't have bosses.'

The man moved away. He sat down on the ground, leaning up against the wall of the house, and took a very crumpled pack of cigarettes out of his shirt pocket. He offered the pack to me. I refused. He took out a cigarette and lit it:

'Smoking kills, it says here. You know what you call that? False advertising. A guy buys a pack of cigarettes, meaning to kill himself, naturally, he goes home and smokes the whole pack, and what happens? He's still alive. If he's lucky he'll die twenty or thirty years later. Imagine you buy some product to whiten your teeth, and the advertising assures you that this will happen, that this product will indeed whiten your teeth. You use this product and nothing happens. And only then do they explain to you that to get your teeth impeccably white you'll have to use this product every day for twenty or thirty years. Would that be right? Fuck, no, it wouldn't be right. And look, it's the same thing with cigarettes.' He smoked his cigarette in silence. He tossed the fag-end into a plastic bin a couple of metres away. He turned back to me. 'Bitterness kills too. It killed me. Your friend, Mauro – that is, Brian – handed me over to the English. I spent twenty years in the shadows. Four comrades died because of him. When I got out the world had changed. I hadn't. I was still the same, only not sleeping, and I was seriously pissed off. I asked a few questions, here and there, and in a short time I had the traitor's records. I sold my parents' house and set off. I'll spare you the details, I don't want to bore you. I travelled a long way to get here. You know what he did, or does, or will go back to doing, your friend?'

'He's not my friend. I've never spoken to him.'

'Brian McGuinness is involved in a network of child pornography. A monstrous thing, that stretches from Luanda to London, that involves some very powerful people and has been operating for more than ten years with complete impunity.'

Perhaps he expected me to look shocked. He wanted my rage, my incomprehension, eventually the consoling solidarity of a hug: 'Don't worry, man, you did the right thing, the guy was a scoundrel.' He just didn't seem to me to be all that different from the rest of humanity. I shrugged my shoulders, said to him:

'I don't give a damn.'

I turned my back on him, walked to the car, got in, put the key in the ignition, and Malembemalembe started up. I left without looking back. I think on all this now, my eyes fully open, as the morning unfolds in light colours from here where I'm sitting over to the immense ocean. If the Irishman had pointed a gun at me, what is it he'd have read in my eyes?

Luanda, Angola
16 February 2007

(Dancing with frogs)

I woke up in the middle of the night to the hoarse clamour of frogs. The apartment where I live is situated right opposite the Largo do Quinaxixe, in a building part-way through its transition to capitalism – that is, with its façade still dirty and embittered, falling to pieces, but with many of its apartments already completely restored by the new bourgeoisie. The back gives onto an obstinate lagoon. In the fifties a powerful mermaid lived in these waters. People left it offerings at the crossroads, food, some money, which the poor settlers, recently arrived from the metropolis, would steal as night fell. At the time the building was being built the engineers in charge of the work opted to drain the lagoon and replace it with a spacious covered patio. After independence, however, the waters rose again with renewed vigour. They swallowed everything up. I've seen a little yellow bus – one of those school ones that form part of American mythology and that at some point for whatever damn reason sprang up on Luanda's streets too – I've seen a bus like that totally swallowed up in a few months by that dark water, tall grass and sugar cane, the wild water-lilies. The wretched inhabitants of the upper floors, those that still resisted selling up, would throw all sorts of evacuations into the lagoon, from the 'foul-smelling dross of their being alive', to quote Jorge de Sena once more, to old furniture, mattresses, empty bottles, or gas canisters. The lagoon accepts all this. Gigantic amphibious rats slip through it, with webbed feet, or so assured me the Professor, an old man from the fourth floor, a retired mathematician, a slow and tenacious Marxist, Secretary General of a certain Light of Salvation Communist Congregation Party.

The Professor dedicates almost every hour of his day, and I suspect of his night too, to sitting on the veranda studying the exotic fauna of the lagoon. On one occasion he showed me a little notebook with a black cover filled with whimsical drawings in pencil and India ink, some of them watercoloured, of birds, lizards, bats and giant rats. Looking more closely I noticed that they were, many of them, unlikely animals, others of them mythological ones. The first that I thought was a lizard, for example, had little membraned wings hunched in to its body. A bird with a red breast and a hard beak showed sharply pointed teeth. Further on there was a minutely detailed drawing of a mermaid, seemingly dead, and on the very next page an impressive watercolour showing the same creature dissected, and demonstrating how the tail fits with perfect logic into the muscular system.

A while back a boy disappeared in the lagoon. They say the mermaid took him. He reappeared hours later, disoriented, dumb with fright, his skin still reflecting the glow of the mermaid when he goes close to any water source.

So, I woke up in the middle of the night, in air that shuddered with the anxiety of the frogs. I got up, went through the kitchen, opened the door and went out onto the veranda to take a look. The male frogs were fighting for the females. There must have been thousands of them, many thousands, in a frantic bacchanal. The darkness stirred down below, as the tumult increased. What I saw was a kind of inverted night, with crystals of light glimmering, and going out, tiny black explosions opening the water. All of a sudden I noticed the silhouette of a woman, standing out faintly in the exact centre of the lagoon. She was dancing. Her arms raised, undulating; her hands: butterflies fluttering their wings. Her feet floating over the mysterious denseness. I recognised her by her posture, by the sweetness of her gestures, and not, of course, by the features of her face which couldn't be made out from here: the Dancer!

I don't know how long I let myself just stop there, astonished, watching a spectacle that seemed to have been put on just for me.

(The true story of Faustino Manso)

The afternoon on which she told me the true story of Faustino Manso, Dona Anacleta gave up her heavy widow's mourning clothes. I imagine this must have been a bit of a scandal among some of her friends, but wouldn't have surprised those closest to her. Dona Anacleta never had much time for convention. Her father, Joffre Correia da Silva, a very fun, rebellious sort, passed on to her a certain disdain for established values. A Treasury functionary, and a compulsive fan of adventure fiction, he had read her the complete works of Emílio Salgari to get her to sleep, before she was nine. Later he set up a hiking group, The Road-Runners, with which almost every weekend he'd organise picnics in the outskirts of Luanda. In the holidays they'd travel all over the country: Benguela, Moçâmedes, Sá da Bandeira, but also to the north, as far as São Salvador do Congo. Joffre hated priests and soldiers, with an identical fervour, and often printed anti-religious leaflets which he'd then distribute to his friends. He was also a member and prime mover of a so-called 'Esperantist Society', which aimed to disseminate Esperanto, the language of universal brotherhood, which in the not too distant future would be spoken by the whole world. Dona Isolda, his loyal wife, struggled to contradict, or at least to contain, her husband's libertarian impulses, but without much success. She did, however, manage to persuade him to place Anacleta – the only girl, youngest of four children – at the São José de Cluny School, run by nuns. Every day the girls had to pray in the chapel, their hair covered in a black veil. Forgetting the said veil was considered a serious fault, punished with the penance of a heap of Ave Marias and Our Fathers, knees on the hard flagstones. It was because of this veil that young Anacleta met Faustino Manso and fell in love with him. One morning, realising (alarmed) that she had forgotten this accessory of faith, young Anacleta went into a fabric shop located not that far from the school and was served by a tall, thin young man, with a long face, and big dreaming eyes. His voice struck her even more than his eyes – a voice that was serious, serene and warm, like the voice of a double bass:

'How can I help you, miss?'

She immediately noticed his fingers, long and fine, darker at the joints; she noticed how they moved nervously, tapping along to an internal rhythm, with their own intelligence. She sighed:

'Are you a musician, sir?'

'That's my dream, miss. How did you guess?'

His fingers caressing a piece of cloth. Her eyes fixed on his fingers. Faustino went to fetch the veils. He chose the best, a fine silk, very soft, dark as the darkest night; in her hair, he assured her, the stars would shine – and wouldn't let her pay. A week later Anacleta reappeared, accompanied by a friend, to buy fabric for a skirt. This time she agreed to reveal her name to him, and learned his. Faustino invited her to a dance at the African League, the following Saturday. The girl said no; he insisted, eyes lowered; she liked that mixture of daring and shyness, and said to him that she'd think about it, already knowing in advance that she'd be there, even if she had to sell her soul to the devil to do it. Her father, however, put up no resistance at all. Her mother did, demanding that the girl be accompanied by her younger brother whom everyone called The Admiral, because of his way of going everywhere dressed in white, and all stiff and proud.

At that time Faustino still only played guitar, but already had impressive style. He could play a popular rumba, a fashionable little samba, or whatever, and it was as though he was inventing it at just that moment. Anacleta felt that the boy was fingering not the strings of the guitar but her heart. That was what she said to me:

'It was as though the music came out fully formed, at its purest, from out of my breast. I can't even explain it to you, my child, it was as though the music was already there, asleep, and he awoke it with his fingers on my poor heart.'

That night she went to bed in a state of anxiety and had trouble getting to sleep. She dreamed that she was being pursued by a legion of angels, or of grasshoppers, or by some angels then some grasshoppers, with both having their heads covered with very dark veils, as though they had night itself rolled around their heads, with all its stars, its dazed planets, the immensely old confused constellations with which God throws dice to combat tedium. She awoke bathed in tears, and continued to cry for the rest of the day, at how much – she was sure – she was going to suffer over her choice:

'I never cried again after that.'

She didn't even cry that Sunday afternoon when Faustino Manso, having lunched on a plate of stew with a glass of red wine, asked to put his head in her lap and slept. It had been his habit for many years. He would take his siesta stretched out on a long divan, his head in his wife's lap. Anacleta would make the most of this time to read. She would often read aloud till her husband fell asleep. That afternoon she was re-reading *Pedro Páramo* by Juan Rulfo: 'Now here I was, in this soundless village. I heard my footsteps fall on the round paving-stones that paved the streets. My hollow footsteps, repeating their sound in the echo on the walls tinged by the evening sun.' She paused a moment, and re-read that second sentence, thinking there was something about it that wasn't right, the pleonasm, 'the round paving-stones that paved the streets,' when Faustino gave a little groan and then settled in her arms forever. She understood then that she'd never stopped loving him, since that cold, dry, grey and melancholy morning when she'd admired his fingers for the first time. She'd continued to love him with the same immoderate madness, without faltering, without hesitation, even for the twenty-two years, two months and thirteen days during which the unhappy man had wandered adrift round the south of Africa, fleeing from her, trying to forget her in the arms of innumerable women. She'd loved him even more knowing that he'd had children with some of these women – loved him for the immense ingenuousness, for the goodness and stupidity, the absolute certainty that when he gave himself to these women, to them all, it was her that he was looking for and no other.

'Did you know that your husband wasn't able to have children?'

Anacleta smiled:

'What I did know for sure was that I was not infertile myself!'

She very much wanted to have children. And as for Faustino, he loved children. He spoke of nothing else. 'I want you to give me at least five children,' he said to her, on the day they shared their first kiss.

Ah, the first kiss. The radio in the living room was softly playing Caubí Peixoto, singing *The Ninth Commandment*, the samba of the day:

Lord,
here I am down on my knees
bringing my eyes red
from weeping, for I have sinned.
Lord,
for the error of a moment
I have not kept your commandment
The ninth of your law.*

Joffre Correia da Silva liked the lad, who was the son of a colleague of his, Guido Lopo Manso, better known as Louco Manso – Crazy Manso – a nickname he earned by his frequent bouts of somnambulism that had him leaving his house in the middle of the night in his pyjamas, only to wake up later in the most unlikely places: on top of a pedestal to the fighters of the Great War at Quinaxixe, incorrectly known as *Maria da Fonte***, on which today there's a rather crude statue raised to Queen Ginga; in the topmost branches of a tall mango tree; lying down beside the altar at the Carmo Church; on the sands of the Island. One morning he even woke up in his neighbour's bed, between the neighbour and his wife, but managed to get out before they'd noticed him.

Dona Isolda, as ever, took longer to accept the relationship. She had doubts about the future of a young man whose greatest ambition – not to say whose only ambition – was to be a musician. What future could a

---

* When I got to the hotel I went to look this up on the Internet and came to the conclusion that this can't have happened. Caubí Peixoto only made his first record in 1952. *The Ninth Commandment*, a samba song by René Bittencourt and Raul Sampaio, wasn't composed till 1957. However, when I phoned Dona Anacleta to make her aware of this anachronism she was offended: 'Nonsense!' she said to me. 'I'm absolutely certain that Caubí was singing when we kissed for the first time.'

** Maria da Fonte, a woman of the people, a native of the parish of Fonte Arcada, in Minho, had been the instigator of a popular uprising which took place in the spring of 1846, which led to the overthrow of the government of Bernardo da Costa Cabral. The reason the statue has taken on this name relates to the main figure, an athletic-looking and determined woman, who holds up a sword. Maria da Fonte was destroyed immediately after independence, and replaced by a military tank.

musician have in a country like Angola, in 1946? Nevertheless she too did end up being seduced by Faustino's elegance and his sweetness.

The marriage of Faustino and Anacleta took place on 5 October of that year in the little Nazaré Church. The ceremony was attended by two dozen closest friends and relations. I've seen the photographs, as I said before: Faustino, really thin, a long shadow dressed in black; Anacleta resplendent in his arms. Ernesto, Faustino's younger brother, as thin as him, but somehow more solid, I'm not quite sure why, perhaps because of the firmness of his gaze and the clear smile with which he confronts the lens of the camera. I also noticed a slightly bald man, elegant, hugging Faustino Manso in one of the photographs. I noticed him because he looked like a casting mistake: English cashmere trousers in combination with a Panama hat and silk tie, two-tone shoes; fingers discoloured by vitiligo, and the natural arrogance of a lion tamer.

'And this one, who's he?'

'Him?! Ah, this man's a key figure in Faustino's career. His name is Archimedes Moran, and he was the man who taught my husband to play the double bass…'

'The American sailor who gave Faustino his bass?'

'Exactly. You must talk to him!'

'Talk to him?! This man's still alive?'

'Thank God! He was at the funeral, actually. Archimedes has no intention of dying. He always says that dying is too much like hard work.'

'And where does he live? Did he go back to the United States?!'

'Archimedes?! No! Archimedes doesn't even remember that he used to be American. He lives in Cazenga, he's lived there for more than thirty years, in a house that's falling apart. The best thing about it is the yard. That's where he is all day, in the yard, talking to the birds and the neighbours.'

I had thought that the Sailor had been a genial sort of invention of Serafim Kussel's; him and Walker, the magical double bass. I couldn't hide my amazement:

'And the double bass?! Someone told me in Cape Town, an old musician who worked with Faustino, that Walker – the double bass – had a mind of its own…'

'Oh, that.' Dona Anacleta smiled with studied indifference. 'Stories Archimedes liked to tell. Why don't you all talk to him?'

I wanted to know whether Faustino had continued to play double bass after returning to Luanda in 1975. Dona Anacleta confirmed that he had. He played, but mainly at home, with groups of friends. The revolution hadn't done music any good. Later – by now in the nineties – he started up a jazz band, the Society of Nations, with a Cuban pianist and a Portuguese drummer, and went back to playing in bars and at weddings. In the later years Merengue used to sing with the band, with increasing success.

'Merengue sings very well. She seems to have many voices in her throat, and sometimes uses them all at once. I don't think it's common at all.'

I didn't reply. I don't like Merengue. The two of us sat in silence. Then, suddenly, Dona Anacleta seemed to take a decision:

'Sis' Fatita, you met her, I presume...'

I assented. Her hands were trembling. She took one in the other and set both in her lap. Her voice lowered:

'Faustino had been going around with that lady, even before he and I started going out. It's a man thing. Sis' Fatita, her name tells you something, she must have been a fairly liberal woman for the time, more liberal than me, at least. What we know for sure is that Faustino married me, but she's the one who got pregnant. I married in October, and in November Pitanga was born – Sis' Fatita's first child. I knew about it, of course, I knew right away. People learn these things right away around here. I was very young, I was twenty, and I panicked, I thought I was going to lose him, he so wanted to have children. Years passed, and I wasn't getting pregnant. I lost weight, I began to lose my taste for life. Ernesto worried about me. He'd often come and have dinner here at the house, and after old Guido died even moved in to live with us. Guido Lopo Manso had a stupid death. He fell from the top of a cupboard where he'd gone to sleep. He died because they woke him and he was startled. His head hit the corner of a bedside table and he died instantly. They had no mother. Their mother had died when they were both very young. Cancer.'

Another silence. I knew it wasn't the death of Faustino's mother that was occupying her thoughts. I realised – with disgust! – that my role there was like those journalists who hang around the rubbish bins of movie stars in search of clues that would allow them to construct any kind of little scandal. I didn't know what to do: get up and leave? Ask her to stop? Or the opposite, help her to say something? Perhaps the talking was doing her good. After all, it had been her suggestion. She'd promised to tell me the true story of Faustino Manso. She let me sit there in silence, immobile, pretending to read what I'd written in my little notebook. Finally Dona Anacleta broke the silence.

'You already know what happened, don't you?'

It happened unhurried, and the decision had been hers. Dona Anacleta insisted on that. The decision had been hers. One morning when Faustino went out to work – in those days he no longer worked at the fabric shop but at the post office – Anacleta went into the room where Ernesto was sleeping and when he opened his eyes he saw her standing there in front of him.

(Family tribunal)

When I arrived at my mother's house, I found General N'Gola's car
parked at the door. Caveira, the driver, was leaning on a wall picking his
teeth. His face would in fact remind you of a *caveira* – that is to say, a skull
– hence the nickname, were it not for the lively eyes animating it. The
three vertical scars on each temple, the sharpened canines, this all makes
him look even more ferocious. He smiled, seeing me, with a cruel
grimace; then with his right hand made the gesture of someone holding
a blade and slitting his own throat (but it was mine that he was symboli-
cally slitting). His voice happy:

'Hey, little Bartolomeu! The General's going to kill you!'

I get along well with him, but at that moment I had to restrain myself
from landing two punches on his skull. Fuck, I thought, I shouldn't be here.
Then I rang the bell and my mother came to open the door. She took me
to the living room, and with a severe gesture made me sit down beside her.
On the other side of the table were my uncle, my aunt, and Merengue,
pretending to be upset. No one said anything. Then my youngest uncle,
Johnny, appeared, fat and jocular. He came in from the kitchen with a
bottle of beer in his hand (Cuca – he only drinks Cuca). He stopped in the
doorway, and seeing us couldn't keep in a resonant laugh:

'Fuck, looks like there's going to be a storm!'

He sat down beside me:

'I'm here as the arbiter. So let's see. So Merengue has announced to
the family that she's pregnant and that you're the father. Can you confirm
that?'

He put the bottle down on the table. I remember thinking that the Cuca bottles are different from all the others. The factory was established in the forties. Perhaps it's even still the original model. The shape of the bottle, as well as the logo – a cuckoo with its wings spread, on a red and yellow background – has a very retro look about it, which I like. My memory is immediately filled with images of women with big round hairdos held in place with a lot of lacquer (in those days people used to say, 'Poor so-and-so, she fell over and broke her hair'), enormous *brassières*, extravagant hats and gloves, which back then were every lady's indispensable accessory. Indeed I was never able to understand how it was possible to put a hat – however remarkable – onto such tall, well-worked hairdos. My memory, including my historical memory, acquired in its entirety from the movie theatres, is guided by the female universe. I remember thinking all this as I raised my eyes to Merengue, my aunt and my uncle. I murmured:

'If that's what she says…'

My uncle lowered his hand to his waist. I imagined him pulling out his famous Magnum and placing it with a thud on the table. They say that's how he used to resolve problems, during the war, in the so-called operating theatre, when he appeared in front of senior military chiefs to justify some manoeuvre or other or to demand more resources. However, he limited himself to pulling out a white handkerchief and wiping his face. That gave me courage. I raised my voice, looking him in the eye:

'I'm very sorry. The child is mine. I assume all responsibilities. But marrying Merengue – that's just something I'm not going to do!'

Merengue jumped up from her chair:

'Son of a bitch!'

Her father held her shoulders, making her sit down again.

'And you, you clown, you really think I'd allow you to marry my doll?! Who do you think you are? A brown-noser! What am I saying, not just a brown-noser, a greenhorn, yes, that's it, a yellow-bellied, brown-nosing greenhorn, who couldn't even do his military service.'

Johnny clapped his hands to restore order:

'Calm down! Calm down! We've going to have some calm or I'm going to suspend this session…'

My aunt, Dona Mariquita, a woman to whom tears come easily, began to cry. My mother began to shout at Uncle Johnny, Merengue to shout at me, N'Gola to shout at everyone, and I stood up and left.

(Rusty dreams, and other dreams)

It wasn't hard to get to talk to Archimedes Moran: he has a cellphone. In Luanda everyone has a cellphone. In the old days, Bartolomeu told me, the consumer goods most strived for by poor people – of those consumer goods within the reach of poor people, of course – were bicycles and battery radios. Today it's cellphones. Dona Anacleta gave me Archimedes' telephone number. I phoned him and explained that we were making a documentary on the life of Faustino Manso, and that we'd like to interview him in his own habitat, at home. He didn't seem surprised:

'I live just off Fifth Avenue!' he laughed. His accent is totally Angolan. 'Fifth Avenue in Cazenga, of course. Ask for me near the baobab tree, someone will point you towards my house.'

Bartolomeu assured me he knew Cazenga. He'd filmed there countless times. Better still, he'd already been in old Archimedes' house. He'd searched him out occasionally at the request of foreign friends visiting Luanda.

'A seriously knowledgeable, demanding crowd,' he clarified, without actually clarifying at all on what matter his friends were so knowledgeable and so demanding. A moment later he insisted. 'Really, a seriously demanding crowd, auntie. I've never seen anyone leave old Archimedes' house disappointed.'

I thought people in Luanda lived hard lives until I went to Cazenga. I thought that the slum houses that peeped boldly out between the corners of buildings (grey, dust-covered shacks) were the worst there was here, the worst it was possible to have anywhere in the world. I was wrong. I under-estimate – as I almost always do – the evil of mankind. Cazenga extends for interminable kilometres of chaos and nightmare. The rented jeep in which we were travelling, with Bartolomeu at the wheel, advanced along a network of holes which you couldn't call roads without a certain amount of irony. We overcame slow torrents of mud, thick marshes covered in water-lilies, and holes again, ditches dug into the rubbish itself, millions of crushed soft-drink cans, plastic bags, bottle-tops, cadavers of dogs, thirty years of detritus waiting to be dealt with.

It was late afternoon and everything was covered in dust. The light itself seemed to be floating, fragmenting in the dust particles, giving the whole picture a depth, the vigour of an epic painting, reminding you of the photographs that made Sebastião Salgado famous.

Low houses on both sides of the road. Crooked palms bursting out of yards. A Beauty Salon here (if you believe what it says on the sign – which does require a lot of faith); a barber's there, with a broken mirror, and a poster on the door: 'Arrive ugly, leave beautiful. We do plaits and perms, crimping, curling and waves. We do extensions. *Curly* used here.' Beyond, the headquarters of a political party. Then the 'neoclassical' façade of a Kingdom of God Church. Everywhere the multitudes, all going in different directions, carrying baggages on their backs, arguing, laughing, some even dancing.

'Here it is!' announced Bartolomeu, stopping the car.

We got out. An old man, sitting on a brick, with an MPLA T-shirt and shorts, was witnessing – perplexed – the clamorous collapse of the world. Bartolomeu greeted him respectfully; he wanted to know if Archimedes was home. The ancient man had a look of discouragement about him. He complained of pains in his soul, or at least that's what I gathered, he complained that he was short of breath, complained about modern times, and about how his old comrades-in-arms had been forgotten; finally he pointed unenthusiastically to the house behind him, and sighed:

'In there…'

We went in. It was a yard crammed full of mysterious rusty mechanisms. A fine-looking fig tree in the centre cast a dark shade. Behind it you could see the hard pink trunk of a guava tree. There was also an Indian jujube tree and two or three enormously long papaya stalks. A hammock hung between the guava and fig trees. I thought the hammock was empty, until I saw leaping out of it – dressed only in a pair of very worn jeans – a wizened old man, completely bald, his skin marked like a dalmatian's, with a braided grey beard that came down to his navel. There are people who expand with age, others who contract. Some explode, some implode. Archimedes Moran had imploded. At least physically, compared to the photograph I'd seen at the house of Dona Anacleta. Inside, however, he was boiling over with energy. He came towards me in little leaps. I offered my hand. He grabbed it, pulled me towards him, with surprising strength for someone who looked so fragile, and kissed me noisily on each cheek.

'So you're the youngest, Laurentina? My comrade really knew how to make children. Once I had some visiting cards printed to give him for his birthday. They said: "Faustino Manso / Independent Reproducer."'

He made us sit at a plastic table, in the shade of the fig tree. The house had its door and windows wide open. In one of the windows a woman was plaiting a girl's hair. In another two young women, very young, were resting naked on a very dirty mattress (even at this distance it was possible to see how dirty the mattress was). A girl of about twelve came out of the house, her arms filled with beers, and arranged them on the table in front of us. She brought me a Coke. It was ice-cold. Mandume, intrigued, pointed to a complex piece of equipment, burning with rust, made up of a series of levers and pistons and cogs, half hidden behind the foliage of the mango tree.

'And that, what's that?'

Archimedes Moran shrugged his shoulders.

'A dream. A mechanical dream. I left it there to remind me that dreams are consumed by rust too. Rust never sleeps.'

He rolled a cigarette and lit it. A sweet, very strong smell spread into the air. Bartolomeu smiled:

'That shit's good!'

The little man looked at him, indignant:

'What do you mean, "good", boy?! It's the best! You know perfectly well there's not a place on earth with better pot than I produce here.'

Mandume was shocked:

'Pot?!'

'You didn't tell them?' Archimedes Moran leapt up. He grabbed me by the arm. 'Ha – come! Come on! I'm going to show you my plantation.'

The three of us followed him. We went into the house, passed through a corridor in darkness, a ruined kitchen – two women were slaving over a huge pan, boiling over a lit fire on the ground – and finally came out into the yard. I was dumbstruck. In one of the corners there was a long greenhouse, tall, about to burst with the exuberance of the green. It was as though they'd packed the whole Amazon jungle in there. In another corner, leaning on the wall, stretched a piece of equipment that seemed to me to be for drying leaves. The rest of the space was occupied by the same bushes with the elegant serrated leaves that threatened to explode the greenhouse.[*]

'I have here several dozen different varieties of cannabis,' Archimedes Moran bragged. 'Some that haven't even been classified yet. Did you know that cannabis has been cultivated for more than four thousand years? The Chinese were already making paper from *cannabis sativa* eighty centuries before Christ! To tell the truth, the history of civilisation is directly linked to the cultivating of cannabis. To fight against cannabis-growing is an act against history and against civilisation. Growing it is an act of resistance against the barbarians.'

He went over to one of the bushes, separated from the others by a little plastic net, and caressed its leaves, lovingly, as you might pet a dog:

'This one here, this is a variety I've been improving over more than twenty-five years. I have one customer, in Rio de Janeiro, who has offered me a fortune for the seeds. But I won't sell. I sell him the leaves, of course, but not the seeds. It would be like selling the chicken who lays the golden eggs. This client, my best client, was a sort of hippy, he made and sold perfumes in the streets and markets of Paraty, until about ten years ago when he inherited a large fortune. So he hired a Portuguese agronomist, a drunken rascal, Antunes, whose only job is to travel around the world choosing and gathering cannabis seeds and leaves. I visited him once, my client, over in Rio de Janeiro. He lives, quite by chance, in an area called Jardim Botânico, named for the Botanic Gardens nearby. A real little palace! Here in Luanda I don't think houses like that even exist, with swimming pool, sauna, movie theatre, library, and – this is the best part – smoking room. There, in the smoking room, that's where he keeps the cannabis leaves Antunes collects for him. You know what I call that? *Savoir vivre*, just like that, in French, because only in French can you say utter nonsense – even obscenities – without ever seeming stupid or common.

---

[*] Composite leaves, finely denticulated, serrated, axillary influorescences, and rounded achenic fruits, according to my beloved Houaiss. Pure poetry!

(Deposition of Archimedes Moran)

I wasn't born in Nouvelle-Orléans. Yes, I prefer to call it Nouvelle-Orléans, I like it more. I was born in a peaceful little town on the banks of the Mississippi called Ethyopia, but I was brought up in Nouvelle-Orléans. I remember the river, a slow flowing of mud, but I'm not even sure if I remember it really remembering it, or if I remember it from hearing my mother tell me so often how she used to take me for walks along the bank. She'd always say that at dusk, when it was touched by the lazy light of the sun, the muddy current would transform into pure gold. So when I think of Ethyopia what I see is a golden river slipping by. My father was a magician, not a real magician, not a medicine man, of which there are so many real ones around this country, but a fancy-dress magician, one of those who pulls rabbits out of top hats. My beloved father pulled rabbits not out of top hats – he never used top hats – but from out of his mouth – he vomited them up. He threw up little white rabbits, very tiny but very perfect. But he didn't throw himself out of the window, no, not with eleven rabbits*, he was taken away by drink, cirrhosis of the liver, before he was fifty.

I entered the world of show business very young. At seven I was already playing piano, with a certain amount of talent, in my father's shows. Till one day when a friend, an older guy, a journalist, took me to a dive where the New Orleans Rhythm Devils were playing. I was stunned. I saw Sylvester Page behind the bass, and knew at once that that's what I wanted to do for the rest of my life. At the end of the show I went up to talk to him and asked him if he'd teach me to play the instrument. I think Sylvester was amused by my enthusiasm. In those days there weren't many people interested in the double bass. We became friends. When he died he bequeathed Walker to me. That's when my career – or I should say, my brief career – really began. I played with the Original Dixieland Jazz Band, and with James France Durante – old Jimmy – in the Original New Orleans Jazz Band. As soon as the war started, I joined the navy. But I didn't like it. I hate war. Any sort of violence. And I hate patriotism even more, and discipline and uniforms, all reference points essential to the success of an

---

* This is obviously a reference to the main character in the story 'Letter to a Young Lady in Paris' (*Bestiary*, 1950), by Júlio Cortázar.

army. So when the ship on which I was serving docked in Luanda, I disembarked, with a group of comrades, just to blow off some steam, and I never went back. I met Faustino Manso that same morning. I went into a bar to think, to think about what step I should take next…

…I remember, my stomach ached from so much anxiety…

I didn't have much money, didn't speak a word of Portuguese, and I was afraid the police would find me and hand me over to the Americans. There I was, absorbed, drinking a beer and eating lupine seeds, when I saw a young man come in with a guitar on a shoulder strap. I'd brought my double bass, with the pretext that I had a musician friend in the city and I'd promised to play with him at a wedding party. Well, that was just what happened. It was the only time I ever told the truth thinking I was lying. Faustino saw me sitting beside Walker, I'd caught his attention, and he came over to me. Right now, as I tell you this, I can hear his voice again. A beautiful voice, the voice of a hypnotist, you see? Calm and very sure. He just had to speak, for people to like him. To me, the great seducer Faustino Manso was sixty per cent voice, thirty-five per cent charm and five per cent sweetness. The charm – what we usually call charm – is no more than good manners together with a good bearing. Faustino had good manners, and good bearing, and he was a very sweet man, though never stopped being very masculine. But the voice, oh, that voice! His voice was his main weapon. He got to where I was sitting, looked at my double bass, showed me his little guitar, and said:

'I have to admit, yours is definitely bigger than mine!'

In Portuguese, of course. Then he noticed my expression, my look of alarm, and translated into English. By this time Faustino already spoke reasonable English. I didn't find it funny at all, but I laughed too. What I most needed at that moment was a friend. A few minutes later we were already talking as though we'd always known each other. And we probably had. I believe in reincarnation, or something resembling reincarnation. Anyway, not to lose the thread in the middle, after a few minutes and two or three beers Faustino told me he had to stop by at home to change his clothes and then had to go and play at a wedding, and invited me to go with him. It was his wedding. You know, music is a universal language, and the universe is a musical language, that's something else I believe, so that it wasn't at all hard for me to transform myself in just a few months into a guy who was indispensable at all the parties that were held in this city. And let me tell you, they were great parties. Apart from that, people liked American music, there were already half a dozen people who listened to jazz, I even met someone who tap-danced, honestly, Liceu Vieira Dias, the great Liceu*, so that without even trying I found myself transformed into a sort of prophet for the younger generation. For the first few years I lived slightly fearfully, afraid that the police would track me down, I was in Luanda illegally, remember, but as soon as I'd learned to speak Portuguese, and to disguise my accent, I went to register as Angolan – or rather, as Portuguese. In those days it was quite common for people to reach adulthood without ever having had any papers. No one asked me any questions. They gave me the papers I needed, in the name of Arquimedes Mourão, and I never worried again. Today only the older generation know that I'm American. I married, married the way they do it here, married several times, had many children.

Homesick?!

Homesick for the United States?! Girl, I don't feel homesick at all! And when it happens that I do feel homesick, you know what I do? I turn on the TV, look for CNN, listen to Bush speaking, two minutes, three minutes, I don't deserve more than that, no one does, and I thank God I no longer have anything to do with that country.

But to get back to Faustino, yes, of course, I was the one who taught that sweet son of a bitch to play the double bass. But from a certain point, to be honest with you, I was the one who was learning from him. Faustino possessed a natural talent, he surrendered himself to the instrument, like – if you'll excuse the poverty of the metaphor – like a bird surrendering itself to the skies. He was the music while he was playing. I used to meet Faustino in the late afternoon at the Café Rialto, because it was – it still is, invincible! – right by the post office where he worked. You know who else worked at the post office in those days, in the treasury? Ilídio Machado; they say that it was in his house that the MPLA was founded, but I think that's slander.

…Hm, I'm kidding! Better cut what I've just said, I don't want any trouble…

The thing was, though, Ilídio did work at the post office and everyone loved him. Sometimes he'd show up at the Rialto too. It was on one

---

* Carlos Aniceto Vieira Dias, better known as Liceu, one of the founders of modern Angolan urban popular music.

of those occasions, having already had a lot to drink, that Faustino made up a whole story about how my double bass, Walker, was haunted by the spirit of Sylvester Page and anyone who played it was transformed into a kind of zombie, an empty shell which the spirit of Page would occupy to play his instrument again. All nonsense, the whole thing, the imaginings of drunks, but people believed him. There are still people who repeat that story today.

It's getting late. Soon you won't have enough light to film. You must want to know why I gave Walker to Faustino Manso, right?

Then I'll tell you: because I invented another life for myself, and Walker was a useless and inconvenient reminder. An impediment, in this case a very bulky impediment. A double bass is only useful for two kinds of person – for a double bass player or for a castaway. A castaway can float in it as far as a desert island and then use it to make a fire. I was a castaway who played double bass.

But then I transformed myself into something else.

And ultimately because Faustino deserved it more than I did. If he'd been American he would have been Mingus. But he was Angolan, my dear girl. In a sense he went further than Mingus did.

He was Faustino Manso.

(Diamond hunters)

Brand Malan was waiting for me, sitting with legs crossed, smoking a cigar, at one of the tables of the Vida e Caffe – spelled just like that, with two f's – which is one of the few places in Cape Town where you can eat a good cream pastry and taste decent coffee. He got up to greet me:

'Good to see you again, Pouca Sorte.'

I sat down, and at once one of the waiters brought me a coffee and a cream pastry. Brand smiled:

'See how much I like you? You don't have to say a word. I know just what you want, I'd already ordered for you…'

'Do you know what I want now?'

'I think I do.' He took a book from out of a little rucksack and pushed it over towards me. 'With my father's compliments.'

Diamond Hunters, by Wilbur Smith. Senhor Malan has a well refined sense of humour and self-mockery. I opened the book and saw the envelope wedged between the first pages. I closed the book again and put it away carefully in my folder. I drank the coffee and ate the cream pastry while I listened to Brand talk about how he'd entertained himself those past days, dancing in clubs and seducing chatterers. Chatterers is my word. What sort of woman could be interested in a country-boy like Brand?

Tomorrow we travel together, back to Angola.

(A grey day)

There are mornings that seem to come from very far away. They arrive tired and cold, dragging along the ground the serious bridal veil of a fine lacy mist. These mornings certainly come from some other season, far to the north, like migrating birds, or like expatriate blondes, very white-skinned, still confused, scared, waiting in line for their turn to show their passport.

For example: this morning.

I looked out of the bedroom window and saw Luanda floating above the dirty waters of the bay like a sad Ophelia. Mandume found me like that and noticed something wrong:

'What's going on?'

(I, the sad Ophelia.) He's been asking me the same thing for days. For days I haven't been answering him. He went off, shaking his head. He's been strange, too. He met a street girl and decided to save her. It would seem the girl's contracted AIDS. A tragedy. One among ten or twelve thousand other tiny tragedies, as many as the Angolan lives that half a dozen nationals and another half-dozen foreigners keep in extreme wretchedness out of their sheer greed. She, the girl, has these huge eyes, much more mature than the rest of her body. I get the impression she's in love with Mandume.

I called Bartolomeu and asked him to come see me. Something in my voice frightened him. Half an hour later he knocked on my door. I let him in. He sat on the floor, leaning on the bed. He prefers sitting on the floor. I was going to say to him, 'I'm pregnant,' but he got in first.

'I've screwed up, my love! I've got Merengue pregnant!'

315

'What?!'

'Merengue's pregnant.'

'How long have you known?'

'A few days. I should have told you before, you're right. But I'm still a bit dazed. I can't think straight.'

'Well, I'm pregnant too!'

Bartolomeu began to laugh, but then he saw the very serious look on my face and paled. Then he did something I hadn't expected. He got up and put his arms around me. Like a man puts his arms around a woman. And I – what do you expect? – I dissolved into tears.

(A surprise)

The postman was waiting for me in the lobby of the hotel. He stood up when he saw me arriving. His name is Hipólito, and he's just as you'd imagine a proper Hipólito should be – a tall, gangly man, with a long horse's face and slow, ceremonious gestures. One of those people who seems always to be dressed in suit and tie, all sombre-coloured, as he would do even if he were wearing not so much as a pair of underpants.

'Laurentina, miss, this arrived for you.'

He held out a brown envelope. I read the name of the sender, Seretha du Toit, and I knew at once what it was. I gave five hundred *quanzas* to good Hipólito; he thanked me with a small bow and backed out. It was as though he were my personal mailman. He insists on delivering the correspondence into my hand, waiting for me as long as is necessary. I pay for his attention, of course, and that way I can be sure that no letter goes astray.

Inside the envelope there was a postcard from Seretha. A roaring lion, a big golden mane, red-hot eyes, and on the back, in violet ink, the chore-ographer's imperious handwriting:

My dear,
As promised here are copies of some of the letters Faustino sent me. I've chosen the ones that would be of most interest to your work, and to you in particular. I presume that by this point you must already know the truth, or something or other that resembles the truth, about your father. I hope you don't give up on the documentary. Faustino Manso was an extraordinary musician. He

317

was above all a good man. In our countries, in these parts of Africa that are always so convulsed, memory is not considered a staple necessity, you can't eat it, it won't protect you from the cold, nor from sickness or calamities – we despise it. And yet you can't build a country without investing in memory. I see you as a sort of constructor of memories.

Please accept my friendship, and in solidarity my woman's embrace,

Seretha du Toit

(The letters from Faustino Manso to Seretha du Toit. A few fragments.)

Lourenço Marques, 1962

'[…] On some nights my dreams are red. Serious voices emerge and I hear them, fearful. I fear for you, and at the same time my poor heart fills with pride. I know you will triumph at the end. I should have stayed at your side, but I am not – I have never been – capable of any act of courage. Forgive me.'

'[…] It wasn't hard for me to find work at the post office. I can still sense in this country – compared to mine – a greater racial antipathy, a distrust (looks aslant, whispers), compensated for by the solidarity of some metropolitan colleagues who make a point of being seen with me in public places. It reminds me a little of South Africa, the difference being that this is secret racism, without arrogance, as the official discourse here glorifies the idea of mixing races. They call it Luso-Tropicalism. I prefer it this way. That is, between a racism that's ashamed and a racism that's proud, I choose the ashamed one. I'd rather suffer the little betrayals, a base comment in a hushed voice, than clear aggression, than explicit blows. Any insult hurts. But a blow hurts much more.'

'[…] I've discovered a place where they play some jazz, nothing like District Six, of course, but quite interesting nonetheless. Walker has awoken a natural curiosity among the natives. Let's see what happens in the coming months.'

'[…] When I think of you and Cape Town, which is what always happens when I'm not thinking of you and Cape Town, what I miss most is everything that has anything to do with you – the friends, the long conversations at Trevor's house (in the kitchen), drinking and smoking, and smoking and drinking and smoking. Every once in a while Thulisile would make a cake. She'd serve us little plates of cheese. Trevor and Thulisile smoking dope. Milton drunk already, repeating the same unfunny anecdotes, and laughing at them, on his own, shaking with laughter. His laugh always provoked a sort of anxiety in me, it was a way of crying. I wasn't surprised to learn he had committed suicide. You remember one time when Frank turned up and played piano and I accompanied him on Walker, and you finally joined us on the saxophone? I don't remember who the saxophone belonged to. But I remember that you surprised everyone. Not me, who always admired your breath – and your fire. Your intimate fire. Ah, my dancer, how I miss you!'

'[…] I've been sleeping very badly. The nightmares have come back. Or rather, the nightmare, for as you know it's always the same one, even though it assumes very different shapes: that morning when I got home with my arm injured, after having fallen on my scooter, and found my wife in Ernesto's bedroom. If I'd gone to work, even with my injured arm, I never would have left Luanda. And of course, I'd also never have met you. You see how things are? A driver loses concentration at a crossroads, looking at the curves of some woman, and he hits a poor fellow on a scooter. Nothing serious, just a few scratches on the right arm of the man he hit, and everything's resolved quickly with a sincere apology and an exchange of impish comments on the dangerousness of mulatta women. The mulatta could have stayed home one more minute fixing her make-up, and nothing would have happened. The driver could have been held up shining his shoes while he had his espresso, at the usual café, and nothing would have happened. I myself could have limited myself to stopping by a chemist's for a quick dressing, and then gone on to the post office. I think of this a lot as I'm lying in bed at night trying to elucidate the nightmares.

I remake – minute by minute – the day of that driver and that girl. It's a kind of game. I call it the Game of God and Coincidences. I imagine that if I could play it with sufficient conviction, I would wake up the following morning next to Anacleta.'

'[…] It has just occurred to me that coincidences preclude God, and God coincidences. As for me, I believe in God more than in coincidences, but I fear coincidences more than I fear God. The fact that it's not possible to believe simultaneously in God and in coincidences is something that doesn't trouble me. We Creoles – that's how a friend of mine, Mário António de Oliveira, one of Angola's greatest intellectuals, defines us – we Creoles manage to reconcile the irreconcilable. We are a triumphant paradox.'

Lourenço Marques, 1963

'[…] I promised to be honest with you and to tell you everything. I will be honest. Some days ago I fell ill. Pains all over. Shivers. I immediately thought it must be malarial poisoning, but that I could get better without any help. The next morning, however, I was even worse, burning with fever, so I telephoned a friend and he took me to hospital. I think I was there quite some time. At one point I thought I had died. I remember opening my eyes to find myself floating between the soft brilliance of very white clouds. I thought, 'So death is white after all.' Then I saw her: a black angel, and remembered the song by António Machín, *Angelitos Negros* – Little Black Angels. She's called Elisa and she's a nurse. Still a girl, but as strong as you, and without the nuisance of scruples. She will go far – in any case, further than you.'

Lourenço Marques, 1965

'[…] The Mozambican nationalists are already operating in Niassa, along the lagoon, and they're threatening the railway terminals on the Nacala line. The whites are going around nervous. Occasionally I surprise one or other of them looking at me with distrust, but also (it's curious) with a kind of fearful admiration. It seems incredible, but many settlers didn't believe that the Portuguese (or so-called Portuguese) blacks could revolt, and that this revolt could call into question their presence here. Even now many believe that Portugal will stay in Africa forever.'

Lourenço Marques, 1969

'[…] Don't be angry with me, my love, but it's happened again. What do you expect? Nature has given me an untameable heart and the good fortune of attracting the attention of women. In this case she appeared from the air, the sky is her element, and for this reason more than any other I think there was some justification in having mistaken her for an angel. There are a lot of angels, I know, I can hear your quite reasonable protests from here. There isn't a chicken coop big enough to keep them all. And yet, I'm sorry to insist: Alma is special, so special that I will never have her all to myself, I know, but I can aspire to live for some moments – those moments when I am with her – and hibernate the rest. […] Do you want me to describe her? I'll try: slender and supple and very fair, a smile like flowers in the desert. You look at her and you feel she isn't subject to the forces of gravity, not to any forces at all, to tell the truth. She truly isn't. She left her parents' home in Moçâmedes very young and hitchhiked to Johannesburg. She worked as a waitress at a restaurant, at the same time as taking her pilot's licence. I met her at the Polana, where as I've already told you I've been working. A pianist ends up meeting so many people.'

Lourenço Marques, 1970

'[…] I'm leaving Lourenço Marques. Elisa invited me to move out. I suspect that for several months she's been having a love affair with a lawyer who's quite well known hereabouts. In any case, our marriage, if I can call it a marriage, was already dead and had started to smell. I'm sorry because of the children, but also as far as they are concerned I don't have any other choice. I don't have the weapons, or the courage, to fight Elisa. She was very clear: "You're slowing down my life," she said to me. "You're harming the children's future." Elisa says these terrible things, and others that are even worse, without ever raising her voice. Her voice remains just the same, slight and soft as it has always been; her body, yes, her body has changed. It's like imagining a lion managing to impose its authority while mewing like a cat.'

'[…] I've decided to settle in Quelimane. A friend, a Goan, offered me a partnership in a fabrics business. He has a shop in Quelimane and needs someone to manage it. I don't know if I ever told you this, but I do have some experience in the field, I began my working life in a fabric shop in Luanda, belonging to a brother of my father's.'

Quelimane, 1970

'[…] Here I am, beside the Bons Sinais river, in yet another reincarnation. Yes, I am still Faustino Manso, musician and composer, but I'm also Senhor Faustino from the Central Bazaar — a better respected person, actually, than the musician was. I managed to get a room in an old colonial mansion, a magnificent building belonging to a family that was once prosperous, now almost ruined. The last descendent of this family is an attractive young woman called Ana, Ana de Lacerda, who lives here in the company of an old nursemaid. Ana is a well-travelled woman. She studied in Paris and was there in May '68 when the students set the streets on fire. Those days have marked her. She too was on the barricades. She hurried back to Mozambique to be with her mother in her last days and this — if you ask me — saved her from the revolution. She has a poster of Mao in the dining room, alongside a portrait of her grandfather, a gentleman with ample moustaches, and serious, curious eyes. Deep bags under his eyes. I'm sure he doesn't approve of his granddaughter's ideas.'

'[…] There's a new tenant in the Lacerda mansion. A pleasant Portuguese teacher, called Dário, who seems to be making a better impression than I with the women. We play chess, after dinner, while we drink our tea. We talk a lot about everything and more, except politics. Neither he nor I understands much about politics.'*

Quelimane, 1972

'[…] I spend my weekends, all the free time I have, on Mozambique Island. I'm in love with that piece of land, by the sea, an emerald-green I've only ever seen in your eyes. I dive into the sea imagining that I'm diving into you, that I'm navigating your dreams and your secrets. Come and see me again. It was so good seeing you again. If you come I promise to write a song for you. If you don't come – so much the worse – I'll go to see you, even risking myself falling foul of the Immorality Act. Of every law. The brutish beast of stupidity.'

Quelimane, 1973

'[…] I heard from Thulisile about your imprisonment. It was also her who gave me the address where I'm now sending these few words. I hope they reach you with all the strength with which I'm putting them down on the paper at this moment. I love you very much, I love you hopelessly, and without promises, which is the purest and most authentic kind of love a man's heart can experience. To know that you are in prison is to know that I am in prison. I walk the city with my thoughts on you. "Where have you been?" they ask me, and I reply, "I've been at Seretha," and there are now some people who think that must be some suburb of Quelimane. I've learned so much from you, above all the value of dignity, so that when I look back I don't even recognise who I was before I met you: I love you!'

---

* This reference to my father left me numb with shock for a few moments. I sat down to reread the letter, this passage, again, and then again, and then – suddenly – I understood why Juliana looks so like me (or I like her).

Quelimane, 1974

'[…] This morning a colleague interrupted one of my lessons. She called me to the door and whispered to me, "There's been a revolution in Portugal, but we still don't know if it was the right or the left." I ended the lesson and went straight home to listen to the radio. I found Ana tremendously excited. She hung a Liberation Front banner at the window. She shouted to me:

"It's now, it's independence now!"

When you receive this letter there will surely already be more news from Lisbon. I don't even know what to think. You help me […]'

'[…] The confusion has begun. At this moment I'm listening to the Mozambique Club Radio. A woman's voice is asking the population of Nampula to unite against the government. "This spontaneous movement has triumphed everywhere," the woman says. Now it's some Commander Roxo speaking: "Attention Niassa, attention Reservists and Special Forces, this is your Commander Roxo speaking, this is your Commander Roxo speaking, from here in Lourenço Marques, be ready for action if necessary. People of Niassa unite and demonstrate in favour of the Mozambique liberation movement."

Ana is walking round the house, shouting: "Reactionaries! Fascists! They want to transform Mozambique into another Rhodesia. They will not pass!" And then, mocking, "They're crazy! With a man like Commander Roxo where do these guys really think they're going?" What I most admire about her is that she's able to see the ridiculous side of things, even when the things' teeth are more visible than their ridiculous side and they're getting ready to bite. The settlers occupying the Club Radio also seem capable of some sense of humour, albeit involuntarily. Their slogan is "All United Together, We Will Never Be Betrayed". It would make you want to laugh, were it not for the fact that this comedy gives every indication that it will end in tragedy.'

Mozambique Island, 1975

'[…] My love, I am in desperate need of your lucidity, of your counsel. The last three weeks have been the most difficult and turbulent I have experienced since leaving Luanda. A month ago I was expecting another child, from a liaison with a girl from this island, Alima; I was seriously thinking of marrying her, really getting married, asking Anacleta for a divorce and getting married, when I got sick and following a series of medical tests came to discover something that left me prostrate for several days – I'm infertile. I always have been. That's how I was, shut in at home profoundly depressed, when I received a phone call from Luanda informing me that my brother, Ernesto, had been murdered in his own home, the victim of a stray bullet. A few days later a letter came to my hands from Anacleta. She asks my forgiveness, swears that she always loved me. What there was between her and Ernesto was a pact – she called it a pact – because she loved me very much, and she was afraid I would leave her if she didn't give me children.

What should I do?

I haven't been able to sleep for days. I feel my head splitting. I lie on my bed and it's as though the night were lying on top of me, as if the night were crushing me with all the weight of its darkness.

Help me, please. You're the only person I can rely on.

Meanwhile there's a world coming to an end out there, and another preparing to be born, and I don't really know to which I belong.'

Luanda, Angola
4 March 2007

(An email from Karen Boswall)

I'm still working on the dugong documentary. As you know, the sailboats of the Arabs cross more or less the same waters, warm and well-protected, between the Tropic of Capricorn and the Tropic of Cancer, that are frequented by dugongs. What you might not know is that there's a law – still in force today – according to which it's illegal to have sexual relations with dolphins and dugongs on the boats. It occurred to me that perhaps mermaids were born from just such carnal transactions, not just peculiar but illegal too. Perhaps, over the course of the centuries, some fishermen had taken pity on, or fallen in love with, one female dugong or other. It may be that after having raped them they threw them back pregnant into the sea.

In the interviews I carried out with the Bazaruto islanders, they all insisted on the idea that it's impossible to confuse a dugong with a mermaid. 'What a stupid question!' they said to me. 'They're completely different. Dugongs have large breasts and when they have babies they dive on their backs with a baby suckling on each side.'

Did you know that the box where they found the stones on which Moses wrote the Ten Commandments was made with dugong skin?

I hope to be able to tell you much more soon, in person.

Kisses,

KB

(Senhor Malan)

Me and Senhor Malan. The two of us sitting on the cliff and in the distance, ahead of us, the smooth endless sea. Senhor Malan has a white beard, which every once in a while he strokes with his left hand. In his right he is holding a pipe. I could have written here 'a pensive pipe', exchanging the cigarette for a pipe, so that you could tell that I have also read Eça de Queirós. A pensive pipe, then. He says to me:

'We Africans...'

He speaks to me in English. He speaks English as though he had stones in his mouth, which is the way these people, his people, speak English. He says to me:

'We Africans, we know that the best ground is almost always covered in thorns.'

He looks straight at me, looks into my eyes with his frank, very clear eyes, while he says 'We Africans'. I understand what he wants. I think I understand. This one too, like that other white man back in Karoo, wants me to come over to his side. I'm not, however, on any side. I'm in transit. Which is not to say I'm currently in a state of being in transit, but I'm someone who is in transit by nature, which is quite different. I'm someone who has no place anywhere. But I still agree, with a slight nod, I agree with him as a matter of courtesy. My agreement (my courtesy) heartens him. His voice rises a little:

'When I talk of good land I could be referring, for example, to the Angolan people. The thorns, they are the people running this country' – he laughs. 'You know very well, Albino, you know that I came here in good faith, my heart open, I worked hard, but when I noticed they'd stolen everything from me. My factory, that factory, have I told you about it? There wasn't another like it either here or in Namibia, not even in South Africa. As long as it didn't create profits, as long as it only created work, I had no trouble. But no sooner had I started earning money, suddenly the governor appeared poking around, interested, and then a general, and then someone higher up still.'

I know the story. History never changes, all that changes are the names. I even know the official version by heart: it falls to us, the effort of constructing a national bourgeoisie, and that quickly, and the means hardly matter. Other countries, very well respected today, went through similar processes. Respectability is the name rich people give to forgetfulness. It's just a matter of recovering what's been stolen from us. That sentence, then, I think it's perfect. I've heard it – delighted – from a whole range of different people. Some with tears in their eyes, sincere, their hearts in their hands:

'It's just a matter of recovering what was stolen from us.'

Others with a complicit smile, finding the whole thing hilarious:

'You get it? It's just a matter of recovering what colonialism stole from us.'

Leaving aside the blatant colour, I recognise that the skin of a settler doesn't sit well on Senhor Malan. I'm well aware that if I were to dare to defend him with such an argument (which I wouldn't do, I'm not an idiot) no doubt someone would immediately retort:

'He's not a settler?! Well then he's worse, he's a white South African, he didn't steal from us but from our black brothers in South Africa. And besides you've forgotten that in '75 they came in here, to spoil everything, from Moçâmedes to Novo Redondo. It's time for this one to pay. He's paying for the others.'

Right. I shake my head again slightly, a sign of agreement. Senhor Malan is no longer paying attention to me. He's gone off:

'...so that actually what I'm doing can't even be considered stealing. I'm just recovering what they stole from me...'

Ah good! Right. It would appear the line is even more popular than I'd imagined. With a slight adaptation here and there it can be used for all sorts of thieves. As for me, I don't give a damn. Senhor Malan discovered diamonds and knows how to extract them without raising alarums. All I have to do is hide them in the van and get to Cape Town with them. I do it easily, I've never had the slightest trouble, for a good five years. It's easy, lucrative work. Bit by bit, I'm building up my retirement. In five or six years I will have enough to buy myself a property in Cape Town, facing the sea. I will be able to sit in the garden, reading and watching the boats pass by. I will – finally – be able to begin forgetting, and being forgotten.

(Almost at the end, or perhaps not)

The light – or what is left of it: a thread, a supposition – rises through the open windows, mixed with the humidity and the salty murmur of the sea, and then lets itself fall exhausted onto the very white sheets. Alfonsina is sitting on the bed, her legs crossed and back straight, in the lotus position. I have my back to her, but I can see her reflected in the mirror of the wardrobe. The air seems to be burning (it must be the mirror), dark with rust.

'Well?' she whispers. 'Now can you kiss me?'

Now, that is, now that I know that Alfonsina's thin body does serve as the prison for a thirty-year-old woman, thirty-something. Now that I have confirmed the extraordinary story of her life, as I've seen documents, and I've heard her speak of events that a girl of eleven, practically illiterate, couldn't possibly know of.

Tiny albino mosquitoes, little shy butterflies, are floating all around. They're frozen still. It is as though they are frozen still. Time stops, but my heart continues to beat. My hands are damp (I wipe them on my trousers). A weight on my chest. I remember an episode I hadn't thought of in a long time. I was a child, I can't have been more than five, and my parents had left me at the house of a friend. She had lost a daughter and had a room filled with dolls. They lay me in a little bed, in the room of the dead girl, and I fell asleep. I awoke in the middle of the night, not knowing where I was, and looking around me saw the dolls, dozens of them, all around me, very blonde and pale with huge eyes. They were watching me. I don't think I slept again that night, terrified, or I did sleep but it was as though I didn't because no sooner had I closed my eyes than the dolls were transported into my dreams. I don't know why I remember the dolls. I make a huge effort and return to Alfonsina. I sit on the bed, the other end of the bed.

'I don't know,' I say to her. And I really don't. 'I don't know if I can.'

Alfonsina gets up, takes her dress by the hem and pulls it over her head. Now, I think, now that I know everything. This morning Laurentina said to me, 'We have to talk,' and she started talking before I had time to protect myself. I didn't let her get to the end:

'I know. Don't say any more. I know everything.'

Or nearly everything. All I have to do is to watch back (and I've done it, tirelessly, in the past few days) over the hours and hours I filmed of her, to know at exactly which minute, in which place, I began to lose her. I see her smile opening in her dark face, her eyes lighting up (16:52), and I hear her say:

'My God! Your country's so beautiful!'

Her mouth in close up. Red lips. Teeth like flashes of light. Then the camera pulls away and an imposing range of mountains begins to rise up, in the far distance: harsh, yellow cliffs, cut out against the brilliant blue of the sky. New scene: it's raining. Eucalyptus trees embrace the road. Cows cross the rain like slow boats in a placid river. Her hand is on Bartolomeu's shoulder (17:32). Images distorted by the water running down the windowpanes.

Yes, my love, I just don't know – and want to continue not knowing – the details. That night, in Cape Town, I was awake when you came in, at three something in the morning. I heard you in the hallway, talking to Lili (Lilith?), the Portuguese redhead, the historian or librarian, I can't remember any more, in whom Bartolomeu showed an interest (or vice versa). I said nothing to you, neither then nor the following morning, because I didn't want to embarrass you. I also said nothing when I discovered, by chance, opening up one of the books you'd been reading (*Ada or Ardour*, by Nabokov) the positive result of your pregnancy test. You were inattentive even in your betrayal of me.

I close my eyes, and when I open them again night has fallen. I close them again and night has fallen. I don't fancy ever opening them again.

(Moran's invention)

In Cazenga, as we were saying goodbye to Archimedes Moran, I asked him what the strange machines abandoned in the yard were for. Bartolomeu had asked him the same question when we'd arrived, but the old man had dodged a reply:

'Dreams,' he'd retorted. 'Old rusty dreams.'

With me he was more explicit. He told me he had invented a machine capable of producing rainbows. This machine, he assured us, was capable of producing not just normal rainbows, but also double and triple ones, even inverted ones, or ones rolled up at the ends. This latter kind he named 'perverse rainbows', which I think is going back to the etymology of the word 'perverse', turned inside-out, not because these colourful fantasies were somehow capable of offending against public morals and good manners.

Archimedes Moran believed that his machine could be transformed into a wonderful public entertainment, exceeding even the interest in fireworks. Unfortunately he decided to build his machines at the end of the seventies, in the middle of the Marxist dictatorship, a period which wasn't too favourable towards poetry. He was completing his final proto-type when a group of state security agents entered his house. A neighbour had denounced him. According to the neighbour, an American citizen, most likely a CIA agent, he'd been constructing in his yard strange contraptions for communicating with the enemy. Moran was immediately cuffed and led to São Paulo prison. For three weeks he shared a tiny cell with a tall, very thin young man, very feverish and excited, who explained to him the difference between communism and socio-fascism, and why the revolution had foundered in Moscow but triumphed in Tirana. At the end of this period of involuntary revolutionary instruction they led him to a man who was simultaneously 'very pleasant and very unpleasant'.

'Sit down,' said the man, gesturing to a chair. 'I've learned about you, comrade. I know that you've ended up here after a regrettable mistake. These are difficult times, these times of ours, difficult times for dreamers. I saw you play a few times in the colonial days. In my opinion, comrade, the fact of your having abandoned the capitalist domain and chosen to live among us, chosen to be Angolan, represents an enormous victory over American imperialism. Unfortunately not all our comrades think like this, they're behind the times, they're cretins – what can you do? – so I recommend a certain amount of caution. There's a car outside to take you home. Please, forget that you were ever in this place. It was a bad dream. It's over now…'

I was struck by a premonition. I asked him whether, by any chance, the interrogator's name was Monte. Magno Moreira Monte. The old man looked at me, with a little start:

'Exactly. I see him now and then, here and there, especially at the few jazz concerts that take place in the city. We greet each other with a nod. We both pretend that what happened never happened. You know, Monte was at Faustino's funeral too, he came over to me then and told me he'd rescued some old papers, from when he worked for the government, papers linked to Faustino Manso, and that he wanted to hand them over to the widow.'

'And did he?'

'No. I advised him not to trouble Dona Anacleta. You know, Miss Laurentina, times change, it might not look it but today I'm a much stronger man than he is. I live in this house, like this, in these conditions you can see, because I want to. Because I like living here. But I've made plenty of money these last years. I know all sorts of people, the crooks who made good and the ones who didn't. Monte, on the contrary, he's a poor wretch. So, I told him not to trouble Dona Anacleta, I want my friend to live her remaining years at peace. Why bother her with the past?'

'And the machines?' Mandume wanted to know (he seems ever more uninterested in the story of Faustino Manso). 'Do these machines really work? Did you never think of restoring them?'

Archimedes Moran looked at him, bored:

'I've already told you, dreams can't withstand rust either. I've grown old. I've come to understand the obvious. True beauty can't be imprisoned, can't be repeated, can't be predicted. A rainbow is beautiful as long as it remains untameable.'

(In which Albino Amador's secret is revealed)

I arrived in Luanda yesterday, after ten hours on the road. I left Benguela at nine, and it was already gone six in the evening when I finally reached the gates of the city. Then another two hours to get through the traffic. Convulsed metals and lights, the multitude exploding with hatred. The radios screaming inside the cars. On one bend in the road pieces of twisted iron. Dark blood shining in the light of the headlamps. I've been around this for years and I don't get used to it. The good news is that the Chinese workers are making a lot of progress on the reconstruction work on the highway. I think this was my last time facing the Canjala potholes.

This morning I met Bartolomeu at the Café del Mar.

'So congratulate me, pal!' he said. 'I'm going to be a father.'

He's started addressing me informally again. In truth he speaks to me as though we'd always known each other. Perhaps he thinks we're friends. We're not, but it's not up to me to tell him that.

'So you got Laurentina pregnant?'

He looked at me surprised, even a little mistrustful:

'How do you know it was Laurentina?'

'My feminine intuition…'

'Feminine?'

'Indeed, feminine! My feminine side is the best part of me. If only every man could understand summer as the apogee of spring.'

Bartolomeu can't listen to much Gilberto Gil. It's a generational thing. He looked oddly at me – as you'd look at a gentle lunatic – but he didn't reply. Instead, a triumphant smile:

'The truth is, I'm a father twice over. I got Merengue, my cousin, pregnant too.'

I felt nauseous. My voice came out hoarse:

'So this irresponsibility of yours, it fills you with pride?'

'What do you mean?!' He paled. 'What the fuck kind of talk is that?'

'You're right. It's nothing to do with me. It's your problem.'

'Nothing to do with you at all! So are you becoming a priest again or what? A relapse? Anyway, who are you to give me morality lessons?'

I got up, took out some money and put it on the table. Bartolomeu got up too. He held my arm:

'Don't get annoyed, Pouca. It's not worth it...'

I didn't even reply. Mandume left two days ago. Shame. I would have liked to have said goodbye to him. When I got home I found Mephistopheles extremely agitated. Mephistopheles – I've not told you about him before – is a cat. Well, not exactly a cat: let's call him a cat, but luxuriously dressed in a deeply black fur on which little white spots stand out like stars shining in the night. I found him in Canjala, lying out on the berm of the road, a leg broken. He offered no resistance at all. I picked him up and put him in the seat beside me. As soon as I arrived in Luanda I took him to a vet, a friend of mine, and she treated him.

'This animal isn't a cat,' she warned me. 'The moment he's recovered you'll have to take him back to the forest.'

I wanted to know why, so resembling a cat as he did, apart from the outfit, Mephistopheles couldn't be considered a cat. She laughed:

'Because he has other habits. The habit doesn't make the monk, but the habits – the good and bad habits – do.'

Mephistopheles calmed down after seeing me. He stretched out at my feet and went to sleep. I suppose he likes me. We are made of the same stuff as nightmares, and he knows that. In 1988 I killed a kid. It was an accident. He was blackmailing me. He had compromising photographs and was threatening to release them. For six months I gave him money. Quite a lot of money. One night he turned up at my house and I told him that I had no intention of paying him another dollar. We argued. The lad was a delinquent, a little thief, who went around armed. He pointed a gun at me. And I was so desperate that instead of trying to appease him I reacted. I fought, we fought. We both fell to the floor and then the gun went off and he was still. That's how it was. As simple as that. Death is very easy. I spent seven years in prison. I lost my future, my friends, my family. I lost everything, everything but my memory.

(Mandume's last word)

I only understood that I was no longer myself, or that I was someone else, early this morning when I disembarked in Lisbon. A very clean light rose unhurriedly up the hills of the city. The silence seemed strange to me, the clear geometry of things. The roads sliding by in a gentle murmur. I couldn't help myself, I exclaimed happily:

'Lisbon is so beautiful!'

The taxi-driver turned to me (against me), indignant:

'What's that you said?!'

'Lisbon! It's so beautiful!'

'Lisbon's beautiful?! Beautiful?! How can you say such nonsense? It's never been so bad, such riff-raff! You only can't tell because you're foreign…'

'I'm not foreign, my dear chap, I'm Portuguese!'

'You're Portuguese?! Ha! Ha! Then I'm a Swede!'

Three months ago I might perhaps have chosen to ignore his comments. Not now. I explained to him that I was born in Lisbon, the son of Angolan parents, which meant that I could have chosen to be Angolan. But I'd chosen to be Portuguese. He, the wretch, had no choice – he was Portuguese through an imposition of destiny. The man looked at me, stunned, and didn't reply.

Alfonsina came to say goodbye to me at the airport. I made her accept all the money I had with me (of course that's not the solution, there is no solution!), and promised her that I would go back soon.

I won't go back, of course.

343

(Faustino Manso and national security)

I'll admit that after everything I'd heard about Magno Moreira Monte I
was a little afraid of meeting him alone. That was why I insisted on
Bartolomeu going with me. After all I found him uncommonly sophisticated and attentive, even though, yes, the eyes – the way they skewer their
interlocutor – they're a bit scary. Excluding the eyes he's an insignificant
sort of man physically: wizened, almost bald, with a rough grey beard
badly trimmed, like a retiree in pyjamas. He got up as soon as he saw us
arriving, hurrying to pull up a chair for me to sit down.

'Please, miss, do be so kind…'

A crude bar, set up on the pavement, high up in Quinaxixe, with a view
over the chaos of the city, and half submerged in the violent noise of the
traffic. A hut with a canvas roof, pyramid-shaped, three plastic tables, half a
dozen chairs. The outfit is called Chapeuzinho – the little hat – and I
wouldn't even have noticed it had it not been for Monte's directions.

'So you're Faustino Manso's youngest?'

I nodded, privately ashamed at the little lie. Monte seemed to scent my
hesitation. He leaned over me:

'I saw you at the funeral. I imagine all this must have been very hard
for you. Finding your father and then losing him immediately after.' He
leaned back again and shut his eyes. With his eyes closed he was
completely harmless. 'Faustino Manso was an extraordinary musician but,
unfortunately, not many people realised it.'

Bartolomeu, who had hardly spoken till now, wanted to know
whether Monte had brought the papers about which he had told

345

Archimedes Moran. The ex-policeman threw him a vague look of scorn and ignored him. He continued to speak to me, only to me, as though the two of us were alone, as if we weren't here suspended above chaos but were instead in an elegant café, exchanging opinions about the political situation in southern Africa, films and books and curiosities of the animal world. What did I think of Kapuściński? Had I read *Ulysses*, by James Joyce? And *The Book of Disquiet*? In his opinion, the fact that Fernando Pessoa never referred to his childhood in Africa, since childhood is such a fundamental reference point in the construction of an identity, this mysterious ellipsis explains the appearance of his heteronyms (to tell the truth I didn't really understand the relationship between one thing and the other); he also spoke at length about butterflies and beetles, about ants and ants' nests, bees, mermaids and sirens and how to distinguish one from the other. Finally he fell silent. He smiled, opened a leather case, very thick, and took out from it a small green-covered dossier.

'They're copies, of course. In here there's plenty of material about your father. Reports of telephone taps, a few letters apprehended by the now defunct Information and Security Directorate, agents' reports, I don't know what else – have fun.'

Have fun?!

'Tell me one thing, Senhor Monte. Why the hell would the Angolan secret police be interested in my father? To the best of my knowledge he never demonstrated the slightest interest in political matters...'

Monte shuddered, nervous. Then he smiled:

'You're very young. You have no idea what those days were like. A country threatened from all sides. External enemies and internal enemies. If it hadn't been for us, none of this would have existed.' He pointed out to the square, to the city that stretched out dirty and wretched as far as we could see. 'None of it! Try to understand. Faustino reappeared in Angola in 1975, shortly before independence, after many years' travelling around southern Africa. It occurred to us that he might be an agent for apartheid.'

'My father, an agent for apartheid?!'

'What can I say? You think South Africa's Bureau of State Security – the famous BOSS, of which you've naturally never heard – you think they'd send to Angola an agent who'd fit the popular impression of what an agent should look like? If I were to send an agent to infiltrate the middle of the forest I'd want him to look like a tree, or like a little bird, like a mouse, I wouldn't want him to look like a lion, mainly because we don't get lions in our forests.'

I had nothing to reply. Bartolomeu grabbed the dossier and got up: 'Shall we go?'

Monte stood up hurriedly and came to help me pull back my chair. As he said goodbye, with a slight bow, simultaneously haughty and beggarly, he added that he'd only handed the documents over to me as a sign of the great appreciation he felt for my father's memory. I was glad not to have to shake his hand.

(Excerpt of a report from the Information and Security Directorate of Angola, the DISA, on citizen Faustino Manso, musician and public functionary. Report is unsigned.)

'[…] The individual in question is frequently seen in the company of a certain Archimedes, an anti-social element who became known in the last years of the colonial-fascist period as a provider of traditional narcotics (*liamba*) to the white bourgeoisie. This man is an American citizen. According to a neighbour, Baptista Batista, editor on the *Jornal de Angola*, Archimedes had been constructing a complex optical mechanism for sending military information to the racist apartheid regime. It is noted that Faustino Manso lived for several years in South Africa, and subsequently in Mozambique, having returned to the country only recently. We believe that he operates as an infiltrating agent in cooperation with the above-mentioned Archimedes […]'

(Excerpt from a telephone call between citizen Faustino Manso, musician and public functionary, and Fátima de Matos, maid, his lover, or ex-lover, in Benguela.)

Faustino Manso: Hello, Fatita?
Fatita de Matos: Hello – is it you, Faustino?! My God, is it really you?
Faustino Manso: I'm still me, my love, though it's harder to be every day. I'm old.

Fatita de Matos: Don't talk nonsense. A man like you doesn't get old. Old is what I am. Old and finished. Where are you?

Faustino Manso: In Luanda, my angel. I've come back to Luanda.

Fatita de Matos: You've gone back to Anacleta?

Faustino Manso: I have.

Fatita de Matos: After everything she did to you?

Faustino Manso: She did to me just the same as you did. You both deceived me, right? But I would like to believe that you too did it out of love...

Fatita de Matos: I don't know what you're talking about.

Faustino Manso: You do know, my angel.

Fatita de Matos: I've forgotten what I know. I'd also like to forget all those nights I slept alone, filled with cold, a horrible coldness, the coldness of not having your arms around me. You know what my life has been? A sad samba, that's what my life has been.

Faustino Manso: I'm very sorry. Truly. I'm sorry from the bottom of my heart. I would have liked to have given you a different life.

Fatita de Matos: Are you coming to see me?

Faustino Manso: I can't...

Fatita de Matos: You can't, or you don't want to?

Faustino Manso: I can't. I can't make another mistake.

Fatita de Matos: You can't make a mistake? You can't make a mistake with Anacleta, is that it? Because I'm a mistake, I've always been a mistake in your life [...]

(Excerpt from a report of the Information and Security Directorate of Angola, the DISA, on citizen Faustino Manso, musician and public functionary. Report signed by agent Ermelindo Lindo, known as Caxexe.)

'[...] Since I have been tasked with the secret mission of tracking comrade musician Faustino Manso, suspected of collaborating with the racist regime of South Africa, it falls to me to report that I came across him at the Biker beer-house, in friendly fraternisation with a young soldier by the name (or nickname) of Babaera. This Babaera – as I later discovered – being a native of the extreme south, the border with South-West Africa, a territory illegally occupied by the racist apartheid regime, I strongly suspected that he might be passing information to the enemy. Comrades of his, however, assure me that the above-mentioned soldier faced the South African troops with extraordinary bravery when they invaded the country in 1975 [...]'

(Letter from Alima to her daughter Laurentina)

My dear daughter,

I write you this letter with the help of a Brazilian nun based here on the Island, who knows her letters better than me. I don't want to stumble in my Portuguese. These last days, since you left, I've lived in great unease. I hope to be able to see you again soon. To talk with more time. To recover the years when we were lost from each other. However, I feel I owe you a truth – about your origins. I know they told you your father was an Angolan musician, who I met as a child (I was still a child), called Faustino Manso. All this time I have allowed people to believe this, even my family, to protect the only man I loved in all my life. This man was married when I met him. By chance his wife became pregnant at around the same time as me. He, your father, is Portuguese. He left before I regained consciousness (I spent several days in a coma, between life and death), in all that independence confusion, and I never heard of him again. He is called, or was called, I pray every day for his health, Dário Reis. Perhaps you will be able to find him.

I am sending this letter to the address you gave me.

I kiss you with much love.

Your mother,

Alima

(Laurentina meets her father again)

Dário was waiting for me at the airport. We got into a taxi and went to my flat. I was cold, distant, and he could tell at once, I'm sure, but he said nothing. It was only when we sat at the table, in the kitchen, to have some tea, that he dared to ask me, shyly, how the trip had been, whether we'd been able to gather enough material to put together the documentary.* Finally he coughed, took courage and asked me if something had happened, what was troubling me. I looked at him, enraged:

'Alima,' I said to him. 'Alima told me everything.'

'So you found her.' He got up and went to the window. 'I supposed you'd be able to find her.'

'And what else did you suppose?'

He looked at me with hurt surprise:

'What do you mean?'

'You didn't by any chance suppose that Alima deserved to know the truth?'

'Try to understand, my child. At the time I thought it was the best solution. After all, I couldn't keep you both, right?'

'Actually all three of us, now. You left another daughter, Juliana, in Mozambique. I met the mother, Dona Ana de Lacerda. You do remember her, don't you?'

Dário turned to me. I noticed he was leaning on the wall. He took two steps and sat down again.

---

* Yes, we have enough. Dona Anacleta did, however, refuse to tell 'the true story of Faustino Manso' in her deposition.

353

Then I fired:

'I'm pregnant. I'm going to have a child.'

'Very good!' He sighed. He must have thought the worst had passed. 'That sounds like good news to me! And can I know when you're going to introduce me to the father?'

I smiled. I don't know where I found the strength to smile. Perhaps from the despair felt by all his women. I looked him in the eye and said only:

'Never. My child has no father.'

Hotel Terminus, Lobito, Angola
16 March 2007

(Maritime phosphorescence)

I arrived yesterday in Benguela to visit a friend. I'm staying at the Hotel Terminus, with the innocent intention of recovering some childhood memories. I haven't met with much success. I remember only that in those days the hotel was bigger. The world, as we know, shrinks the more we grow.

I went down to the beach after dinner. There was no one about. Stars shone in the limpid hugeness of the firmament. I managed to make out the Southern Cross, and Venus, whom the ancients used to call Lucifer, the bearer of light. I undressed and went into the sea – the water was smooth and warm – with the feeling that I was immersing myself in night itself. Or 'nyte', as they used to write it in the fifteenth century. Let's say, then, that I was immersing myself in nyte, sucked in by its dark vortex, and that I closed my eyes and that when I opened them again I saw the stars spinning about me. I moved my arms, and each movement seemed to generate a tumult of stars. I know people who go through this experience and go into a panic. Others into an ecstasy. Many people talk about intoxication, most people about dreaming. The phenomenon is caused by a little single-celled organism, the noctiluca, capable of emitting luminescence, and it's called maritime phosphorescence – or, in southern Portugal, 'agualusa'. I spent a long time in the sea, enjoying myself, like a little inclement God, creating and unmaking constellations. As I got out, I noticed the thin shadow of a woman stretched out on the chair beside the one where I'd left my clothes. I recognised her as soon as I approached: the Dancer. She was in a little black bikini, with appliquéd

355

glass beads, or some other similar material, which seemed to sparkle vaguely like glow-worms under her dark skin. I sat down beside her, in silence, and this time it was she who spoke first.

'You should take dreams seriously,' she whispered. 'There's nothing so true that it doesn't deserve to be invented.'